Judy

"Sir, I believe you must have confused me with someone else. I can't possibly . . . "

~~~

"Why ever not, love? You're *here*, aren't you? And we seem to have developed a rather intoxicating rapport."

"Here? Where is *here*, exactly?"

Seger's expression darkened. "You don't know where you are?"

"I'm afraid I don't. I would appreciate it if you enlightened me."

All the warmth and seduction from only seconds ago vanished from his voice like a drop of water on a hot stove. "This is a private ball, madam. Only those with an invitation are permitted to enter." He closed his eyes. "Please tell me you're married."

Clara's brows flew up under the half-mask, which suddenly felt very tight on her face. "Married!" She lowered her voice to a whisper. "No! And if I were, I would certainly *not* be here having this indecent conversation with you!"

He took her by the elbow and began to escort her back to the ballroom. "You need to leave. Don't speak to anyone else. Get out of here now, and for God's sake, don't tell anyone where you were. Do you understand?"

"What I understand is that I should never have danced with you."

He stopped and looked down at her, his eyes fierce and dark. "You were, in fact, very *fortunate* to have danced with me. You are a tempting little flower, and another man might not have been so understanding. Or so apt to let you go . . . "

W9-BRC-151

Other **AVON ROMANCES**

ATTENTION: ORGANIZATIONS AND CORPORATIONS
Most Avon Books paperbacks are available at special quantity discounts for bulk purchases for sales promotions, premiums, or fund-raising. For information, please call or write:

Special Markets Department, HarperCollins Publishers, Inc.,
10 East 53rd Street, New York, N.Y. 10022–5299.
Telephone: (212) 207–7528. Fax: (212) 207-7222.

JULIANNE MacLEAN

AN AFFAIR MOST WICKED

AVON BOOKS

An Imprint of HarperCollinsPublishers

This is a work of fiction. Names, characters, places, and incidents are products of the author's imagination or are used fictitiously and are not to be construed as real. Any resemblance to actual events, locales, organizations, or persons, living or dead, is entirely coincidental.

AVON BOOKS
An Imprint of HarperCollins*Publishers*
10 East 53rd Street
New York, New York 10022-5299

Copyright © 2004 by Julianne MacLean
ISBN: 0-06-052705-6
www.avonromance.com

All rights reserved. No part of this book may be used or reproduced in any manner whatsoever without written permission, except in the case of brief quotations embodied in critical articles and reviews. For information address Avon Books, an Imprint of HarperCollins Publishers.

First Avon Books paperback printing: February 2004

Avon Trademark Reg. U.S. Pat. Off. and in Other Countries, Marca Registrada, Hecho en U.S.A.
HarperCollins® is a registered trademark of HarperCollins Publishers Inc.

Printed in the U.S.A.

10 9 8 7 6 5 4 3 2 1

If you purchased this book without a cover, you should be aware that this book is stolen property. It was reported as "unsold and destroyed" to the publisher, and neither the author nor the publisher has received any payment for this "stripped book."

This one is for Stephen,
the great love of my life.
I'm so glad I married you.

Special thanks to Kelly, for your insightfulness and intelligence as an editor, and your ability to think outside the box. Thank you, Paige, for being the kind of agent I always wanted—someone I could work with as well as laugh with. Thank you, Jo Beverley, for your generosity as an author; Cathy Donaldson, for your journalistic talents in my neck of the woods; and lastly, thank you, Michelle, for being my lifelong pal—the best friend anyone could ever ask for.

Prologue

London, 1883

Lady Berkshire stood outside her bedchamber in the full light of the afternoon, and gathered her wrap around her voluptuous naked form. She leaned a shoulder against the doorframe and sighed contentedly as she handed her lover's greatcoat to him. "Come back on Thursday?"

Standing tall and sumptuous in the corridor, his golden hair spilling onto his shoulders in unfashionable disarray, her lover smiled. His devilish charm filled the corridor like a beam of sunlight, radiant and warm.

Lady Berkshire, who was still flushed from their afternoon frolic, melted like hot butter before him, for she had just experienced, firsthand, the validity behind the rumors.

Yes, it was all true. The beautiful marquess had a flare for the erotic. An intensity in the bedroom. A talent for lavish, liberal lovemaking.

He was Seger Wolfe, the Marquess of Rawdon, and among the ladies who liked to whisper in the dark corners of London's late-night drawing rooms, he was England's most coveted lover.

With boyishly appealing green eyes, he watched her run a slender hand seductively down the front of her neck and along her collarbone while she waited eagerly for his reply.

"I'm afraid I have an appointment on Thursday that cannot be postponed," he said.

"Friday then? I'll have strawberries." Beneath the melodic intent to entice, her voice was laced with pleading.

Seger considered her invitation with care. It was not his habit to see any one woman more than twice in the same week, and never under any circumstances exclusively. Most women knew the boundaries merely by instinct. They knew not to ask, and not to become possessive if they wanted him to return another day, which almost invariably, they did.

Because of his ability to give more than he took, they all agreed.

He inhaled deeply and sighed, surprised by a sudden twinge of discontent that was unusual at a time like this.

Lady Berkshire took a sultry step toward him and grasped his hand. "Please?" She brought his forefinger to her lips, drew it into her mouth, and suckled on it.

"Perhaps on Friday," he said softly.

Lady Berkshire gleamed with anticipation. "Friday, it is."

She stepped back into her bedroom and closed the door behind her with a quiet click.

Seger stood for a moment, staring down the long length of the empty corridor, questioning his response just now. Something had lately been missing from his usual enthusiasm for trysts like this, which made no sense. Lady Berkshire was a skillful, enthusiastic partner beneath the covers. The climaxes today had been both potent and plentiful for both of them.

He continued to stand outside her door, staring at it. Then he realized something. He barely remembered what it felt like to make love to a woman because he loved her.

Her.

Seger inhaled deeply. God. How long had it been, and why was he even thinking about it now?

Bloody hell, he knew how long. Right down to the day. It was just under eight years. Yes.

Thankfully, eight years of superficial encounters and casual intimacies for the sole purpose of pleasure had for the most part emptied him of all memories of her, and he was glad. There was no point pondering them now. She wasn't coming back. Death was rather firm in that regard.

He buttoned his coat and turned to leave, telling himself that this feeling of dissatisfaction would pass, probably as quickly as it had set in. Everything was fine, as it had been for the past eight years. Seger was content. He knew how to enjoy himself, and enjoy himself he did. He found pleasure with women and gave them immense pleasure in return. He liked the superficiality of his life and his relationships. The women he flirted with were always cheerful and smiling. Nothing was ever complicated or distressing.

To be frank, he wasn't certain he would know how to understand a woman's deeper emotions even if he wanted to.

Not that he wanted to. He didn't.

Seger descended the stairs and, with firm resolve, expelled those thoughts from his mind. They did him no good.

He let himself out the front door of the fashionable London house, glanced up and down the street, then crossed to where his coach was waiting a few doors down.

He reminded himself that there was much to look forward to this evening. He had a particular ball to attend—a Cakras Ball. As always, it promised to be a tantalizing feast for the senses. Exactly what he needed for distraction. He would no doubt meet a number of interesting women there. Beautiful women. Adventurous women.

He climbed inside his coach and signaled to the driver to move on. His blood quickened as he anticipated the evening ahead.

Chapter 1

The London Season
May 1883

Dearest Adele,

It is finally upon me—my first London ball. You cannot imagine how my hands are trembling, for I fear that I will not fit in, that everyone will see through me and know that I am not one of them.

I hope that will not be the case, of course, for I do long to be a part of the Society here—the daily rides in Rotten Row, the receptions, luncheons, and evenings at the theater. It has been an exhausting but glorious experience so far, Adele, though I admit most of my acquaintances have been frustratingly superficial.

I realize, of course, that that is to be expected. I am in England after all, and people are extremely reserved. I suppose my frustration comes from what occurred with Gordon two years ago. I must be an oddity. I crave adventure and my heart wants it, yet I know how dangerous it can be.

*Good gracious, listen to me. I must strive to move
beyond that mistake if I wish to live a proper and
virtuous life. I only hope that my heart has not become too complicated for this distinguished place.
Sometimes I find it difficult to just smile and be
pretty, which is what is expected of me. I want something deeper than that. Something more honest.*

Indeed, what a challenge this is going to be. . . .

Your loving sister,
Clara

Already late for her first ball in London—quite notably
the most important ball of her life—Clara Wilson stood in
the doorway of her sister's boudoir, watching her chaperone, Mrs. Gunther, flip through a huge stack of invitations.

"I'm sure it's one of these," Mrs. Gunther said, spilling
a few of them over the edge of the silver salver onto the
mahogany desk. "It has to be."

Mrs. Gunther was a staunch woman—the only person
her mother trusted to act as Clara's chaperone in London.
She was a great social matriarch in America and came
from a very prestigious family with very *old* money, but
unfortunately for Clara, her memory was not as sharp as it
once was.

"It was at—or somewhere near—Belgrave Square. I at
least know that. I remember Sophia describing it."

Clara's tiny heels clicked over the marble floor as she
crossed the room to peer over her chaperone's shoulder.
There were certain to be a number of balls 'at or somewhere near' Belgrave Square this evening. "Is there any
way I can help you remember, Mrs. Gunther?"

They had to find it soon, for they were already late.

Mrs. Gunther flipped through invitation after invitation. They all looked the same—square, ivory cards with fancy titles in lavish print, and they all belonged to Clara's older sister, Sophia.

Three years ago, Sophia had become the first American heiress to marry a duke. She and her husband, James, were immensely popular among the Marlborough House set, and there were never any shortages of social engagements to attend at any given moment. Which made the task of finding the correct invitation all the more difficult now.

"The Wilkshire Ball, the Devonshire, the Berkley . . ." Mrs. Gunther said. "No, no, no. The Allison Ball. Could that be . . . ? Wait, Lord and Lady Griffith . . . was that it?"

Mrs. Gunther continued to guess haphazardly at the names, and Clara's hopes for the evening took a deep, sickening dip and settled uncomfortably in her belly. Everything depended on this one night, and if Clara did not reach that ball tonight, there might not be a second chance. For Clara—the latest American heiress to invade aristocratic London—had to pass the test. In order to be accepted and welcomed into British society like her sister had been, Clara had to glide into a London ballroom and win the approval of the Prince of Wales. Or end up returning to New York, where her position in society was fragile, to say the least.

She shook away the shiver, for she could not afford to have her mind congested with misgivings tonight. The past was in the past. It was time to move forward.

"Ah." Mrs. Gunther turned to face Clara and handed her the invitation. "Here it is. The Livingstons on Upper Belgrave Street. I'm certain this is it. We can go now, my dear."

Releasing a deep breath she hadn't realized she'd been

holding, Clara smoothed a gloved hand over the antique lace on her French silk gown, and touched the glittering diamond-and-pearl choker at her neck. She led the way out of her sister's boudoir, the precious ivory invitation safe in her hand.

A moment later, they were stepping out of the brilliantly lit manor and into the dark, still night. Mantles buttoned at their bare necks, ivory fans dangling from their wrists, they walked down the stone steps to the coach.

As soon as Clara stepped onto the sidewalk, however, her heel imposed upon a crack and she stumbled. The invitation went sailing out of her gloved hand, and she toppled sideways into a tall, extravagantly liveried footman who caught her and righted her before she even had a chance to notice him there.

Clara collected herself. "My word. Thank you! What a decidedly convenient place for you to be standing just then!"

Without a hint of a smile, the young man nodded.

Clara gazed at him for a moment, but he stood like a palace guard, his face made of stone.

Clara sighed hopelessly. *The English.*

Pray, the people she would meet tonight would have a little more personality. A sense of humor at least.

Clara picked up the invitation. She looked at it more closely, and pointed a finger. "What's that symbol in the corner?"

Mrs. Gunther squinted at the small triangular medallion printed on the card, with the letters MWO above it. "I don't know. I'll ask Sophia when we see her."

The footman handed them up into the crested black coach with shiny silver fittings, then hopped onto the page board as the vehicle lurched forward and turned toward Belgravia.

A short time later, they pulled up in front of a grand manor house, lit up like a sparkling jewel in the night. Clara could hear the music from the orchestra inside. Couples moved past the large windows, twirling on the dance floor to a Strauss waltz. A mixture of excitement and apprehension sizzled through her veins, and she gathered up her silk skirt to follow Mrs. Gunther out of the coach and onto the sidewalk.

They made their way up the stone path to the front door beneath a massive portico. A broad-shouldered, bald man with an earring stood at the entrance, and when Clara and Mrs. Gunther approached, he stepped in front of the door, which was closed tightly behind him.

Mrs. Gunther rolled her shoulders in that haughty way of hers, a skill she had perfected to a science. "We are here for the ball," she said in her best matriarchal voice, with one intimidating eyebrow raised.

"Do you have an invitation?" His deep, booming voice didn't intimidate Mrs. Gunther. She kept her eyes on his as she reached into her gleaming silver purse.

"Here." She handed it to him.

He glanced over it, then lifted his narrow gaze to assess each of them individually. Clara felt a prickling of dread, as if they were about to be turned away. Was this how her Season in London was to begin? A failure, before she even set foot in the door?

There was suspicion in his voice. "You're American?"

"Yes," Mrs. Gunther replied.

"You'll be a novelty, then." He stepped out of the way of the door and opened it. "You'll find the masks on the oak table just inside the entrance."

Mrs. Gunther eyed him incredulously. "Masks?"

Clara nudged her through the door before she could question him about the mask theme, for Clara did not want to appear as if they did not belong. She wanted to fit in.

Once they were inside, Mrs. Gunther said, "I did not like that man."

"Neither did I. I'll feel much better when we see Sophia and James."

They found a large crystal bowl full of feathered masks just inside the door, and Clara chose a cream-colored one to bring out the auburn highlights in her dark brown hair.

A woman walked by while they were donning their masks, and Clara could have sworn she wasn't wearing a corset. Clara's lips fell open, and she was about to say something to Mrs. Gunther, but caught herself and didn't mention it. Surely, she had been mistaken.

They withdrew to the cloak room to freshen up, then made their way across the crowded grand hall toward the ballroom.

As soon as Clara stepped inside, her mood instantly lifted. She relaxed, clearing her mind of all the rules she had been going over in her head and all the mistakes she was sure she would make, for what a dazzling room it was. Couples swirled around the floor in bright splashes of color and glitter. The music from the orchestra seemed to come from the blue beyond, so skilled were the musicians, and all the ladies and gentlemen looked elegant and happy.

A footman approached with a tray of champagne, and offered glasses to Clara and Mrs. Gunther.

Mrs. Gunther shook her head and waved a hand to decline. The man's brow furrowed, and he looked at them as if they possessed antlers.

"Really, you must," he said in a pleasant tone, raising

the tray toward them again. "Lord Livingston would be disappointed if you didn't try it."

Clara, still wanting to fit in, took a glass of the bubbly and carefully sipped, savoring its delicious taste and delighting in the way it poured heat through every limb. The footman winked at her as he left.

"Did you see that?" she said to her chaperone.

Mrs. Gunther touched her arm. "Pardon me? Oh, my dear, you don't have a dance card." She stopped a lady passing by, and asked her.

Clara left the issue of the winking footman alone.

The woman, wearing a black and white feathered mask and a garnet gown trimmed in velvet, merely laughed. "We don't bother with names *here*," she said, then continued on her way.

Clara suddenly felt as if she'd just followed Alice down the rabbit hole.

"Perhaps it's because the Prince is coming," Mrs. Gunther surmised. "They say he is not at all as prim as his mother, and prefers to move with the fast set."

"What if someone asks me to dance?" Clara whispered. "What about introductions?"

"No one else seems to be bothering with them." Mrs. Gunther's concerned gaze swept the room, and her voice took on that haughty tone again. "This is highly improper. Where is Sophia? I would like her to explain what we are expected to—"

At that moment, a young gentleman with gold spectacles and fair hair approached and bowed. "May I have the honor of a dance?"

Clara glanced at Mrs. Gunther who hesitated at the man's informality, then nodded, albeit reluctantly. Clara was surprised her chaperone allowed it without a proper introduction, but she supposed the woman felt as anxious and out of place as she did, and didn't want these eminent lords and ladies to know it.

So, not wishing to defy her chaperone, Clara allowed the gentleman to take her champagne glass and set it on a table, then accepted his gloved hand and walked onto the floor with him. They danced a waltz—she had yet to see any other dance performed—and when it ended, he escorted her back to Mrs. Gunther, thanked her, then went on his way.

"That was lovely," Clara said, "but this is not at all how Sophia described it. She said the necessity for social graces was as bad if not worse than New York, and she'd had a terribly difficult time. That man did not even know who I was, nor I he." She leaned closer to Mrs. Gunther, and whispered, "A few of the gentlemen aren't wearing gloves. Look at that man there."

Another couple twirled by.

Mrs. Gunther raised her chin in the air. "I don't know what the world is coming to. We may be approaching the end of a century, but I hardly think society should act in such an uncivilized manner—noble or otherwise. Why, at one of *my* balls . . ."

Just then, a tall, imposing gentleman entered the ballroom. Clara's attention flitted away from her chaperone's social commentary and landed lightly upon the man now standing just inside the doors. He wore a black suit with tails and a white necktie and waistcoat, and his hair—golden and wavy like ripe wheat in the wind—was an unfashionable length, reaching his shoulders. He stepped into the room with his hands clasped behind his back and tossed his head in a most arrogant manner, throwing an errant lock of that golden hair away from his face.

He wore a black mask that matched his attire, and consequently Clara could only see his chin and mouth. It was a beautiful mouth, she decided as she watched him move closer and smile and nod at a passing gentleman. A mouth with full lips and perfect, white teeth. There was a deep dimple centered on his chin, and his jaw was firm and angled. Clara took another slow sip of the champagne.

He must have sensed her staring, for his gaze swung around the room and came to rest intently upon her.

For a long moment they watched each other, to the point where it almost seemed improper, yet Clara could not bring herself to look away. Not that she was feeling brave or daring. Quite the contrary, she was dumbfounded and completely stuck, like a butterfly with its delicate feet caught in honey.

Gracious, but he is handsome. She knew it in the unexplored depths of her being, even though he wore a mask.

He wasted not a single second. He set out on a path around the ballroom, straight toward Clara, his eyes never veering from hers. She sucked in a short, shaky breath, oblivious to whatever Mrs. Gunther was now going on about. All Clara could do was watch that beautiful man saunter like a lion across the floor, his shoulders broad beneath his jacket, his gait slow and sure and languid.

He stopped before her, said nothing, and held out his hand.

Mrs. Gunther stopped talking. She saw the gloved hand beside her, and turned to look at the man who belonged to it. He simply nodded at her, then lifted his hand another fraction to pull Clara out of her stupor and boldly indicate that he wanted to dance.

In complete silence, Mrs. Gunther stared at the impossibly gorgeous gentleman. Clara could only presume that her chaperone was caught in the honey, too, for her lips were parted, but no words were coming out of her mouth.

Laying her gloved hand in his, and without an introduction, Clara allowed him to lead her onto the floor.

She picked up her train and looked into his eyes, then they glided harmoniously into the waltz. They went around the room a few times before he spoke.

"You're a fresh face at one of these things."

"I've only just arrived from America," Clara replied. She would have liked to add "my lord," or "sir," or maybe even "Your Grace," but without the introduction, she didn't know what to call him.

His lips twitched with what looked like pleasant surprise. "America, you say. Allow me to be the first to welcome you to England. It's enlivening to meet you."

"Thank you," she replied, somewhat abashed by his choice of words.

This was not at all how Clara had imagined this night would begin.

"I'm visiting my sister," she told him.

He did not ask who her sister was.

They continued the dance, swirling around the room with such fluid grace, that Clara did not feel the least bit dizzy. Her partner was by far the most skilled dancer she had ever encountered. His hand held the small of her back firmly yet lightly, guiding her around the room as if she were as light as fairy dust.

When the waltz ended, they came to a graceful finish near a large potted tree fern. Another waltz began—a slower one—and her partner inclined his head at her. "Shall we dance another?"

Again she was surprised by this blatant disregard for the rules of etiquette. He should be returning her to her chaperone now. She glanced over at Mrs. Gunther, who was trying most unsuccessfully to look at ease. Clara remembered the old adage, "when in Rome," and decided she should simply follow this Englishman's lead.

"I would be honored."

They moved into position again, and a shiver of excitement moved through Clara as his strong arm encircled her corseted waist and his hand returned to the small of her back. He led her into the center of the ballroom, where they moved about at a more relaxed pace.

"I must say," he commented, in a deep, sultry voice, "you are an extraordinary dancer. I was fortunate to have found you before some other man. I believe I would like to keep you."

Clara laughed. "You cannot keep me."

"Ah, but I wish I could. At least until you tire of me and send me on my way."

Clara felt a hot thrill at his flattery. "Sir, you are flirting with me, quite shamelessly."

"Because I am a shameless man—at least in the wake of your exquisite charm. You are undeniably the most intriguing creature I've encountered all evening. All year to be precise."

Clara's cheeks felt like they were on fire. "I don't know what to say in response to such overdrawn compliments. You don't even know me."

"Overdrawn? You underestimate your allure. You should allow me to prove it to you."

"Prove *what* to me?"

"That you are exquisite."

Their conversation was decidedly out of her realm of experience, and though it was exhilarating in ways she had only dreamed of, it was most definitely improper. She urged herself to remember that. He was a complete stranger. Did he not realize the scandalous nature of his flattery?

And yet, she could not bring herself to change the subject. "How will you prove it?"

He considered it a moment. "How would you like me to?"

Clara gazed at him, not quite sure she could speak, even if she knew how to answer such a slippery question.

"I am completely yours," he said, his expression friendly and open—a delightful change from what she was accustomed to since arriving in England. "I am at your disposal. Your humble servant. Here for your pleasure."

She stared in shock for another few seconds, then couldn't help herself. She laughed out loud. Maybe it was nerves. "I've never met anyone quite like you."

And who was he, exactly? All she knew was that he was someone very daring and very grand. Everything about him was exciting and magnificent and lordly. He was such a resplendent change from the ordinary.

He gazed at her. "Look around you. Every gentleman on the floor is taking notice of you here tonight, and wishing he had spotted you first. They are each hoping that I will soon disappear and leave you free once again."

Clara did look around. The other gentlemen were simply dancing with their partners; not looking at her. "I'm afraid I don't see it."

"No? How else can I prove it to you, then? I know. Feel my heart. It's racing." He pulled her hand to his chest and held it there. Firmly.

Stunned by the physical intimacy in the middle of the crowded ballroom, and flustered by the feel of the man's hard chest against the flat of her hand, Clara tried to pull it away.

He held her hand where it was.

She felt his heartbeat. It was not racing. He was as calm as a lake in the deep of night.

Utterly beguiled and falling into a lazy daze, Clara missed a step.

Her partner righted her and continued on without missing a beat, holding her hand out again, where it should be.

Clara's mouth suddenly felt dry. In fact, she could barely breathe. Did this man always have this debilitating effect on women? If so, she was in for an engaging, perhaps difficult, first season here if she ever encountered him again.

They danced a little longer, and she noticed his pace was slowing, growing more and more leisurely with every musical bar of the waltz.

Clara found herself now avoiding his gaze. He had knocked her off kilter with that last little flirtation.

The waltz ended, and the orchestra paused. The sound of pages turning filled the silence. Clara raised a hand to her cheek, feeling a bit faint in the moist heat of the room. Or perhaps it was this beautiful man's profound effect on her that was causing her to feel fuzzy-headed.

He sensed her distress with perfectly timed precision. "Would you like a cool drink? There is a punch bowl in the supper room."

"Please," she replied.

He offered his arm, and she permitted him to escort her into the next room, where a long clothed buffet table was overflowing with tea cakes and crumpets, huge bowls of colorful fruit, clotted cream and towers of frosted peaches. There were shellfish on silver platters, cheeses and meats, and cakes and candies and berries.

The gentleman led her to the punch bowl, filled a glass and handed it to her. She took three large gulps before she realized it was burning her throat. It tasted bitter with some kind of spirit.

She tried to swallow without croaking or making any facial contortions, then smiled politely at him and carefully set the cup on the table. She wasn't about to have any more of that beverage, whatever it was. She didn't want to end up smelling like a distillery.

"Better?" he asked.

"Yes, better." *Except that my throat is on fire!* She tried to clear it. "Thank you." Her response barely squeaked out of her.

"Would you like to see the Fuseli? It's in the main hall."

She swallowed again. "I'm not sure that I should be away from my—"

"You can't come to Livingston House and not see the Fuseli."

Clara looked up at his elegant mouth, heard the sound of his seductive voice, and felt a buzzing sensation somewhere deep within herself, along with a desire to follow him wherever he led her.

"I suppose I could go and have a peek."

" 'Have a peek.' What a charming American expression."

He offered his arm to her again, and she went with him to the main hall, determined to take one look at the Fuseli, then politely thank her partner and ask him to escort her back to Mrs. Gunther.

Out in the hall, other couples were whispering quietly in corners, and Clara found the whole atmosphere somewhat dreamlike. The ladies seemed to float around as if bewitched by something, and the gentlemen spoke in hushed tones. The masks gave it all a rather mysterious flavor, as if they were all supposed to keep some great collective secret.

Clara attributed her odd perceptions to the few sips of champagne she'd had, and that scalding beverage in the punch bowl.

Her handsome escort stopped before a painting that hung at the bottom of a wide, circular staircase. "Here it is."

Clara looked up. "It's *The Nightmare*."

She sensed the gentleman quietly studying her face. "You know your art."

"Yes, though I've only read about this one. I had no idea it would be so . . ."

"So what?"

"So . . ." Dare she say it? She looked up at the curvaceous contours of the sleeping woman's breasts beneath her gown, her arm limp and flung down to the floor. "So erotic."

She continued to stare in silence at the details: the grinning devil, the luminescent horse entering the bedchamber from some other, unnatural world.

She could feel those gleaming green eyes beside her, watching her, taking in her response to the painting.

He leaned closer. "Some say it leads to the dark recesses of the mind."

The heat of his breath in her ear caused a torrent of gooseflesh to surge like a tidal wave down the entire left side of her body.

He moved silently behind her as she studied the painting, and his presence at her back was more unsettling than anything she saw in *The Nightmare*. For the man standing at his ease behind her was true flesh and blood, sumptuous and beautiful, and he was breathing hotly against the damp back of her neck.

"God, but you are lovely," he whispered.

Unaccustomed to such potent, open flattery, Clara grew breathless. "Thank you."

"Your perfume is like strawberries."

She turned to meet his gaze, and could not stop herself from staring up at his mask, trying to imagine what he would look like without it. He must surely be the handsomest man in all of London. He certainly had more charm and appeal than anyone she had ever met in New York or Paris.

"Come with me, darling," he said softly.

He was smiling now, like that grinning devil in the painting. He took her hand and slowly backed up. Captivated by the playful glint in his eyes and the appealing way he looked at her, as if she were the most beautiful creature in the world, Clara followed him around the bottom of the staircase and along the side of it.

Suddenly, with a hazy, besotted awareness, she realized, with some distress, that he was leading her away, into the dim, private shadows beneath the stairs.

Chapter 2

Warning bells rang and clanged inside Clara's head, but a more willful part of her nature—a part that wanted to experience what this man offered—somehow managed to silence them.

The man backed up against the wall, pulled her toward him so that her breasts were pressed firmly, thrillingly against his chest, and with a smile, he leaned closer for a kiss.

It was one of those life-altering moments, when all that a person believed about one's self was about to be tested, delusions revealed and insight gained.

Clara should have stopped him then. She should have stepped away or placed her hand on his chest and pushed him back, but alas, she did not. She did nothing to stop the snowball from rolling, did not even try to overcome her teeming desires, for here in the dark, she and this gentleman were hidden from view.

He was the most exciting man she had ever encountered. After two long years of self-inflicted emotional repression to try and fit into a strict, upper-class society, she couldn't resist the opportunity to taste freedom. She wanted to burst forth like a white-water flash flood, breaking through a dam.

She gazed into the man's eyes and felt her proper convictions break.

His lips were still parted with a smile when he kissed her. His tongue swept in and touched hers with the confident skill of an experienced lover, heating her blood and igniting a blazing fire that roared like a monster in her ears. She swayed into the kiss and into his body, relying on his strong hands around her waist to keep her steady through her knees, which incidentally, in the last few seconds, had turned to pudding.

Sweet Jesus, she thought, as his huge hand came up to gently stroke her neck, sending waves of tingling, wicked delight down her spine.

She had to stop this now. Her brain was screaming for attention, but lusty curiosity wouldn't allow her conscience to gain a foothold.

The delicious rush of desire mounting inside her was more exciting than anything she'd ever known. She'd never imagined a London ball would be quite like this. It felt like she was dreaming. Or drowning.

"Ah." He sighed against her cheek. "That was the most enchanting kiss I've had in . . . I don't know how long. You are extraordinary."

He pressed his lips to hers again, deepening the kiss, closing in on her with his whole body, and sending a sweet pounding arousal straight to her core. She wrapped her arms around his neck and reveled in the pleasure of his hot, moist mouth, while she tried to ignore her conscience, scrambling helter-skelter to dig in its heels.

Groping for self-restraint, Clara managed to drag her lips away for a moment. "Sir, I must ask you to—"

"Come with me upstairs," he whispered in her ear. "Then you can ask me to do whatever you like."

"Upstairs?" she blurted out. She took a step away from him, but he still held her hand.

"Yes," he replied, sounding amused. "It's still early, love. I doubt all the rooms would be taken yet."

"All the rooms? Taken?"

Panic pooled suddenly in her belly.

"If we're going to go, we should go now. The hall is getting crowded. All the corners have been taken up."

He stepped away from the wall to collect Clara, as if he fully expected her to follow him. As if this little tryst they were having were perfectly acceptable.

Clara had had a feeling earlier that something wasn't quite right about this ball, but she hadn't been sure what to do about it. She had hoped Sophia and James would arrive and make sense of it for her. Now, the need for action was weighing down on top of her like a piano on her head.

"Sir, I believe you must have me confused with some-one else. I can't possibly—"

"Why ever not, love? You're *here*, aren't you? And we seem to have developed a rather intoxicating rapport."

She realized with stark regret that she should have lis-tened to her instincts sooner. Something was very wrong.

"Here? Where is *here*, exactly?"

He gazed at her for a long moment, then the set of his jaw changed. His expression darkened.

"You don't know where you are?"

"I'm afraid I don't. I would appreciate it if you would enlighten me."

All the warmth and seduction from only seconds ago vanished from his voice like a drop of water on a hot stove. Clara's stomach lurched.

"This is a private ball, madam. Only those with an invitation are permitted to enter."

Clara backed away from him and moved out of the shadows and into the open hall. A sick feeling crept into her belly as she watched him follow her.

"I did have an invitation," she told him.

"Was it yours? How did you get it?"

"It was my sister's."

He stopped following and closed his eyes. "Please, tell me you're married."

Clara's brows flew up under the half-mask, which suddenly felt very tight on her face. "Married!" She lowered her voice to a whisper. "No! And if I were, I would certainly *not* be here having this indecent conversation with you!"

He glanced this way and that, as if he weren't sure what to do with her. After some brief contemplation, he took her by the elbow and began to escort her back to the ballroom. "You need to leave."

"But what is this place?"

"Not the kind of place you should know about." He quickened his pace, and Clara had to struggle to keep up with him.

"Don't run," he said. "You'll attract attention."

"How can I help it? You're practically dragging me on my knees!"

"Don't speak to anyone else. Get out of here now, and for God's sake, don't tell anyone where you were. Do you understand?"

"What I understand is that I should never have danced with you."

He stopped and looked down at her, his eyes fierce and dark. "I must correct you on that point. You were, in fact, very *fortunate* to have danced with me. You are a tempting little flower, and another man might not have been so understanding, or so apt to let you go."

He marched her back to Mrs. Gunther and gave a polite bow.

He lingered a moment, staring at Clara as if he weren't quite ready to leave. Then his shoulders heaved with a deep intake of breath.

He redirected his gaze toward Mrs. Gunther. "Good evening, madam. It is my understanding that you are in the wrong house this evening. I implore you to take your charge and leave here. Immediately."

With that, he turned and walked off.

With trembling hands and a throbbing pulse, Clara walked into the Witherington Ball only moments after their footman informed them that the Prince of Wales was not at Livingston House. He had arrived not long ago at the house two doors down.

Clara was breathing hard, partly from her hasty escape, but mostly from the memory of following a handsome, seductive stranger into the dark shadows beneath a staircase, and feeling the shocking, sizzling lure of temptation.

She had thought she was stronger than that.

Groping for some semblance of normalcy, she glanced around the room in search of her sister, Sophia, the Duchess of Wentworth, and spotted her near the orchestra, conversing with her husband, James.

"There she is," Clara said to Mrs. Gunther, who was still unaware of what had happened to Clara while she had supposedly been sipping punch, and was now pressing Clara for answers. "Let's go and tell her we're here."

Mrs. Gunther led the way around the perimeter of the

room. Sophia's face lit up with a radiant smile when she noticed them. Wearing a spectacular Worth gown with gold lace and jewel trimmings, topped off by a sparkling tiara—a requisite among married ladies when royalty was present—Sophia came to meet them halfway, leaving her husband to socialize with a group of older gentlemen.

"Where were you?" Sophia asked, meeting Clara and taking both her hands. "You were supposed to be here an hour ago."

Clara labored to keep her voice steady as she explained. "We went to the wrong ball."

"The wrong ball? Which one? And why do you look so pale, Clara? Are you feeling unwell?"

Mrs. Gunther leaned forward to speak softly to Sophia. "It was a disgraceful ball."

Clara gazed imploringly at her sister, who knew her well enough to guess that she wished to speak privately. Sophia smiled gratefully at Mrs. Gunther. "Thank you so much, Eva. Perhaps Clara and I need a moment alone. Would you excuse us?"

Mrs. Gunther's brow furrowed, but she nodded in agreement and snapped open her plumed fan. "I shall wait by the fountain."

As soon as Mrs. Gunther left them, Sophia took Clara by the arm and led her to a private corner behind some leafy potted plants.

"What happened, Clara? You look as white as pastry dough, and you're perspiring." She reached into her jeweled purse for an embroidered handkerchief and used it to dab at Clara's forehead. "Perhaps we should go and find somewhere to sit down."

"I don't need to sit, I'm fine. I just need to know where I was."

Sophia paused. "How can I possibly—"

"We had to wear masks, and there were no dance cards. Everyone was drinking a tart punch that kicked like a mule, and no one wished to be introduced."

Sophia covered her mouth with her gloved hand, her expression coloring as what Clara described to her sank in.

"What was it?" Clara asked. "Please, tell me."

"Heavens above. Don't tell me you went to Livingston House."

"Yes, I did, and what do you mean, 'Heavens above'? Tell me, Sophia, before I lose my mind!"

"You went to a Cakras Ball, but how in the world did you get in?"

"We had an invitation."

"From where?"

"Mrs. Gunther picked it up from your desk. She couldn't remember the address of where we were supposed to meet you, so she went through your invitations and thought that Livingston House was the place."

Sophia shook her head. "Do you still have the invitation with you?"

"Yes, here." Clara pulled the tattered card out of her purse.

Sophia examined it and touched the small medallion in the corner. "Oh, Clara, I can't believe you went there. Did anyone see you?"

"Yes, but we were wearing masks."

"Did you talk to anyone?"

The panic in Sophia's voice was making Clara more and more nauseous with every passing second. "Yes, I danced with a couple of gentlemen."

"That's all? You just danced?"

When Clara didn't answer right away, Sophia grabbed

hold of her upper arms and held her firmly, forcing her to meet her gaze. "Clara, what happened? Are you all right?"

The room seemed to be spinning. Clara nodded. "I'm fine."

"Thank goodness."

"But I was very lucky."

"How?"

"I danced with a man who was charming and wonderfully handsome, and he took me for a glass of punch."

"That punch," Sophia said quietly, "is pure rum, with a little juice added for color."

"I only had a few sips. But then the gentleman escorted me to look at a painting, and we lingered there a while . . . He was very handsome and—"

"Clara, what did you do?"

"Nothing! Or rather, I followed him under the stairs."

Sophia blanched. "Did he kiss you?"

Clara's inability to answer the question said everything that needed to be said. She gazed at her sister imploringly.

"Was it very awful?" Sophia asked. "He didn't hurt you, did he?"

Clara shook her head. "No, it was nothing like that, and that's the worst part." She lowered her voice to a whisper. "I don't understand what happened to me. I *wanted* him to kiss me, Sophia, and I was powerless to resist, even when I knew it was wrong."

Sophia stared at Clara, then pulled her into her arms. "Is that all that happened? Just a kiss?"

"Yes. I managed to put a stop to it. Eventually."

"Hush, now. I'm sorry. I know how important it is to you, to be cautious and prudent. But take heart, it could have been worse. He might have believed you wanted more and demanded it."

"I think he did believe it. At first anyway."

"But you told him otherwise? And he accepted that?"

"He was surprised, but as soon as he discovered I was not married, he took me back to Mrs. Gunther immediately, and insisted that we leave."

Sophia shook her head in disbelief. "You were very fortunate to have met *him*, Clara, whoever he was."

"That's exactly what he said."

The two sisters stood in silence for a moment, listening to the orchestra play a Minuet. Finally, Clara's heart rate returned to a less expeditious pace.

"It felt like some kind of dream world," she said. "What are these Cakras Balls?"

Sophia glanced over her shoulder to ensure no one was listening, and leaned in to whisper in Clara's ear. "The Cakras Society is a secret, exclusive club, that no one is supposed to speak about outside the gatherings, so I must be very quiet. They hold balls where the guests may leave the ballroom for trysts in corners or in the bedrooms of the house. The MWO stands for 'married women only,' and all social rules are relaxed in favor of anonymity and liberation, but most importantly, in favor of pleasure."

Clara stared dumbfounded at her sister. "Do husbands and wives go there together?"

"Some do, but I suspect that most who attend keep their spouses in the dark about the whole thing."

"That's appalling. You mean to tell me that each and every person I saw there was cheating on their spouse?"

"Not all of them. Like I said, some married couples go together, and many single gentlemen attend."

"But how do *you* know about it, Sophia?"

Sophia colored, and began to walk along the edge of the ballroom. She whispered to Clara, who walked beside her. "James belonged to the society, when he was younger."

"James? Your *husband*, James?"

Sophia nodded. "Yes, and . . . well . . . we attended a few of the balls together when we were first married."

"*You* went there? I thought *I* was the only one who had ever done anything wild."

Sophia glanced over her shoulder again. "We stayed together all evening, of course, and I must admit, it was wicked fun. We danced as much as we wished, drank champagne, and slipped away when we felt like it, finding some dark alcove to be alone."

"Sophia, I'm surprised. You've always been so responsible."

"There's nothing wrong with enjoying one's husband," Sophia replied, smiling deviously, "and allowing him to enjoy you. It keeps marriage interesting and exciting, and a happy marriage is a gift to everyone involved, including one's children."

Clara laughed quietly. "Leave it to you to find the charity in lovemaking."

Sophia inclined her head at her sister. "You can find anything you desire in lovemaking, Clara, but I should not be telling you these things. Mother would throw me to the hogs if she could hear me now." Sophia stopped and nodded at a lady across the room. "The point is, you should not have gone to that ball."

"I'm fully aware of that, Sophia, but it cannot be undone. You must help me get out of this as smoothly as possible. The last place I want to be is at the center of a scandal. I've already come close enough to that fate and skirted it. I doubt I would be so lucky a second time."

Sophia nodded, and continued to walk with Clara

around the room. "You told no one who you were? You wore your mask the entire time?"

"Yes."

"We are fortunate in the fact that most people who attend a Cakras Ball do not attend any other social functions in the same evening, to prevent being seen and recognized. We must pray that everyone will be judicious tonight."

"There's a chance they won't?"

"A chance, yes. Some people simply don't care. Either way, it wouldn't hurt to burn that dress you are wearing, and don't wear that diamond pendant again. And that comb in your hair—toss it out."

Perspiration began to stifle Clara. "I should leave right away." She glanced anxiously around the ballroom.

"You can't leave now. You still have to dance with the Prince." She began to primp the trimmings on Clara's gown. "He has an open mind when it comes to foreigners, being half German himself, and thankfully for us, he has an eye for pretty ladies. You, my dear sister, are among the prettiest." She smiled, but Clara knew her sister well enough to see the concern in her eyes.

"Now, you must try to forget about what happened tonight," Sophia continued, "and bring some color back to your cheeks. I have already spoken to the Prince about you, and he has requested a spot on your card, so you cannot leave without insulting the Crown."

Clara nodded. "I'll do my best."

"Good. Then let us find James. It's time for your Season in London to begin. This time, we'll begin it properly. Then we'll get you home."

Chapter 3

Dearest Adele,

I miss you, dear sister, and I take back what I wrote before about London gentlemen being as dull as the Knickerbockers. I met a most fascinating man just the other night. I won't tell you how I met him, only that he was very exciting . . .

Clara

"It has become a verifiable stampede."

Quintina Wolfe, the Marchioness of Rawdon, tossed the *Morning Post* down onto the breakfast table and reached for her gold-trimmed teacup. "Have you read this yet, Seger?" she asked her stepson, the marquess. "Another American heiress waltzed into a ballroom last night and danced with the Prince of Wales, and she's made headlines because of it. I ask you, what is the world coming to?"

Seger Wolfe, the Marquess of Rawdon, had not read the

society pages. He never read *anything* in the society pages, nor did he ever wish to, but when his stepmother spoke about it this morning, he found himself diverted. He glanced up from his own copy of the paper.

"I beg your pardon, Quintina? Did you mention an American?"

God, he had not yet managed to sweep last night's brief but consequential encounter from his mind. He could still hear the woman's deep, sultry voice in that irresistible American accent, and the appealing way she'd purred and shivered when he had whispered in her soft, dainty ear.

He had returned home early from Livingston House, for he had lost all interest in 'dancing' with anyone else after she'd left, but a lot of good that had done him. Last night, in bed, he had smelled her perfume on his hands. He had remembered the luster in her unfathomable brown eyes. It was the kind of luster he'd only seen once before in his life, and it had bloody well kept him awake and tossing like a flounder all night.

Quickly, he attributed his sleeplessness to the fact that their "encounter" had been cut short, and because of that he was frustrated. He was, after all, not accustomed to being refused. He had become an expert at spotting fruit that was ripe, and ripe fruit was generally eager to be picked and tasted. Not in many years had he bothered to approach the type of woman who would not be willing or able to carry things to the finish. What in God's name had induced him to mistake a debutante for a seasoned trifler?

Perhaps it was because she resembled Daphne in certain ways—her dark hair and brown eyes, and her facial expressions. He supposed he had needed a closer look.

Quintina stabbed the paper with her long, bony finger. "It's all there in black and white. Read it yourself. Another tart with obnoxious manners and objectionable breeding has arrived with trunkloads of American dollars, hoping to become one of *us*. Pox on her. She's a trollop, like all the rest. Honestly, what can they be thinking?"

Seger reached for the open paper, barely listening to his stepmother ranting openly about the Americans. He had learned to ignore her tirades in that regard—ever since that cocksure Californian had purchased her parents' family home after her father died. It had been the talk of London for a while, and it was no secret how Quintina felt about her neighbors overseas.

"Did you know," she said, "that she's the sister of the Duke of Wentworth's young American wife, who came from a hovel somewhere in the middle of the country, where her ancestors were bootmakers and butchers. But then again," she waved a hand, "the duke was not exactly in an enviable position in society, was he? Being so deeply in debt. . . ."

Seger picked up the paper and found the headline: AN- OTHER AMERICAN HEIRESS JOINS STAMPEDE TO ACQUIRE ENGLISH TITLE.

The article went on to describe the estimates and sources of her father's wealth, the young woman's unparalleled charm, and the details of her attire, mainly her exquisite Worth gown. "It was the color of a fresh magnolia," the writer said, "with pale blue flower sprays. She wore pearls and lilies in her thick, mahogany hair."

Seger's gut began to twist and roll as he read word after word of the excruciatingly disturbing article. Her name was Clara Wilson. *Clara.*

It was her. The beautiful, bewitching—and idiotic— young temptress.

What the bloody hell was wrong with the girl? Didn't

she know she would attract attention by dancing with the Prince of Wales, and that every gentleman who had laid eyes on her at the Livingston Ball would be making the connection this morning, licking his chops and planning how he was either going to ruin her altogether, or use what he knew to squeeze the largest wad possible from her rich American father?

Dammit, everyone had seen him dancing with her, too, and Seger was more than recognizable, even in his mask. He was one of the regulars at the Cakras Balls, and had never bothered to try and hide that fact. All of society knew he avoided ambitious single women like he avoided the plague, for he was not interested in being anyone's prized acquisition.

He knew what real love was. He'd had it once, and he knew it could not be arranged, nor bought, nor snuffed out by a strict and sometimes cruel social code.

He would not marry to please his tenants or the royal court or his stepmother. Especially his stepmother. Such a path had been forced upon him once, and it would not be forced upon him again. It was a matter of principal now. He would not surrender to it. Besides, he preferred his life exactly the way it was.

He gazed coldly at Quintina. There were still so many things not yet forgotten. Or forgiven.

Seger raked a hand through his hair and pushed the still-glowing embers of resentment down into the deepest corners of his being where they belonged. They did him no good out in the open. What was done was done, and he could not change the past. It was best left forgotten.

He turned his attention back to the paper and read the rest of the article about the American. He pinched the bridge of his nose.

No doubt, there would be conjecture about his intentions if their encounter at the Cakras Ball became known. Everyone would wonder if he would marry her; some would expect him to, for he had compromised her reputation by disappearing with her under the stairs.

"Bloody hell." Seger crumpled the paper in his fist, whirled around and threw it into the fire.

This was precisely why he did not flirt with debutantes. He did not wish to marry until he was good and ready, and he was not ready now. He would not be forced. His marriage would be on his own terms.

Seger watched the newspaper shrink as the red flame consumed it, then he faced the table again.

His stepmother was staring at him in stunned silence, her thin-lipped mouth dangling open.

After a second or two, she raised an eyebrow. "That's exactly what *I* wanted to do with that paper." Then, with notable concern, she glanced up at Gillian Flint, her niece, who was just entering the breakfast room. Gillian removed her spectacles, smoothed her skirt and sat down.

Seger nodded at Gillian—the daughter of his stepmother's dead sister, Susan, who had been Lady Hammond. Gillian was visiting from Wales, enjoying her first Season here in London under the chaperonage of her aunt. From what he'd heard from his stepmother, the young woman had been a great success so far.

Quintina furiously buttered her roll. "I wish we could do the same to that American heiress, and all the others like her. Throw her into the fire. We have our own English girls to arrange into marriages, and we should not have to suffer this kind of vulgar, garish invasion. They think they can *buy* their way in. It is simply shocking."

Nostrils flaring, she returned to her breakfast, and Seger turned his attention away from her.

He could not eat another bite, however, for now he knew the American girl's identity, and her blossoming notoriety was prime fodder for a scandal.

Seven days later, Clara waited in the drawing room at Wentworth House for Sophia, James and Mrs. Gunther, for they were about to embark upon another exhausting evening of society balls and assemblies.

Tonight Clara wore a pale yellow, short-sleeved satin gown with a tight *cuirasse* bodice and an off-the-shoulder, lace-trimmed décolletage, ornamented with a deep silk *fichu*. Her skirt was draped and caught up at the side, with a flounced train decorated with lace and velvet ruching.

She gazed at herself in the enormous gilt-framed mirror above the fireplace, fiddling absentmindedly with one of her earrings, and wondering if the mysterious masked lover she had met a week ago would recognize her if they met again.

Thankfully, no one else had recognized her. At least she didn't think so. There had been some concern after that crass article in the paper, but when Clara went out the next evening and the evening after that, nothing untoward had occurred. It seemed the English were as discreet and reserved as they led the rest of the world to believe. Or perhaps no one wanted to stir up a scandal and make a fool of the Prince of Wales.

Clara moved away from the mirror and sat down, wondering who she would meet tonight, and if any of the gentlemen would intrigue her.

She had met dozens of young aristocrats the past week,

but none had possessed the striking charismatic presence of her secret paramour, or the tantalizing features of his person as a whole. As a matter of course, she forgot the plain gentlemen she had met this week very quickly after the initial introduction and the obligatory brief but polite conversation. She could picture none of their faces now, even though she had been able to look at them fully and without restrictions for a good many minutes.

Contrarily, the only face she could conjure in her imagination possessed a pair of striking green eyes and a full mouth, a deeply dimpled chin and a strong, square jaw below a narrow, black mask. Clara knew she would spend most of her evening thinking about him, searching ballroom after ballroom for that thick, golden hair and that confident, sensual walk.

Sophia, James and Mrs. Gunther entered the room, and in minutes, they were all walking out the door and stepping into the coach.

Four drawn-out hours later, Clara entered her third ball of the evening. She was exhausted from the constant string of introductions and the challenge of making conversation with English gentlemen while remembering to curtsey to this one, not to curtsey to that one, and for pity's sake, not to become distracted and call an earl a "sir-something" or a baronet a "lord."

She had danced with a number of men, but had not yet found the one she had been searching for.

She later sat down with Mrs. Gunther to catch her breath and cool herself. She clacked open her plumed fan and sat for a time, watching the dancers while she absent-mindedly stroked the smooth jewel in her drop earring with a finger and thumb.

Her mind returned again to the vision of that incredible

man, sauntering across a glittering ballroom toward her. It all seemed like a ridiculous fantasy now, even though she knew it had been real. Perhaps the champagne and the punch had rattled her senses and made it all seem more magical than it had been—at least up until the moment he'd invited her under the stairs.

Or perhaps it truly had been magical.

Certainly, the man's effect on her had been. She had not been able to extinguish the confusing, sweet ache that emerged every time she thought of him, every time she reminded herself that she did not even know his name, and that it was a very real possibility she would never see him again.

Still, Clara continued to dream of that night, imagining in great detail what would have occurred if she had gone with him to one of the private rooms when he had suggested it, if she had not revealed her innocence to him.

She envisioned a night of abandoned morality, bold and daring quests for pleasure she could not begin to understand, and quests for knowledge, so that she *could* understand the longings inside her—longings that were growing more and more intense as her fantasies became more adventurous.

But that's all they were, she reminded herself. Fantasies. She knew nothing about the man beneath the mask, except that he had not ravished her when he'd had the chance.

And for that—despite all her daydreams that indicated otherwise—she was thankful.

She also felt justified in her private affection for this stranger, for at least she could tell herself that he possessed some integrity, and that he was a true gentleman. A hero who had pulled her from the fires of scandal, just like her father had done two years ago. If that mysterious gentleman had not marched her back to Mrs. Gunther and insisted that they leave immediately, who knew where Clara might be today? Perhaps on a steamer somewhere in the middle of the Atlantic, on her way back to America, her chances of marrying a decent man all but washed away.

On the other hand, her heroic fantasy man could have been married.

Married. She hoped he wasn't. Pity the poor wife if he was, for how could any woman survive the knowledge that a husband like him was unfaithful and uninterested in her?

Sophia approached at that moment, her cheeks flushed from a dance with her husband. "It's almost time to leave, Clara. Have you danced enough?"

"Enough? Most definitely. I'm exhausted." Yet, the thought of leaving drizzled disappointment over Clara, for another night had passed and her dream lover had not materialized.

"Shall we go?" Sophia asked.

Clara pasted on a smile. She closed her fan, gathered up her skirts, and followed her sister out.

As they drove home in the dark carriage, Clara continued to ponder the situation. She could not continue this way, dreaming about a mysterious stranger, while heaps of opportunities for acquaintances with perfectly respectable gentlemen passed her by.

Later that night, not long after she'd changed into her nightgown, Clara padded down the corridor in bare feet and knocked on Sophia's door.

Sophia opened it and raised her index finger to her lips. "Shhh." She held her second son, John, in her arms. He was wrapped up in a blanket.

She carefully handed the sleeping infant to his nurse,

Louise, who headed for the door to take him upstairs to the nursery. Clara closed the door behind Louise.

Sophia pressed the heels of her hands to her eyes. "Sit down, Clara. What is it?"

Clara sat on the bed, not altogether certain how to explain her feelings to her sister, who already had enough on her plate with two babies barely ten months apart. All she knew was that she needed to do something to get over this foolish infatuation, because it wasn't going away on its own.

"I'm sure you've noticed," Clara said, "that I've not been remotely interested in any of the gentlemen I've met this week, and I've met quite a few very nice men."

Sophia covered Clara's hand with her own. "Correct me if I'm wrong, but I suspect it's because you're still thinking about *him*. Am I right?"

"Is it that obvious?"

"To be honest, yes. You gaze off into space most of the time, and if you're not doing that, you're surveying ballrooms, searching hopefully with your eyes."

"I want to find a good husband, I truly do, but how can I, when I can't get a certain fantasy man out of my mind? None can even compare to my memory of him." Clara cupped her forehead with her hand. "I know it's ridiculous, because I'm sure that everything I believe about him is exactly that—a fantasy. Let's face it, he was present at one of these improper balls, and therefore is probably one of two things: a rake who carries on affairs with married women, or a husband who cheats on his wife. Neither of those possibilities are attractive to me. I want to marry a decent man who will be faithful to me and be a good father, and yet . . ."

"You can't stop thinking about him."

Clara sighed. "Something needs to be done. I need to get him out of my head."

"How can I help?"

Standing and crossing the room, Clara glanced down at the stack of cards on Sophia's desk. "I don't suppose you've gotten any more invitations for a *you-know-what*."

Sophia rose from the bed and joined Clara at her desk. "I know very well *what*, and I thought you said those balls were appalling."

"Well, they are, at least for married people who go there to be unfaithful."

Sophia slowly shook her head. "No. Absolutely not. You can't take a risk like that. What would Mrs. Gunther say?"

"You could be my chaperone, Sophia. We could go just for an hour or so. You said you're anxious to start going out more since John was born, and James is usually at the House until quite late many nights."

"I couldn't go to a Cakras Ball without James, nor would I even want to be seen there without him. People might presume we are inconstant. Which we are not."

"We could wear wigs and put on English accents. No one would recognize us."

"Have you lost your senses? Even if we did manage to get there without anyone knowing, what are the odds that you would see this particular man again? He might not even be there."

"Can't we try? I must know who he is—a name at least. What if he's the man I'm destined to marry?"

"Then you will meet him in a respectable situation."

"How can you be sure? Maybe he only goes to the Cakras Balls."

Sophia sighed with frustration. "What about everything you just said, about him being either a rake or a philanderer?"

Clara waved a finger at her older sister. "You told me James used to go to those balls when he was younger, and now look at him. He's a perfect husband, Sophia. What if you had dismissed him because you'd discovered he attended those parties?"

Sophia was quiet for a moment. "I suppose you have me there."

"I just want both of us to keep open minds." A thrilling ripple of anticipation shimmied up Clara's spine. "So you'll come with me?"

Her sister hesitated, then went to her desk to sort through the invitations. "The Cakras Balls don't always happen regularly. Sometimes I don't get an invitation for months on end."

She continued to flip through, then stopped and stared at Clara. She handed her a card. Excitement twittered in the air.

"Or sometimes, they come just when you want them to."

Chapter 4

Dear Clara,

Please be careful. Do not forget what happened two years ago. You craved excitement and you wanted to break free of society's strictures, and you came very close to complete ruination. Remember that where young women like us are concerned, society's strictures exist for our protection. . . .

Love,
Adele

"If Mother could see us now, she'd forget to breathe and turn blue." Sophia glanced out the dark window of the carriage as Livingston House came into view, then arranged her rhinestone and feather mask on her face. "And I don't know what James will think when I tell him where we went tonight. I hope he won't be angry."

"You can blame it all on me," Clara replied. "Besides, it's not as if you're sneaking out behind his back. In fact, we would have brought him with us if he hadn't gone to Yorkshire."

"I suppose. Nevertheless, I'll explain it all when he returns home and hope for the best. We're here. Are you sure you want to do this?"

Clara tried to suppress the nervous butterflies in her stomach as she, too, arranged her mask. She was about to take a huge risk by sneaking into a Cakras Ball, but she was also—if luck was on her side tonight—about to see her handsome paramour again.

Anticipation quivered up her spine. All this was both imprudent and exhilarating. Who knew what could happen in the next few hours?

"I'm sure. I need to see him in order to forget him and get on with my life."

Sophia faced her squarely. "You can't fool me, Clara. You're not here to forget him, you're here to see him again because you want him. I know you too well, and all I see in your eyes at the moment is desire. You're dreaming that he'll be here tonight and lead you under those stairs again."

Clara stared speechless at her sister.

"And as your chaperone," Sophia continued, "I shouldn't let that happen. I should be telling you that you can dance with him, but under no circumstances should you be alone with him. This is a dangerous place, Clara, and if he's not to be trusted—"

"Don't worry, I won't do anything foolish, and I'm grateful to you for bringing me here. But I don't want to presume that he's not to be trusted, either. He didn't ravish me the last time."

"That was the last time. What if—when he sees you here after you'd been warned—he presumes you're looking for a dalliance? He might think you're fast."

The carriage stopped in front of the dimly lit mansion. Clara gathered up her purse. "I'm not fast. I am morally upright, in perfect control of my impulses."

Sophia smiled and raised a delicately arched brow. "Then what, pray tell, are we doing here?"

Clara smiled in return, surrendering unequivocally to her sister's acute observation. They knew each other too well, and sometimes all that was necessary between them was a certain look to communicate what they were each thinking, which was usually the same thing.

"I've missed you," Clara said.

Sophia hugged Clara. "I've missed you, too. I'm so glad we're together again and I'm glad I can help you tonight, because despite my warnings, I do know how you feel. I felt the same way about James when we first met. I could barely survive each day, wanting him the way I did." She squeezed Clara's hand. "Who knows, maybe this man *is* your destiny. My, what a romantic I am."

Clara sighed. "Or maybe I'll discover that he's the worst rogue in the world and he's here tonight cheating on his wife, after losing half his fortune playing cards, and on top of that, when he sleeps, he snores like a buffalo."

They shared an affectionate smile, then Sophia pulled on her long gloves. "With any luck, we'll find out soon enough—at least about the first two things."

The carriage door opened, and the ladies stepped out. Clara looked up at the huge stone front of the mansion, where the same burly man as last time stood in front of the door.

Sophia straightened her mantle. "You're absolutely positive?"

"Yes. Let's go and get this over with."

They picked up their skirts and walked up the steps. A delightful shiver of anticipation ran through Clara. She could hardly believe she was here again, in this scandalous, forbidden place.

Sophia presented their invitation. The next thing they knew, they were inside, standing on the shiny, black and white checkered floor in the wide hall, handing their mantles over to the masked butler while the music of flutes and violins flitted to their ears from the ballroom.

"Does Lord Livingston ever greet his guests?" Clara asked as they ascended the stairs to the drawing room.

"No, there are never any introductions. Both Lord and Lady Livingston follow the same rules as everyone else. They mingle and dance with whomever they please, but no names are ever spoken."

"You mean to say they carry on affairs under each others' noses?"

Sophia sighed and leaned in to whisper close to Clara's ear. "This country is different from ours. I'm afraid adultery is not all that uncommon among the nobles here, especially the men, and any public recognition of it by their wives is practically a cardinal sin."

Clara immediately thought of her sister's own marriage. "James isn't like that, I hope."

"Absolutely not. James was different from the rest. I knew it the first moment I met him."

Clara considered this. If she herself married an Englishman who was later unfaithful, would she even be *capable* of ignoring it? She had been brought up with a radically different ideal, as all American girls were, with a Puritan attitude toward adultery as a Scarlet Letter sin.

They entered the crimson and gold drawing room, where elegant chintz fabrics covered all the chairs and chaises as well as the windows, and the walls were painted scarlet with gilt crown moldings. Clara tried to forget about her high ideals for the moment, reminding herself that Sophia had managed to find an honest, faithful English husband. Surely not all of them would turn out to be philanderers.

She glanced up at a huge crystal chandelier hung low in the center of the room. Most of the guests stood close to the walls, whispering and giggling in the dimly lit corners. The air was charged with the heat of secretive, wicked seductions.

"I don't see him," Clara whispered. "Maybe he's in the ballroom."

"Or maybe he's in one of the private rooms already."

Clara didn't want to think about him in a private room with another woman, but she had to face the fact that that was a very real possibility. It was late, after all, and the night he had made advances upon her, he had moved quickly and effectively. By this hour, they had already ventured under the stairs. "Let's try the ballroom."

They smiled and nodded at the people they passed, and to make sure they fit in, accepted glasses of champagne from a footman who offered it.

Clara and Sophia entered the large ballroom and watched the couples waltz around the polished floor. The same orchestra that had played the last time was here again tonight, and the music was equally stupendous.

Clara couldn't help thinking that from her vantage point, it could have been any other respectable ball—if not for the couple huddling behind a potted tree fern not three feet away from where she stood. Kissing.

A mixture of shock and fascination struck her.

She knew she should look away. She wanted to, but couldn't.

The gentleman's arms slid around the lady's waist; she combed her fingers through his hair. Their mouths were open, as if they were famished and trying to gobble at each other.

Clara continued to stare. Even though she was uncomfortable with the spectacle and felt wretched for watching, it was the most erotic, stimulating thing she had ever seen.

Were those two people married to each other? she wondered, still staring at their mouths in motion.

All at once, she noticed other people staring, some moving closer to watch openly, others whispering and pointing. Clara's cheeks suddenly ignited with an almost scalding heat.

Sophia leaned close and took her by the arm. She led her away toward the other side of the ballroom.

"Can you believe that?" Clara whispered. "I've never in my life seen anything like it."

"I thought your mystery man kissed you."

"He did, but I didn't get to see what we looked like from afar. And at least he found us some privacy, so that we weren't out in plain view." She couldn't help glancing over her shoulder again at the couple. They were now merely conversing and smiling. "It's shocking that a place like this exists."

Sophia smiled at a gentleman as he passed. "Yes, especially when you consider the social caliber of the guests. There are some very powerful, influential people here."

They continued to move around the perimeter of the ballroom, watching the dancers. A gentleman caught Sophia's eye and approached. "Care to dance?"

Sophia smiled graciously at him and disguised her

voice with an English accent. "Please do except my apologies, sir, but I must decline at the moment. Perhaps later."

He bowed cordially before moving on.

"I won't be dancing with anyone tonight," Sophia said, "and neither should you, except for the man we're here to see. We must stay focused."

"I agree entirely."

They finished their champagne and set their empty glasses on a passing tray.

Clara continued to search the room with her eyes.

"Do you see him?"

"No. He's not anywhere," Clara replied, hearing the disappointment in her voice.

"Don't give up yet. We'll stay for a little while. Maybe he's just late."

"Or maybe he was here early, and left already." She didn't want to get her hopes up and feel even more disappointed later on.

Just then, a very grand-looking, golden-haired man in a black mask strolled into the ballroom. Looking relaxed and confident, he picked up a glass of champagne and let his gaze sweep around the room. Clara's eyes narrowed.

She knew that walk . . . that hair . . . that body. It was him. *He was here.*

A hot thrill rushed through her, shooting into her belly like a firebrand. She stood motionless, intently watching him, not sure if she'd be able to move her legs if she tried. She was fixed to the spot, staring at all of him, from his beautiful head down to his shiny black shoes. He looked as handsome as she remembered. More so, after the week spent dreaming about him. She was completely thunderstruck by his powerful, breathtaking presence.

"Is that him?" Sophia asked. "The man who just came in?"

Without taking her eyes off him, Clara nodded.

"My goodness," Sophia said. "No wonder you couldn't forget him. He's incredible."

Clara managed to find her voice, and smiled. "So it's not just me."

"I should say not. Pardon my vulgar tongue, but *Lord Almighty*."

The two of them watched him saunter around the room looking composed and at ease, his golden hair falling about his shoulders in wavy disarray. Clad in the usual formal wear—black jacket, white waistcoat and white necktie—he raised his glass to a gentleman on the other side of the room, who raised his glass in return before continuing his conversation with a lady.

"Do you know who he is?" Clara asked. "Have you ever seen him before?"

"Never. I only attended a few Cakras Balls with James over the winter, and I don't recall seeing this man, though James and I weren't exactly here to socialize with other people."

"What about during the Season last year?"

"I never saw him at any of the parties or balls I attended, though perhaps he had shorter hair then and that's why I don't recognize him." Sophia studied him further, then tilted her head to the side. "He certainly wouldn't have attended society balls looking like that."

Clara wondered why he kept his hair so unconventionally long. "Perhaps he's married. If he doesn't feel the need to keep up a respectable appearance and frequent the Marriage Mart. . . ." She took a deep breath. "What's wrong with me? My stomach is rolling!"

"It's called lust, Clara, and you're infected with it." Still watching the gentleman, Sophia shook her head as if she couldn't believe anyone could be such an extraordinary feast for the eyes. "But I can see why. Let's walk this way so you can have a chance to collect yourself before you speak to him."

Speak to him. At the mere mention of it, Clara's stomach careened again.

They strolled casually around the ballroom in the other direction, so they wouldn't meet him face-to-face as he circled toward them. Clara struggled to resist the urge to turn around and look at him again. She didn't want to be caught staring like an imbecile while her heart was doing back flips.

"What will I say? I can't ask him his name. That would be against the rules. How will I find out anything?"

Sophia discreetly glanced over her shoulder. "You'll have to be creative. Do you think he'll recognize you in that wig?"

"I don't know, but surely when I speak he'll recognize my voice and accent. Do you think he made the connection and figured out who I was after the article in the paper?"

They continued to wander around the room. "Hard to say."

Clara's insides continued to whirl until she almost felt dizzy. "That's it, I can't take it anymore. The anticipation is killing me. Let's get this over with."

They both turned. Now, they were walking straight toward him. Tall and broad-shouldered, he towered over everyone in his path.

"I hope you're ready," Sophia said.

Clara found herself again caught in the sticky web of his unparalleled good looks and his debilitating sexual allure.

"Heaven help me, I could never be ready for a man like him."

It was the perfume that gave her away as she brushed by his elbow, in a ridiculous dark wig, no less. She smelled of strawberries again.

A brief glance at her mouth confirmed it. Indeed, it was the American.

Seger inhaled deeply, then frowned. He stopped and turned around to look at her from behind after she'd passed by.

Contrary to common sense, his body reacted to the familiar fragrance. He'd never smelled a perfume quite like it before, only on her, and it brought back all kinds of full-bodied recollections about touching her and tasting her in the dark. Kissing that lush, open mouth. Caressing the soft, supple skin just below her earlobe. Then having it all cut short.

He felt the immediate stir of a lingering, unfulfilled arousal, but knew better than to let it take hold. He shifted the direction of his thoughts.

She was with a friend tonight instead of the older woman from the week before. No, not a friend. Seger's brows drew together as he noticed the wig on the other woman as well. She was probably Miss Wilson's sister, the Duchess of Wentworth.

At that precise instant, the heiress turned around and glanced over her shoulder. Their gazes met and locked, and recognition occurred. She stared at him for a few heated heartbeats, then quickly, almost as if in a panic, she faced front again.

Seger shook his head. What was she doing back here? It was a well known fact that American heiresses were bombarding London in a mad dash for husbands with titles. Why would she come here to look for one, and risk her reputation? Did she not realize that skirting a scandal last time had been a complete miracle? Did she not know how to quit while she was ahead? The duchess should have known better.

Or perhaps that's why she was here in the first place. To stir up a scandal and force someone's hand.

Well, it wouldn't be his. He had spent the past eight years learning how to guard himself against that kind of thing.

Unfortunately for her, however, it probably wouldn't force anyone else's hand either. Most of the gentlemen here were not in possession of a great deal of honor when it came to young ladies and scandals. They would simply watch from the shadows as she danced in her noose. Besides that, most of them were already married.

Just then, in his peripheral vision, Seger noticed an older gentleman making his way toward Miss Wilson. It was not surprising. Even in that horrid wig, she was gorgeous. It was only a matter of time before every other gentleman in the place would want to experience her delights, for she was a rare contradiction. She had the look of a professional beauty, yet with innocence. And those lips were enough to bring any man to his knees.

The man bowed before Miss Wilson, and held out his ungloved hand.

Seger tensed as he watched.

Miss Wilson smiled, but politely refused the gentleman, who nodded courteously and backed away. Seger exhaled a breath he hadn't realized he'd been holding. She was lucky that time, but how long would that luck hold out?

Seger downed the rest of his champagne in a single gulp

and set the glass on a table. He hadn't come here tonight to play hero, but he supposed it couldn't be helped. He would dance with her once and do what he could to talk some sense into her. Then he could at least say he tried.

He approached the ladies and made a bow. "Good evening."

"Good evening," they both said simultaneously.

He offered his hand to the heiress. "Shall we?"

Clara's whole body stiffened as she gazed up at her dream lover in a shock-induced stupor. She hadn't expected him to approach her after he'd been the one to march her back to Mrs. Gunther the first time they'd met. She was surprised he hadn't turned and run in the opposite direction when he'd recognized her a few minutes ago.

But who was she to refuse such a gift? All that mattered was that he was here, and she was going to dance with him.

She placed her gloved hand in his. He led her onto the floor and stepped into a slow waltz.

They danced for a moment or two before he finally spoke. "Clara, isn't it?"

Stifling her surprise and struggling to gather her wits, she cleared her throat. "You've been reading the papers."

She couldn't believe how calm she'd managed to sound on the outside when she was squealing like a schoolgirl on the inside.

"I have, along with everyone else. You're quite a sensation."

She raised her chin. "I assure you, it was not my aim to attract so much attention, and I was quite surprised by all of it. The London press is very aggressive."

He inclined his head. "Indeed it is. Which makes me wonder why you took such a huge risk coming back here tonight. I thought I'd made myself clear the last time, and warned you about the dangers of a place like this for a woman like you. Did you not understand my meaning?"

"I did."

"Then why have you returned, may I ask?"

Clara rummaged around her muddled brain for an answer, when she didn't want to be *giving* answers, especially to difficult questions like these. She wanted to be the one asking the questions.

Maybe she could turn things around. "It seems, sir, that you know all about me, yet I know nothing of you. That's hardly fair, is it?"

She barely recognized the bravado in her voice, the deep, almost seductive timbre. She had no idea where it was coming from. She wasn't exactly experienced with this sort of thing.

Perhaps it was something in the air. The whole room reeked of pure, unhampered sexuality.

"There are rules here," he replied. "Identities are to be kept secret."

"But you broke the rule when you revealed that you knew my name."

The corner of his mouth turned up in a wicked grin. "You're not going to report me, are you?"

She returned the smile with an equal dose of charm. "Good gracious, no. Not unless you want me to."

He chuckled. "I think not. Only because it would put you in the spotlight more so than me, and I don't think that's a wise place for you to be at the moment. Not among these people. They have no mercy when it comes to the violation of their rules."

Clara tilted her face upward, remembering how gloriously indulgent it had felt to be kissed by those beautiful lips. "I must thank you, then," she said sweetly, "for being my champion a second time and warning me away from danger."

"Not that it did any good the first time. All you did was leap back into the fire. Strange, you don't strike me as the type of woman who enjoys things hot and hazardous."

"No? How *do* I strike you?"

"As the type who doesn't usually take risks. You seem fresh and free of sin. To tell you the truth, you stick out like a sore thumb."

Clara pursed her lips. "I'm not sure if I've just been insulted or paid a compliment."

"It was, for all intents and purposes, a compliment."

They continued to dance around the room, and Clara considered all that he had said and realized she still knew absolutely nothing about him. Sophia had told her to be creative. How the blazes was she supposed to do that?

"Obviously," she said, "you don't attend many balls other than these ones, or you would not find me so fresh. I'm no different from most other young ladies my age."

"I beg to differ."

Still no new information. What would it take?

"Shameless compliments," she said. "Are you always so blatantly charming to the ladies?"

He didn't reply. The waltz came to an end, and her mystery man looked up. "Blast it, I had intended to talk sense into you, and all we've been doing is flirting with each other. Stay for one more."

He was certainly direct. It was refreshing.

Another waltz began and she could not even think about refusing. "But wait," she said, stepping back. "If I am to stay for your lecture, I would have you tell me something about yourself first."

"Is this a negotiation?"

"I believe so."

He wet his full lips. "All right, then. What would you like to know?"

She considered it for a few seconds. "If you won't tell me your name, tell me why neither my sister nor I have never encountered you out in society."

"Because I prefer to avoid the Marriage Mart. Come, let's dance."

She finally stepped into his arms and let him whisk her across the floor. "Because you're already married?"

"No."

"You're not married, then? You've never been?"

He shook his head and Clara's heart rejoiced, but there was still so much more she wanted to know.

"Why won't you tell me your name?" she asked.

"Because that's not what we do here."

"I don't care. I'll probably never come to one of these things again, and I would at least like to know the name of the gentleman I danced with this evening. You're not a criminal, are you? A fugitive from justice?"

"No."

"A spy for the British government?"

He laughed. "No, I'm afraid not."

"Then why must you be so secretive? It's not as if I couldn't find out who you were if I asked enough people. You must be the only man in London with hair down to your shoulders."

He said nothing for a few minutes while they continued to dance, then finally, when the waltz was nearly at an end, he said, "It's Seger."

Clara felt the color rush to her cheeks. "Seger?"

"Yes."

The music stopped, and they stepped apart. Clara gazed at his face, wishing she could see what he looked like without the mask. Wishing she could reach up and touch that strong chiseled jaw and those perfect, masculine lips.

"Now, since you didn't allow me to lecture you, it's your turn to do something for me," he said.

"All right."

"Leave, and don't come to one of these balls again."

His blunt request hurt, even though she knew he was only thinking of her well-being. Further contemplation made her feel flattered that her well-being even mattered to him.

Clara knew she should do as he asked, but wished it did not have to be so. There was still so much about him she didn't know, and how would she ever find out if he never ventured into society? How would she survive another week of longing, because this feeling—unwise though it may be—was not going away. Not the way things stood now, when all she wanted was an ambrosial repeat of last week's escapade under the stairs.

In the end she agreed because he was right, but she wasn't happy. She held out her hand. "Thank you, Seger. I enjoyed myself."

Eyes never leaving hers, he kissed it. "As did I."

At the touch of his lips, a shiver of delight coursed through her. She began to walk away, but he stopped her. "Wait."

She turned.

"Why *did* you come here tonight?"

Clara stared at his green eyes beneath the mask. Her heart began to pound. "Haven't you guessed?"

He merely stared at her, waiting for her reply.

"I came here because I couldn't stop thinking about you." With that, she walked away.

Chapter 5

Dearest Clara,

You must be more careful about breaking the rules, and I am not just referring to your foolish intention to go to that scandalous ball. Even the smallest mistake matters. Just the other day, Mrs. Carling gave Mrs. Jenson the cut direct, because Mrs. Jenson had worn her diamonds in the morning. (Be sure not to do that.)

Now that I have dutifully said my piece, you must tell me all about your adventure. Was he there?

Love,
Adele

"Did you see the Duke of Guysborough last night?" Mrs. Gunther asked, looking up from her embroidery to peer across the breakfast parlor at Sophia. "Did he attend the assembly?"

Sophia picked up her teacup and sipped from it, a faint

smile touching her lips. If the Duke of Guysborough had been at the Cakras Ball, she and Clara certainly hadn't known it.

Sophia set down her cup. "No, we didn't see him."

"I wonder if he'll be at the Tremont assembly this evening. He's a handsome gentleman, don't you think? And widowed."

Sophia raised her eyebrows. "You think he would be a good match for Clara?"

"Naturally, don't you? Your mother would be pleased."

"He's rather old."

"Nonsense, he can't be a day over forty-five."

"But he has children already from his first wife, who passed away not that long ago. Do you think he wishes to remarry?"

Mrs. Gunther poked her needle into the fabric on her lap and looked up. She spoke in a lowered voice. "I've been making inquiries, and from what I've learned, he has only one son and four girls. No spare, so to speak. I would think he would be inclined to marry again, and Clara is certainly a beauty."

Sophia dabbed at her mouth with the corner of her linen napkin. "I hadn't considered the duke. I don't know him very well. Do you really think he's handsome, and doesn't seem too mature?"

"To a woman of my age, he's barely more than a schoolboy."

Just then, Sophia's husband entered the breakfast parlor. "James, you're back!"

He smiled. "Yes, I decided I missed my wife and sons far too much to spend another day away from them trying to calm my fanatical steward. He's in a panic about the cottage renovations, you know. I believe your extravagance has taken ten years off his life."

Sophia rose from the table to embrace him.

They sat down and discussed the renovations at Wentworth while James ate his breakfast. As soon as he laid down his fork, Sophia stood. "Shall we go and see the boys?"

"I would like nothing more." Together, they excused themselves from Mrs. Gunther's company and left the room.

As soon as they were alone in the corridor, James took Sophia's hand, kissed it, then held it as they walked. "Perhaps next time you'll accompany me to Wentworth," he said, "and spare me the anguish of sleeping alone."

Sophia's voice was flirtatious. "Is that the only time you missed me, James? In bed?"

He kissed her hand again. "You know I think of you always. There was a time I never imagined that being a husband and father could add such joy to my life."

Sophia gazed lovingly at him. "And I think of you always, too. Which brings me to what I must tell you now. I hope you will not be angry, James, but I took Clara to a Cakras Ball last night, and I'm worried that I might have done the wrong thing."

James stopped and let go of her hand. "You went to a Cakras Ball? Why in the world would you do that?"

She had taken a few steps ahead, but halted to turn and face him. "It's a long story, James, but I must tell you all of it, for I worry that the situation could become dangerous if we don't soon learn about a certain gentleman who has made an impression upon Clara."

"Ah. This gentleman was at the Cakras Ball?"

She nodded.

"But why did you take her there, Sophia? The Cakras Society is supposed to be secret."

Sophia explained the whole situation—how Clara had gone to the wrong ball a week ago by mistake, how she had not been able to forget the gentleman who'd informed her of her error, and how they went to last night's ball to try and discover his identity.

After reminding Sophia of what she already knew— that going to a Cakras Ball had been a risky thing to do— James took her hand again. "Did you discover the gentleman's name?"

"Only his Christian name. It's Seger."

James thought for a moment. "Seger. The only Seger I've ever heard of is Seger Wolfe, the Marquess of Rawdon."

"He's a marquess?"

"If he is indeed the same man."

"Have you ever met him?"

"No, he doesn't sit in the House. He's not interested in politics from what I gather, or perhaps he simply doesn't like to show his face. He was involved in a divorce scandal a few years back. He and a few other gentlemen were called to court as witnesses, to testify for a particular lady's husband, to prove the woman's adultery."

Sophia tried not to sound glum as she walked slowly down the long corridor beside James. "So he's not respectable?"

James inclined his head. "As I said, I've never met the man, so I can't say. But do warn Clara to be careful if she encounters him again. Just in case. Especially considering what happened to her before. Is that what has you worried?"

Sophia inhaled deeply. "You don't think she'll make a mistake like that again, do you?"

"What I think, my dear, is that you should try to have confidence in her. She is an intelligent young woman, and is no longer naive. She has been quiet and careful for the past two years, choosing to postpone her first Season. That is self-restraint at its best, especially for a romantic young girl like Clara, who attended our wedding with dreams of romance in her eyes, longing for such happiness for herself. We must trust that she will be prudent, for she has said on many occasions in her letters to you that it is her greatest wish to be sensible."

"Yes, but she is inherently passionate, and sometimes love can turn one's head."

"Like it turned yours?" He squeezed her hand.

"You were a good man, James. We don't know anything about the marquess, and I fear that I might have become caught up in the excitement of her infatuation and advised her poorly. Perhaps I should have set a better example and refused to let her return to that place."

"She saw him again, I presume."

"Yes, they danced twice and he again asked her to leave. She was in a romantic daze the whole way home. I'm worried, James."

He nodded as they reached the door to the nursery. "You mustn't let yourself be troubled, my darling. We will do what we can to help Clara. I will make inquiries about the marquess. Now let us dispense with worries for the time being and see what our sons have accomplished today. Perhaps John has discovered his thumbs."

"I have good news and bad news," Sophia said to Clara that afternoon, as soon as they were out of earshot of the groom, who rode behind them in Hyde Park.

Both in their riding habits, crops in hand, they sat high

in their sidesaddles, maintaining a leisurely pace along the bridle path.

"Did James know anything?" Clara asked.

"Yes, if he was talking about the same Seger. The good news is, he's a peer. His name is Seger Wolfe, and he's the Marquess of Rawdon."

"Truly. A marquess, you say. Mother would swoon."

"Yes, she would, but I must inform you that James wasn't particularly pleased to hear that you were at a Cakras Ball. He warned me to be more careful from now on, and suggested that you be especially careful if you ever see the marquess again."

"Gracious. He has a reputation, then." Their horses' hooves tapped lightly over the soft ground. "What about the bad news? Did he lie to me about not being married?"

"That, I don't know, but it would be very easy to find out now that we know who he is. All I know is the bit of news James reported to me—that the marquess was involved in a divorce scandal a few years ago, called to the witness stand to admit to being a certain lady's lover—or one of them—to prove her adultery. It is said he seeks only physical pleasures, that he finds no joy in sentiment. That is surely why he's not invited into polite society."

Clara digested this news with some disappointment, though she knew she shouldn't be surprised. She knew the marquess seduced married women regularly at the Cakras Balls. That sort of behavior was bound to ruin a man's reputation eventually. Even in London.

"Will society not let him back in?" Clara asked. "Or is it his choice to scorn invitations?"

"I wish I knew."

Clara gazed up at the sky. "I wonder if he learned a lesson from that scandal. Perhaps he's more careful these days. He must be, given the way he tossed me out the door when he discovered I was unmarried—a hot potato to him apparently."

"You are not a potato, Clara, and you're still hoping for the best where he's concerned, aren't you?"

"I can't help it. He's still the most intriguing man I've met since I've arrived here. I have a profound desire to understand why he is what he is, and I can't seem to shake myself out of it."

Sophia regarded her sister. "What about the Duke of Guysborough? I only mention him because Mrs. Gunther asked about him this morning. She wanted to know if we'd seen him last night."

Clara laughed. "Wouldn't she be surprised to know why we didn't see *anyone* where we were."

"Indeed. Do you remember meeting him last week?"

"The tall fellow with the dark mustache?" Clara said. "Yes, I do."

"What did you think of him? He would be an excellent catch, given his rank. His title is not quite as old as James's, but he's favored by the queen I understand. Her Majesty admired his wife for her charity work. She passed away just over a year ago."

"A widower." Clara ducked below some low hanging, leafy branches. "I hadn't considered marrying someone who had been married before. I suppose it is an option."

"Did you find him attractive?"

Clara shrugged. "Not as attractive as the marquess, though he would probably be a more sensible choice."

"Yes," Sophia agreed, gazing directly into Clara's eyes, "and I do want you to be sensible. I know I was supportive about going to the Cakras Ball, but when I think about what could have happened if we were discovered. . . . I don't wish to take that kind of risk again."

"I'm sorry to have put you in that position, Sophia."

She sighed. "It was my decision to take you there, so don't apologize."

They rode in silence for a few minutes, enjoying the cool breeze.

"I just wish," Sophia said, "that there was a way for you to see the marquess again without risking another appearance at a Cakras Ball."

"If only he came out into society."

Sophia smiled mischievously. "We could hide in a parked carriage across the street from his London residence, and simply wait for him to come out, then follow him. With any luck, he'd go into a shop or into the park, and we could pretend to bump into him by chance."

Clara shook her head at her sister. "How decidedly deranged. I can just picture us sitting for hours in the rain, then getting arrested like a couple of Peeping Toms."

"It was just a thought. Not exactly sensible, was it?"

"I think I'd prefer something a little more direct."

Sophia considered it. "Well, there's always the obvious. I could hold an assembly and send him an invitation. He knows I'm your sister. If he's interested in seeing you again, he'll come."

"He told me he despises the Marriage Mart."

"That may be so, but if my eyes were telling me anything last night, it was that he was as taken with you as you were with him. You might be the very thing to bring him out of his shell. Perhaps deep down, he wants to be accepted again, and we can help him. The worst thing that could happen is that he could simply not attend, in which case we will at least know he is determined to remain alone."

"Or that he is not interested in me."

Sophia urged her horse into a gallop. "Not a chance."

Clara began to gallop her horse, too.

"Shall I arrange an assembly then?" Sophia called out to Clara as she came up beside her.

Clara tingled with a thrill of anticipation, and smiled. "Most definitely."

Seger sat down for supper in his dining room, with his stepmother, Quintina, at one end of the table and his cousin by marriage, Gillian, to his left. Lobster puffs with hollandaise sauce were served, followed by tarragon chicken with artichokes, at which time Quintina set down her wine glass and broke the customary silence.

"I received an assembly invitation today, from the Duke and Duchess of Wentworth."

Seger paused from his chewing, then swallowed. "You don't say."

"You don't sound surprised."

He did not look up from his plate, for there was very little he ever chose to reveal to his stepmother. "Should I be? I wouldn't know, since I haven't been following your social calendar."

Quintina bristled. "Surely you know that I do not receive invitations from dukes or duchesses, but we won't go into the reasons why." She gave a cursory glance to Gillian, as if she didn't want to soil the girl's virgin ears with talk of Seger's personal exploits.

Instead, she'd cast the blame without actually saying it, which was her way. She blamed Seger for the family's social descent, all because of what had occurred three years ago with Lord and Lady Edmunston.

Though if one was to be analytical, one could go back much farther than three years and find another source for blame. The true origin of Seger's current manner of existence. Why he preferred to remain an island.

"The odd thing about it," Quintina said, "is that the invitation was addressed to you and me both."

Seger leaned back in his chair.

"*Now* tell me you're not surprised," Quintina said, lifting a dark, arched eyebrow.

Seger wiped his mouth with his napkin. "All right, you win. I am indeed surprised."

Surprised? Bloody hell, yes. He hadn't been invited into that upper echelon in years. The duchess couldn't actually be playing matchmaker for her sister, could she? He wasn't exactly a respectable catch, although he did hold a title, and that was the whole purpose behind most of the American heiresses' shopping excursions to London. Perhaps she or the duchess didn't care about his reputation.

Or didn't know about it.

Not that any of it mattered. He was not interested in being bought for cash. He was one of the few English aristocrats who had enough cash of his own to paper every last wall of his sprawling country house. Twice.

"So what do you make of it?" he asked.

"I would call it a freakish and fantastic gift. Despite the unpleasant fact that the duchess is an American, it is at least a chance to get our toes through the upper doors, which is an opportunity this family desperately needs. An opportunity Gillian needs." She smiled warmly at her niece. "After all, I promised Susan on her deathbed that I would do everything I could to see her daughter married well, and yet, I have been opposed at every turn in that regard. This is Gillian's first Season and I must seize this opportunity."

Seger glanced at Gillian, who kept her gaze lowered and said nothing. She was a quiet little bird at the table most nights. Barely noticeable sometimes, almost like she wasn't there. *Shy,* Seger thought. Though not unattractive in a youthful way.

"You'll go, I presume," he said to Quintina as he leaned forward to reach for his glass of wine.

"Naturally. But may I ask that you, on the other hand, decline?"

He raised his eyebrows. "Decline? The first decent invitation I've received in years, and you want me to decline? What was all that talk about finally getting the Rawdon toes back through the upper doors?"

To be honest, he didn't care a whit about sticking his toes through anybody's upper doors; he wasn't interested in going to a stuffy Mayfair assembly where most of the old matrons would likely hiss at him anyway.

He would, however, like to see the lovely masked creature who'd been keeping him up most nights for the past two weeks. He had still not gotten over her departing words the last time they'd spoken—that she had come to the Cakras Ball to see *him*, and had risked her reputation in the process.

To say he was flattered was an understatement. More accurately, he had been knocked clear of his equilibrium. He hadn't expected her to say such a thing. He had expected some roundabout answer, maybe an aloof claim that she was simply looking for adventure, because that's what most women said to him when flirtations began. They knew by instinct that that was what would lure him into their bedrooms.

Clara however, had been fearless. She had dashed to the point and told him in no uncertain terms that she had come to the ball because she'd desired *him*.

He, in turn, had been more than impressed. He'd been bowled over, aroused by her instinct to surprise him with such a comment, then instantly turn around and walk away. She had not waited for his reaction, nor had she asked for a reply, and the effect was to leave him dumbfounded and wanting more.

He remembered suddenly that she had reminded him of Daphne the first time they'd met. He realized with some relief that he no longer saw the resemblance.

"I do want all of us to be invited through those doors again," his stepmother said, ripping him out of his reverie, "but your presence at this early stage might evoke whispers. I want our re-entry to be smooth and gradual. Certain people will not take as much offense with Gillian and me as they might with you, and I want to do what is best for Gillian."

He glanced at his cousin again. She smiled sheepishly.

"And what would you have me do, Gillian?" he asked.

Seeming surprised that he had spoken to her at all, she paled. "I . . . I would have you do whatever pleases you."

He leaned back and nodded.

Quintina was quiet for a few seconds. "There is another more important reason why you shouldn't go, Seger."

"And what, pray tell, is that?"

Her narrow shoulders rose and fell as she took a deep breath. "I suspect that the real reason we were invited was because of the duchess's sister—that garish girl we read about in the paper. The duchess is holding this assembly to gather all the unmarried peers in one room, so they may be sized up like merchandise. Surely, you would prefer to avoid such a vulgar affair."

Seger slowly blinked. "Ah. You don't want me to meet the American. Afraid I'll become infatuated with someone inappropriate?"

Her voice was cool and subdued. "It's not as if you haven't made that mistake before."

Tension curled around the table. Seger made a fist on his lap. "You're right, Quintina, and there were disastrous consequences."

His stepmother's cheeks flushed red with fury. "Seger, for eight years you have refused to take a respectable wife and produce an heir. Don't you think you have punished this family for those consequences long enough? Consequences that no one could have predicted?"

"Her death was more than just a consequence, Quintina. I loved her. She was taken from me, and she died." Seger tossed his napkin onto his empty plate and stood up. "I believe I am finished. I'll skip dessert tonight. If you will excuse me." He bowed politely to Gillian. "Enjoy the rest of your dinner."

He left the dining room and went upstairs to reply to the Wentworths' invitation, and graciously accept.

Chapter 6

Dear Adele,

That exciting man I told you about? I hope to see him again tonight. . . .

Clara

Clara stood beside James and Sophia inside the wide double doors of the drawing room, greeting the assembly guests as they filed in.

The sheer splendor in the room was beyond anything she had ever seen before, and she'd seen a great deal of splendor in New York. Tonight, beautiful women in jeweled, luxurious, low-necked gowns with trains and long white gloves glided about, laughing and conversing, while the gentlemen strolled around in their black and white formal attire.

In addition to the sparkling finery on the guests, the drawing room was garnished with a number of immaculate tables, covered with silk tablecloths, stacks of fruit and trays of desserts that looked more like colorful works of art than actual food.

This had to be one of the most exciting and disquieting nights of Clara's life. The anticipation to see Lord Rawdon again had reached an incomparable pitch, and her heart lurched in her breast every time a new guest approached the door.

Would he even come? she wondered. He had replied to Sophia's invitation and said he would, but Clara nevertheless found it almost impossible to believe, for he had become something close to a fairy tale prince to her. He seemed to exist more in her imagination than in reality, and to conceive of seeing him here tonight in the flesh without the mask seemed too much to hope for.

Perhaps he had reconsidered and changed his mind. It wasn't every day, after all, that a man re-entered a society that had rejected and expelled him.

If he did come, however, she would know that there was indeed something between them.

A gentleman stepped up to the door. The majordomo announced, "His Grace, the Duke of Guysborough."

James and Sophia greeted the older gentleman, then Sophia turned toward Clara. "And you remember my sister, Clara Wilson?"

He bowed elegantly. He was one of the gentlemen under consideration as a possible husband, at least by Sophia and Mrs. Gunther, and this made Clara pay attention.

He was, she supposed, a handsome man. With dark hair and mustache, he possessed a certain impressive maturity. There was something about him, however, that made her uncomfortable, as if she would always have to sit up straight when he was around.

"Indeed," he said, "it is a delight to see you again, Miss Wilson. We will have a chance to talk later this evening?"

"That would be splendid, Your Grace."

As soon as he moved on, Clara glanced at Mrs. Gunther across the room, sitting alone. She was leaning forward, watching Clara's every move. She leaned back, however, after the duke turned away.

"It's getting late," Clara whispered to Sophia when there was a free moment. "Do you think he changed his mind?"

"I don't know. I hope not."

At that moment, an older woman approached the door with a younger lady at her side. The woman was of medium height and proud looking; the girl appeared shy and nervous.

The majordomo announced: "Lady Rawdon and Miss Gillian Flint."

Clara's stomach went *whoosh*. It was Seger's stepmother.

Clara sensed her sister's sudden, intense awareness as well. "Lady Rawdon, welcome," Sophia said.

"Thank you, Your Grace. May I present to you my niece from Wales, Gillian Flint." She gestured toward the girl behind her, who curtsied.

Sophia smiled. "It's a pleasure to meet you, Miss Flint." Then she turned toward Clara. "This is my sister, Clara Wilson."

The older woman smiled but glanced sidelong at Clara as she passed. The younger Miss Flint followed with her head down.

"That was Lady Rawdon," Clara whispered, leaning forward to see out into the center hall. "His stepmother. I wonder if Seger will be next."

Pulse pounding, she watched the top of the stairs, but a

group of ladies ascended. No wild-looking, wavy-haired gentlemen in sight.

Another half hour went by, and the frequency of arrivals began to diminish. Clara's feet were getting sore. *He's not coming,* she thought. *He changed his mind.*

The disappointment was difficult to keep at bay, though she did her best not to show it. She glanced at Lady Rawdon across the room, talking to a group of older women.

Suddenly Sophia nudged her. Hard.

Knocked slightly off balance, Clara stepped to the side, then turned toward the door just as the majordomo said, "The Marquess of Rawdon."

The whole world seemed to hush. All Clara heard was the noisy, thunderous rush of blood in her ears.

It was him. *Him.*

Her gaze went first to his eyes, for she had never seen them before without the mask, and what eyes they were. Deep green and large and expressive. She had known before that he was handsome, but this was mind-altering. He was everything she had imagined and more, with the divine presence of a Greek god.

Her entire body pulsed with sizzling, nervous excitement; her blood rushed through her veins like a flash flood, her stomach whirled with butterflies.

It wasn't until a few seconds later, as he was shaking James's hand and saying something that made James laugh, that Clara noticed he had cut his hair. Though it was by no means short, it was not wild about his shoulders any longer.

Had he trimmed it because of this single assembly? Had he gone out and changed himself just for her? Or would he have done it for any other invitation?

Either way, the gesture touched her. She wanted to laugh. He had come out of hiding.

She wondered yet again . . . had he done it for *her*?

Clara watched numbly as he greeted Sophia. "Duchess, it is an honor."

"The honor is mine," Sophia replied, turning casually toward Clara. "May I present my sister, Clara Wilson of New York. This is Clara's first Season here in London, Lord Rawdon."

He moved to stand before her, so tall, so grand and sophisticated that she barely remembered to breathe. She glanced up at his beautiful face, felt her heart pulverizing her ribs, and despite all the panic from inside, felt overtaken by an instinctively flirtatious behavior that emerged from some primitive element of her being. What was it about him that brought that out of her each time she met him?

She smiled and lifted an eyebrow. He smiled in return, bowing slightly. His eyes never left hers as he whispered, "At last."

A shiver tingled all the way down to her toes. She sucked in a quick breath.

"Welcome to Wentworth House," she said.

He stood before her, staring.

Locked in his smoldering gaze, Clara melted at the grandeur of his face—the masculine line of his jaw, the discerning intelligence in his eyes—and as she stared at him, Clara felt as if she were looking into the swirling, red-hot center of a volcano, feeling a senseless impulse to leap.

Neither of them spoke until the moment was broken by Sophia, who cleared her throat. Clara felt wrenched out of a trance.

The marquess smiled again, more broadly this time, as if he had noticed her start and known that she was enamored. Not that he hadn't seemed enamored himself, but perhaps that was just his way. Perhaps he was enamored with all women.

The divorce scandal of three years ago entered her thoughts. She reminded herself to be prudent.

The marquess let his gaze sweep the room, but before he ventured inside, he faced her one more time. "I hope to hear all about America this evening, Miss Wilson, if you would be so inclined to describe your home to me?"

"I will seek you out," she replied.

"I'll look forward to it with pleasure."

He fully entered the room, and Clara faced the door again to greet another guest. She smiled brightly at the lady, while struggling to wipe the silly smile off her face and quiet her trembling heart.

There were very few people whom he could talk to, Seger realized as he crossed the crowded drawing room and felt more than a few disapproving gazes follow him to the buffet table. He had not attended a proper assembly in three years, and consequently did not move in these circles. His acquaintances were of a different breed now— not so strict and straight-laced, less judgmental of others—and his entertainments were less correct. Apparently most of these people knew it.

Did they think he wanted to be accepted again? He hoped not, for he had never wished to reconcile with them. He had never really cared. They had forsaken him, as was their prerogative, and he had accepted that. Being accepted by them was not important to him. He was accepted in other places. He was here for quite another reason this evening. To satisfy a lusty curiosity. Quench it if he could, for he was not interested in marriage for profit.

Yet he could not deny that he was interested in *something*.

He noticed his stepmother and Gillian in the far corner, but was not inclined to join them. Instead, he reached for a glass of champagne as a footman passed, and downed it in one gulp.

Setting the empty glass down on a table, he slowly made his way around the perimeter of the room, feeling very much like an outsider. The only pleasant distraction was Miss Wilson still at the door, teeming with charm as she greeted the last few guests. She had smelled like strawberries again.

Her sister, the duchess, was also enjoyable to look at. She had welcomed him without a hint of contempt.

The duke had been cordial as well. Seger wondered if His Grace knew about his wife and sister-in-law attending a Cakras Ball. From what Seger knew about the duke, he was not the sort of man one kept secrets from, nor was he the sort who would remain in the dark for long about any and all events involving members of his household. Regardless, if His Grace had known about his wife's little adventure, he certainly hadn't revealed it. Still, he was a man Seger should not underestimate.

Seger did manage to meet a few gentlemen he knew from his own social circle, gentlemen who had the rare ability through certain connections to cross over from one sphere to the other. They were surprised to see him at the duke's assembly and made no secret of it as they waved him into their conversation.

There, he was introduced to a few respectable ladies and gentlemen, and the first crack in the barrier of his expulsion became visible to both himself and others in the room. He wasn't sure how he felt about that. He had not come here to chisel his way back in.

A short time later he felt the sizzle of Miss Wilson's approach. He turned slightly to watch her cross the room, her gaze locked on his from yards away, her eyes smiling with mischievous anticipation. His loins stirred with sensual awareness of her as a woman. He turned away from the laughing gentlemen to walk toward her.

They met in the center of the room, but did not settle there. Seger led her toward the wall.

"You wanted to hear about America," she said cheerfully.

He grinned at her. "That, and whatever else you want to tell me about. I'll listen to bible recitations if it would please you."

Her whole face beamed. She gazed over her shoulder at the other guests and spoke softly. "I wasn't sure if you'd come."

"I wasn't sure myself, but I'm glad I did. I had no idea that without the mask and ridiculous wig, you would be more beautiful than I had imagined."

She sighed. "Still full of compliments, I see. I thought you might be more reserved in a more . . . *normal* situation."

"You call this normal?" He glanced around. "I had forgotten how completely *abnormal* these things could be. No offense meant to the hosts."

"I'm sure none would be taken. My sister is American, as you know, and I assure you, all this was a culture shock to her in the beginning."

"And what about you? You're American as well. What do you make of our English ways?"

She paused. "I don't know yet. I'm still trying very hard to fit in. I wish I knew how to act blasé."

"I'm glad you don't."

Clara smiled at the compliment. "May I just say that you have given me hope, my lord, that not everyone is as reserved as they pretend to be."

He pushed away from the wall. "No, I suppose I am not as reserved as most of the people here tonight, and I can certainly feel the chill because of it. Perhaps we should take a turn about the room. I forgot that lingering in private corners for any period of time with unmarried ladies is frowned upon."

He offered his arm to Miss Wilson. She laughed. "You certainly *have* been out of circulation if you'd forgotten something as fundamental as that."

"I have indeed."

They walked through the crowd, nodding politely at people as they passed.

"I heard about your court scandal three years ago," she said quietly, when they were out of earshot of other guests.

Seger felt his eyebrows lift. "Good heavens, are all Americans as blunt as you? Don't you know how to talk about the weather with gentlemen you've only just met?"

She touched his arm with the closed fan that hung on a string from her wrist. "Yes, but you and I have met before and we are beyond what is proper. To try and act otherwise would be hypocritical. Besides, I've already discussed the weather at least fifty times tonight, and your scarlet past is much more interesting."

A smile touched his lips. "I suppose my scarlet past is the subject matter of most conversations here tonight. Were you shocked to hear about it?"

"I was, but I'm over it now. You see, I didn't learn of it tonight. I learned of it from my sister a week ago, after she asked her husband about you."

Seger glanced at the duke on the other side of the room. "And he knew everything? I'm surprised he invited me into his home." He gazed down at Miss Wilson with a devious smile. "He doesn't know what happened between us that first night, does he? Perhaps that was his motivation to bring me here—to either squash me like a bug or force me to propose."

She laughed again. "No, my lord. My brother-in-law is a very open-minded man. He was on the fringe of good society himself at one time. He believes there is more to a person than what first appears on the surface. He believes in second chances. That is why he invited you."

"Do you believe that, too?"

"Of course. People are not all good or all bad. They are more complicated than that, but we seem to have strayed off topic. I was hoping you would tell me about what happened three years ago and why you felt you could not re-enter society."

He shook his head in disbelief. It felt odd and out of kilter to discuss such a thing in a place like this, but Miss Wilson, he supposed, was not like other debutantes. She was not like any other woman he'd ever met, to be honest.

Nevertheless, she seemed genuinely eager to hear about it and far be it for him to disappoint a lady.

"It's not that I felt I couldn't re-enter," he said. "I simply did not wish to. It was my choice, and I believe my lack of penitence exasperated certain self-righteous people who would have liked to see me beg."

"So it was your pride that kept you out? You would not apologize?"

"Partly. But mostly, the scandal was more of a final

straw. I had been displeased with society for a long time before that. As I told you before, I never wished to be a part of the Marriage Mart." He was surprised he was telling her all this. It was not why he had come. He had intended to enjoy a lighter, more frivolous encounter.

"You don't ever intend to look for a wife?" she said.

He felt his shoulders stiffen. "Not among society in this manner, when everything is a mad scramble for position. I admit I am jaded. When it comes to marriage, I will take my chances with fate."

She seemed to accept that.

"But don't you wish to hear about the actual scandal, my dear, or at least my side of it?" He wanted to steer her away from the deeper, more ancient issues regarding his lifestyle choices.

She looked him directly in the eyes. "Yes, I would like to hear your side."

They moved to a vacant sofa in the corner and sat down. "First, tell me what you heard and I will tell you whether it's true or not."

Keeping her voice very low, she explained what she knew—that he had been called as a witness in a divorce case in court, to prove a lady's adultery.

Seger leaned back. "All true."

Miss Wilson's voice lost its confident coquetry. She suddenly sounded like an innocent child. "So you *were* the lady's lover?"

He did not flinch. "I was."

She nodded and lowered her gaze to her gloved hands in her lap. She became very quiet.

Seger swayed closer to her. "You were very liberal a few minutes ago. Now you're different. Are you horrified?"

She shook her head. "I'm not horrified. I knew it had to be true. Consider where I met you."

He leaned back again. "Ah, yes, in a den of wickedness. So there you have it. My character unveiled. Be warned, I am depraved."

"I was warned already. Many times, in fact, by you and by my sister and by my own self."

His voice became a husky whisper. "So you know I am a scoundrel. Why, then, are you sitting with me?"

She seemed to consider the question for a long time, then she finally looked up and met his gaze. "If our acquaintance were of the more conventional sort, I would tell you that I am sitting with you because I believe no man is ever completely irredeemable. But since we are being liberal and honest and admitting to all kinds of depravities, I will confess that I am sitting with you for the plain and simple reason that I find you attractive."

Seger smiled. The heiress was delicious. Her paradoxical combination of feral sexuality and sweet innocence was like ecstasy to his senses.

His predatory instincts began to hum. He leaned toward her, close enough that he could smell the fresh, clean scent of her skin. So close, that he was pushing the limits of propriety. "Then I believe we have something in common."

She inched away from him and glanced around self-consciously. "And I believe, sir, that you should sit back. We are not at one of your Cakras Balls."

Taking a deep breath to overpower the intense desire welling up inside of him, Seger forced himself to rise. He held out his hand. "You are absolutely right, and a bloody shame it is, too. Hungry?"

She gave him her hand. "Ravenous."

He led her toward the buffet table. Seger picked a few

red grapes from a large bunch and offered them to Miss Wilson in his open palm. Eyes never leaving his, she took one and popped it into her mouth.

He watched her moist, pink lips as she ate the grape, felt a stirring of arousal in his groin. What he wouldn't give for the honest liberties of a Cakras Ball now.

Miss Wilson swallowed. "My lord, despite the fact that I've witnessed your debauched societal underworld, I will have you know that I am a respectable girl. Pardon me for saying so, but you shouldn't be looking at me like that."

"In my defense, you shouldn't be licking your lips like that."

She grinned, then became more serious. "I'm not looking for trouble."

God, how he wanted to touch her. "You're trying to tell me something."

"Yes."

"That you have no intention of taking any more risks?"

Just then, an older woman approached. Seger recognized her from the first night he'd met Miss Wilson. She was the chaperone.

"Good evening, my dear," the woman said. "You've found the grapes, I see. They are delicious, are they not?"

Miss Wilson seemed to tense at the woman's question. Seger cursed to himself. No wonder he'd not missed the Marriage Mart. The frustrations were unbearable.

"My lord," Miss Wilson said, "may I present Mrs. Eva Gunther? Mrs. Gunther, the Marquess of Rawdon."

They greeted each other. It was clear to Seger that the older woman recognized him as well, though naturally she did not acknowledge it.

She stayed to make conversation for a few minutes, then gestured toward the other side of the room. "I believe

there are some ladies who would like to make your acquaintance, Clara. Would you be so kind as to excuse us,
Lord Rawdon?"

Seger recognized the obvious intent to pry her out of
his company. He was not surprised. He smiled and inclined his head.

"Perhaps we can continue our conversation later?"
Miss Wilson said.

"I'll look forward to it." He bowed and turned away.

The marchioness watched her stepson turn away from
Miss Wilson. "They *have* met before," she whispered to
Gillian. "I'm sure of it. Did you see the way she traipsed
across the room to talk to him? It was the crudest thing
I've ever witnessed in my life. God help us all if she's
picked him out of the crowd." Quintina glanced toward
the fireplace, where a group of gentlemen were standing
in a circle. "Why isn't she hounding after the Duke of
Guysborough, for pity's sake? He's the best catch in the
room."

"For the same reason as myself, I believe, Auntie. He's
not the one she wants."

The marchioness clenched her teeth and sighed. "I hate
to say it, Gillian, but you could learn a few things from the
American gels, despite their brazenness. In fact, I believe
that brazenness is precisely what has all our unfortunate
gentlemen tripping over themselves to talk to them." She
squinted her eyes in disgust. "It's because those gels are
smiling and laughing all the time, telling stupid, unbelievable stories. My word, I *despise* Americans."

Gillian regarded her aunt.

Quintina's jaw clenched. "They don't know their place.
They are overconfident. They think they can buy their

way in with the money they earn—*working*, might I add? You have no idea how it broke my heart to see my family home go to a vulgar American laborer, who earned his fortune panning for gold. Panning! I hate that word. I've never so much as touched a pan in my life. Nevertheless, Americans remind me of leeches. They're here to latch on. They don't realize the greatness of England."

"You forget Yorktown, Auntie."

Quintina raised her chin. "Hmph. Do you have any stories to tell, Gillian? Have you never done anything wild or different? I heard for example that the duchess, before she came to London, went on a buffalo hunt once. She said she knew how to throw a tomahawk. What is a tomahawk, by the way, do you have any idea?"

Gillian shook her head.

"No, I didn't think you'd know. It's just as well. It's probably an American sport of some kind."

They sat down on a settee. "You're going to have to try harder to *say* something," the marchioness said to her niece. "And keep your head up. You never look at him when he talks to you."

"I can't help it, Auntie, I become nervous."

She patted Gillian's hand. "I understand, my dear, but you must endeavor to get over that. You must try harder to put a sparkle in your eye. It looks as if Seger is finally ready to move forward with his life. The fact that he came here this evening was astonishing, to say the least, so you must be the first to take advantage of this opportunity. Watch the American gels and see what they do. Perhaps I'll have a few new gowns made for you, like the ones they are wearing. Would that help, do you think?"

"I believe it would, Auntie. Thank you."

"Well, well, well," she replied, patting her niece's hand

again. "It's the least I can do. You have no mother to see to your future, and if she were alive—my dear, dear sister—she would want you to be happy, to get what you want. You're a good girl, Gillian. You deserve a husband you can be proud of, and I would like to see our family's bloodline continue in such a prestigious vein. I wasn't able to give the marquess any children, but you could be the one to provide the next heir. We shall not give up hope, darling. Now do as I say. Watch the American, and see how she handles herself."

As an afterthought, Quintina added, "She looks a little bit like Daphne, don't you think? It's rather disconcerting."

Gillian turned her gaze toward Clara Wilson, the famous heiress, the sister of the Duchess of Wentworth. The girl was surrounded by a crowd of doting gentlemen, all of them laughing at her stories, enchanted by her smile, just as Seger had been only moments ago.

A tiny muscle twitched at Gillian's jaw, and she squeezed her reticule so hard that she broke the looking glass inside it.

Chapter 7

Dear Adele,

Sometimes I feel so out of place here. I am not like the other English ladies. I try to be reserved, but at heart I know that I am not. What I really want is to be an open book with those I care about, and I want to find a husband who is that way, too. I'm tired of talking about the weather. I want a soulmate, Adele, someone who will not be superficial.

The marquess, interestingly enough, is not afraid to break the usual rules of conduct. He's different from the rest, but I fear that Mrs. Gunther does not approve. . . .

Clara

"Is it time to continue our conversation, yet?" Lord Rawdon whispered in Clara's ear.

He had come up behind her unexpectedly, startling her with the moist heat of his breath against the side of her neck. Her entire left side erupted in tingling goose-flesh.

Champagne glass in hand, she turned. "I'm willing if you are."

He smiled and offered his arm. They walked into the music room where a German pianist was scheduled to begin playing shortly. "Shall we take our seats?"

"Yes." Clara allowed him to lead her to the front row.

They were the first guests to sit down. The pianist's assistant was arranging sheet music; a liveried footman stood near the open doors.

"You've been very popular this evening," Lord Rawdon said. "Why is it that Mrs. Gunther has never dragged you away from any of the other gentlemen? She doesn't disapprove of me, does she?" His last comment dripped with sarcasm.

Clara tried to attach an apology to her smile. "She is on a mission for my mother, I'm afraid. She wants to be sure I am married off to the highest ranking peer possible, and the most respectable."

"Ah, and the respectable part . . . that is where I fall short."

Clara tried to explain. "She's a very proper lady. She comes from old money. Mother was thrilled when Mrs. Gunther agreed to accompany me to London. She knew Mrs. Gunther would have the highest standards conceivable, and she felt I needed someone with a very strong hand to lead me in the right direction."

His eyebrows rose. "And she took you to a Cakras Ball?"

Clara gave him a quick heated glare, then returned her cool gaze to the front of the room. "That was a mistake, and I do *not* thank you for reminding me of it."

His lips curled up in a sexy grin. "Now this is becoming

very interesting. Your mother felt you needed a strong hand. I detect something naughty in your past." He leaned forward and she felt his masculine presence roar like a lion beside her. "Why didn't your mother accompany you herself?"

"Because she is with my sister, Adele, who is having her own first Season in New York."

"You didn't wish to debut in London together?"

Clara felt her spine bristle at the direction of their conversation, and his mischievous curiosity. Unlike most of the other Englishmen she had met, he had no qualms about asking intrusive questions. They were heading into dangerous territory.

"No," she tried to explain. "We did not wish to debut together." She glanced uneasily at him.

"I see," he replied, his scrutinizing gaze moving all over her face.

"I wanted her to have her own special time," Clara explained. "Without her older sister around. Things didn't go that well for me the year before last. Hence Mrs. Gunther's strong hand."

Clara didn't know why she was telling him this. It pointed back at her mistakes.

She supposed she felt that he of all people would understand.

Maybe that's why she was so attracted to him. He didn't make her feel inadequate. He lived by his own rules and did not judge her or anyone by society's strictures.

Most people—if they knew the whole story—would call her fast or unprincipled, which she was not. Yes, there was a thrill-seeker lurking in her heart, but she was not fast. She believed in fidelity and she wanted a decent man for a husband.

That was her struggle, she supposed. Her desires weren't quite as black and white as the rest of the world's.

"How in the world could a Season not go well for you?" the marquess asked. "You are the most lovely creature I've seen since . . . well, since forever."

She warmed at the compliment, but still wanted to be cautious where her heart was concerned. She stared straight ahead at the piano.

"What, no answer?" He leaned forward to try and urge her to look at him. "Don't tell me you botched it up. Made a few social blunders?" He sat back and laughed. "Is that why you're here? Because you can't show your face in New York? That's the best thing I've heard all day."

"Stop teasing me!" she said, slapping his arm with her fan. "I can certainly show my face. I just wished for different surroundings and fresh conversation this year, that's all."

He gave her an exaggerated nod as if he didn't believe her. "You must realize that now you *have* to tell me what happened, and spare nothing, I need all the grisly details."

She glared at him, astounded. "Sir, you are very rude. And there are no grisly details."

"There must be. You're blushing. There are red blotches on your neck, right there."

He pointed at her cleavage.

Excitement swelled in her veins, but she forced herself to ignore it. She slapped his hand again. "Do you mind? You are uncontrollable!"

He smiled and leaned back again. "Yes, I suppose I am, but you still haven't told me how you stumbled and landed on your face during your New York debut."

"I did not land on my face."

She said nothing after that.

He continued to stare at her, waiting.

"All right. A man proposed to me—a very unsuitable man my parents did not approve of. He did not move about in polite society."

She felt rather than saw his face go serious. "That's hardly your fault."

"Some would argue that I encouraged him, and maybe I did. My sister had just married a duke and I was feeling pressured to follow in her footsteps and marry well."

"So you rebelled."

She clenched her jaw at the simple discernment, felt her nettle rise up. Not at the marquess, but at the plain, all too honest subject-matter of their conversation. Why were they talking about this? She had wanted to forget it.

Yet she had wanted to be an open book.

He raised his hands in mock surrender. "Don't give *me* that look. I'm on your side. I believe in a good rebellion from time to time. God knows the whole world has witnessed a number of my minor social revolts. You didn't marry him, I take it."

"Of course not."

She chose not to tell him how close she had actually come. How her father had arrived just in time and caught her on a ship bound for Europe, with plans to get married on board.

Thank God for her father.

"The story has a happy ending, then," Lord Rawdon said, whispering in her ear. "And you had an adventure. Good girl."

Clara couldn't help smiling as her anger began to drain away. The tension in her shoulders disappeared, and she was finally able to take a deep, calming breath.

The marquess was certainly relaxed about so-called

scandals and social blunders, which was probably a good thing. She doubted she would ever tell any of the other London gentlemen what she'd just told the marquess. She certainly couldn't imagine telling the Duke of Guysborough.

"So if your sister doesn't succeed in America this Season," he asked, "will she come to London next year?"

"Probably."

He glanced in the other direction. "The newspapers were right, it is becoming a mad stampede for titles."

Clara threw him a cantankerous look.

He chuckled. "What, that's not why you're here? To bounce back from your close brush with social pauperism and, like you said, marry well?"

She shook her head at his insolent manner. "I am here to find a decent and respectable man to spend my life with. It doesn't matter to me if he has a title or not." She shifted on the chair, raised her chin high. She felt his unwavering gaze on her profile and turned to look at him when she sensed his amusement. "You don't believe me!"

Still smiling, he shook his head. "To be honest, no. You seem like the ambitious kind. The kind who wants the very best, especially after coming a little too close to disaster once before."

"What I consider to be the 'best' might surprise you. Perhaps it has nothing to do with a mere accident of birth, my *noble* lord."

She heard the sarcasm in her tone and knew she was the one being insolent now, but she couldn't help it. It seemed like he was always teasing her and trying to provoke her. She suspected he liked to see her fight back. It amused him. She suddenly felt very American next to his Englishness.

And she could not deny the fact that this unrestrained dynamic between them amused her, too.

He crossed one long, muscular leg over the other. "I don't think anything could possibly surprise me about you."

Clara lowered her voice. "Why are you harassing me like this? It always feels like you want to get me into trouble. You say the most improper things. Or maybe it's the way you say them."

"Because I like to see your cheeks flush."

Other guests, two by two, began to trickle into the room. Clara sat up straighter in her chair, resolving not to get pulled into the tempting heat of his flame just yet. She had to be more careful. She was still not sure she could trust the marquess to be "decent," therefore she could not allow her passions to lead her into what might be a dangerous, ruinous place.

"I would prefer it if we changed the subject now, my lord."

They said nothing for a few minutes.

Lord Rawdon stretched his legs out in front of him. He began to look bored. "All right, all right. A decent and respectable man you say. I guess that counts me out."

He was unbelievable. "And you are no doubt relieved."

"Intensely."

The room filled up and they had to refrain from speaking so candidly with each other. It was time to stop, anyway. Clara recognized the marquess's body language and the tone in his voice and knew that he was both pulling back and pushing her away. Their conversation had become too personal, and he wanted only to flirt with her.

She felt a stab of disappointment.

From everything he'd said tonight, it was easy to gather

that he wanted only brief, frivolous affairs, not deep soulful ones. He was not the sort of man who was suited to a marriage based on fidelity—like that of Clara's sister, Sophia, and her husband James. They were devoted to each other in every way. They knew each other's hearts as well as they knew their own, and they had no desire to stray.

Feeling discouraged, Clara watched the pianist cross the room and take a seat on the piano bench. He laid his fingers on the ivory keys.

Clara realized miserably that her desires were caught in a paradox. She craved excitement. In her heart she wanted to burst out of the box of polite behavior, yet she wanted to be respectable. She wanted a man who believed in piety and the instituition of marriage. She wanted a morally upright man, but not a dull one, which was a difficult combination.

Gordon had been wild, but he had not possessed any honor. She had learned a sturdy lesson with him. Because of that, she was determined now. Just as the marquess had said, she was ambitious toward that end and would not settle for less than what she wanted.

She felt another wave of disappointment move through her. She did not believe the Marquess of Rawdon could be what she wanted. Like Gordon, he was far too wild. He did not seem interested in what was socially proper. He did not seem inclined toward true intimacies of the heart, only pleasures of the flesh. He continually pushed her away when she tried to take a step forward and move away from flirting. He had said he was relieved he was not the kind of man she would want for a husband.

But oh, he was so beautiful, and so far he was the only man in London who made her heart go pitter-pat.

Well, at least now she knew. The fantasy of him was indeed just that—a fantasy. He could only be a lover in the physical sense. She had to keep her head on straight about that.

What a shame, she thought. What a sad, disappointing shame.

The very next day, a letter arrived for Clara. Not recognizing the penmanship, she took it upstairs to her room to read on her bed.

She flopped down on her belly and broke the seal.

My Dear Miss Wilson, it began . . .

Clara's heart began to pound.

You must forgive me this indulgence, but I could not resist the inclination to write to you and tell you how thoroughly I enjoyed our discourse last evening at your sister's assembly. I had considered calling on the duchess today, but decided against it, as I felt it was too much progress for a man like myself, in too short a time. I cannot, I'm afraid, delve into a complete recovery from my wicked ways and evolve overnight into a proper gentleman who pays calls to respectable young ladies, sipping tea in brightly lit drawing rooms.

Instead, I chose to write you a letter, where I would be free to say the things I would have wanted to say, had I been in your delightful, delectable company this afternoon.

Why am I writing this? you must be wondering. I am wondering that myself. I have no idea. As I mentioned last night, I am not presently seeking a wife and I usually confine myself to less perilous associ-

*ations. Perhaps it is the French wine I am sipping.
No, it is not. It is you. You enchant me.*

Clara's heart did a back flip inside her chest. A huge,
goofy grin split her face. She rolled over and sat up, then
walked to the window to read more.

*I have no wish to spoil your chances of meeting the
decent and respectable man you desire, yet I find I
cannot sit idly back and accept that I will never see
you again, or—forgive me for my plain manner of
speaking—kiss you again. I could not stop looking
at your lips last night. I wanted to find another dark
staircase.*

*But I digress. As you see I am too frank for the
society you accept as your own. If I were like other
gentlemen, I would say goodbye to you now and
wish you the best. But I have not behaved as a gentleman for many years, and I find myself plotting
mischievous ways to kiss you again and satisfy my
passions without causing too much damage in the
process. Do you understand my meaning? Do you
have any ideas?*

*Sincerely,
S.*

Clara squealed. Was this some kind of joke? Was he serious? Surely not! This was scandalous! She could not reply to something like this. What if someone found out?

She read the letter again. Good God, her blood was rushing so fast, it was surely turning white-hot in her veins.

This was insane. She could not take part in a wild and wicked affair. She'd brushed too close to scandal once before and did not wish to do so again. She had come to England to avoid that sort of thing. How had she managed to stumble across the worst rogue in London? And allow him to kiss her!

She paced back and forth across the room, telling herself that she should not under any circumstances reply to this letter. That would be social suicide. She must break all contact with him, for it was clear he was exactly the kind of man she should avoid. The kind of man she had initially feared he was—a rake and a libertine. The kind of man who was very dangerous to her, for over the past week, she had discovered that she was not as strong as she thought she was. Where the gorgeous, tempting marquess was concerned, she was actually quite weak.

Clara squeezed her eyes shut and breathed deeply. She must concentrate on meeting the *right* sort. The kind of man she had hoped to meet when she'd steamed across the Atlantic dreaming of a beautiful future. She wanted a man who would be faithful to her. A man who would have the integrity not to stray outside of his marriage, because that's what it took to be faithful. Honor and integrity. Everyone felt passion and temptation. Those with honor did not act upon it. The marquess seemed to act on every base impulse he felt.

Clara read the letter again. It was shocking. She lifted her chin and folded the paper and stuffed it way into the back of one of her drawers.

No, that wasn't a good place. Her maid might find it. She pulled it out and stuffed it under her mattress, then made a firm decision to thrust the Marquess of Rawdon out of her mind once and for all. For good. For eternity. She would not think of him again. No. She would forget him. He was not the man for her.

There. She went to her door and ventured out into the corridor to join Sophia for tea.

He was forgotten.

The next day she read the letter again. It had taken every ounce of self-control she possessed not to pull it out in the middle of the night and read it. Somehow she had resisted and had congratulated herself in the morning.

It was almost noon now, however. She had not been able to get through even half the day.

I could not stop looking at your lips last night. I wanted to find another dark staircase.

Her toes curled inside her shoes. Something tingled in her nether regions. She should not have read it. It had been a foolish thing to do. She was weak, to have been seduced from clear across the city by ink and pen. Weak, weak, weak. He was an expert at lovemaking to be sure.

She should have known better. She should have burned his wicked words right after she'd read them. She should not be infecting her brain with them now.

She read the letter again.

What a scoundrel he was. *Any ideas?* he had asked. As if she would entertain such thoughts.

God help her, she had quite a few.

But she would certainly *not* tell him what they were.

That night, by candlelight, Clara dipped her pen in the ink jar and paused above her stationery. How to begin, how to begin. It was necessary to inform him that she was not interested in anything untoward, and that she would prefer it if he refrained from any further insinuations in the future.

She looked at his handwriting again and felt a flutter within her breast. This was his personal penmanship. The ink on this paper had come from his very own desk. His huge, masculine hands had touched this paper not long ago. Perhaps he had blown gently on the ink to dry it.

Her belly quivered as she imagined all that.

Clara shut her eyes and shook her head, forcing herself not to think about him sitting at his desk writing to her, or doing anything else for that matter. She had to focus on the task at hand.

If only she knew what to say. There was a part of her that did not want to end this. It was exciting and invigorating and flattering. He was a grand and beautiful man and he found her attractive. All her sexual instincts were telling her to encourage him and see where this would lead, but her head was telling her to be careful and prudent and not be foolish. She wanted so very badly to be virtuous.

Lord. She was having a barrel of a time listening to the right voice.

Sighing deeply, hoping she was not doing anything *too* terribly risky, she lowered her pen to the page. Then it came to her. She smiled and began to write.

My lord, you are very naughty.

Sincerely,
C.

The next morning, another letter bearing the marquess's seal was brought by a footman to Clara's boudoir,

who picked it up off the silver salver and calmly thanked
the young man. She set the letter on the corner of her desk
and feigned disinterest until the footman left the room and
closed the door behind him, upon which time she couldn't
help herself. She snatched up the letter, rose to her feet
and tore at the seal. She read Lord Rawdon's brief reply:

Miss Wilson,

*I laughed out loud when I read your note. You are
enchanting. Again I implore you. Any ideas?*

S.

Clara covered her mouth with her hand to smother the
urge to shriek. She'd never felt like this before. What was
it about this particular man that brought out such strong
sexual impulses in her? She hadn't felt like this with Gordon. It had been naiveté and the pressure from her parents
that had caused her problems with him, not this kind of
blatant, hungry desire. She should not be communicating
with this man in this way.

She stuffed the letter under her mattress with the last
one and tried to go back to her respectable correspondence. That was impossible, however, with her mind
where it was at the present time—frolicking in the house
of sin, entertaining all kinds of lewd, indecent thoughts
about a golden-haired marquess, lying naked in his bed.
He was so impossibly gorgeous.

Ten minutes later, she realized she was still resting her
chin on her hand, staring blankly at the wall. She felt
inebriated.

She shook her head at herself and realized she could not

possibly resist replying to his letter, depraved as it was. She pulled a blank piece of stationery out of her desk drawer.

For a moment she sat there tapping the clean end of her pen against her lips, wondering if it was possible for the marquess to ever be faithful to one woman. Perhaps he had simply not met the right one yet. All boys grew up to be men eventually, didn't they? Wasn't it possible he could be at that crossroads? She was his first debutante, after all, or so he claimed. Perhaps he was ready to change. Perhaps she could teach him about real love. Was she foolish to hold onto that hope? Probably.

Nevertheless, she dipped her pen and began to write. She forced herself to be serious and scrupulous.

Lord Rawdon,

You must realize that this manner of correspondence is utterly inappropriate. I do not wish to continue this, as I have explained that I am not interested in any kind of immoral affair. If you wish to see me, please do so in a proper, respectable place, at which time I would be happy to converse with you.

C.

She congratulated herself on her most inspiring self-restraint.

Another reply arrived that very afternoon.

But I don't wish to see you in a proper, respectable place. I wish to be quite alone with you, my dear, so no one will witness my hand sliding up your dress.

S.

Clara shook her head in total disbelief. Of all the shocking, cheeky nerve! The audacity! What kind of wanton woman did he think she was? She would not be lured into sin because he simply requested it in a note, no matter how clammy her palms were at the moment, or how loopy she felt.

Congratulating herself again for her impressive iron will in the face of such astounding provocation, she picked up her pen to reply:

My lord, your suggestions are appalling. Is it your intention to ruin me?

C.

Clara received the marquess's reply the next morning. She had to admit, she was exceedingly curious about how he would respond to her blunt accusation. She tore open the letter and began to read:

Dear Miss Wilson,

I apologize if I gave the impression that I wanted to ruin you. I have no desire for such a thing. You have my word that I would do everything in my power to prevent it. I am discreet and I know how to give

*pleasure without destruction. You may trust me com-
pletely in that regard.*

                                                    S.

Clara couldn't believe the marquess's reply. He was
still trying to seduce her after she had clearly, in no uncertain terms, told him no. Had he no shame?

The time had come to end this. For real this time. She
could not see him again.

She was about to write another reply and say just that,
when a knock sounded at her door. A maid said, "Miss
Wilson, the duchess requests your presence in the drawing room."

Clara called out, "Is it important?"

"There is a gentleman caller, miss."

A swarm of butterflies dashed into Clara's belly. She
rose and went to the door. "Do you know who it is?"

She pulled the door open, but the maid was gone.

Standing motionless holding the doorknob, Clara
blinked. Had the marquess come to call properly? Was he
willing to make this concession, or was it another gentleman calling to pay his respects?

Clara hurried to her cheval mirror to look over her appearance. She pinched her cheeks and smoothed her
hands over her upswept hair. Perhaps it was the marquess.
Perhaps it wasn't. She would know soon enough.

With a hand on her belly to quell her nervous stomach,
Clara made her way into the corridor and walked slowly
toward the drawing room. She entered and saw her sister
sitting near the fireplace pouring tea, laughing at some-

thing, then she turned her gaze toward the other occupant in the room.

Her entire being swirled with a dizzying current of desire. It was indeed the marquess. He was smiling wickedly at her.

She managed somehow to smile in return, then entered the room.

She had not told Sophia about the letters. She wasn't sure why. She usually told Sophia everything—she'd told her every word the marquess had said to her at the assembly—but this was different. Perhaps she was afraid Sophia would begin to disapprove of him, and whether it was wise or unwise, Clara did not want to be told that she should not respond. She wanted to make up her own mind about that.

Sophia stood up. "Clara! How lovely that you passed by. See who has come to pay us a call today. You remember the Marquess of Rawdon? He attended our assembly the other night."

It was all so proper. Sophia was a brilliant hostess. "Of course I remember you," Clara replied. "Good day, my lord. It was kind of you to call."

"It was entirely my pleasure, Miss Wilson."

Not knowing what to expect, Clara took a seat next to Sophia, who poured her a cup of tea. The conversation then turned toward the usual things—the current events in *The Times*, the most recent debates in the House of Commons, and of course, the most agreeable topic that could always be depended upon for propriety—the weather.

At the end of the obligatory fifteen minutes, the marquess reached for his hat and walking stick. "I must thank you, duchess, for a delicious cup of tea. It was second to none."

His behavior was impeccable. He moved toward the door. One would think he'd been a formal member of society forever.

He made a bow to Clara. "Miss Wilson." He turned and left the drawing room.

As soon as the front doors opened and closed downstairs, Sophia rushed to Clara and took both her hands. "He came to call!"

Clara didn't know what she felt. She was in shock. She was confused. What exactly did he want—a torrid affair or a proper courtship? Perhaps he had changed his mind after he'd sent the last letter. Perhaps he was giving in to the idea of reforming himself.

"I wonder if we should call on his stepmother," Sophia said. "Lady Rawdon seemed to enjoy herself here the other night. I believe she was pleased to receive the invitation. From what I've heard, she has not been received in most places, not since the marquess was involved in that beastly court case."

Clara sat down again. She picked up her teacup and took a sip, but set it down when she realized it was cold.

Sophia sat down beside her. "He likes you, Clara."

"But he has a reputation, and I am quite certain that Mrs. Gunther disapproves of him."

"It's your future. You are the one who must choose, and it's obvious that you fancy him."

"But how do I choose when I still know so little about the marquess, except that he is not respectable? The Duke of Guysborough on the other hand is completely respectable, but he does not interest me, not the way the marquess does. Perhaps it's just a foolish desire to possess something that cannot be possessed—like the wind or the sun." She gazed imploringly into her sister's eyes. "I feel like I'm losing my mind, Sophia. My head is telling me he is all wrong, but I can't I stop thinking about him."

Sophia rested her hand upon Clara's. "Sometimes the heart does not make sense. It only knows what it feels. I still believe that the marquess should not be ruled out as a possible match for you. He came here today, which suggests to me that he is at least willing to make an effort to act respectably. Maybe he does want to change. Maybe he was only waiting to be invited back into good society, and now that he has been, he will be able to court proper, unmarried young ladies like yourself and look to a brighter future. Perhaps it just wasn't an option for him before."

Clara narrowed her eyes at her sister. "You think there's hope for him? That I should give him a chance?"

"He came here today, Clara. He made a promising effort. Yes, I do think you should give him a chance."

But you haven't read his letters.

Oh, who was she trying to fool? Clara knew she could no more forget him than she could forget to breathe.

Perhaps she simply had to leap in head first and take a risk. If it all blew up in her face and he broke her heart, well, she would just have to deal with that. At least that way, she would never have to ask herself, *what if?*

She only hoped he was as discreet as he claimed to be in his last letter, and that he would not allow her to be ruined.

Chapter 8

Dear Clara,

The marquess sounds like a very dangerous man. . . .

Adele

Seger had dreamed about her last night.

The memory of the dream hit him just as he was walking out of Wentworth House, away from Clara when every instinct within was urging him to go back inside and fetch her—to take her by the hand and lead her out. To bring her home with him.

That's what he'd done in the dream. He had taken both her hands in his and led her to his bed. She had come willingly, smiling at him with such warmth, it had made him feel dizzy.

He quaked with an intense craving to touch her right now, to feel that joy again. To explore a world of sensuality and delight with this woman who would not leave his mind, even in slumber.

Seger had to shake himself. Had he taken leave of his senses? What was it about Clara that made him dream about her and feel so much? How did this innocent, untouched maiden bring him to such heights of longing? It was entirely out of his realm of experience.

He climbed into his crested coach and tapped his walking stick against the roof to signal the driver, then he tried to ground himself. He labored to remember the kinds of relationships he was used to. The kinds he wanted. He was not like other men. He was not looking for a socially acceptable wife. He liked his life just the way it was.

But good God, he had just taken the first step toward a proper courtship with a respectable young lady, after swearing to both himself and the lady in question, through a number of daring letters, that he was only interested in a brief, sordid affair. The usual stuff where he was concerned. He had made it clear in no uncertain terms that that was what he'd wanted, then at the last minute after he had sent the letter, he had panicked—yes, panicked—and feared he had gone too far, come on too strong. Consequently, he had made a complete about-face and bloody well contradicted himself. He'd called upon her.

He remembered the dream again, and felt a disturbing jolt of confusion. It felt like two musical notes were chiming in his head at the same time. He winced at the discord.

He wasn't even sure what he wanted at this point. It had been a number of years since he'd desired a woman who was innocent—presuming the heiress was in fact untouched, which he did presume, rightly or wrongly.

Daphne had been innocent. He had loved her unreservedly without any thought to whether or not it was wise. It had led to disaster.

He was, however, no longer a boy. He was a man and he was the Marquess of Rawdon. His father was no longer alive to dictate Seger's future. If Seger wished to marry someone completely unsuitable—an American heiress for instance— he could do so. No one would dare stand in his way.

Seger chided himself. He did not wish to *marry* Miss Wilson. At least not at the moment. He certainly didn't need her money. He only wanted her in the physical sense.

He wanted to feel her hands running through his hair. He wanted to kiss the soft, creamy skin between her breasts and taste her moist, honey-sweet lips. He wanted to hear her sigh with contentment after he'd brought her to the most ferocious orgasm she'd ever experienced in her life—all the better if it was her first. What he wouldn't give to show her that kind of pleasure for the first time.

Which was, he supposed, the primary problem. One couldn't enjoy an innocent without repercussions. Without responsibility and commitment and permanence. Without the young woman's expectation of sentiment.

He had been too long living outside the lines. He'd forgotten how to play by the rules. After Daphne died, he'd lived the life he'd wanted to live, without caring what other people thought. Without letting himself empathize or think about how they felt. Women especially. He had forced that particular instinct out of himself and had chosen to give a very specific kind of pleasure instead. He was renowned for it, and the women he associated with rarely expected anything outside of that. They knew the rules, knew what he could give them, and most of them accepted it quite happily without making the mistake of asking for more.

Because he always made it clear he wouldn't give them more.

Wouldn't or couldn't?

He took a small breath. He wasn't sure. It seemed like he had always been isolated. Emotionally removed from everyone—from society, from his family, his acquaintances. He'd never had any brothers or sisters.

Was his lifestyle really by choice, or was he incapable of intimacy?

No, he could not be incapable of it. He had once loved very deeply.

But only once. Eight years ago when he had been devoted to Daphne.

Was it possible for a man to permanently banish from his heart the capacity for true emotional connections with other people?

Seger exhaled and shook his head. Lord, how many times over the past few weeks had he questioned his lifestyle and remembered Daphne? He hadn't thought of her in years, but lately, their relationship had been coming back to him in little flashes of memory.

Perhaps it was the way Miss Wilson made him feel. She, like Daphne, possessed innocence, and consequently whatever existed between them was fresh, not sordid, as most of his relationships had been since Daphne left this world.

Suddenly, he felt dissatisfied with everything about his life. He remembered the things he had wanted when he was twenty, and how eager he had been to become someone's husband. He had wanted Daphne to be his partner for life, to share his joys and pains. He'd wanted a home filled with children.

He sat in silence, staring unseeing out the window at the passing traffic, barely hearing the clatter of the coach or the noise from the street. He had not wanted anything like that since then. He had given the idea of marriage a very wide berth.

Seger tipped his head back against the seat. Daphne disappeared from his mind.

Instead he thought of Miss Wilson sitting in the duchess's drawing room across from him only moments ago, sipping her tea. What a vision she had been, beautiful and charming and glowing with smiles. Intelligent as well, discussing light politics and other things. She was a remarkable woman, and she inflamed his senses like no other. She possessed some kind of magic. A power that he feared could bring him to his knees.

Strange, how he feared it and wanted it at the same time.

Then he thought of Clara reading the last letter he had sent, contemplating his promise not to ruin her, and a shadow moved through him. *I know how to give pleasure without destruction,* he had written. What had her face looked like when she'd read such licentious words? Surely no gentleman had ever written anything like that to her before.

God. He felt a sudden urge to apologize to her—a strange and extraordinary impulse for Seger, who had written similar things to other women in the past and had never thought twice about it. It was a jarring reaction now. He wished he could take the letter back. He wished he could start over where she was concerned and handle everything differently. More politely.

It brought a frown to his face.

Wearing a low cut, royal blue velvet gown and feathers in her hair, Clara walked into the large opera box with

James, Sophia and Mrs. Gunther. Before she sat down, she glanced at the brightly lit theater below, at the blinding glitter of gowns and jewels. People were filing in to their seats. A hum of conversation filled the auditorium while the orchestra warmed up with a dissonant mixture of violins, flutes and trumpets practicing scales.

Many seats below were still empty. Clara gazed across to the other side where the more luxurious boxes were filling up. She found herself staring at every fair-haired gentleman who caught her eye, searching for one in particular.

"It's a lovely theater," Mrs. Gunther said as she sat down and withdrew her mother-of-pearl opera glasses from her beaded reticule. She held them up to her eyes to look at the elaborate set on the stage.

Clara sat down as well, while Sophia and James remained standing at the back near the open red curtain, talking to someone they knew.

It had been a full week since Clara had seen or heard from Lord Rawdon, and she was desperate to know why. She had not replied to his last letter, taking a chance that his unexpected afternoon call had been his way of retreating from the scandalous nature of their acquaintance and perhaps to begin a proper courtship. She had subsequently watched for him at every social event since, hoping he would continue his re-emergence into society, but she had been disappointed.

She began to wonder if she had made a mistake in not replying to his letter. Perhaps he had taken her silence as a rebuff.

It seemed all she ever did where he was concerned was analyze the situation and wonder endlessly what he was thinking or how her actions had been received. If only they could be honest with each other and communicate frankly.

She supposed that was what he had been trying to do when he had written those letters. He'd wanted to escape the pretensions of the Marriage Mart, which he openly admitted to despising.

Just then, someone touched Clara's shoulder. "Your Grace," she said, turning in her chair and looking up at the tall Duke of Guysborough behind her.

"Good evening, Miss Wilson." He moved to the empty chair beside her and sat down. "It's been an exceptional week for entertainment, has it not?"

She had seen the duke at most of the assemblies and balls she'd attended the past few days, and had danced with him a number of times. "Indeed it has been. How is your mother?"

They talked about the dowager's health, then discussed the opera they were about to see. Mrs. Gunther listened politely to all that was said and smiled and nodded with approval. Then the duke gave his farewell and stood up to talk to James for a few more minutes before leaving the box.

"He is a charming gentleman, don't you think?" Mrs. Gunther said, leaning in close.

Almost too charming, Clara thought. Too perfect. Could she live up to that kind of ideal on a daily basis?

"I believe he fancies you."

Sensing that the performance was about to begin, Clara reached into her purse for her opera glasses. "It's difficult to say. He's always very friendly to everyone."

"Yes, but especially to you. I've been keeping track of the ladies he's been dancing with and you hold the highest honor for most waltzes each night."

Clara drew her eyebrows together as she stared at her

chaperone. "You've been keeping track? You surprise me, Mrs. Gunther."

The older woman smiled. "He's a very good catch, Clara. I was curious to know the caliber of your feminine competition, if there was in fact any competition at all. There doesn't seem to be much."

When Clara made no reply, Mrs. Gunther continued. "Has he spoken of his children to you?"

"A few times, yes."

"He has only one son, you know. The boy is eight I believe."

Clara held her glasses up to her eyes and looked at the boxes directly across from where she sat.

"I would expect," Mrs. Gunther said, "that he would wish to have more children, more sons if possible, to ensure the security of his line. One can't take chances with a dukedom."

Clara perused each box and peered down at the audience below.

"You're not listening to me," Mrs. Gunther said, unfolding her own glasses and looking down. "I ask you, what down there could possibly be more interesting than the Duke of Guysborough?"

"I'm just looking at the fashions, Mrs. Gunther. There are some beautiful gowns tonight."

Mrs. Gunther continued to look down at the crowd. "Poppycock. You're looking for that disreputable marquess. Is he there?"

Clara leaned back and stared at Mrs. Gunther. "No, I don't believe he is."

"Good." She leaned back, too, and lowered her voice. "He is not the sort you should associate yourself with, Clara. I realize he is a peer, but his reputation overshadows that fact. There is your own reputation to think of. I would ask that in the future, you cut him."

"Cut him? I couldn't do anything like that."

"But you must, in order to make the message clear. You do not want to sully yourself. You must not do anything to discourage more respectable men—like the duke, for instance—from considering you as a bride. You must convey perfection."

"I'm hardly perfect, Mrs. Gunther. No one is."

"But some people are more perfect than others, and despite his elevated rank, the marquess is very low down on that scale. The gossip about him, may I say, is detestable."

Clara was beginning to feel ill. "Gossip can sometimes be exaggerated."

"Don't defend him, dear girl. Even if it is exaggerated, appearances are as important, if not more important, than the truth."

Clara knew she shouldn't argue with Mrs. Eva Gunther, a grand New York matriarch, but she couldn't help herself. Her hands had closed into tight fists. "How can you say that? What if he is in actuality a good man, merely misunderstood?"

Not that she really believed that herself. She had no idea. Well, she had some idea. Judging by the letters he had sent, he was every bit as notorious as the gossips claimed.

"It wouldn't matter."

The lights dimmed and James and Sophia took their seats. The curtain at the back of the box lowered as if by magic.

Clara sat stiff in her seat, contemplating everything Mrs. Gunther had said. She felt a great pressure squeezing around her heart at that moment—an obligation to ignore what she wanted, and do what was expected of her.

Another part of her, in angry response, wanted to see the marquess again for the single purpose of rebellion. Of proving that he was not all bad, and also to prove that she had a mind and will of her own and and she would not relinquish her personal happiness for the mere sake of appearances.

Clara chided herself. She had felt this way once before, and there had been harrowing consequences.

The opera began. Clara sat agitated for a while, then she tried to calm down and use the time to come to terms with what Mrs. Gunther had said. She took a few deep breaths. She could not fault the woman for acting in a way that she believed was in Clara's best interest. The woman came from a very old family, after all. She had certain values that were not easy to renounce.

Clara sighed.

Who was she fooling? She knew she could never act rebelliously for the mere sake of rebelling. She had learned to be smarter than that. Well, most of the time.

She raised her glasses and glanced at the box across the way and saw the Duke of Guysborough sitting alone, watching the opera. His wife had probably occupied the seat beside him when she'd lived. How sad that she had died so young and left her husband and children behind. Clara felt a strong wave of sympathy for the man.

Perhaps she *was* being foolhardy, dreaming about a wild, dishonorable marquess when a decent, genteel man with proven high moral and family values was within her reach, expressing his interest in her. Treating her with the utmost gentlemanly respect.

She lowered her opera glasses and sighed deeply, then promised herself that she would keep an open mind.

* * *

Three days later, the Duke of Guysborough called on Clara. He sat down on a sofa in the drawing room, and proposed.

Sitting in her chintz upholstered chair, Clara stared at him blankly.

"I would be an excellent husband, Miss Wilson. I am highly regarded by the queen herself. My estate is comprised of some of the most prestigious lands in England, and my children are obedient. You would almost never see them."

Never see them? That was supposed to be a good thing?

"You would become a duchess, like your sister," he added with a proud nod.

Clara tried to think straight. It was the offer of a lifetime. Hundreds of young women on both sides of the Atlantic would give anything to be in her shoes at this moment.

Why then, could she not feel her toes?

Clara tried to smile. "You flatter me, Your Grace. I had not expected such a wonderful speech from you today."

Just before he'd proposed, he had told her she was lovely—a rare jewel.

Purity and perfection.

She was not perfect. She was far from it. Would he still want her if he knew the passions that lived in her heart? Passions of the flesh and mind? She suspected that any wife of his would have to hide or smother that part of herself.

"May I deliver good news to my family this evening?" he asked.

Clara's skin prickled all over. It was too much too soon. How could she possibly accept? At the same time, she did not want to pass up on this opportunity—which was indeed a great boon—and later live to regret it.

"Your Grace, you must give me some time to think about it. I am truly honored by your proposal, but as I'm sure you can understand, I must consult my family on the matter."

He smiled. "Of course you must. It is a momentous decision. I'm sure they will guide you in the right direction. Shall I return tomorrow?"

"That would be very kind of you."

He made a bow and took his leave.

Clara sat in her chair, completely unable to move. The walls seemed to be closing in all around her. The Duke of Guysborough had just proposed marriage to her and before twenty-four hours were out, she would have to make the biggest decision of her life and choose her destiny.

She stood up and went to the window to watch him step into his carriage and drive away. He was a handsome, distinguished man, admired by the Queen of England. Mrs. Gunther approved of him. Clara's parents would undoubtedly also approve. The duke had been married once before and had from all accounts been a good husband.

He was, as some would say, a sure thing. As far as appearances went, he was exactly what she wanted. Or at least what her head told her she wanted. Her instincts told her something else, however. There was something about him that didn't ring true. He was too perfect.

The carriage disappeared at the end of the street, and Clara turned from the window.

Sophia entered. "Well? Did he propose?"

Feeling almost numb inside, Clara nodded.

"What did you say?"

"I told him I would give him an answer tomorrow."

"I see." Looking worried, Sophia regarded Clara. "Are you still thinking about the marquess? Because I don't think he's the kind of man who would propose marriage quite so quickly." She moved fully into the room and stood before Clara, who felt suddenly pale.

Sophia continued. "What do you want, Clara?"

"I don't know. Or rather, I do know, or at least I thought I did. I want to marry a man who will be a good husband. A man I can respect. Everyone is telling me that the duke is that man—he satisfies all my criteria—yet my heart is not quite so certain. He said something about his children today. He said I would almost never have to see them, as if that would make me more likely to accept his offer. What does that say about his love for them, and his devotion to his family?"

Sophia nodded.

"Besides," Clara added, "I am still attracted to the marquess."

Sophia took Clara's hand and led her to the sofa to sit down. "I remember what it felt like when I was falling in love with James. If I had been pressured to marry someone else, I don't know what I would have done. I don't envy you."

"If only I could see the marquess again."

"But would it make a difference? I believe the marquess would require a fair bit of wooing, so to speak, to be enticed into marriage, and unfortunately you don't have time to do that. It's a shame the duke had not waited a little while and given you a chance to get to know him better and figure out what you really wanted. This lays a great deal of weight upon your shoulders, doesn't it?"

"You know me too well, Sophia." Clara gazed down at her hands on her lap. "What am I going to do?"

Sophia shrugged. "Only you know the answer to that question. It's your future."

After a long pause, Clara looked into her sister's compassionate eyes. "I need to see him."

Sophia's breast heaved with a deep intake of air. "I suppose you could send him a note and tell him that you've received an offer. That might give him a little push."

"I don't want to force him or push him into proposing to me. I just want to see him and talk to him. Find out for sure if there is any hope."

"But would you be prepared to refuse a decent man's offer on the off chance that a notorious rake might reform?"

Clara stared out the window again. "I'm not sure. That's what I need to find out."

Clara sat alone in her room that evening and read all the letters again. After some careful contemplation, she knew that the time for playful flirtations had ended. She couldn't go on waiting and hoping the marquess would appear at a society ball. She had to take the bull by the horns.

She dipped her pen in the ink and scrolled a quick note.

Dear Lord Rawdon,

I wish to see you as soon as possible. Can we arrange a time?

C.

Clara sealed the letter and gave it to a footman with instructions to deliver it immediately. He returned an hour later with a reply.

Miss Wilson,

The urgency of your letter intrigues me. My carriage will be outside of Wentworth House tonight at two A.M.

S.

Two A.M.! Clara could barely believe her eyes. Did he think she would be able to convince her chaperone, Mrs. Gunther, to escort her out to a gentleman's carriage at that hour of the night?

Obviously not.

Which was precisely the point.

He expected her to sneak out alone.

Good God.

Clara squeezed her forehead in her hand. Could she do such a thing? Perhaps this was fate trying to give her the proof she needed that the marquess was not the man for her.

Or perhaps it was just the opposite. Fate giving her the chance to meet the *real* marquess. Alone without pretensions. Without restrictions. There was no time, after all, to get to know the real man through superficial encounters in drawing rooms.

He'd told her she could trust him to do everything in his power to protect her from ruin, and oddly enough, she did trust him in that regard. Every instinct she possessed—and she was operating wholly on instinct where the marquess was concerned—told her that he would not ravish her if he had the chance. He had on two other occasions proven that fact, when he'd instructed her to leave the Cakras Balls and not return.

Her belly swarmed with apprehension. Could she sneak out of the house undetected and not get caught?

By God, she was going to try.

Chapter 9

Dear Adele,

Have you met anyone interesting in New York? I hope there are some new faces, because sometimes I fear that I will be a complete failure here, and end up back there before I have a chance to blink.

Love,
Clara

Wearing a dark gown, no jewels and sensible shoes, Clara tiptoed down the stairs, then down another flight to exit the quiet house through the servants' back entrance. She left the door unlocked and moved quickly through the foggy night along the side of the house to the front— where indeed, a carriage was waiting in the shadows across the street, a considerable distance away from the nearest street lamp.

She approached slowly, her heart pounding like a mallet in her chest. This was an adventure, yes, but presently the excitement was translating into a dreadful, nauseating knot in her stomach, for she did not know what to expect. She had never been out alone at night before, nor had she ever agreed to such a scandalous, secret rendezvous with a rake. In his carriage. Just the two of them.

She neared the shiny black vehicle and circled around the back of it. The door opened onto the sidewalk, the light from inside the carriage spilling onto the ground. The marquess stepped out into the chilly mist. He wore formal attire—a black jacket, white waistcoat and white necktie. No hat or gloves.

"I knew you would come." He took a step forward and kissed her gloved hand. "Your carriage awaits."

Clara glanced over her shoulder. The large coach blocked the view of them from the house, so Clara could at least relax about being seen.

He assisted her inside, then climbed in after her and closed the door.

A small lamp gave the lush, velvet interior a dim, surreal glow. Dark, crimson curtains covered the windows. Clara tried to breathe normally as she sat down and arranged her skirts.

"Where are we going?" she asked.

"Nowhere. We'll stay right here. Unless you *want* to go somewhere."

She shook her head. "No, here is fine. Then I can leave when I wish."

You're thinking out loud, Clara.

"Precisely my thought as well." With all his attention focused on her, he leaned in, crossed his legs and rested an arm along the back of the seat behind her.

She stared at his face. He was so handsome in the lamplight, it hurt just to look at him.

"So tell me," he said with a friendly, open expression, "what was the emergency?"

Clara tried to think clearly. She did not want to tell him she brought him here just to inform him that someone had proposed to her. She was certain he would not be attracted to such desperation—a single woman carrying a torch for him, begging to see him immediately and sneaking out in the middle of the night to do so. He'd take off like a fox. He would think she was entertaining foolish, romantic hopes that he, too, would propose, when in actuality, Clara was doing everything possible to shun those hopes.

"It wasn't an emergency," she said, "I just suddenly recalled that I did not respond to your last letter, and since I had not seen you for an entire week, I wondered how you were."

He didn't reply right away. The momentary silence made Clara squirm uncomfortably. She knew she would have to work hard to keep her composure.

The marquess, on the other hand, did not seem the least bit uncomfortable. He was staring directly into her eyes, smiling, then he began to stroke her arm with a finger. "You know, I thought I might have shocked you with my last letter. Did I?"

She cleared her throat. "No. Well, perhaps a bit."

He continued to stroke her forearm, causing gooseflesh to erupt in every nook and cranny under her dress.

"You can take off your gloves if you like," he said.

"Why would I want to do that?"

He shrugged.

She gazed at him for a titillating moment, then swallowed hard and took them off. She set them on the seat beside her.

It was strange that on all their previous encounters—

except the first perhaps—she had felt confident around him and had become bold and flirtatious.

Tonight, she was nothing of the sort. She was nervous and frazzled and shaky. He had all the power.

"You've never been in a carriage alone with a man before, have you?" he said.

Clara's eyebrows lifted. "Certainly not."

"I promise I shall endeavor to make it a pleasant experience. There's nothing to be nervous about."

She swallowed again and wondered if he'd heard the gulp. "Will we talk? Or are you going to kiss me?"

Amused by the question, he chuckled. "What would *you* like me to do?"

"Talk," she said too quickly. "At least, to start off with."

His face warmed. "So you are not averse to the idea of my kissing you. I'm glad to hear it." He leaned back. "Just for the record, I prefer to talk first, too. What would you like to discuss?"

Clara considered it. "Well, here in your carriage at two A.M., I doubt that polite rules apply, so can we avoid talking about the weather?"

"Absolutely."

"Then I would like to ask all the questions I've been told are too forward in polite society. I would like to know more about you, Lord Rawdon. I would like to know about your family and your home and your childhood. I would like to know more about the affairs you've had."

His head tilted back a bit. He still looked amused. "I'm game, as long as you promise to oblige me the same way."

"I'd be happy to."

He casually pushed a lock of hair away from her forehead. His touch made her tingle. "Where would you like me to begin?"

Clara turned slightly to face him on the seat. "Where did you go to school?"

He told her about attending Charterhouse, about his grades. He'd been an exceptional student academically.

"Were you well behaved as well?"

"I was a model student, usually a favorite of my professors and prefects. I was one of the few lucky ones who never once received a caning."

Clara grinned. "An achievement to be sure, but I doubt it was luck if you were well behaved. Did you attend university?"

"Yes, I went to Cambridge, then I went abroad for a few years to Paris and India." He told her about his travels, the things he had seen and done.

Clara listened to everything with keen ears, fascinated by all of it, soon forgetting that she was here on a mission to gather information and decide whether or not he was redeemable. Instead, she merely began to enjoy herself.

They chatted about their favorite pastimes, unusual tastes, embarrassing moments. The marquess had a surprising interest in botany. Clara enjoyed sketching people's faces. The marquess once posed for an inexperienced artist in Paris who was attempting to paint Zeus. It had turned out very badly. Clara had once drawn a picture that made the model look like a pomegranate.

He could be very amusing, she discovered as she laughed at something he'd said. He seemed to greatly enjoy a lot of little things in life, like a perfectly cooked salmon steak, or a quiet ride over the dewy countryside at dawn.

Before Clara knew it, an hour had passed and she realized she had not learned half of what she had wanted to learn about this man. There suddenly seemed to be much more to learn than she had initially imagined.

"Do you have any brothers or sisters?" she asked.

"No. My mother had a difficult time bringing me into the world and the doctor told her not to have any more children. Seven years went by and she made the mistake of forgetting his advice. She and the baby died before she made it to the birthing bed."

"I'm sorry. Do you remember much about her?"

His expression softened. "She was a quiet, unassuming woman, and very kind. When my father remarried, he chose a more outspoken woman—my stepmother—but they were unfortunately unable to have children, which I believe partly explains the marchioness's deep affection for her niece."

"Miss Flint? The young woman who attended my sister's assembly?"

"Yes. Her own mother died a few years ago. She was Quintina's twin."

"Ah, it's no wonder she is close to her."

They sat in silence for a few minutes, then Clara answered the marquess's questions about her upbringing and education in America. She described her early childhood in Wisconsin, what it was like living in a one-room cabin in the woods before her father moved them to the city and slowly but surely earned his fortune on Wall Street. She told him about learning to speak French in Paris with her sisters, and described her etiquette training in finishing school.

Then she decided it was time to broach a new subject.

"What about your affairs?" she asked directly, knowing she had to become more efficient in this conversational quest. "That woman from the divorce case. Did you love her?"

His eyes narrowed devilishly. "Now we're getting

somewhere. No, I didn't, but neither was the sentiment returned."

"How long were you involved with her?"

"Only for a couple of months, but never steadily. She was a regular at the Cakras Balls and when we met there, we often spent time together, but I wasn't the only man she carried on with, nor was I the only witness in court that day." He brushed a fleck of dust off his lapel. "She was a witty woman. She enjoyed limericks."

Clara did not particularly enjoy hearing about him with another woman. She knew, however, that the questions were necessary and she reminded herself that she was a rational woman and that feeling jealous did not make sense. He did not belong to her.

Still, she didn't like it.

"Where is the woman now?"

"I have no idea. She left England after that. She might have gone to Ireland. Her husband is still here, though he stays in the country most of the time. He took a second wife last year and I believe they are expecting their first child."

Clara settled back onto the deeply buttoned upholstery. "Have you never been serious with anyone?"

"Ah. The questions are becoming more stimulating, aren't they?" He gazed up at the ceiling for a moment. "Yes, I was serious once."

Clara sat forward. "How serious?"

"As serious as a young man can get. I wanted to be married."

Clara stared wordlessly at him.

"You're surprised," he said.

"Well, yes." And a thousand questions were darting around inside her brain. "Why didn't you marry her?"

He took a deep breath. "Because I was young, and according to my father and stepmother, not aware of the 'importance' of my marriage. I was heir to a very old title and I had the unfortunate luck to fall in love with a merchant's daughter. Not even a very prosperous merchant, at that."

Still digesting the shock, Clara probed further. "How old were you?"

"Sixteen. I knew within a week that she was the one for me, and I was her lover for four years before I proposed. The marriage was of course forbidden, and she was sent away."

"By whom?"

"My father."

Clara was brimming with curiosity. "Where did she go?"

"She was sent to America, but the ship went down somewhere in the Atlantic."

A lump formed in Clara's throat. She swallowed over it and laid her hand on the marquess's thigh. "I am very sorry to hear that."

He looked the other way toward the red velvet curtains that covered the window. "It was a long time ago."

"Have you never cared for anyone since then?"

His gaze dropped to her hand upon his thigh, then flicked up and settled with intensity on her eyes. "I've cared for many."

Feeling nervous all of a sudden, she discreetly lifted her hand off his leg.

"No need to do that," he said, reaching to take her hand and slowly place it back where it was. "Things were just getting interesting."

Her heart began to pound. "I only meant to offer commiseration, my lord."

"Yes, I know, and you're very good at it. Care to offer a little more?"

He leaned closer. His gaze went from her eyes to her lips, back up to her eyes again. He was so close, his nose was almost touching hers. The proximity stirred her pulse.

"Are you going to kiss me now?" she asked ridiculously.

"Only if you want me to." He remained where he was, gazing down at her lips. Tension seemed to crackle all around them.

"I'm not really sure. It doesn't seem right."

"Sitting in a carriage alone with me at three A.M., asking all kinds of personal questions, doesn't seem right either. But here we are."

"Yes, here we are." His nearness was overwhelming. The rush of blood through her body throbbed in her ears.

Clara moistened her lips.

The marquess smiled.

He was still smiling a few seconds later when he kissed her, his lips touching hers almost experimentally. Clara closed her eyes and gave in to the desire to open for him, to welcome his tongue inside after so many days remembering what it had felt like that glorious first night under the stairs. Now, here it was again—the passion, the eroticism, the sweet, pounding ache of lust being fulfilled.

He cupped her face in his large, warm hands and grinned roguishly. "I had not forgotten how delicious you were."

"Nor I, you," she said, trembling all over, a blush warming her cheeks. She wished she could be more in control at this moment and feel as if she knew what she was doing, but she did not. She had no idea. This was unlike any experience of her life.

"You even taste like strawberries," he said. "I'm afraid

I'm going to have to kiss you again. There's no getting around it."

"Please do." But she pressed her open mouth to his before he had the chance to comply.

The kiss was deep and fierce and utterly intoxicating. A shiver ran through Clara as she devoured his mouth, clutched at his shoulders, realizing she had been starving for this, more than she ever could have comprehended.

The marquess eased her down upon the seat, never breaking the intimacy of their kiss. His hands roamed leisurely over her hips, then he rose up to move her leg to one side and adjust her skirts so he could settle himself between her thighs.

This was wrong, she knew—to part her legs for him like this, to let him lie on top of her, so close—but she couldn't help it. She wanted to feel the weight of him upon her body, to feel his hips near the private place between her legs that tingled and ached for the pressure of his arousal. She had not known that lust could have such an overwhelming effect on all her senses and reasoning.

Laying hot, open-mouthed kisses on her neck, he whispered, "You must tell me how far you wish to go tonight, so there are no surprises or disappointments later on."

"I don't know," she said breathlessly. "I've never done any of this before. I don't even know what should come next. Or last."

He smiled and kissed her cheeks and nose. "You are charming."

"I can only trust you, my lord. You said you could give pleasure without destruction. Can you really? And do you promise?"

"I certainly *know* how to. Whether or not I can remain disciplined toward that end, I'm not sure."

Clara knew her eyes had revealed her sudden fears and doubts, and knew that Lord Rawdon had recognized it. She could tell by the way his eyes warmed.

He kissed her on the lips again, then eased her mind with a tender smile. "I give you my word," he said. "No destruction tonight. I know what to do. But are you sure you want to even begin? It might leave you starving for more."

She nodded. "I'm sure, only because at the moment, I cannot even contemplate stopping you."

He smiled and lowered his mouth to hers, letting out a deep and sensual growl. His tongue in her mouth heated her blood, sent waves of erotic excitement to all her frazzled nerve endings.

"We might as well allow ourselves to get comfortable, then." He unfastened the covered buttons on her bodice one by one, and kissed lower and lower down the length of her neck and across her sensitive collarbone.

When her bodice finally fell open, he thrust his hips against hers and slid his hand up over her corset to her bare neckline. Clara's pulse quickened at the softness of his caress.

He smiled seductively as he kissed the swell of her cleavage, unhooking the corset clasps over her breasts.

Sucking in a breath, Clara marveled at the quivering sensations deep within her belly. This was all so deliciously wicked. If anyone caught them! Oddly enough, the danger only served to pour kerosene on her already flaming desires.

The corset came loose and she reveled in the physical freedom. Seger massaged her breast through the light fabric of her chemise, then tugged at the ribbons to loosen it and pull it down. He took one of her breasts into his mouth. Every tingling fibre of Clara's being cried out with shock and delight at the feel of his tongue flicking back and forth.

"This is inconceivable," she whispered, clutching at his head. The sound of his lapping tongue in the otherwise silent coach, and the feel of his hot breath against her skin caused an ache down lower where his arousal pushed against her nether regions. She had no idea what was happening down there, how he could be so huge and rigid where there had been nothing visible earlier.

Curious and aching to touch him, she let her hand slide down his back, then around to the front. He stopped what he was doing and glanced at her with a rakish grin. "You are absolutely delightful."

"I want to know what you feel like."

"Be my guest."

She slid her hand down inside his pants, without attempting to unbutton them. What she touched was astonishing. He was so smooth and hot and large. She wrapped her hand around him and remained there, very still, holding him.

After a minute or two, he reached down to unbutton his trousers. "I think you need a little more room to maneuver."

"Maneuver?"

His voice was quiet and husky. "I'll show you."

He closed his hand around hers and proceeded to teach her how to touch him. As soon as she caught on, he closed his eyes and returned his mouth to her breast. Clara tilted her head back on the seat, surprised when a tiny moan escaped her throat. It didn't even sound like her.

"Lord Rawdon," she whispered, feeling strange.

"Call me Seger." Then he reached down to lift her skirts until they were bunched around her waist. He slid a hand over her thigh, then into the heated confines of her drawers. "I'll be gentle," he said.

Clara clutched onto his broad shoulders. "Seger . . ."

While he kissed her on the mouth, he stroked her with his fingers, paying particular attention to one spot that seemed more sensitive than anywhere else, causing her insides to quiver with an unfamiliar need.

After a few minutes of that skillful touching, he lifted her chemise and kissed her belly, then went lower down, past her bunched up skirts, until he was pulling her drawers down over her hips and tossing them onto the floor of the coach. Then he began to pleasure her—down there— with his mouth and tongue.

Reeling with shock at the intimacy of such an act, Clara arched her back on the seat. "Seger, what are you doing to me?"

He didn't answer. She didn't mind, not if it meant he would continue whatever it was he was doing.

She could hear the carnal sounds of his mouth on her. Aroused beyond any imaginings, Clara grabbed onto the curtains and squeezed them in her fist.

Soon, all her muscles began to tremble and quake, then an extraordinary sensation licked over her like hot, advancing flames, followed by an intense shudder of release. It was unlike anything she had ever experienced. It was divine, liquid ecstasy.

Afterward, her body relaxed. Seger sat back, draping her legs over his lap. He held her hand.

"Good Lord," she said, feeling utterly depleted of strength. "Am I dying?"

"No, you just had a glimpse of heaven, that's all."

She shook her head in disbelief. "I've never glimpsed heaven like that before. What did you do to me?"

"I gave you an orgasm."

She tossed a limp arm over her forehead. "An orgasm? Did I give *you* one?"

He smiled. "No, my dear."

"Have you ever had one?"

He smiled again. "Yes, and your innocence is enchanting."

"I'm not so innocent anymore, am I?" she asked, then frowned. She leaned up on both her elbows. "I'm not ruined, am I?"

Seger caressed her cheek. "No, darling. You're still a virgin."

She laid back down again. "You'd have to touch me with that other part, wouldn't you?"

He chuckled. "I'm afraid so."

"Well, I don't want you to do that. At least not tonight."

"Have no fear. I've got it under lock and key."

She could sense his amusement. She knew he was pleased with her and she couldn't deny the satisfaction that came with that knowledge.

"But was it enjoyable for you?" she asked. "If you didn't have an orgasm. . . . Do you usually have orgasms with other women?"

"Almost invariably."

She thought about that. "Then this wasn't quite as gratifying for you as it usually is, then."

He touched a thumb to her lips. "It was gratifying enough. I made you a promise."

"But you gave me pleasure. Can't I do the same for you?"

He raked a hand through his hair. "I wouldn't want to overdo it your first time out of the gate."

Clara laughed and sat up. "What if I want to overdo it?

I'm a very enthusiastic pupil. Besides, I'm not ready to go back inside yet. The servants won't be up for at least another hour."

She slid across the seat to take his face in her hands and kiss him again. "Show me what to do," she whispered. "I don't want to go yet."

He responded instantly and lifted her onto his lap, kissing her with unleashed abandon. His hand slid up under her chemise again and cupped her breast, gently pinching her pebbled nipple between his thumb and forefinger.

Feeling aroused all over again, Clara straddled him. Her drawers were still on the floor, so she could feel the rigid length of him easily through the barrier of his trousers.

"What can I do to give you an orgasm, without losing what's left of my virtue?" she asked, blowing in his ear.

He groaned and kissed her neck. "Maybe you should quit while you're ahead, while I'm still in control of myself."

"But there must be some way that you can have a glimpse of heaven tonight, too." She had to admit, she was feeling determined.

"There are a couple of ways," he said into her mouth, "but I think one in particular would be the better choice."

"Show me."

He lifted her up so he could slide his trousers down over his hips. Knees braced on the seat on either side of him, skirts bunched under an arm at her belly, Clara gazed down at the tremendous sight of him in the dim light and trembled with awe.

He didn't give her much time to stare. He slouched down and took her hips in his strong hands, then guided her down on top of him. "Like this."

His erection lay flat on his stomach. She simply covered him with her private center. "Slide over me," he said, "back and forth, but gently and not over the tip."

She understood and held onto his shoulders while she moved. Everything was slick down there. He closed his eyes and leaned his head back on the seat.

Clara began to move in a way that brought the pleasure swirling back into her own senses again. She slid that one sensitive nub over the firm but silky length of him. Her breathing quickened. So did his. Clara let out a tiny little moan.

He began to quickly unbutton his waistcoat and shirt, then pressed both garments open. He inched down a bit more.

Clara gazed in bewildered awe at the sheer beauty of his bare, muscled chest. He enflamed her desires more than she'd ever dreamed possible. Was this love? Was she falling in love with him?

Heart racing, she let her fingers skim over the smooth skin on his chest and pressed her palm over his heart to feel it beating. She leaned forward and kissed him.

"This is as close as one can get to the real thing," he whispered. "But what I wouldn't give to be inside you right now."

She watched his face in the lamplight; he, too, watched hers. The movement took on a life of its own and Clara simply had to thrust her hips in harmony with Seger's. It all seemed so natural. So intimate and tender.

He shut his eyes. She saw the muscles in his jaw clench, then he reached into the breast pocket of his jacket and pulled out a handkerchief.

He was so beautiful. God, how she loved being here

with him and feeling this way. How could she dream of marrying and doing this with another man?

She closed her eyes, too, and rested her forehead against his. Their pace quickened until his grip on her hips grew tighter, firmer, then he let out a groan and pushed her back so she was sitting above his testicles.

He covered himself with the handkerchief. Clara watched his face, felt his hips thrust forward, and knew he was climaxing like she had earlier. It made her smile.

"Did you see heaven?" she asked, a moment later when he relaxed and tossed the balled up handkerchief to the floor.

"God, yes."

"What did it look like?"

"You." He pulled her close and kissed her. She sat forward to throw her arms around his neck and hold him close, to feel the bare skin of his chest against her loose chemise.

"Careful," he said, slipping a hand down to cover himself. "Don't get too close. A virgin can still defy the odds and find herself in the family way."

Thankful for his experience and knowledge in these matters, she nodded and slid off him. He pulled his trousers back on and buttoned them. "Better safe than sorry."

Clara leaned back against the side wall of the coach. "I can't believe what we did, Seger."

His eyes softened. "Promise me you won't feel guilty in the morning. You did nothing but give yourself pleasure, and me as well."

She sighed. "I'm not sure how I'll feel. This was all very new."

They sat in silence for a moment.

"Very new and very marvelous." He slid closer to kiss her, then he kissed down the side of her neck. "I apologize for not paying more attention. Did you have another one while you were on top of me?"

"Another orgasm?" She tossed her head back and reveled in the sweet gooseflesh tingling up her side. "No, but it still felt good."

He continued to kiss her neck and chest. "Would you like another one now? There's time before you go."

He was unbelievable. "You're not tired?" she asked.

He shook his head. "Me? Never."

Then before she had a chance to argue, he smiled and disappeared under her skirts again.

Chapter 10

Dear Clara,

No, there are no new faces in New York, so you had better make a success of it in London. You haven't given up on the handsome marquess, I hope. Have you become better acquainted with him yet? I am anxiously awaiting more news.

Adele

Clara woke to the sound of a knock at her door. She grumbled, rolled over onto her back in her huge bed, and opened her eyes.

The curtains were drawn and the room dim, but the sun was shining outside. What time was it? She squinted at the clock. Almost noon.

The knock rapped again.

"I'm still sleeping!" she called out, rolling to her side and curling up with a wicked little smile, gathering the covers into a ball and hugging them.

"Are you all right, Clara? You're not ill, are you?"

It was Sophia. Clara sat up. *No, I'm not ill. I'm quite the opposite.* "Come in."

Her sister peered inside. "You missed breakfast and you're about to miss lunch, too, if you don't get your lazy bones out of bed."

Clara smiled and waved Sophia in. "I need to talk to you."

"Good Lord, Clara." Sophia closed the door behind her, moved all the way into the room and touched Clara's forehead with the back of her hand. "You look awful. Your eyes are bloodshot. Didn't you get any sleep last night?"

"Not really." Clara couldn't keep from smirking.

"What's going on? You know a secret." She sat down.

Clara arranged the pillows behind her and leaned back. "I do, but if I tell you, you have to promise that you won't be angry, nor will you breathe a word to anyone. Not even James."

"You know I don't like keeping secrets from James."

Clara hated asking her sister to lie, but she couldn't let anyone else find out what she had done.

More importantly, she supposed that she didn't want her brother-in-law—who had always been so understanding and supportive of her despite her past mistakes—to think badly of her. She couldn't imagine anything worse than disappointing someone she respected so very much.

"I don't want James to know because he has always seemed to trust me and believe in my judgment. I don't want to fall short of his generous regard. Besides, there would be havoc if he knew."

"Havoc? Tell me, Clara."

Clara stared at her sister for a moment, hoping she

wouldn't be too shocked by what she was about to hear. "I . . . I did something a little wild last night. Well, something *very* wild."

Sophia covered her face with a hand. "Oh, no."

"Don't worry, no one knows. I was careful."

"What did you do?"

"I snuck out to meet Lord Rawdon."

Sophia's cheeks went pale. "When? How?"

"I sent him a note last night saying that I wished to see him, and he replied by telling me that his carriage would be out front at two A.M. I knew I had to take advantage of the opportunity, since time was an issue regarding the duke's proposal, so I was very quiet and went out a servant's door, and indeed the marquess was there waiting for me just as he said he would be. We didn't go anywhere. We just sat in his carriage out front and talked."

"You talked," she said skeptically. "That's all?"

"Well, no, but I'll explain the rest in a minute. The point is that I've made up my mind about the Duke of Guysborough. I don't want to marry him."

Sophia continued to stare at Clara in shock.

Clara elaborated. "After I talked to the marquess, I realized that we were right about him, Sophia. There is hope. His unconventional behavior makes perfect sense."

"Why?"

"First of all, he was an exemplary child and model student, very well behaved with excellent academic performance. It was only later in life that he began to live recklessly, and there is an explanation for it. You see, he fell in love with someone but was forbidden to marry her because she was considered beneath him."

"I'm still waiting for the reason why you think there is hope."

Clara continued. "The young woman was sent away by Lord Rawdon's father, but she died when her ship went down in the Atlantic. Yes, it's tragic, I know. It was after that that the marquess retreated from society because he blamed its severe, restrictive rules for his heartache. The point is, he loved once before, Sophia, deeply and faithfully. He wanted to marry the girl, and the loss of her cut him so deeply, he has not yet gotten over it."

"And you think this makes him more attainable?"

"Yes. If a man is capable of loving a woman once with intimacy and devotion, he is capable of it again. He needs to be rescued. I can help him, I'm sure of it. It's in his nature to love."

Sophia stood up and paced the room. "This is dangerous, Clara. A woman should never believe she can change a man. When you marry, you must marry the man for who and what he is, not what you hope he will become."

"You rescued James."

"But I didn't know that's what I was doing when I agreed to marry him. I believed he was perfect as he was. It was only later that I realized there was more beneath the surface than I knew. You, on the other hand, know that the marquess is not the kind of man you ever intended to marry. You should not forget that."

Clara tossed the covers aside and stood up. She went to her dressing table to sit down and begin combing her hair. "There is an attraction between us. We could have talked all night long."

"He's a very skilled lover, Clara. That's what he does. He seduces women, makes them feel desirable."

Clara bristled at the words. "No, there was something special between us."

"I'm sure all women feel that way after a night in his arms. He's a very handsome and charming man. Tell me you did not do anything foolish. You didn't give yourself to him, did you?"

Clara turned to face Sophia, and saw the anxiety in her eyes. "You needn't be concerned. I am still a virgin."

Sophia let out a deep breath and collapsed into a chair. She rested a hand on her chest.

"Which is another reason why I believe he is honorable beneath the less than respectable notoriety," Clara said. "He's had three opportunities to take advantage of me, and all three times he has resisted his base impulses and done everything in his power to protect my virtue. I trusted him completely last night, Sophia. There was not a single fear in my mind that he would ravish me against my will or do anything to harm me. The fact that he could act with honor in that way leads me to believe that if he makes any kind of vow or promise, he will be faithful to that vow."

"You think he could be a faithful husband?"

"Yes, I do."

"We're talking about a lifetime, Clara, not one night with a virgin. Maybe he didn't ravish you because he knew that if he did, he'd have to marry you, and the idea of commitment and fidelity outweighed his temporary, base impulses."

Clara pulled the brush roughly through her hair. "There was nothing temporary about what happened last night."

"But you are not experienced with this sort of thing! Some men can make love to a woman and forget her the very next instant! Their dalliances are merely conquests. What did happen, exactly?"

Clara shook her head. "I wanted to tell you before, but now I don't. You'll only disapprove."

Sophia approached Clara and rested her hands on her shoulders. "I only worry that you're going to get hurt. That you're romanticizing what happened."

"You were supportive before. You were encouraging me to find out all I could about him. Why have you changed your mind?"

"I haven't changed my mind, I just feel that you must tread carefully where the marquess is concerned. Guard your heart as well as your virtue until you can be sure he is worthy of you. Be vigilant and act with caution. That's all I'm saying."

Clara knew deep down that her sister was right. Clara's head was in the clouds this morning.

How could it not be? She had glimpsed heaven the night before.

"All right," she said, gazing up at her sister. "I will promise to be careful. But I must refuse the duke."

Sophia nodded. "Mrs. Gunther won't be happy. You probably shouldn't tell her beforehand. She'll spend the whole day trying to change your mind."

"Good point. I'll tell her after the fact, then she'll have no choice but to accept it." Clara sighed heavily. "Well, now that we've got all that out of the way, do you want to hear what happened in the carriage *after* we talked?"

Sophia smiled and sat down next to Clara. "Of course. And spare nothing. I want every delicious detail."

Later that day, the Duke of Guysborough was announced. He entered the drawing room.

With a barely discernible smile, Mrs. Gunther mentioned that she had to go and speak to her maid about something, and left Clara alone with him.

"You've had a chance to consider my proposal?" he asked, looking down at her where she sat on the sofa. He appeared confident. She supposed it was natural, considering his status. Clara was not looking forward to rejecting him.

"I have, Your Grace, and I am indeed flattered."

He smiled and sat down next to her.

A cold knot tightened in Clara's belly. She hated this. "You are a wonderful man, Your Grace, and I am honored by your offer, but . . ." She paused for a few seconds. "I'm afraid I must reject it."

The duke's head tipped back in surprise. "I beg your pardon?"

"I'm sorry."

"Is there a reason? There must be a reason."

"I do apologize. This is most difficult. I . . . I am simply not in love with you."

His eyebrows drew together. "Not in love with me?" He sat in tense silence for another few seconds, then rolled his shoulders as if he were struggling to keep his anger in check. "Perhaps I should have taken more time for a courtship. I've heard that you American women have certain expectations in that regard."

Clara tried to let him down easily. "Your proposal did come rather quickly, yes."

"Because I was certain that if I did not act quickly, someone else would. The competition for you is intense, my dear. You are the talk of the town, so to speak."

Clara was no fool. She knew she was renowned because she was an heiress and it was a well-known fact that her father would furnish her husband-to-be with an inconceivably huge marriage settlement. Her own sister, Sophia, had made James one of the richest men in England; her dowry, if one included the railroad stock, had been the largest in English history.

Clara's would match that.

"Thank you for the compliment, Your Grace," she said.

He was not satisfied. "May I indulge in some hope that you might change your mind if I give you time?"

She didn't know what to say. She hated rejecting the duke, and there was of course a chance that Lord Rawdon would break her heart in the coming weeks. The possibility that she might be burning all her bridges loomed over her.

"I really don't know, Your Grace. I don't wish to give you any false hopes."

He stared into her eyes for a moment. His darkened. "Is there someone else?"

Clara swallowed nervously. "I can't say."

"Can't say?" His voice revealed agitation. Tension moved through Clara's neck and shoulders. "You're making a stupid mistake. You know that, don't you?"

The duke's harsh tone cleared her of any regret about rejecting him. She was now certain that she had done the right thing.

When she did not reply, he grabbed hold of her hand and pressed it against his cold lips. He began to drop hard kisses up her arm. "Maybe this is what a woman like you wants."

His mouth reached the inside of her elbow, and the hairs on the back of her neck stood up in disgust. Heart pounding, she pulled her arm out of his grasp.

The duke's petulant gaze shot to her face. Recognizing

her revulsion, he sat up straighter. "I was right. Your interests do lie elsewhere."

She tried to shake her head, but his eyes narrowed with accusation.

"I want to marry you," he said. "I want to treat you with the respect you deserve. The Marquess of Rawdon does not."

Clara stared at him, dumbfounded. *The Marquess of Rawdon?*

How did the duke know? No one had seen her last night. The marquess had come to call on her once, but surely that wasn't enough to connect . . .

"I beg your pardon, Your Grace?"

"It is your choice, Clara. You can be a duchess or you can be a slut."

Clara sucked in a breath. She had never been spoken to in such a manner. She certainly had not expected this from the duke, who had always appeared to be the epitome of proper, gentlemanly behavior.

Fury began to rage inside her. She stood. "Please leave."

She made a move to walk around the sofa and open the drawing room door for him, but he grabbed hold of her arm.

"I will leave when you've realized your folly. You've attended two Cakras Balls and you have become besotted with a notorious rake. I saw the two of you here in this very room at your sister's assembly. A few others did as well. I assure you, there were whispers. You do not emit purity, my dear. There's something unchaste about you, and you have affiliated yourself with the marquess —a known degenerate. I am willing to overlook that fact because the damage is still reparable at this point, and offer you a respectable escape."

"Respectable escape?" She jerked her arm from his grasp. "I asked you to leave."

"I don't believe you want me to do that."

"And why not?"

"Because I have the power to destroy you, Miss Wilson. To put it in plainer terms, if you do not accept my offer, I most certainly will."

"He said *what*?" Sophia asked, her voice brimming with horror and shock.

Clara sat numbly on the sofa. "He told me that it was my choice. That I could be a duchess or a slut. Needless to say, I didn't tell Mrs. Gunther. She is very curious about what happened."

Hands wrenching together in front of her, Sophia walked to the mantel. "I cannot believe this! The Duke of Guysborough of all people. I always took him for a gentleman."

"So did I. I was stunned."

"As you had every right to be! He behaved deplorably!"

"Yes." Clara gazed around the room. "But I, too, behaved deplorably, and I must accept responsibility for the state of affairs. If I had not lost my head with the marquess, none of this would be happening." She stood up and paced the room. "If you must bar your door to me, Sophia, I will understand. Perhaps I should leave now and go back to America before this spins out of control. I don't want you and James to be sullied by it."

"We will not bar our door to you."

"James might wish it. He has every right to. He might want to protect Liam and John."

"James will not wish it. You are a member of this family, and as far as he is concerned, you are under his protection." Sophia crossed to the sofa and sat down. "Besides, this is as much my fault as it is yours. I should never have taken you to that Cakras Ball. Good Lord, I have been getting rid of Mrs. Gunther whenever possible. I've been a terrible chaperone."

"No, Sophia. If you hadn't taken me to that ball, I would have found some way to see the marquess again, and things could have been much worse. Or maybe I would have accepted the duke's proposal, and paid for such naiveté later."

For a long time, neither of them said anything. The mantel clock ticked and ticked. Clara felt a heavy weight upon her shoulders—the uncomfortable, cumbersome weight of her emotions.

"Sometimes," she said softly, gazing up at the flowers on the mantle, "when I think about the marquess, it feels as if I am possessed. I don't know if it is love or something darker . . . something purely hedonistic. Most of the time, all I can think about is being alone with him again. I cannot suppress my desire to give myself to him in the physical sense. Completely."

She turned her gaze to her sister, expecting to see shock and condemnation in her eyes.

Instead, she saw compassion. "I understand how you feel," Sophia said. "I remember . . . with James." Sophia stood up again and took both Clara's hands in hers. "Do not distress yourself. You are a normal, healthy young woman with very human desires, and I agree with you on one point—that the marquess acted honorably, having spared your virtue when clearly you could have been easily persuaded. Compared to Guysborough, he is a gentleman through and through."

Clara nodded.

"It appears," Sophia continued, "that the marquess and the duke are very different from how they are perceived. Things are not always what they seem, are they?" She hugged Clara. "I've always believed there was more to a person than what they reveal on the surface. That's why I despise the gossip mill."

Clara sighed and stepped back from the embrace so she could look at her sister. "I'm afraid I might be dragged through the gossip mill very soon, if the duke doesn't get what he wants—which is undoubtedly a mammoth settlement from Father."

Pursing her lips, Sophia turned away from Clara. "It is nothing short of blackmail. I will not stand for it. James will not stand for it. We must tell him. He will know what to do."

A wave of apprehension moved through Clara. It was colored with shame and remorse. She hated causing problems for the two people she respected most in the world, and she did not want her sister's husband to think badly of her. "Please don't tell him about my sneaking out the other night. Everything else, but not that."

Gazing uncertainly at Clara, Sophia spoke softly. "Don't worry, Clara, it will not change how he feels about you. James is a man of the world. Besides that, he *must* know, because we cannot allow him to take steps without knowing all the facts."

Clara sat back down. "He won't go to the marquess, will he? I would die if he did."

"I will ask him not to. Either way, it will not be his first priority. The marquess will not be the one to face the core of his wrath today."

* * *

In the end, Clara told James everything that had occurred between herself and the marquess over the past few weeks. She even confessed to the letters and the scandalous rendezvous in the carriage, though she spared him the more intimate details.

Standing by the window in his study, he gave her a responsible speech about the importance of propriety, then made her promise never to do anything like that again.

Clara agreed without hesitation.

James glanced out the window for a brief moment before turning his attention back to Clara, who sat in a small chair.

"You're certain that the duke knows nothing about the meeting in the carriage?" he asked.

Clara nodded. "He would have used it against me if he knew. He only mentioned the Cakras Balls and the way the marquess and I were looking at each other at the assembly."

James folded his arms. "The duke should have known better than to reveal his knowledge of a Cakras Ball and to use it to threaten *anyone's* reputation. He'll pay for that mistake, I assure you. You have nothing to worry about, Clara."

She gazed up at her brother-in-law. "You're sure?"

He smiled warmly. "I'm positive."

"But what about Mrs. Gunther? She has no idea why I refused the duke and she is pressing me to explain."

"I will speak to her and tell her that you simply did not favor the man."

All her fears drained away in that instant, but were quickly replaced by another cause for concern. "You won't intimidate the marquess, will you? As I told you before, he has been nothing but honorable toward me. Well, with the exception of certain things he said in the letters, and inviting me out in the middle of the night, but even then, he did not take advantage of me when he could have. Will you think of that, James?" *When you are face-to-face with him, as I'm sure you will be later today.*

Her brother-in-law stepped away from the window and came around the desk. "I will indeed endeavor to think of it. Now, do not trouble yourself with this disturbance another minute. Guysborough *will* back down, and you have my word that he will behave himself in the future. Go to the nursery now and try to smile, my dear. I believe Sophia is waiting for you to play peekaboo with Liam."

Clara rose from her chair and allowed James to escort her out of his study.

Sickening dread poured through her, however, when she stood at the top of the stairs a few minutes later, watching her brother-in-law slip into his long, black greatcoat and place his top hat on his head, and inform the butler that he was going to take care of a thing or two.

Chapter 11

Adele,

I have fallen hopelessly in love with Lord Rawdon, and everything is in a terrible, terrible mess . . .

Clara

Seated at the desk in his study, Seger glanced up from the newspaper when his butler entered and informed him that the Duke of Wentworth wished to see him.

Seger laid his newspaper aside and inhaled deeply. "Send him in, Cartwright."

As soon as the butler closed the door behind him, Seger stood. "Bloody hell." He went to the sideboard and poured himself a brandy. "Here we go."

A moment later, the duke entered the room. Hands at his sides, he said simply, "Rawdon."

Seger poured another glass of brandy and approached the duke with it He held it out. "I suppose we'll each need one of these."

The duke removed his gloves and accepted the snifter. "Thank you."

Seger noticed the duke's right knuckle was bloodied. "Were you practicing on a tree outside in the garden?"

Wentworth glanced absently at his hand, then took a deep swig of the amber liquid. "It wasn't practice."

For a long moment, the two men regarded each other, then Seger gestured toward the chairs in front of the fireplace. "Care to sit?"

"I would indeed." The duke sat down and waited for Seger to sit before he spoke. "We shall dispense with small talk, then?"

"By all means."

Wentworth nodded. "You're no fool, Rawdon. I'm sure you know the motive behind my call."

Seger swirled the brandy around in his glass and took a sip. "I can hazard a guess. You want me to stay away from your sister-in-law."

Wentworth's gaze narrowed with shrewd scrutiny, as if he were trying to figure out what to make of Seger. "To be frank with you, I'm not certain. I'd like clarification from you first."

"Ah. Concerning what, in particular?"

The duke took another sip. "I shall come right to the point. Clara informs me that she is still in possession of her virtue. Is that true? And I will have the truth, Rawdon."

Seger considered the material facts. Images of every exquisite sexual act he'd performed with Clara in the carriage flashed like fireworks in his mind. He remembered sliding his hand into her drawers, taking them off and tossing them to the floor. He remembered what she'd tasted like and sounded like when she'd climaxed. Then he recalled Clara on his lap, bringing him to an acutely satisfying orgasm.

If anyone had peered in at them, it would have looked like they were having intercourse. They weren't, but it was damn close.

He had certainly taken a good deal of her innocence the night before, but for all practical purposes, he'd left her with the most important part of it—her maidenhead. He'd ensured she would still have choices.

"It's true," he replied, then downed the rest of his brandy in one gulp. "She is still in possession of her virtue."

"Despite your appointment with her last night?"

"Despite that, yes. You have my word that I did not harm her. Most of the time, we talked." That, too, was the truth.

The duke continued to glare at him.

"Do you believe me?"

Wentworth dipped his head. "Yes, unless some evidence in the future points to the contrary, in which case you would deeply regret our conversation today."

Seger understood. The duke would not be lied to.

"So I take it," Seger said, "that you are not here to muscle a marriage proposal out of me?"

"Not today."

"But you do want me to stay away from her."

Because that's what male relations of Seger's paramours *always* wanted.

For a long time the duke stared at Seger, appearing as if he were considering the question. "Clara is my wife's sister. She's a kindhearted, intelligent girl and her happiness is my primary concern. From what I can tell, she has an affection for you, and I will not be the one to tell her that her affections are misguided. I don't as yet know one way or another if they are. I will, however, watch carefully over the coming weeks to ensure that she is not treated in a cavalier manner. You will see her only in respectable situations, and you will not continue to encourage her if there is no future in it. If you do, there will be consequences. Do you understand my meaning?"

"Perfectly."

They were quiet for a moment.

"I must also inform you," the duke said slowly, "that you are very close to the center of another scandal, a scandal I attempted to avert just over an hour ago."

Seger glanced down at the duke's bloody hand again, and felt the muscles of his forearm tighten as he clenched his own hand into a fist. "What kind of scandal? It doesn't involve Clara, does it? Is she all right?"

The duke slowly blinked. "She is fine, and your concern for her does you credit. Yes, it involves her. The two of you were seen together at two separate Cakras Balls, and a certain gentleman who covets Clara's marriage settlement has threatened to reveal that fact. Under other circumstances I would have words for you in that regard, but from what I understand, Clara's attendance at the ball was accidental, at least the first time, and you steered her away and suggested she leave. You did the same the second time, when it was *not* accidental."

Was he receiving a commendation? Seger wondered, staring at the duke's dark blue eyes. Why was he telling him all this?

"You attempted to avert the scandal," Seger said. "You were not successful?"

"I made an impression, but it wouldn't hurt for you to

make an impression as well. I believe we should present a united front."

Seger tried to keep his anger in check. "Who, may I ask, is the gentleman in question?"

"Guysborough."

"The duke? The bloody hypocrite. He, of all people, should know the rules of the Cakras Society. He tried something like this once before, didn't he?"

"Yes, two years ago he was suspended for speaking about a particular lady who had rejected his attentions at one of the balls, but I think in this case, Clara's value financially was worth the risk of being suspended again."

"The Society won't take kindly to a second misdemeanor. A suspension would be the least of his punishments."

"I reminded him of that. Perhaps you should, too. Tell him we spoke."

"Will that do the trick?

"Who's to say for sure? All I know is that I don't trust him." Wentworth set his empty glass on the small table next to his chair, and stood. "Thank you for the brandy, Rawdon."

Seger stood too. "I'll show you out."

They went to the front door where the butler was waiting with the duke's coat and hat.

Wentworth was halfway down the steps on his way to the waiting coach, when Seger called out to him. "Wentworth!"

The duke stopped and turned.

"I appreciated the invitation you sent, for my family to attend your assembly."

A bluebird flew overhead, then swooped down and perched on the stone wall by the gate.

"It was my pleasure, Rawdon," Wentworth replied. He settled his hat on his head and continued toward his coach.

Seger stood there for a moment or two. The meeting had not gone the way he had expected it to.

Finally, he closed the door and returned to his study. All he could think about was Clara and the idea that a scandal had brushed by her, no thanks to him. God! He hated the idea that he had brought her even the smallest measure of grief or anxiety. She had trusted him with her reputation and he had let her down.

Seger sank back into the chair he had occupied a few minutes ago and stroked his chin. He gazed at the empty grate in the fireplace and let his mind wander where it would. He recalled the taste of Clara's open mouth when he'd kissed her the night before.

Remembering her irresistible erotic whimpers when he'd been busy with his tongue in certain places beneath her skirts, he had to fight to suppress the inconvenient surge of arousal that accompanied the heated memories. And the guilt for what she had suffered today.

With firm resolve, he decided that he would take care of the scandal. He would see Guysborough, and ascertain what exactly had happened, then he would ensure the man behaved himself in the future and never so much as looked at Clara again. Then Seger would call on Clara to assure her that all was well.

Oh, who was he trying to fool?

He didn't want to see her to ease her mind about any scandal. He wanted to see her for the simple reason that he wanted to be in the same room with her. Touch her if possible.

With some apprehension, he rose from his chair and

summoned his butler to tell him that he intended to go out, that he had a certain personal matter to attend to.

Just when Clara thought the day could not possibly have been more distressing, a footman entered the nursery. Clara was holding John, singing a lullaby.

The tall footman announced that Clara had a visitor. "It is the Marquess of Rawdon, Miss Wilson."

Clara shot a glance at Sophia, who froze.

"Tell him I'll be right down," Clara replied, and the footman took his leave.

"What's he doing here?" Sophia asked, picking Liam up off the floor and laying him down in his crib. "James hasn't even returned yet. We haven't had a chance to find out what happened."

"You don't think James coerced Lord Rawdon to propose, do you? Because I will not agree to a forced wedding."

"I don't know." Sophia took John out of Clara's arms. "Just go, Clara. Don't keep him waiting. Offer him tea. I'll give you a few minutes before I follow."

"Thank you. You are the best sister."

Clara inhaled deeply and tried to smooth out her hair on the way to the drawing room. Nervous twitters gathered in her belly at the mere thought of seeing Seger's face again.

She stopped and paused outside the drawing room doors, fighting the butterflies, then tried to look at ease as she entered.

The marquess stood at the window, hands clasped behind his back as he looked out. The sunlight shone in on his face, illuminating the square cut of his jaw, his full lips and straight nose. All Clara's senses careened. Such power he could wield over her, merely by standing there, doing nothing.

Then he faced her. They stared at each other for a moment. Excitement swirled up and down Clara's spine.

"What are you doing here?" she asked, moving forward at last.

It was not the sort of question she would pose to a regular caller, but to say anything else to this man—this man she had allowed up under her skirts the night before—would be putting on airs to say the least. They were beyond the usual protocol.

Just thinking about what he had done, however, when he was up under her skirts, caused a sudden, concentrated ache between her legs. She struggled to ignore it.

He took a step forward. "I wanted to see you. Your brother-in-law paid me a visit today."

Clara's stomach lurched. What had occurred between the two men? She couldn't imagine.

"I was afraid he would do that," she said apologetically.

Clara moved fully into the room but kept the sofa between herself and the marquess. She was afraid that if she were within arms' reach of him, she would not be able to resist touching him. "What did he say?"

"Among other things, he came to warn me not to take any more risks where you are concerned, as any responsible brother-in-law would do. I must see you only in respectable situations from now on."

"That's all?"

The marquess sauntered seductively around the sofa. She knew he wasn't trying to be seductive. He simply was.

Clara backed up a step.

Seger stood before her, barely a foot away. "He also informed me that a possible scandal involving the both of us had come to his attention earlier today."

Clara's muscles tensed at the mere mention of what had occurred between her and the duke. She was still shaken by it. "Did he tell you where things stood? Was he able to clear things up?"

Seger's eyebrows drew together. "You don't know?"

"James hasn't returned yet." She began to feel ill, wondering what had occurred, wondering if the rumors had already been circulated and she was about to be sent back to America.

The expression on Seger's face softened. "You needn't worry. It has been addressed."

"By whom? By James, or you?"

"By both of us. Guysborough, if he knows what's good for him, will never speak your name again unless it is to comment on your kindness or your grand sense of morality."

Clara swallowed over a lump of dread. "How can you be sure?"

Seger said nothing for a few seconds, then she noticed a drop of blood on his collar. "Oh."

Seger saw what she was staring at and glanced down at the blood, too. He tried to rub at it. "I do beg your pardon. I hadn't noticed this."

Then he glanced up at her face and his expression paled. "I'm not generally the fighting kind, Clara. But the duke pulled a pistol on me and I had to disarm him."

"A pistol! Good heavens!"

"Don't worry, the pistol went out the window."

"Are you all right?" Clara couldn't bear the thought of Seger staring into the barrel of a gun because of her.

"I'm fine."

"What about the duke? He's not . . ." She couldn't finish.

"No, no. This is the consequence of a mere bloody nose. His, not mine. He didn't take too kindly to losing his pistol, so I had to defend myself."

She decided she did not wish to know any more details concerning his or James's "conversation" with the duke. The bloody nose was more than enough information.

Seger gazed down at her lips. "*You* are all right, are you not?"

She swallowed hard as she nodded.

"Good." He reached out a hand, his eyes locking on hers, warm with an open invitation. "Come and sit with me."

What could she do but follow him? She was charmed by his potent sexuality, by his silky confidence, his inconceivable good looks. She placed her hand in his, and they sat on the sofa, facing each other.

"I am deeply sorry for what happened," he said, "and I accept all responsibility. I should not have come to your sister's assembly. People know what I am, and they are not accepting. I should have remained outside your circle."

"No. You have honor, Seger. Surely you know that. It was Guysborough who behaved badly."

And, she added silently, as far as the social "circle" went, Clara suspected that the very matrons who hissed at Seger would melt like hot candlewax in his hands if he ever so much as smiled in their direction.

With a swift glance toward the door to ensure they were alone, Seger turned her hand over and kissed her open palm. Clara tried to maintain her composure, but it was impossible. Seger stirred everthing that was alive inside her. Shivers of delight trembled through her veins with an astonishing ferocity.

"I will continue to blame myself for what happencd," he whispered, his hot breath trapped in the hollow of her hand and causing a torrent of gooseflesh to wash over her. "I only wish I could make it up to you somehow."

Then he probed her palm with his tongue. She sucked in a breath, feeling as if he could bring her to the heights of orgasm by doing just this.

No wonder every woman in London wanted him. His charm and overwhelming ability to please was addictive. Having experienced his lovemaking in the carriage, it was now impossible for Clara to forget how he had made her feel. How quickly he could become an obsession.

Slowly, he kissed his way to the inside of her wrist and indulged his tongue there as well. "I am deeply sorry, Clara."

Clara's heart thundered in her head. She trembled at the sheer, unbridled roar of her desire just from the feel of his mouth pulsing on her wrist.

She'd never in her life experienced an apology like this.

Her voice was breathless. "You're quite forgiven, my lord."

Just then, Sophia entered and cleared her throat.

Seger reacted calmly, with the unruffled demeanor of a man who had been caught like this a hundred times before. He sat back, then stood. "Duchess. What a pleasure."

Before Sophia had a chance to reply, Mrs. Gunther appeared. Clara—still in a dazed stupor—said a silent thank you that Sophia had arrived first.

The two ladies entered the room and moved around the sofa to sit across from them in two facing chairs. Sophia's face was pale. Mrs. Gunther's chin was high in the air as she glared hotly at Seger. No one said anything for a second or two until a parlor maid arrived with a tray of tea and scones.

"May I pour for you, my lord?" Sophia offered with a

smile, trying to break the tension. It would not be broken, however. Not with Mrs. Gunther's nostrils flaring as she breathed heavily on the other side of the room.

All Clara could do was sit quietly and try to quell her racing heart and force the hot, stinging blush from her cheeks. Her body was still heated with an insatiable need for more. There was some kind of frenzy going on within her. Her mind was besieged.

She glanced warily at her sister. How long had she been standing there?

Without batting an eye, Sophia led the conversation into lighter matters. She inquired about the health of Seger's stepmother and asked polite questions about his home in the country. Mrs. Gunther was grimly silent.

Ten awkward minutes later, Seger set down his cup and addressed Sophia. "I wonder if you would be so kind, Duchess, as to permit me a moment alone with your sister?"

Clara gazed at him in shock. His meaning could not have been more clear. Gentlemen did not request private conversations with unmarried ladies in drawing rooms unless they intended to discuss something personally significant.

Something momentous.

Something that involved questions that were asked on one knee.

Had James forced him to do this?

Heart racing, Clara had to remind herself to breathe. The marquess did not meet her gaze.

All Seger's attention was focused on the duchess as he waited for her reply. He wanted everyone out of there.

"Of course," she said at last, looking uncharacteristically flustered. "Mrs. Gunther, won't you join me in the library for a few minutes?"

The woman didn't move. Eyes wide, she gazed from the duchess to Seger, back at the duchess again as if she were struggling for a way to stop what was about to occur.

But even Seger wasn't sure he knew what that was. He was operating on instinct, being controlled by his desires, his unquenchable lust for this sweet, fresh young woman who had shattered his ability to stave off emotion. When he was with her, he lost all sense of reason and strength of will, and he was astonished by his malleability. He could not be blasé with her, for this entire experience was new. Enchanting. He had not known it was possible to want a woman this badly.

"Mrs. Gunther," the duchess repeated more forcefully, rising to her feet. Seger rose also.

The woman gathered her aplomb and finally stood, sending a seething glare in Seger's direction as she passed by on the way to the door.

He wondered suddenly what he was going to say next. He gazed down at Clara and saw in her vivid eyes a cautious expectation.

So there it was. The first step toward the life he had been avoiding for eight years, the life that went beyond superficiality where a woman was concerned. He realized suddenly that a partial reason for his avoidance of it was to punish his stepmother and his late father for what had happened with Daphne. Even though the old marquess was cold in his grave, Seger had wanted to deprive him of the next heir.

Now, for the first time, that meant nothing to Seger. All

he knew was that he could not bear the thought of anyone else having Clara Wilson. He wanted her for himself. In his bed.

He wanted *only* her.

The thought shocked him. He had never meant for Clara—or any woman for that matter—to ever be so important.

As soon as the duchess and chaperone were gone, Seger sat down again and turned to face Clara. He should end this now . . . say goodbye, but his mental faculties could not gain control over his lust and need. He wanted Clara. He wanted access to her rare inner beauty. He wanted to possess it, and there was no fighting it. All he could do now was try to say the right things without becoming a man he did not wish to become. A man at the mercy of his emotions.

Consequently, he searched for bearings, and fell back into the behavioral habits that had become the foundation of his existence. He reached for his charm, and forced a lid on anything deeper.

Clara's thoughts were screaming inside her head. What were his intentions? Was she being presumptuous, thinking that he meant to propose?

"I don't wish to cause any more scandals," he said.

"Then maybe we shouldn't be alone right now."

"But we must be, if I am to say what I wish to say."

She had to struggle to keep her voice steady, when every nerve in her body was buzzing like an electric current. "And what is that, my lord?"

Looking relaxed and confident, he smiled. "That I desire you. That I want you."

Despite her anxiousness, she somehow managed to return an equally confident smile. "You didn't need to come all the way over here to tell me that. I already knew it. You made it more than clear to me last night."

His brow lifted with amused admiration. "I've never met a woman quite like you. Marry me."

Clara's body seemed to stop functioning. Everything within her went still.

"Marry you? Just like that? No romantic proposal? No attempt to win me over with a few choice compliments?"

"You said yourself that you already know how I feel about you, and you don't seem like the kind of woman who needs to dance around a point before coming straight to it. There is scandal on our heels, and it is certain to catch up with us again if we continue in the direction we are going. I desire you, Clara, and since I am now confined to seeing you only in respectable situations, I will have to make everything respectable, because I do intend to see you. Quite often, in fact. Every night in my bed, if I must be blunt."

He was certainly that.

Clara stood and walked to the window. Her body had started working again. Her heart was now racing, her thoughts swimming. She had never truly expected a marriage proposal from Seger, at least not so soon. She had thought she'd have to do some clever operating to encourage him to reform, and she'd expected that to take some time.

Then again, she hadn't expected James to learn all about their secret encounters either, and visit the marquess. Nor had she expected the Duke of Guysborough to try to blackmail her into marriage.

She faced Seger. "What is the real reason you want to marry me?"

"The real reason?" He stood also and moved to stand before her at the window. "Because as I said, we are heading for scandal, and I desire you too much to give you up."

"What do you mean, heading for scandal? Do you mean the duke's threat to reveal our acquaintance, or do you mean something else? Some future scandal?"

"Both. I cannot promise that I will be able to behave myself if and when we meet again." He considered that statement, then added with a captivating smile, "Actually, I can quite assure you that I would not."

Clara felt dazed by his suggestion. It was no wonder every hot-blooded woman in London wanted him. They knew what he offered just by the look in his eye. His appeal was unquestionable. She felt the debilitating power of his attraction like a tremor in the ground beneath her feet.

"My brother-in-law didn't put you up to this did he?" she asked. "He didn't give *you* a bloody nose, I hope."

"I assure you, our conversation was non-violent. In fact, he has no idea I am here, let alone proposing to you. I'm not even sure he would approve if he knew."

Breathing deeply as she gathered the facts—and her composure—Clara groped for understanding. She needed to know what this was about and how the marquess truly felt about being attached to her for a lifetime.

"I don't want a forced marriage," she said. "I want my husband to be sure that he wants me."

"There are no worries there. I am sure."

She narrowed her gaze at him.

"You want more from me, don't you?" he asked. "You want me to pour my heart out to you?"

Clara saw the reluctance in his eyes and knew that he had already said more and done more than he ever intended to say or do with any woman.

A sudden thought of all the other women pummeled her confidence, and she reminded herself what kind of man he was. She told herself it was dangerous to hope for too much.

Seger moved to the mantel. "I am not a romantic, Clara, nor am I interested in lying to you. On top of the reasons I already gave you, I have always known that I must marry eventually. I require an heir."

Even when he was giving her the cold, hard truth, he was delivering more flattery than she'd ever known in her life. He looked at her like he wanted to devour her, and it made her weak in the knees. She felt as if he could pull a yes from her lips with a mere smile.

"So it is duty," she managed to say.

"Partly."

"And desire."

"Definitely. I can't resist you."

She took some pleasure from the compliment, for he was in his own way telling her that she was special. She had done something no other woman had been able to do. She had gotten a proposal out of him.

"What about the marriage settlement that is sure to come?" she asked. "Have you been seeking that all along? Did you somehow manipulate all of this to cause a scandal and force my hand?"

"Good God, no. I have enough money of my own. I don't dabble in politics, so I dabble in other things. The American stock market for one. I am probably as rich as your father."

Clara's eyebrows lifted. "I had no idea."

"Not many people do."

She moved away from him to pace around the room. "So you're not one of the infamous impoverished English lords? That will certainly surprise the New York newspapermen," she said with bite. "They don't seem to believe that any Englishman would marry an American for anything other than money."

"We will break the mold, then."

Clara stared at him for a moment, considering all of it. "What about love?" she finally asked, knowing she was pushing the limits. "Since we're being blunt . . ."

If he was unnerved by her question, he didn't show it. He seemed more amused than anything by her "negotiation."

"I had wondered if you would bring that up." He gazed out the window for a moment, then looked directly into her eyes as he spoke. "I won't coddle you, Clara. You're an intelligent woman, and you must realize that we barely know each other."

"I do."

"And as I told you last night, I've only loved one woman in my life, and it ended badly. I will admit I am jaded, but that doesn't mean our marriage cannot be a success."

He was being honest and sensible, admitting that he did not truly love her, and she couldn't deny she respected him for that. If he'd told her he loved her, she probably wouldn't have believed him and would have felt as if she were being patronized or lied to.

But still, in her deepest heart of hearts, this was not what she wished they were saying to each other right now. She didn't want to hear about the other women in his past, not to mention the woman he had once loved—the only woman he had *ever* loved. The mere mention of her cut Clara to the quick. She had dreamed of so much more where Seger was concerned. *She* wanted to be the only woman in his heart and mind at this moment.

"Are you suggesting that you would grow to love me?" she asked.

A reasonable question that she hated asking. It hurt. It made her feel rejected. It humiliated her to have to ask it.

"Possibly."

Possibly. Not definitely. The response sank like a cold, hard stone into her belly.

Would the mere possibility of love be enough? Could she take such a risk with a man like him? What if he only grew bored with her?

Seger must have recognized the doubts in her eyes, for he strode toward her and spoke firmly. "I would treat you well, Clara. You would become a marchioness and live here in England near your sister. It would be a life of privilege and grandeur. In addition to that, I desire you and you desire me. Can't that be enough, at least for now?" He gazed at her for a turbulent, fleeting second, then said, "Imagine the pleasure, Clara."

Oh yes, she could definitely imagine that.

He gently lowered his lips to hers and kissed her. The feel of his mouth upon hers was so right, so wonderful, that she couldn't stop herself from devouring him. She wrapped her arms around his neck and let out an involuntary moan.

Holding her face in his hands, he pulled back from the kiss. "I want to marry you, Clara, because I am starving for you. I must have you. I want you for myself in my bed. I want no other man to ever touch you but me. Yes, I need a wife and an heir, but this is not just about duty. Believe me, I crave you."

It was about passion, but not love. Could she live with that? She had wanted love.

But wait, no, she had not. She had wanted a decent man who would be a good husband and father. A man who would be faithful to her.

Seger's heart was decent. She was certain of that—as certain as she could be where any man was concerned. He had always kept her best interests in mind, doing what he could to protect her when she'd ventured outside the safe circle of her proper world. He'd even tried to push her back in. Except for last night in the carriage, when he had led her out, but that was because he desired her. *Craved* her, as he put it.

Perhaps it would not take much to turn that craving into love.

So his heart was decent and he desired her. She could try to be patient in regards to a deeper love.

But was she certain he could reform and be a faithful husband? Or was that simply what she wished? Everything to do with him had been a fantasy for so long. She couldn't be sure where the fantasy ended and reality began.

He was very passionate, that much she knew. He enjoyed pleasure. He enjoyed women, so much so, that he broke all of society's rules to satisfy his urges. Would she be enough for him? Would she be able to keep him satisfied for the rest of their lives?

He kissed her again and she melted in his arms. "Say yes, Clara."

Senses blazing, she returned the kiss with abandon and wrapped her arms around his neck. Then, before she realized what she was saying, she blurted out, "Would you be faithful to me?"

This, she realized, was the final question that would determine her future.

He pulled back to look at her. For a long moment he

considered her question while her stomach turned over with a sickening fear that his answer would be no. Or that he would say yes, and she would know he was lying.

"That's a difficult question, Clara. I don't have a crystal ball."

She wasn't satisfied. "Answer the question, Seger."

His shoulders rose and fell with a deep intake of breath. "I would try to be."

Clara knew it was as honest an answer as she would ever get from *any* man. He was right about the crystal ball. No matter who she married, there would never be any guarantees. Marriage, by nature, was for everyone a leap of faith.

He kissed her again and she gave herself up to the passion, for that was the one thing she knew they shared, then she let that passion bring her to a decision. Somehow, she managed to speak.

"I believe, my lord, you've found yourself a wife."

Chapter 12

Dear Clara,

You said in your last letter that everything was a terrible mess. I hope things have improved. Just remember, don't do anything hasty. Be careful in your decisions. Be sure to listen to the advice of Sophia and James. They have your best interests at heart. . . .

Adele

Clara, Sophia, James, and Mrs. Gunther gathered in the drawing room after Seger left. The tea was now cold, but the parlor maid had not been allowed in to take the tray away.

"Sophia," Mrs. Gunther said, as if Clara were not in the room, "you must realize the mistake your sister is making. The Duke of Guysborough proposed first. He is the better choice. He outranks the marquess, not to mention the fact that he is respected by society, where the marquess is not even invited into it."

James was quiet for a long moment, then he strode to the mantel. "May I remind you of the old adage not to judge a book by its cover?"

"How else can one judge it, when appearances mean everything?"

Everyone was silent. "Not to me," Clara said softly.

"Or me," Sophia added, gazing up at her husband, who smiled down at her.

"You have lost your senses, all of you," Mrs. Gunther said. "Your Grace, you must do something. They are smitten simply because the marquess is an attractive man. They must be made to understand."

Hands behind his back, James moved to stand behind his wife's chair. He rested a hand on her shoulder. "I believe, madam, the only one here who must be made to understand anything is you."

"I beg your pardon."

"I mean no offense, Mrs. Gunther, but you are not in full possession of the facts, and it is time someone enlightened you. The duke acted in a most unseemly manner, and threatened to destroy Clara's reputation if she did not accept his proposal. There. Now may we dispense with the arguments?"

Mrs. Gunther stared blankly at Clara and Sophia. "Is this true?"

"Yes," Sophia replied. "He knew about Clara attending the wrong ball that first night. He threatened to use it against her."

"But did he actually threaten it," Mrs. Gunther asked, "or merely suggest that she would be better off avoiding the possibility that such a thing might get out?"

"It was a threat," Clara said firmly.

Mrs. Gunther's voice took on a desperate tone. "But he

is the Duke of Guysborough. You should not have crossed him by refusing him, Clara."

Everyone, including James, gaped at Mrs. Gunther.

"Are you saying I should have accepted his proposal, regardless of his behavior?"

"*His* behavior? *He* was not the one with the scandalous secret, Clara."

For a moment Clara thought her chaperone was referring to what had happened two years ago when she almost eloped with Gordon. Then she remembered that Mrs. Gunther knew nothing about that—no one did, except for Clara's family. Mrs. Gunther was talking about the Cakras Ball, nothing more.

Still, her meaning was the same. Make a mistake and pay the price.

James held up a hand. "I believe this discussion is over. Clara has made up her mind."

"But Your Grace, the duke is. . . . Well, he's a duke."

"Meaning what, exactly?"

She shifted in her chair. "Meaning Clara would be a duchess. Imagine, two American duchesses, and sisters! It is too good an opportunity to—"

James narrowed his gaze at her. "You would have Clara marry a man who threatened to publicly destroy her?"

"No one would ever have to know."

"But I would know!" Clara said. "I wish to be happy, Mrs. Gunther, and I would not be happy with the Duke of Guysborough."

The older woman's cheeks flushed with smug condescension. "Why? Because he is not as handsome as the marquess? Mark my words, Clara, a handsome face will not keep you happy when your husband is cavorting with other women right under your nose."

Clara bristled.

James held up a hand again to hush everyone. He turned toward Mrs. Gunther. "I believe, madam, that your duty to my sister-in-law has been fulfilled."

Though she spoke to James, Mrs. Gunther turned her admonishing gaze toward Clara. "She is making a grave mistake, Your Grace."

"I do thank you for your attendance to her," he added.

After some deliberation, the woman rose from her chair and smoothed her hands over her skirt. "If you will excuse me, I am suddenly in need of a rest. I will be in my boudoir."

She turned to leave, but James took a step forward. "I will send a footman to ascertain the time of the next crossing to America, Mrs. Gunther. I am sure you are anxious to return home."

Mrs. Gunther halted, but did not turn around. "Thank you, Your Grace," then she walked out with her nose pushed high in the air.

Clara sat in silence staring after her chaperone, and felt the impossible weight of her own doubts descend upon her.

After Seger broke the news of his engagement to his stepmother, he retired to his study and realized that the expression on her face had been the same as it had been eight years ago when he'd told her he intended to marry a merchant's penniless daughter.

Only Clara wasn't penniless. She was, however, American and not "one of them."

Quintina—after she had realized she would not be able to change Seger's mind—had made a point of mentioning that at least with an American bride, their vulgar in-laws would remain on the other side of the Atlantic, and wouldn't be dropping by for tea. She'd actually accepted the fact that she would have to abide by his choice this time and make the best of it.

He sat down at his desk and realized with some chagrin that he was experiencing a slightly perverse pleasure from that fact.

A knock sounded at his door just then. "Come in."

Quintina entered. She strode all the way in and stopped before him with her hands clasped in front of her as if she were nervous.

"Yes, Quintina, what is it?"

She hesitated a moment. "I believe, Seger, that I . . . would like to invite your fiancée as well as the Duke and Duchess of Wentworth to dine with us one evening this week."

Seger leaned back in his chair and stared. "I beg your pardon?"

"You heard me the first time. You're just making me repeat it to punish me further."

"None of this is intended to punish you, Quintina. I want to marry Clara Wilson because she delights me. It's as simple as that."

She nodded quickly, almost as if she needed to hush him, as if she did not wish to hear any explanations of that nature. "Either way, if we are going to be related, we must come to know these people."

He supposed it didn't hurt that Clara's sister was a duchess. American or not, a duchess was a duchess. That was likely what was behind this.

Well, he'd take it. "Magnificent. Send the invitation first thing in the morning."

She turned to leave. "I will, Seger, and . . ." She stopped at the door. "Congratulations."

He gazed with scrutiny at his stepmother, feeling uneasy with her remark, for he knew it was taking every kernel of will she possessed to say it.

"Thank you, Quintina," he replied.

Quintina walked out of her stepson's study and closed the door behind her. She met Gillian in the hall and stopped abruptly. The girl's eyes were red and puffy. She was clutching a handkerchief.

Quintina felt her heart throb painfully.

"Well?" Gillian said in a shaky voice.

Quintina put her arm around her distraught niece and led her toward her boudoir.

"Don't worry, my dear. Dry your eyes. I will handle this. I have an English acquaintance—a woman currently abroad in America. She will be a useful connection in New York. Everything will work out just fine. You'll see. Now let us go and fix your hair. From now on, you must always look your best. Come, we will talk about what you need to do."

Clara entered Rawdon House with James and Sophia, and handed her cloak over to the butler. She looked up at the crystal chandelier over her head in the entryway, and the numerous, huge family portraits that lined the wall up the wide, carpeted staircase. It was difficult to believe this was going to be her home one day, when she became Seger's wife.

Never in all her life had she imagined such a future for herself, certainly not when she was a child living in Wisconsin, where stories of princes and dukes and duchesses with coronets on their heads were merely fairy tales.

Then, after what had occurred two years ago just after

Sophia had married James, Clara had thought her future was doomed. She had never expected to marry a man she adored. She had expected to have very little choice in the matter and consider herself lucky if anyone even asked her. Or she had expected not to marry at all.

But two years had passed and that particular time seemed like someone else's life. It was ancient history. She could barely remember Gordon's face. Thank goodness she had been able to move on.

Clara walked with Sophia and James as the butler led them upstairs to the drawing room. She continued to gaze at the portraits on the second floor. Everyone was very grand. Her belly quivered suddenly at the daunting idea of becoming part of a family such as this.

She followed the butler toward the double doors of the drawing room and tried not to feel intimidated. Instead, she focused on the crude and simple fact that in the near future, she would share a bed with Seger and it would all be perfectly respectable.

That was the best part in all this. She would not need to worry about being ruined. In fact, it would be her duty to let him "ruin" her. She could hardly wait.

The butler showed them into the drawing room where Lady Rawdon stood by the window, and her niece, who Clara remembered from the assembly, sat by the fireplace. She stood, however, when they all walked in.

"Your Grace," Lady Rawdon said, turning toward them with a warm smile. She approached with her hands outstretched and greeted each of them, then invited them in to sit down.

The woman's gracious manner and her amiable welcome caused a whole slew of Clara's apprehensions to drain away. She found herself smiling in return as she shook hands with Gillian, realizing that this shy young woman was her future cousin by marriage.

Just then, Seger appeared in the doorway. Clara's heart tumbled over itself at the mere sight of him looking so handsome in the light from a wall sconce next to him. He wore a formal black jacket and white waistcoat. His face was pure perfection—all fine lines and classical elegance.

But beyond his physical beauty, he possessed a free and open disposition that was such a large part of his extraordinary charisma. In this era of restraint and sexual repression, he was the opposite. He called out with an offer of pleasure and laughter.

That, perhaps, was what made people uncomfortable around him. He drew attention. He was extreme in his pursuit of gratification, and he made women think lustful thoughts. Perhaps they worried that it showed. Perhaps they felt their cheeks flushing with desires for this-that-and-everything, and they feared the whole world would know.

His gaze fell upon her, and he smiled. "Clara."

All her senses trembled at the husky sound of his voice and the fierce intensity of his eyes as he entered and approached her, kissed her hand, then greeted James and Sophia. He was so suave and irresistible, he took her breath away.

Oh, she hoped Mrs. Gunther had been wrong about him. Clara prayed she was not making a serious mistake, agreeing to marry a man who would have the power to break her heart into a million tiny pieces, because she adored him so much and he was not so ardent in the return of his affections.

He'd told her he would *try* to be faithful. *Try.*

How hard would he try?

A footman entered the room and brought a tray of champagne around. Clara gratefully accepted a glass.

They all stood and talked about the wedding plans and about Clara's family: when they would be able to come to London, where Clara planned to purchase her wedding gown, and other topics related to the upcoming nuptials.

Had they set a date yet? someone asked. Why not next spring? Lady Rawdon suggested. Sooner, Seger had replied, gazing seductively at Clara.

She felt as if she were watching the conversation from a great distance away.

A short time later, Seger lured Clara to the other side of the room and glanced over her shoulder at the others, as if to make sure no one was watching.

"You look positively luscious tonight," he said, running a finger along her forearm and up to the top of her long glove. "But you always look luscious. You make me hungry."

"Thank you. I'm nervous, Seger."

"Why? We are engaged now, all is right and proper."

She glanced uneasily at the others, laughing about something. "Yes, but it all happened so fast. Aren't you worried? You don't have cold feet?"

He smiled. "No. If anything, I want to move the wedding date forward. That's how badly I want you, my dear. I am aching for our honeymoon."

Glancing at the others again, he snuck the other hand up to touch her briefly behind the ear and send a wave of gooseflesh down her leg, then he touched her cheek with the backs of his fingers before dropping his arm to his side. It was all done so quickly, so discreetly, that it left her trembling with desire for something more.

How skilled he was at seduction. He could reduce her to a blob of pudding with a single touch.

Would he ever do something like that to another woman in another drawing room one day? Was that how easy it would be?

No. She had to stop thinking those things. He had told her he would try to be faithful. He had told her he wanted her more than he wanted any other woman in a very long time. She would be content with that and enter into this marriage with favorable expectations.

Still trembling from the way he had touched her, she swept all that nonsense away. "I admit, I am looking forward to our honeymoon, too."

"Then let's get married in September."

"Your stepmother suggested the spring."

"Yes, but she's not thinking about what I'm thinking about."

Suppressing a chuckle, Clara said, "I'm afraid to ask."

"Good, because I don't think there are words for it."

They walked leisurely around the room, aware of the others talking and laughing.

"October, then?" Seger asked.

Clara raised an eyebrow. "A wedding should not be rushed. There are things to plan, like flowers and music and food."

"It can all be planned in a day if one is focused."

"My gown must be designed and made. That can't be done in a day."

"It can be done in a week for the right price."

"A week! You'd have me wear something plain or unoriginal?"

"I'd have you wear nothing at all if we could do it in private. Honestly, all that wedding business is just for show. I've never cared what other people think and I would marry you tomorrow in the back garden with only the necessary number of witnesses if you would agree."

She took a sip of her champagne and spoke with a teasing tone. "Are you afraid I'll change my mind?"

He pressed a hand to his chest as if he had been shot. "Good gracious. I hadn't thought of that. Now that you mention it, I suppose I must consider the possibility. How will I ever keep your interest through the winter, which is so dashedly long and cold?"

"I think the question of the hour is 'how will I keep *your* interest?' " she replied.

He stopped walking and leaned in closer. "That will be very easy. Just smile like that, wear more dresses like that, and every once in a while, send me an indecent letter."

Clara laughed out loud. The others quieted and glanced at them, then resumed their conversation. Seger and Clara began walking around the perimeter of the room again.

"I would give anything to be alone with you right now," he said softly. "I fear this proper behavior where you are concerned will be the end of me."

"I wouldn't want that, my lord."

His gaze was hot and sexy. "Then marry me in September."

"You are very persistent."

"When I want something, yes. September?"

"But it is now June. That gives us little over two months."

"That's two months too long. Let's tell everyone tonight. The wedding will be in September. I can make arrangements for our honeymoon immediately. Would you like to go to Italy? Or perhaps to America? You choose, as long as it's in September."

She shook her head at him in disbelief. "Do you never give up?"

"Not when it comes to what I want. Will you agree?"

His tenacity was amusing and flattering and left her feeling warm and excited inside. Unable to resist his enticing, pleading expression, she set her empty glass down on a table and grinned wickedly. "Yes."

"Superb. Now that leaves us two whole months to figure out a way to avoid another scandal."

"What do you mean?" she asked, concern suddenly clouding her thoughts.

"You don't expect me to survive that long without kissing you, do you? I believe I would collapse in painful, throbbing agony, and I mean that quite literally."

Clara laughed again and tapped his chest with the tip of her closed fan. "What are we going to do about that?"

He touched her arm where it was bare, just above the top of her glove and below her short, lacy sleeve. She felt instantly aroused and glanced at the others to make sure they weren't looking.

Seger leaned down and whispered in her ear. "I still know how to give pleasure without destruction, and I believe you know how to accept and enjoy it. All we require is a location."

She gazed up at him in disbelief. "You're not trying to lure me out to your carriage in the middle of the night again, are you?"

"Actually, I had somewhere else in mind. Somewhere much more comfortable, but a good deal riskier. How about tomorrow night?"

Could she even pretend not to be interested in hearing his shocking and appalling plan? Not a chance.

Her mouth curled up in a smirk as she flicked open her fan and waved it in front of her face. "All right. I'll bite. What, pray tell, are the scandalous particulars?"

Seger awakened the next morning feeling energetic and famished. His future wife was turning out to be a bold and adventurous woman, unlike any of the appropriately insipid debutantes he'd ever met.

He was not sorry, he decided as he sat down in the breakfast room and picked up his newspaper. He needed a woman like her as a wife, someone who would enjoy a little spice in their marriage. Or presently, their engagement. He could never have married a tame and spiritless young woman. He needed excitement, and Clara, innocent as she was, was proving to him again and again that she suited him absolutely. She had agreed to his shocking proposition—even *he* thought it was shocking—and he would see her tonight. In private.

Maybe with a few well-timed trysts like these, he would survive until September after all.

Though it would be a challenge not to deflower her completely. Could he survive that? He had already plucked a good number of petals.

He supposed he would have to. There was always the off chance that something could happen to him—he could get hit by an omnibus or something of that nature—and he couldn't leave her alone in the world, unmarried and possibly carrying his child. He would marry her first.

He looked up from his newspaper when Gillian walked into the breakfast room. Under her arm, she carried a large, heavy package wrapped in brown paper, and set it down on the chair beside her.

"Good morning, Seger," she said in her quiet, childlike voice before she sat down at the white-clothed table across from him.

"Good morning, Gillian. Did you sleep well?"

"I did, thank you." She waited for the footman to set her plate down in front of her, then reached for her fork. "It was a lovely dinner last night. Did you enjoy yourself?"

He glanced up from his paper again. His cousin did not usually ask questions at meals. She was very quiet and shy, and this surprised him.

Seger smiled, folded his paper and set it aside. "I did enjoy myself, and what about you?"

Though she usually did not meet his gaze directly when she spoke to him—or anyone else for that matter—this morning she did. At least a few times, anyway, over the top of her plate.

It was a shame she was so painfully shy. She was not an unattractive young woman, if only she would smile occasionally and speak up more often.

"It was delightful," she said. "I must say, I like Clara very much. She's lovely."

"I'm glad you think so."

The conversation stalled for a moment or two while Gillian ate her breakfast. Seger considered picking up the paper again, but did not wish to be rude. He sipped his coffee instead and stared out the window.

"September is a lovely time for a wedding," Gillian said, surprising him by resuming the conversation. "Will all of Clara's family come over from America? I understand she has another sister."

"Yes, her name is Adele and she's eighteen. I'm sure she will look forward to meeting you. She is out this year for her first Season, just like you."

"I wonder what it would be like to have a Season in New York," Gillian replied. "America sounds like an exciting place. I would love to visit it sometime."

"Perhaps you will."

She smiled across the table at him, though he saw very little joy in her eyes. He had never seen her sparkle the way Clara sparkled, not once in all her life, and he'd known her since she was an infant, when she came with her mother from Scotland to London to attend Quintina's marriage to Seger's father. Seger had been seven at the time.

Seger suddenly recalled the day they buried Gillian's mother two years ago. Gillian had wept silently through the entire service. Seger had been sitting in a pew across from her and had watched her wipe her cheeks incessantly under the black netting of her hat, though she'd never made a sound.

She, like him, was an only child, except that she had been extremely close to her mother. Quintina had explained the uncommon bond between them when she'd received the telegram about her sister's death. Seger had marveled at the bond, realizing he was not able to understand what it could have been like growing up in a house where one did not feel completely alone. Seger had grieved deeply for the young woman's loss.

She must feel very alone now, he thought with more than a little sympathy, even though Quintina did her best to be a mother figure whenever Gillian came to visit.

Gillian finished her breakfast and set down her fork. She reached for the large package beside her. "I have something for you, Seger. It's an engagement gift."

She brought the gift around the table and handed it to

him. He gazed up at her with surprise. "My word. Thank you."

Gillian sat down in Quintina's usual spot.

Seger used his breakfast knife to cut the string, then opened the package. "An Atlas, and a very good one. What a perfect gift, Gillian. How did you know I enjoy maps?"

"I've noticed that you read a lot of travel books, and the Atlas you have is very old. This one is new and has more detail."

He leafed through it. "I dare say it does. This is magnificent. Thank you again." He smiled at her, reached across the table and patted her hand. "I will treasure it."

He saw her eyes light up at the compliment, and was glad to at last see some spark.

Chapter 13

Dear Clara,

Mother is determined to train me to follow in your footsteps next year. She has hired an Englishwoman as my new governess. Mrs. Wadsworth is helping me to learn all about aristocratic etiquette. Just today I learned that if I was ever to break a vase or a glass in a noblewoman's home, I should not offer to pay for it. That would be very bad form. So keep that in mind if you are ever so clumsy, dear sister . . .

Love,
Adele

Shortly before three o'clock in the morning, Clara quietly tiptoed downstairs to open the door she and Seger had decided upon—the same one she had sneaked through the night she had ventured out into the fog to meet him in his carriage.

Tonight, however, she would not go outside. He would come to her. For one hour, while everyone slept, he would share her bed.

It was wanton and irresponsible she knew, but she could not resist the thrill that came with knowing she would be alone with him tonight, touching him in the darkness. Smelling him and kissing him. Bringing him into her private world.

She tried not to feel too guilty about her willingness to do something so wildly improper. They were engaged, after all. It was not as if she were doing this with a stranger. Seger was going to marry her.

They simply had to do something to get through the next two months, for the entire foundation of their relationship was based on lust, and their present geographical separation was becoming impossible to bear. At least for Clara.

Besides that, it was never too soon to start building on the foundation that she hoped would evolve into something more.

That was perhaps her primary objective, why she couldn't help but be accommodating to his needs, which at the moment were solely physical.

Consequently, she had given him detailed instructions on how to make his way through the house in the dark tonight, and how to find her room. She'd told him she would leave her door ajar and light a candle. She'd explained which steps and floorboards creaked, and which doors were routinely left open. Thankfully there were no dogs in Wentworth House to raise a ruckus, so Seger could be quite sure of reaching her room without incident.

Clara sat on her bed on top of the covers, her nightgown unbuttoned at the collar, her hair freshly combed, feeling as if she were waiting for a train to blast through her room and screech over her bed. Her heart was pounding, her senses humming as she listened for the slightest sound from outside her door. The nervous excitement rushing through her veins was enough to make her giddy.

The clock chimed three times in the entryway downstairs, then a few more drawn out minutes ticked by. Anxious about Seger's safe and undetected arrival, Clara slipped off her bed and padded to the door to peer out into the hall.

He wouldn't forget, would he? she wondered uneasily, fearing that he might not be as enthusiastic as she was about spending this brief hour together. Maybe all his flattery was mere habit. Maybe it was in his nature to make women feel attractive and alluring. Maybe he did this sort of thing—snuck into ladies' bedrooms in the middle of the night—all the time and it was a mere walk in the park. Easy to disregard. He might have fallen asleep. He might be out at a party somewhere and had lost track of time.

She suddenly felt foolish to think that he might have been anticipating this encounter as ardently as she, thinking of nothing else but this for the past twenty-four hours. This was nothing new to him.

But suddenly, without warning, there he was. He appeared like a ghost at her door.

She had heard nothing—no floorboards creaking, no footsteps tapping up the stairs. Before she could comprehend that he had not forgotten her, the door behind him quietly swung closed and he was holding her face in his hands, kissing her with his hot, wet mouth, parting her lips with his own.

"I managed to get here," he whispered. "Let's just hope your maid is a sound sleeper and we are not interrupted."

The image of them being interrupted jarred her brain. What exactly would they be doing? she wondered with a sharp thrill, imagining all kinds of interesting things.

He left her breathless for a moment while he went to lock the door, then returned to fill her senses with pleasure and ecstasy using the inconceivable skill of his kiss.

He backed her up to the bed and eased her down upon it, then stood looking down at her while he removed his jacket and waistcoat, and pulled off his boots.

A few seconds later, he was lying beside her, leaning on one elbow and running his forefinger down her open collar to the center between her breasts. "I don't suppose I can convince you to let me stay for two hours?" he whispered.

"In a few minutes, you'll be able to convince me to do anything, Seger, so give me your word right now, while I still have my head. One hour, then you must go. We're taking enough of a risk as it is."

He nodded and unfastened another button on her nightgown, gazing flirtatiously into her eyes the whole time. He slid his warm hand inside to her breast, massaging it gently and sending waves of heat straight to her core. "I'm always making promises where you are concerned."

His mouth covered hers and she drank in the exquisite male taste of him, washing her tongue over his.

"Are we not going to talk tonight?" she whispered as he reached down to gather her nightgown in his fist and slowly pull it up past her waist.

Smiling down at her, he shook his head. "We can talk at the next assembly, or you can write me a letter. But this . . ." He urged her up onto her knees so he could pull her nightgown off over her head. "This can't be enjoyed in public, and since we have only one hour . . ."

Suddenly she was naked in the candlelight, allowing

him to gaze openly at her body. Sitting back on her heels, she realized she had never imagined couples did this sort of thing together. She'd imagined that everything would take place in pitch darkness, under the covers, with the lovers' eyes closed.

On top of that, she had never imagined she would ever do such a scandalous thing in her sister's house while everyone slept. The danger made it all the more exhilarating.

"You are lovely," he whispered. "You will pardon me if I don't waste a single minute?" Then he eased her back down onto the soft mattress and his tongue licked, and licked eagerly, and moved in circles over the rigid peaks of her breasts. Clara wriggled and fought to keep herself from letting out an impassioned groan. She would have to work hard to remember to keep quiet during the next glorious hour.

He continued to plunge his face into her breasts and suck until she was breathless with desire. She twisted lasciviously as his tongue lifted from her erect nipple and slid into her mouth.

The sheer pleasure of being naked beneath him was enough to drive her into the beyond. She groped for his neckcloth and tore at it, then sat up again to pull his shirt off so she could rub her hands up and down his beautiful muscled chest.

"Take everything off," she whispered, overcome with an intense, instantaneous need. "Let's be naked together."

She saw doubt flash in his eyes. He seized both her hands in his and held them. His voice was husky, yet gentle with a warning. "That might be dangerous."

Clara stilled, not really understanding what it would be like for him. "I don't want to make it unpleasant for you. I just want to lie naked with you. Can we do that?"

He hesitated a moment, then smiled and let go of her hands. "None of this could ever be unpleasant, Clara, even if it killed me. Perhaps just my shirt."

He pulled it off over his head.

A moment later he was lying on top of her, kissing her, stroking her thighs with his warm, gentle hands and flicking his tongue over her swollen nipples again. The feel of his skin against her chest, so hot and moist and close, made her quiver with delight and wrap her legs around his pelvis.

He still wore his trousers, and she suspected it would take a great deal of convincing to get him to take them off. The thick fabric was their last line of defense.

But oh, how her body yearned for more, though more of what she had no idea. There was still so much she had yet to experience, though she remembered certain things he had done to her last time and longed to do them again. A sweet ache began to pulse and drip between her legs as he wrapped his arm around her waist and drew her close, caressing the soft flesh of her bare bottom.

"Oh, Seger, I love the way you touch me. I want more."

"Then more you shall have."

He inched down her belly, laying kisses around her navel and stroking her breasts with his expert fingers, gently pinching them and squeezing them. Clara spread her thighs and ran her fingers through his hair, and could not stop herself from thrusting her hips in eager, twisting circles.

Soon, she was persuading him in a southerly direction, longing for the feel of his head between her thighs. Lord, how she craved the exquisite pleasure of his mouth kissing her in that most sensitive, private place, the same way he had pleasured her in the carriage.

At last she felt his tongue probe the soft center of her

desire, and her breath caught in her throat. Her heartbeat quickened in erotic response as he explored the damp folds of her flesh. Almost of their own accord, her thighs spread wider, her legs bent at the knees as she held onto his head and strove to open herself still more to him, if it were possible.

This was some kind of seventh heaven of rapture, she thought as she squeezed her eyes shut and arched her back and tossed her head to the side on the pillow. Seger mouthed her and pleasured her, his face buried between her legs. The mere sound and feel of his breathing was enough to drive her wild with delight. He seemed to be able to go on forever doing what he was doing.

"Do you enjoy this?" she found herself asking in a breathless voice. "Or is this just for me?"

He stopped only for a second to reply. "I enjoy it immensely."

Then he dove in with even more devotion to the task.

She held his head tightly against her and wrapped her legs around his shoulders, feeling the oncoming tidal wave of the ultimate crest of passion. She fought to push it away, for it was too soon. He'd only just gotten here. She wanted to draw the pleasure out a little longer. "Stop," she whispered. "Come here."

He gave in to the pull of her hands on his arms, bringing him up to lie on top of her as before. She kissed him deeply, tasting the flavor of her own feminine arousal and losing control of all her senses.

"Please, take these off," she pleaded, tugging at his trousers. "I just want to touch you and feel you against me. Can't we do what we did last time, with you on top?"

"Darling, with me on top, things would most assuredly get out of hand."

Seger felt his defenses slip, however, beneath the sheer erotic force of her plea and the pounding ache in his loins. He could not seem to locate the will that had always been his unwavering armor. It was that very will that had protected him from ambitious debutantes or lonely wives of philandering husbands. He had managed to live a gratifying eight years without ever causing an unwanted pregnancy.

Yet here tonight, he was suddenly willing to risk it all. Consequences meant nothing. He wanted this woman, who was his future wife. Couldn't he relax just this once? God, he'd earned it. Couldn't he begin their journey now? Why wait for the marriage papers? They were just a formality. Even if he got her with child, they could simply claim that the baby had come early. It happened all the time, didn't it?

God, he was making excuses.

He would say anything to justify making love to her now, and being free to shoot his seed into her with unfettered abandon.

Clara, delightfully wild thing that she was, began to tug at his trousers. He grabbed hold of her hand with the tiny speck of restraint that was still glimmering faintly in his muddled consciousness.

"What are you doing, darling? We're treading on a fine line here."

"I don't care," she said. "I want you, Seger. We're engaged. Why not? I've heard it's painful the first time. Why not get that over with now, so I can enjoy our honeymoon without any fears or anxieties? The time is right. I can feel it. Let's just do it."

She was thrusting her hips against him while she begged. God.

God.

God!

"I'm not made of steel," he whispered into her mouth as she kissed him aggressively.

"Good."

Then she reached down into his pants and grabbed hold of his firm shaft and toyed with his heavy balls.

"Please," she whispered urgently in his ear, her hot breath making him even more stiff than he had been before.

The bed seemed to shift beneath him.

That was that.

He reached down in a fumbling panic that was completely outside his usual smooth approach, and ripped his pants off like a randy schoolboy, clumsily kicking his legs in frustration to get the damn pant legs off his ankles.

How much time did they have, he wondered? A quarter of an hour? Let it be more than that.

A second later he was nude and pulsing on top of Clara, pressing his erection into the soft, hot cleft between her thighs.

"Are you sure?" he asked one last time, suckling her breasts and praying she wouldn't change her mind now.

Thankfully she nodded and nibbled on his earlobe, driving him down and down into a swirling eddy of pleasure until he was long gone, far beyond the turning point.

His whole being shook with excitement as the swollen head of his desire came to a quiet pause at the entrance to her dark, divine haven. Slowly he edged himself into the tight opening as wave upon wave of unyielding temptation enveloped him. He kissed her deeply, pressing his tongue into her mouth in a fervent attack that she met with equal ardor. Her legs wrapped around his buttocks and she pulled him into her, her fingernails digging into his firm flesh.

The throbbing sensation in his loins intensified. Her body arched into his. He shifted, hesitated for one final second, then thrust his hips and drove in, but only halfway into the sweet, tight hollow between her thighs, for he felt the rupture of her delicate opening.

Clara whimpered in his ear. He knew she was biting back a pain-wracked cry so she wouldn't wake anyone in the house, and the idea that he had hurt her made him stop.

He kissed her neck and whispered, "I'm sorry."

She clung to his shoulders and squeezed him tightly with her legs. "Don't be. I want this."

Pushing himself up on one elbow, the other arm stretched across her, he lifted his head and gazed down at her face in the flickering candlelight. She was the most beautiful creature he'd ever laid eyes upon. So remarkably beautiful, she made his chest ache.

She took his face in her hands and stroked his cheek, then closed her eyes and inhaled deeply. A single tear trickled down over her temple, and it wounded him to see it.

"Are you all right?" he asked.

She nodded. "Yes, it's not what you think. It feels good, Seger." Then she wiggled her bottom beneath him in a bid for more of his thick, firm length inside her.

Feeling a passionate jolt in his loins and awakening from what felt like a dazed stupor, Seger paused for a moment to think, realizing this was only the second time in his life he had taken a woman's virginity. It had been twelve years since the first time, and he had not thought about it in ages. Tonight, he felt almost like a virgin himself.

Lowering his mouth to hers, reveling in the drenching sensation of their lips and tongues meshing together,

Seger pushed firmly, all the way into her soft, hot depths. Clara whimpered again and clutched onto him. He could feel her muscles tensing around him, then a second later they relaxed. He thrust again, careful not to hurt her, but needing to appease the stinging excitement that was pulsing inside him.

She opened her legs even wider and thrust her hips to meet each of his own gliding penetrations. Together they moved in harmony, seeking a satisfaction they had both been craving since the first night they'd met and kissed under the stairs.

They had come so far since then. She was his now. Forever. She would be his wife and he would make love to her just like this every magnificent night for the rest of their lives. He wanted it to begin now. He didn't want to wait two months, but this was how the world worked, he supposed.

Suddenly a pounding wave of pleasure crashed down upon him and he quickened within Clara, feeling an impossible rush of need. He began to stroke faster, and at the same time, she dug her fingernails into his back and pushed her hips upward, squeezing around him, clenching tight until her head came off the pillow and slammed back down.

He felt her orgasm as it pulsed around him. The sight and sensation of her pleasure drove him into his own private heaven, where he quaked and spilled forth in pure, unparalleled ecstasy.

Just then, he heard a clock somewhere in the house chime four times. He collapsed upon her, completely and utterly spent.

Clara wrapped her legs around him even tighter. She tried to lift her head off the pillow, but it fell back. "You're not going anywhere," she whispered.

"But you made me promise," he replied, ribbing her on, without withdrawing from the tight, sopping heat of her womanhood.

"This is one time I think I'll let you break your promise."

"The only time, I presume."

"Yes, unless we are in this same situation again, in which case I hope you will do whatever I ask." Her voice trailed off. "*I had no idea. . . .*"

He kissed her cheeks and nose and felt a great, splashing torrent of affection.

She'd said *she* had no idea, when in fact it was he who was bewildered beyond any imagining. He had just made love to a virgin—a virgin he had already proposed to—and he felt joyful. Wholly content. All was right with the world, except for the fact that he would have to rise from this bed very shortly and walk away from her.

His gaze roamed possessively over her face, then he gently rolled off her.

He was more than a little accustomed to this routine—rolling off a lady, then reaching for his trousers and making himself scarce—but tonight it felt wrong and frustrating and the reaction was completely foreign to him. He felt like he was already home and he should not have to leave.

Home. This wasn't even his house, dammit, and if anyone discovered him here, the dangerous Duke of Wentworth would probably beat him to a pulp.

Yet Seger felt like he was home. He was farther gone than he'd thought.

Clara rolled over to lay her cheek on his chest. "That was wonderful, Seger."

He spoke very quietly. "It wasn't too painful for you?"

"Only for a moment, then the way you moved inside

me. . . . It was the friction I believe. It seemed to make the pain go away." She lifted her chin and rested it on her hands, which she laced together on his chest. "When will we be able to do this again?"

He couldn't help chuckling. "Sooner rather than later, I hope. Let's not wait until September."

"How soon are you thinking?" she whispered.

He lifted his eyebrows. "Tomorrow would be nice."

"Tomorrow would indeed be nice, but my mother arrives tomorrow."

"Then let's not wait until September to get married. What about next week by special license?"

Her eyebrows lifted. "All of my family needs to be here."

"They could get here within a week."

She stared at him for a moment, considering it. "Your stepmother is making plans for September."

He touched her cheek. "Plans can be changed. There is no reason to wait. In fact, it's dangerous to wait because I am sure I won't be able to stay away from you, and we can only risk our luck for so long. We'd get caught eventually, and on top of that, we'd each go insane. Well, I would at any rate."

"I would, too."

He held her soft cheek in his hand. "Then marry me in a week. Put me out of my misery."

"There would be talk."

"You know I don't care about that sort of thing."

Clara sat up. "Why are you so persistent all the time? I can never say no to you."

He held a finger up to his lips to remind her to speak softly. "I don't want you to say no. I want you to say yes."

"I already said yes. To everything so far. We have to draw the line somewhere."

He frowned. "But why draw a line? Why deny ourselves? Why not simply have what we want?"

She stared at him in the candlelight, then her face changed. Her voice lost its playful tone. "You're used to that, aren't you?"

"What do you mean?"

"Taking what you want without considering the practicalities or social restrictions. Must everything be about pleasure and self-gratification? Is that all you want?"

"Clara," he whispered as he sat up. "Don't."

She continued whispering angrily, as if he hadn't spoken. "Can you not abide by society's rules just this once and suffer through the usual betrothal?"

She reached for her nightgown and pulled it on over her head, then climbed off the bed and walked to the window. She stood before the drawn drapes.

Seger raked a hand through his hair. "Something tells me there is more to that question than the obvious."

It almost seemed like she wanted to make him wait in order to use their engagement to test his ability to resist temptations.

She only shrugged.

He climbed off the bed and went to her. He stood behind her, feeling the soft fabric of her gown against his nude front. He tried to ignore the urge to take her into his arms, carry her back to the bed and plunge into her again, to go back to the way they were feeling only moments ago.

"I don't deserve this, Clara," he whispered. "I have never taken what I wanted from you when I had every opportunity. Even tonight I would have resisted, if you had not been so persistent."

The fact that he was actually discussing this was astonishing. Any of his previous lovers would be shocked to see him defending himself. It was a huge concession, and he wished she knew that.

She dropped her face into her hands. "Maybe you should go."

"Go? Why?" He tried to keep the shock and anger out of his voice because he was afraid that if he didn't, someone might hear them. He had to keep this argument to a whisper. "What's this really about?"

She said nothing for a few seconds, then she turned to face him. Her eyes were filling with tears. "I'm nervous about marrying you."

He tried not to let her comment aggravate him, but it did. It damn well did. He had come forward leaps and bounds to reach this point with her. He had proposed, for God's sake!

She bowed her head. "You can't blame me for being unsure. I am a prime target for fortune hunters, and you have made it clear that you don't truly love me. How can I be sure you will be a good husband?"

He backed away from her. "I am no fortune hunter. You know that."

She merely stared at him.

"This is about my being faithful to you," he said.

God, women were so bloody complicated. Normally, he would walk away when his bed partner began to talk like this, or even hint at talking like this, but with Clara, he couldn't. He was in for the long haul and there was no turning back now. Not after what they'd done tonight.

Her shoulders rose and fell with a deep intake of breath. "If you can't make it through two months, how can I be sure you could make it any reasonable length of time in a marriage? Sometimes there are temptations, and I'm afraid you are not even going to bother to try and resist them. What about when I am enormous with child and unable to perform my wifely duty? What if I become ill? I won't be attractive to you then. Will you go back to your usual entertainments?"

He turned away from her and picked up his trousers. "Maybe I *should* go."

She watched him pull them on. The volume of her voice rose a fraction. "Wait, Seger."

"The servants will be up soon."

He put on his shirt, then sat down on a chair to pull on his boots in a hurry. He wanted to get out of there. He felt her hovering over him. Women never did that to him. They knew better than to push. They knew that if he was going to return another day, they would have to let him go without a fight.

He felt impatient with Clara, for he was not accustomed to rules or controls. For eight years he had lived freely. He had steered away from responsibility and commitment.

He didn't like feeling impatient with Clara. She was different from the others. He didn't want to feel this way with her, but he supposed that deeply ingrained responses were not easy to change.

Clara followed him around the bed. "I didn't mean to make you angry. It's just that a lot has happened these past few days, and we just . . . we just . . ."

Her voice shook and he immediately looked up. She was distraught. He'd just taken her virginity and all her choices were gone. She was probably sore down there for God's sake. She probably felt vulnerable and confused.

Bloody hell, he was an idiot. He knew nothing. In eight

years, he had never let himself feel responsible for a woman's comfort or happiness. He'd avoided women who pushed toward intimacy and sentiment. Now suddenly here he was, up to his ears in sentiment and obligation and probably tears, too, if this continued in the direction it seemed to be going at the moment.

Lord, this was not at all what he was used to. He was completely out of his realm of experience. He was fine with seductions and physical attachments—more than fine—but he didn't know the first thing about emotional intimacy and how to handle a woman who was upset. He was not the kind of man to stay around for that, but now he was to be someone's husband and he had no choice but to stay. He couldn't don his boyish charm and tease his way out the room like he usually did.

He suddenly felt as if he had bitten off more than he could chew.

Then he saw Clara's nightgown quiver and knew she was fighting a full-blown sob.

He couldn't let her cry. Someone would hear.

He felt a shamelessly shallow need to stop her from crying only to keep the silence, and an even more shallow need to get out of there as soon as she collected herself.

Something else took over, however. Perhaps it was compassion or affection for Clara. Perhaps it was merely the need to fix the situation. He had no idea.

Before he knew what he was doing, he had crossed the room and was taking her in his arms. All that mattered to him at that moment was her comfort and happiness. Her needs became more important than his own. It was all very new.

His voice was gentle and soothing and completely unrecognizable to his own ears. "Why did you insist we make love if you weren't sure?"

She shook her head and whispered, "I couldn't think about anything except that I wanted you. Now it's settling in, and I think I've just realized the gravity of what we've done, and I suddenly feel very alone."

Alone. She felt alone.

His heart began to pound. It was a first for Seger, who never, ever experienced any kind of panic in a woman's bedroom. Not even when the husband's carriage pulled up outside, because there was always a back door.

"But I can't do anything about it," she continued, wiping under her nose, "because I can't turn back the clock."

He rubbed her shoulders and stroked her hair. "And the fact that you can no longer change your mind about marrying me has spooked you."

She nodded.

It bloody well spooked him, too, but he knew enough not to say it.

"There is nothing to fear, Clara. We are going to be married. If we hadn't done this tonight we would have done it eventually—on our honeymoon at least, which is only two months away. A mere fragment in time. Do not feel that you are alone."

But how would he ever make her not feel that? *Jesus.* He was here with her, he'd just made love to her, and she felt alone. Lonely. Even though he was holding her in his arms.

Seger lifted her chin with a finger and kissed her gently on the lips. "You are my fiancée, and tonight you gave me something very precious. You shared a part of yourself with me. I am deeply touched."

But she felt alone.

Clara nodded, and he relaxed somewhat, knowing he

had eased her mind a tiny bit, and given her at least a particle of comfort.

Still, the urgent compulsion to leave continued to poke at him, and he wasn't sure how much of it was a result of the servants' impending appearance, or the subject matter of this conversation.

Either way, he had to go and she knew it. At least he had a good reason to slip out without tramping cruelly on her feelings.

He quickly pulled on his waistcoat and jacket while she watched him in silence. "I really do have to go before people are up and about."

"I know." She crossed toward him, looking vulnerable and uncertain. Even her voice had changed. It did not hold her usual confidence. "I'm sorry, Seger. Now I feel foolish for the things I said. I wish you didn't have to go."

He gathered her into his arms again. "No need to feel that way. You did something you hadn't planned to do tonight. It's only natural."

Natural that she would regret what they'd done.

Something tightened in his gut, but he tried to ignore it because he didn't understand it. He'd never felt uncertain after making love to a woman. He'd always walked out with the secure knowledge that he had pleased his partner and the session had been a success. He'd always walked out with an uncomplicated smile on his face.

He should walk out now. He wanted to, but he couldn't seem to do it. He couldn't leave her like this. "Let's do it sooner."

Her eyes were wide with innocence as she blinked up at him. "Do what?"

"Get married, like I said before. I know that's what started this argument, but you don't need to make me wait to test my discipline against temptation. Let me marry you and prove that I am completely devoted. If I were not, I would be putting it off. I want you and no one else. That is what lies at the heart of this. It's why I want to skip the elaborate wedding and keep it simple. We could do it next week."

What the bloody hell was he doing? The more uncertain he became, the faster and deeper he dug the hole.

"Seger, you don't have to say that to make me feel better."

"I'm not trying to make you feel better." But he was, and he knew it. "I just don't want to wait, it's as simple as that. Besides, you might be carrying my child."

Worry flooded her eyes.

God, it was wretched of him to resort to that.

Nevertheless, he forged ahead. "Let's just do it. We'll be joined legally and morally. You will have my total commitment and all these doubts and fears will disappear."

What he really meant was that if he put the ring on her finger, signed the papers, she wouldn't feel guilty about making love to him, and they wouldn't have to have this difficult conversation again. They could go back to laughing and smiling.

"You will be my wife," he said, "and we will share a bed like a normal, respectable married couple."

That at least got a smile out of her. "I think I'd like to be respectable."

Seger chuckled. "*You* would? Lord, I'm about to enter a whole new world."

The tension lifted and she rested her forehead on his chest. "What about the honeymoon? You've made arrangements for September."

"We'll simply wait and go then. This way, you'll have time to settle into your new home."

She laughed at the absurdity of such a rushed affair. "Go, before someone catches you sneaking out of here."

"Not without an answer."

She shook her head. He wished he could see her face.

"An answer, darling. Next week?"

She gazed up at him in the candlelight, then at last she replied, "All right, but only because I want to be in your bed again."

Her answer relieved him greatly. What could he say? He was a man, and the bed was the one place he felt confident in knowing his way around.

He turned to leave, but Clara stopped him with a question. "Seger? Was I your first virgin?"

He halted and closed his eyes. He wished she had not asked him that. "What does it matter?"

He did not see the point in the question.

"Well? Was I?"

He slowly turned to face her. "No."

"Have there been many?"

"No. Only one."

He saw her Adam's apple bob, as if she had difficulty swallowing over his reply. Finally, she nodded. "Daphne?"

"Yes."

Her chest rose and fell with a deep sigh.

Hearing a thump in one of the upstairs bedrooms, Seger knew he had to leave. He hesitated a moment, however, for he could see the distress in his future wife's eyes, and wished he could stay to make it disappear. He wanted her to know that Daphne was deep in his past. She was forgotten. There was no need for Clara to feel as if *she* were not the most important woman in the world to him.

Another thump sounded over their heads.

He had to go.

He kissed Clara on the mouth, then backed out of the room. He noted however, that he left without his usual indulgent, postcoitus smile.

When the news of her stepson's sudden haste to marry the American reached Quintina's ears the next day, she gazed helplessly across the breakfast table at Gillian. Time seemed to stand still for a few seconds.

An *American*. Quintina could have spit on her toast.

All was quiet, until Gillian burst into tears and ran out.

Quintina sat in her chair, staring blankly at the wall. She felt numb. Sick. Disgusted. How could this have happened? Marriage terrified Seger. He had never been willing to face the permanence or the commitment. Nor had he been willing to let go of the past, in particular the daughter of an insipid, working-class merchant.

At least *she* was English.

Quintina had thought she had all the time in the world to make Gillian the next Lady Rawdon. She had thought her niece was the only young woman with even the slightest chance with him, because she was the only one Seger spent any time with on a regular basis—the only unmarried gel who didn't apply any pressure, the kind of pressure that always made him rebel into extreme bachelorhood.

Quintina had also believed she could put an end to his engagement to the American and send Gillian in to take over where the heiress had left off, after having lit the stove, so to speak.

A sudden heated rage rose up within Quintina. No! Gillian had been waiting forever. She'd wanted him since she was a girl!

Quintina rose from her chair, picked up a vase full of flowers from the sideboard, and smashed it on the floor.

The American. Next week. It couldn't be true!

She took in a number of deep breaths to calm herself, then left the breakfast room and informed the house-keeper that she required a carriage right away.

She had to send an urgent telegram to America. She could not let this marriage take place.

Chapter 14

Dear Clara,

He must truly love you, if he is willing to give up his way of life for you. You must believe that in your heart if you want to be happy.

Love,
Adele

Beatrice Wilson of New York stepped out of the large coach and onto the sidewalk. Wearing an excessively flounced traveling gown that made her look even shorter and plumper than she already was, she gazed up at Wentworth House from beneath a wide brimmed, purple plumed hat.

This was the home of a duke. Her daughter's home.

A great wave of satisfaction moved through her.

Her maid stepped out behind her just as Beatrice's two daughters came running out the front door to dash into her open arms.

"Mother!" Sophia said. "You're here!"

All three of them hugged and laughed, until Clara and Sophia stepped back to give their mother room to breathe.

"You both look beautiful," Beatrice said. "Congratulations, Clara. I can't wait to meet this marvelous man you have caught, and Sophia, I must see my grandchildren."

"Of course. Come inside."

A footman took care of her trunks, while the housekeeper greeted Beatrice's maid and showed her to her room.

A few minutes later, Beatrice was in the nursery picking up her newest grandson, John, second in line to a dukedom. "You're such a beautiful boy," she cooed, letting him clasp her finger. "Sophia, what an accomplishment. The dowager must be pleased. Two sons in two years."

"She is, Mother. We've become very close."

Clara gathered Liam into her arms.

"And you . . ." Beatrice said, turning to face Clara, "you are to marry a marquess. My two girls. What legends you have become back home. Sophia tells me your marquess is handsome. No doubt your children will be the envy of all the mothers in England."

Clara smiled, wondering uneasily if the future heir to the title was already planted in her womb. "He is indeed handsome, Mother. I'm very happy."

"I'm glad. You deserve it, darling. The world has come around right, has it not?"

"Yes, Mother," Clara replied, knowing her mother was referring to that disagreeable time two years ago, when it had felt like all joy in her life had come to an end.

"How is Adele?" she asked, wishing to change the subject.

"Adele is having a grand time going to parties and balls, but she has not given up the idea of coming here next year to enjoy what spoils London has to offer—spoils which seem to be quite impressive, judging by what you two have achieved."

She winked at Clara and swayed from side to side to rock the baby. "I've hired an English governess for Adele," she continued, "and the woman is spectacular. She knows all about the aristocracy and tells me she has connections here as well. Though of course, what better recommendation can a young woman have than to be the sister of a duchess and a marchioness?" Beatrice's eyes glimmered with pride. "I am so proud of both of you."

"You will be even more proud tomorrow night," Sophia said, "when you meet the marquess and his family at the Wilkshire Ball." Sophia gave her sister a knowing glance. "May I be the first to tell you that the date of the wedding has been moved up since yesterday. They're going to be married next week, Mother. They are that much in love."

Beatrice's mouth fell open. "You don't say. Then it is true."

"What's true, Mother?" Clara asked.

"That it really is a love match. The newspapers in America are churning the story out like cheese."

Clara laughed out loud. "But where would they hear such a thing?"

"Heaven knows. The only thing that matters is that you are the latest American heroine, darling." She affectionately wiggled Clara's nose. "I can't wait to meet this man of yours."

Sophia approached and put her arm around Clara. "You will approve of Lord Rawdon, Mother. I am sure of it."

"A marquess? You needn't even wonder if I will approve. Handsome or not, I will adore him."

She did, of course, adore him. Clara watched her mother curtsey before Seger in the ballroom with a look of pure wonder teeming from her eyes—a look that had more to do with how handsome he was than the simple fact that he was an English lord, which was an astonishment to be sure.

After their engagement was announced, everyone seemed to suddenly share her mother's opinion. It had been a number of years since Seger had frequented society ballrooms, and Clara guessed that most of these people were finally admitting to their fascination with him, for he was like no other man in London.

And now he was accepted. The powerful Duke of Wentworth had welcomed the fallen marquess into his family, and people were at last free to admire him.

Clara stood off to the side alone, watching Seger dance with his cousin, Miss Flint, and watching his stepmother smile. The woman certainly seemed proud to see her son moving in good society again. Clara was glad she had played a part in that.

Just then, an attractive woman wearing a dark crimson gown, with rubies sewn into the skirt, moved up beside her. Clara remembered meeting her when she had arrived. Lady Cleveland was her name. She was exceptionally beautiful.

"You mustn't stare," Lady Cleveland said. "Everyone else is doing a fine job of that, and you shall have him all to yourself soon enough."

Clara turned to face her.

The woman raised a coquettish, arched eyebrow. "You must tell me how you did it, Miss Wilson."

Clara tried not to squeeze her champagne glass too tightly. "I beg your pardon?"

"How you snared him. He doesn't need your American money, so however did you manage to turn a man who has such a great predisposition toward bachelorhood into the marrying kind?"

Clara could barely swallow as she gazed at the woman beside her, whose eyes raked over her with a sneer. "I didn't snare him."

The woman smirked. "Well, whatever you did, I could kill you for it. I only hope you will allow him some freedom, and won't be one of those jealous wives."

Clara had to fight to breathe over the fury welling up inside her. "If you would make your meaning clear, Lady Cleveland."

The woman kept her gaze on the dancers as she sipped her champagne. "I thought I already had."

The dance ended and Seger escorted Miss Flint to Quintina, then immediately made his way across the floor to where Clara was standing with Lady Cleveland.

"My lady," he said, bowing over her hand and placing a kiss on her gloved knuckles. "It is a pleasure, indeed."

"The pleasure is all mine, my lord," she replied in a deep, throaty voice that held a dozen-and-one hidden meanings. It was more than clear that these two had a history together and Lady Cleveland wanted it known. "I believe congratulations are in order."

"Yes, I see you've met my fiancée."

The woman turned and gave Clara a haughty look down the length of her nose. "I have indeed. She is very sweet, Seger. Not your type at all."

The way she used his given name right under Clara's nose made all the hair on the back of her neck stand up. She would have liked to empty her champagne glass over the top of the woman's head, but she resisted the impulse, tempting as it was.

Seger merely laughed. "You're incorrigible, Lady Cleveland. It's been too long since we've seen each other. Where have you been these past months?"

She shrugged. "Here and there. Mostly there."

"Well, I hope to see you more often, now that I am finally 'out.'"

Lady Cleveland threw back her head and laughed, revealing a mouthful of huge white teeth. "And a magnificent debut it was, Seger." She discreetly squeezed his arm as she moved around him to take her leave. "I hope to see you later. I believe after supper, I'll be in need of some entertainment."

Clara watched her fiancé's eyes follow the other woman across the room, then he picked up a glass of champagne from a passing footman and turned his attention back to her. "What's wrong?"

"You have to ask?"

He glanced back at Lady Cleveland. "She bothered you? There's really no reason not to like her. She's just bored, that's all."

"She said she hoped I wouldn't be a jealous wife, and that she didn't think I was your type."

"She didn't mean anything by it. In fact, I would take it as a compliment."

Clara watched the woman on the other side of the room. "She didn't mean it as a compliment. Not if she considers herself your type."

"She doesn't. She's just a friend."

"A friend? I hardly think so."

Seger finished his champagne and set it down. "So you *are* going to be a jealous wife after all. Heavens, how will I ever live up to my reputation after next week?"

Clara's eyes widened in horror until she realized that Seger was joking. He was gazing down at her with a teasing smile.

"Why don't we dance?" he said. "Are you free for the next one?"

"I am."

She followed him on to the floor and worked hard to stifle her suspicious misgivings. She did not wish to sound like a nagging shrew. She wanted to be an agreeable, amusing wife he would enjoy more than any other woman. A wife he would feel close to. A wife who would become his best friend.

She also wanted to trust Seger, and making accusations like these would not foster a sense of confidence between them.

She shook her head at herself. "I do apologize, Seger. I'm afraid I've been thinking too much lately."

He pulled Clara into his arms. "Let's not talk about Lady Cleveland. Let's talk about you. Your mother is delightful," he said. "She is everything I imagined she would be. Energetic and cheerful, and thoroughly American."

Clara tried to push Lady Cleveland from her mind. "Mother liked you, too. I could tell."

"But does she know you refused a duke before you accepted my proposal?"

Clara sighed at the reminder. "I told her everything this morning. She is not like Mrs. Gunther. My mother covets British titles, certainly, but to her, one is as good as another. Precedence is merely incidental."

They moved to the center of the ballroom, and Seger held Clara with confidence as he led her through the dance.

"When will your father and sister come?" he asked.

Clara began to feel a distance between them tonight that hadn't existed before. She knew it was because of what had happened the other night, when she'd made demands upon him. And what just happened with Lady Cleveland didn't help matters either.

But perhaps this change was a good thing, she tried to tell herself. Perhaps they were moving beyond the surface flirtations and she was getting to know the real man beneath it all. Perhaps it was time to be serious.

"They'll be here for the wedding," she replied, "but with not an hour to spare. My father is a busy man. He works very hard."

"I don't doubt it. To have built such a fortune from nothing, he must be ambitious."

Was she being foolish, or did this feel like polite small talk between strangers?

"Speaking of fortunes," Clara said carefully, "I read in one of the New York newspapers Mother brought, that you turned down what my father offered as a marriage settlement. It was the biggest headline on the society page."

Seger gazed into her eyes. "We live in strange times indeed if you hear of those details in the newspaper. How in the world did something like that get out?"

Clara shrugged as she let him lead her through another turn. "What I want to know is why you turned it down. The newspaper called it a love match and we both know that's not true."

His brow furrowed at her comment and the tone with which it was delivered. "You sound cynical, Clara."

"I don't mean to. I knew what I was getting into when I accepted your proposal. You've been honest with me, Seger, and I respect that. I just didn't expect you to turn down the settlement. Why did you do it, and why didn't you tell me the other night?"

She stopped on the dance floor.

Seger stopped, too, and looked tired all of a sudden. His shoulders rose and fell with a sigh. He glanced around the room. "It was unimportant—a discussion that took place between solicitors."

"But *why* did you turn it down?"

He took his time answering. "I suppose I didn't want there to be any speculation that I married you for your money."

"I thought you didn't care what other people thought."

He was quiet for a few seconds. "Just so. Come, we're missing the dance." He gathered her into his arms again and moved across the floor.

"I still don't understand," she said, knowing she should let it go. She was pushing him to talk when he didn't seem in the mood. This—after she'd just told herself to find her composure and be light and airy. To amuse him.

Lord, she should just give up now. Call the whole thing off. It was one thing to hide a lack of confidence from your fiancé during a one week engagement, but quite another to paste on a smile and pretend things were fine every day for the rest of your life, if they weren't fine. Clara knew she could not possibly keep up that kind of superficiality.

"It's just not the way these transatlantic marriages are usually done," she said with resignation.

Seger spun her around. "You've been reading too many stories in the society pages, darling. Don't worry, your father didn't get off entirely scot-free, and you won't have to decrease your spending. He insisted on providing you with a monthly allowance for his own peace of mind, and I agreed. You will, like your sister, have your own bank account and your own money, so you will have the freedom to spend what you like without having to ask your husband for a handout."

Clara absorbed his meaning and gazed up at him with consternation. "No, no, that's not why I'm asking you about the settlement. I don't want you to think that I'm worried about my financial situation. Truly, I wouldn't have minded having to ask for things."

He raised a flirtatious eyebrow at her and smiled. "I'm glad. But why don't you save your requests for the bedroom?"

His seductive gaze traveled over her face and caused an intense flare of heat inside Clara. It was the first time he had flirted with her all night and she was surprised and concerned by how relieved she was to bob back to the surface—back to the superficiality. She was relieved that he was behaving more like his old self, the exterior self that was pleased to be marrying her and pleased to be flirting with her.

She only wished she knew for sure how the interior felt about it.

The following week passed quickly for Seger, with decisions to make about the honeymoon and ten dozen details about the ceremony to work out. He was glad. Glad to be busy, glad to be one day closer to the finale. He would be even happier when it was completely over, and all this commotion would at long last settle down.

He woke on his wedding day, however, to the startling sound of thunder booming just over the house. It was the worst commotion he'd experienced all week. Rain beat noisily against his window and poured down the panes, almost as if someone were standing on the roof, dumping buckets of water, trying purposefully to give him a headache.

He tossed the covers aside and sat up on the edge of the bed. Sleepily, he walked to the window. The fog was so thick, he could not even see the street. Lightning flashed, then thunder boomed again.

A fine day for a wedding, he thought.

He washed and ate breakfast in silence in his room. Calmly, he read the newspaper. An hour later, he decided it was time to dress. He was about to summon his valet when a knock sounded at his door and a footman entered carrying a silver salver with a letter upon it. A telegram, Seger discovered when he picked it up.

It was from an anonymous person in New York.

YOU SHOULD HAVE TAKEN THE SETTLEMENT STOP
YOUR BRIDE IS A LIAR STOP
YOU'RE NOT THE FIRST STOP
ASK HER ABOUT THE EMBEZZLEMENT STOP

He read it again. "What the bloody hell?"

Seger turned it over, looking for a clue about who would send such a thing, but there was nothing to reveal who had written it.

Perhaps it was a scandalmonger who had read about their marriage in the newspapers and wished to create havoc.

He flipped it over again. *You're not the first.*

Of course he was the first. He knew he was. He had made love to Clara a week ago and she had been a virgin. There was no doubt about it.

But what the hell was the person referring to, and what embezzlement?

Seger rose from his chair and walked to the window. Looking out at the storm, he made a fist and tapped it a few times against the dark oak frame. They were to be married today. In three hours to be exact.

He felt a deep need to know the facts behind this note before he said I do.

A half hour later, he was stepping out of his coach in front of Wentworth House and dashing through the cold, hard rain to the door. He noticed the look of concern on the butler's face when he informed him that he wished to speak to Miss Wilson, but paid it no heed. He followed the butler upstairs to the drawing room, where he had to wait a significant number of minutes before Clara appeared.

Finally she walked in wearing a simple green morning dress. Her hair was elegantly adorned with pearls and white flowers and combs that sparkled.

God. He was interrupting her wedding day preparations. He saw the apprehensive expression on her face, watched her wring her hands together in front of her, and felt instantly guilty for coming here unexpectedly and in a panic, and for seeing her this morning when she would have preferred not to be seen—at least not by her bridegroom.

He was surely causing her great distress at the moment. She probably feared he was going to call everything off.

"You look lovely," he said, crossing the room to take her hands in his, kissing them and hopefully easing her mind.

She spoke with shaky uncertainty. "Thank you. Why are you here?"

He tried to convey warmth with his voice and expression, for he did not wish to cause her any further anxiety.

Surely a woman's wedding day was filled with enough anxiety as it was, without the groom barging in to the bride's house two hours before the ceremony to ask intrusive, accusing questions. He would try not to let it sound that way, at least until he knew the particulars.

"I received a telegram this morning from someone in America, but it was anonymous. I wanted to speak to you about it. They suggested I ask you about an embezzlement."

Clara felt her heart go *thump* inside her chest. All she could do was stare bewildered at her fiancé, and wonder how and why this telegram had come to him today at the worst possible time.

She had told Seger about Gordon proposing to her, but she had not told him everything. She had not explained all the details and complexities. Now she wished she had.

Looking back on it, however, there had never been an opportunity to bring it up. After Seger proposed, she thought she could tell him later, when it would hardly matter.

It hardly mattered now, she tried to tell herself. The embezzlement had nothing to do with her, after all. She had known nothing. She had been innocent.

She would tell Seger that.

Clara sat down on the sofa. "You remember the man I told you about? The man who proposed to me two years ago?"

Seger remained standing. His expression was calm. "Yes."

Clara's heart began to race. "Well, the reason I didn't marry him was because he was arrested for embezzlement."

The room seemed suddenly very quiet. Seger stood motionless, staring down at her. She tried to stay calm.

She gazed into her fiancé's eyes. He did not seem angry. He didn't seem anything.

"It's a rather strange story, actually," she said with a smile, trying to keep things light.

Oh, she hoped he would be understanding about this. He, of all people in the world, should be. He—the king of scarlet pasts. . . .

"Tell me."

She nodded and complied. "His name was Gordon Tucker, and when he proposed, my father refused to let me marry him. I told Gordon I would marry him anyway, despite my parents wishes, but he knew he could never afford to take me away, so he stole from his employer. I assure you, I knew nothing about it. All I knew was that he had somehow managed to pay for our passage to Europe. He told me he was in possession of enough savings to tide us over until he could find work when we got there. We were going to get married on board the ship. I suppose he thought that once we were married, Father would have no choice but to provide us with an allowance."

Seger's eyebrows drew together, and for the first time, she saw mild anger in his face. "So you *wanted* to marry this man? Enough to elope with him?"

Her nerves tensed immediately. "Yes."

"Did you love him?"

She bowed her head and paused a moment before answering. She had been enamored with Gordon, certainly. He was handsome and he knew how to charm her, how to manipulate her, but she had never been in love with him.

"No," she answered at last.

"How can I be sure you are telling me the truth?"

"All you can do is trust me and believe me when I tell you that I was nauseated getting on the ship with him, and

I wept with relief when my father came to take me home. When I said yes to Gordon's proposal, I only wanted to escape the pressure."

"The pressure to marry well."

"Yes."

He took a moment to consider this, while she sat helplessly, not knowing what to say, wishing she knew what was going on inside his head. Was he furious with her? Did he hate her?

Or was he hurt?

"So you didn't love him," Seger said. "Did you desire him? Did you ever let him touch you?"

The question unnerved her. It was clear that for Seger, desire was paramount.

She shook her head. "Never."

He stared at her for a moment, then, appearing satisfied, turned toward the window. "Where is this man now?"

"He went to prison for the embezzlement."

Seger faced her again. "Prison? Good Lord. There was a trial? Were you involved in the scandal?"

"No, my father took care of that. I was removed from the situation."

Seger's broad shoulders rose and fell. He looked fatigued. "So there was much more to this than what you told me at your sister's assembly. This is very serious, Clara. You should not have kept it from me."

She saw the disappointment in his face and wished more than anything that she had told him about it sooner. She hadn't set out to keep a secret from him. She had simply pushed it out of her mind.

Pushed it out of her mind. Perhaps it had been her way of pretending—at least to herself—that it hadn't happened, because she was not proud of it. And she had been afraid that if he knew the magnitude of the situation, he wouldn't want her.

"I couldn't tell you at first," she said. "I barely knew you. It's not something I talk about with strangers. Then, when things started to progress between us, I simply forgot about it when we were together."

"Forgot about it." He said it like he didn't believe it, then he faced the window again. "Have you told me everything?"

"Yes."

"Are you sure? There is nothing else I should know about? Because whoever sent this telegram knows about what happened, and if you are guilty in any way . . ."

"I am not guilty."

"You're telling the truth?"

"Yes!"

Clara wondered again if he was hurt. If he was, he certainly wasn't showing it. He was focusing on the facts, not his feelings. She should not be surprised.

"Who do you think would have sent this?" he asked. "And why?"

"I don't know."

"Perhaps it was your jilted lover."

"Perhaps." She hated to hear him use the word *lover* to describe another man.

Seger paced about the room, considering everything. "Do you realize that in my position, I would be perfectly justified to call off our wedding?"

His coarse words embedded painfully into her heart. She nodded.

"But we have already made love," he continued, "and

you were, as it turned out, a virgin." He paced around the room, thinking for a long time.

She waited nervously for him to make a decision. What would it be? He had been hurt once before in regards to a woman. Perhaps he felt defeated again. Powerless. Perhaps he was disappointed in Clara, and would not be able to forgive her. Or maybe this turn of events had spooked him and reminded him of why he had spent the past eight years avoiding marriage.

This was torture.

At last, he stopped behind the sofa where she couldn't see his face. She could only hear the deep timbre of his voice and feel the intensity of his presence curling around her.

"I believe we are tied to each other," he said.

Clara closed her eyes. Of course, that was how he would see this. He would not speak of hurt feelings or disappointments. He would speak only of the necessity of duty in these circumstances.

"I never wanted to trap you," she said.

He did not respond to that. He merely went on talking as if she had not spoken—with a notable lack of sentiment in his voice. He could have been speaking about a pot of tea that had gone cold.

"I am hardly in the position to call any kettle black, so we will be married. We will hope that this matter will not arise again after today, and that whoever sent this telegram will let it die. If not, and there is a scandal, then I will deal with it accordingly."

"I don't wish to be a problem you have to deal with," she said.

"Scandal is rarely a problem for me. I have learned that

one can be perfectly happy outside of society. Sometimes I wonder why I ever wanted to venture back in. Oh, yes. Because of desire."

Now because of obligation. Her mood sank.

He came around the sofa and stared down at her with cool, detached eyes. He looked very different from his usual self. She had never seen him when he wasn't exuding his famous charm.

"We must simply put this behind us, Clara. You are a beautiful woman and I still desire you."

Was that all? A basic physical attraction? Had this conversation spoiled their chances for anything deeper?

She felt as if she had taken one step forward with Seger—they were getting married after all—but two steps back as far as moving toward anything beyond desire.

Finally, a small fragment of affection found its way back into his eyes, and he kissed her hand. "I will see you in a couple of hours?"

Feeling numb, she stared up at him. "Yes."

"Good."

With that, and nothing more, he walked out, leaving Clara feeling as if she knew him less now, than she had the first time she'd seen him.

Chapter 15

"Icannot believe he is going through with it," Quintina said to Gillian in the carriage on the way to the church. "What in God's name did she say to him to prevent him from calling it off?"

Gillian gazed listlessly out the rain-soaked window. "Maybe she lied."

"We can only hope. If she did, there might be a chance for an annulment. He could claim fraudulent misrepresentation or something of that nature."

Gillian turned to her. "How do you know about that sort of thing, Auntie?"

Quintina's eyes bored into Gillian's. "I've been reading up on it, dear, trying to find ways to shift things in our favor. The last time this happened, Henry—God rest his soul—had used an iron fist to stop Seger's marriage, but I don't have that option. Seger is a man now, and has an iron will of his own. We must be more conniving and move him to end it himself. Believe me, if there is any way to terminate this, I will find it. I am not one to give up hope."

"But he is going to marry her today, Auntie. After that, there won't be any hope."

Quintina gazed at her niece, saw the despondent look in her eye, and remembered the day the gel's mother— Quintina's dear, dear twin sister, Susan—had died. A sickness had spread through her body, and for weeks leading up to the end, caused her excruciating pain that made her writhe hideously on the bed. Quintina had found it difficult to stay with her, for it had been too unpleasant to watch. Grotesque, really. She had not been there when Susan died, though Susan had asked for her repeatedly.

Quintina still felt guilty about that. Susan had been her twin.

At least Gillian had been there at her bedside the entire time, waiting, praying, and hoping. She had been dutiful to the end.

There was such finality in death, Quintina thought as she watched her niece stare out the window at the passing traffic. No wonder the gel found it difficult to hope now.

Quintina squeezed Gillian's hand again. "Do not despair, dear. This is happening very quickly, and a man who marries in haste often finds himself nursing regrets later on. Fortunately for us, Seger is not the type to worry about divorce scandals. I believe he would be the first to leap on an opportunity for freedom if he is not happy." She leaned back and pulled on her gloves. "We must hope there won't be any children right away. That would only complicate things."

"What are you saying, Auntie?"

"I'm saying that even if he does marry the American today, it doesn't mean he will stay married to her. I know, I know, it sounds scandalous to even think of a divorce in our family, but I cannot bear to see you hurt. You have been hurt enough, with your dear mother departing this world and your father nothing but a cruel brute, God rest his putrid soul. You mother was my twin, and you are as precious to me as my own daughter. You deserve to get what you want, Gillian, and you have wanted Seger your entire life."

"I've more than wanted him, Auntie. I've loved him." The carriage swayed back and forth and rumbled over the bumpy cobblestones. Gillian smiled at Quintina. "Do you remember when I was twelve, and I fell in the courtyard at Rawdon Manor and cut my knee?"

Quintina nodded, her heart squeezing with sympathy as she recalled that cloudy afternoon.

"I remember how much it hurt and that I couldn't get up, and how badly I wanted to cry, but I couldn't because I was afraid Father would find out. He always got so angry when I cried. Then Seger appeared out of nowhere and scooped me up in his arms and carried me inside. I buried my face in his coat collar, and he said, 'Don't worry, Gillian, I've got you. You'll be fine,' and I burst into tears. Nothing ever felt so good as to cry that day. My knee was throbbing, and all I could think about was how wonderful Seger was, saying to me, 'there, there now,' and rubbing his cheek against the top of my head.

"Then he came back to check on me that afternoon and the next, and that's when I fell in love. No one knows what he's really like, Auntie. Not like I do. I know the real Seger. Society has always judged him wrongly."

Quintina tried to keep her voice from quaking. She remembered that day. Very well. That's when the seed had been planted, and it had grown into something far too substantial to be ripped from its roots now. Especially by an American.

Quintina straightened her shoulders and spoke with fresh resolve. "This is impulsive for both of them. There is room to maneuver, Gillian, and to manipulate the situation. We will all be living together in the same house very soon, and I for one will not simply hand the reins over to a vulgar, opportunistic foreigner. She has no heart invested in this marriage, while you have half of your lifetime invested in loving Seger, deeply and truly. It is not fair, and we will do what is necessary to find a way around this obstacle. You will have him. It won't be difficult. With all that we know about that woman and her past, we *will* find a way to put an end to this."

He should not be troubled, Seger told himself, as he spoke his marriage vows in front of the reverend and the small number of guests. Clara simply had a blemish in her past, which was nothing compared to the complete discoloration of his own tainted history. He should think of it as further proof that they were a good match. She was a kindred spirit, so to speak. She was by nature impulsive and somewhat rebellious toward social restrictions, even though, since the near brush with scandal, she had tried to walk the straight and narrow.

He had witnessed that wild impulsiveness in bed a week ago, when she had pleaded with him to make love to her, and he'd given in and had delighted in it. He had delighted in her passion.

What was the problem now? he wondered, resisting the urge to rub the tense muscles at the back of his neck. Why did he not feel elated on this day when he was securing a beautiful, spirited woman as his bedmate, and he was removing the cloud of duty that had hung over his head his entire life—the duty to marry and produce an heir and continue his line.

He should be relieved. He should feel that a great weight had lifted, but he did not. He felt only apprehension.

Perhaps it was because he was entering into a permanent relationship with a complicated woman, and he would have to deal not only with the problems of life, but with her resulting emotions.

He'd dealt with a problem this morning, and it had not been a pleasant discussion. He hadn't enjoyed asking her those questions. He'd tried to be impartial, and had wanted the same from her in return, for he had only once let himself near a woman's emotions, and in doing so, he had fallen in love. Then he had been devastated beyond contemplation when it came to an end.

No, he said to himself as he slipped the ring on his bride's slender finger. He should not feel apprehension or any other convoluted emotions. This was all very simple. Clara had made a mistake once, and almost married a swindler. She did not care for the man, and it was ancient history. He knew about it now, and he would very quickly forget it.

In fact, he should try to see this as a good thing. Clara's secret had put some distance between them. They did not really know each other, and this morning that truism had been brightly illuminated.

Yes, he should be able to relax somewhat. There was a small measure of space now.

So. All he had to think about was taking on the very pleasant task of providing his line with the next Marquess of Rawdon. He would devote himself entirely to her pleasure, hour upon hour, until she was completely satisfied and sighing in his arms.

Not such a terrible fate after all.

* * *

Clara waited in her room that night for her husband to come to her.

Her husband. It hardly seemed real. One day, she was adoring him from afar, not even knowing his name. Now, only weeks later, she was married to him—married to her mysterious dream lover.

Just then, the door knob turned and her husband entered the room. Her breath caught in her throat at the awesome sight of him. He wore a black silk robe and approached the bed like a panther—all confidence and seduction. If there was any resentment in his mind left over from this morning, he certainly didn't show it. He looked completely at ease and full of sexual anticipation.

"You were right," he said, sitting down on the bed. "It was a good idea to consummate our marriage a week ago. Now you'll be able to enjoy our wedding night without any pain. There will only be pleasure."

Pleasure. It was always the priority.

She gazed at him with a sense of bewildered blankness. This was her wedding night, but she did not know how to feel. She couldn't be frightened, because they'd already made love, and there was nothing to fear as far as her body was concerned. She should be looking forward to the pleasure he had given her a week ago, and promised to give her tonight.

Or perhaps she should be worried. Worried that he did not trust her and they would never be able to move beyond this wrinkle in their relationship. Perhaps she should be worried over the fact that he seemed completely at ease with everything. He was as charming as ever. As charming as he had been with Lady Cleveland. This was his persona, she supposed. The persona he revealed to strangers.

As his wife, was that all she would ever know? The same Seger half the pretty women in London knew?

She wished she knew him better. She wanted to *be* more to him.

She wanted to know the Seger that no one else knew.

He rolled onto his side, resting his cheek on his hand and gazing at her with rakish eyes.

She couldn't help smiling. She snickered, even, because he was in the mood for fun, and it wasn't much of a stretch to find her own desire for such pleasures. This was the basis of their marriage, after all. At least so far.

Seger raised a finger and stroked her cheek. "I thought it went well today. The food was superb."

"Delicious. I especially liked the cream cakes."

"Ah, you like desserts. I knew it," he said wickedly.

"Knew what?"

He ran his finger down along her jaw to her neck and caused a torrent of gooseflesh to rush over her shoulders. "Some women like appetizers, some like the main course. But you . . . I had you pegged for a dessert woman."

"We women fall into such simple categories."

Seger laughed. "It's true, isn't it? You look forward to the dessert, even when you've eaten enough and you're full."

Yes, she did.

"What do *you* like, Seger?" she asked in a sultry voice.

He sat up and helped her remove her nightgown. "I'm not sure, I keep changing my mind. I do like the appetizer, but then when the main course comes I think it's the best—the most substantial part of the meal."

He gazed at her naked form in the flickering lamplight. Clara laid her head back on the pillow, enjoying the way he admired her with such voracity.

"Tonight I'll be your appetizer, main course and

dessert," she said, "if you wish it. Consider it a very personal wedding gift." She tossed her arms up behind her head and crossed one leg over the other.

Seger's face lit up with anticipation. He quickly removed his robe and tossed it to the floor.

Lord, how she loved that she could have this effect on him in bed. This part of their marriage, at least, was flawless.

If only that flawlessness could spill over into everything else.

Naked and already firm with an appealing erection, her husband rolled on top of her and pressed his mouth to hers. The heavy weight of his hot, hard body awakened her senses. Before she knew it, she was parting her legs, wrapping them around his hips and locking her ankles together behind him.

"Ah, Clara, you are delicious."

She felt the tip of his arousal poised at her eager opening.

"Perhaps we could forego the appetizers this time around," she said. "After a week away from you, my darling, I'm afraid I am craving the main course."

He laughed as he devoured her mouth with his own. "You are a dream."

Swiftly and smoothly, he entered her in a single thrust. Clara sucked in a breath, surprised at the shock of how completely he filled her, stretching her, rubbing, then pressing hard against the outer reaches of her womanhood.

It was the single most erotic sensation of her life. Pleasure shot straight to her core. Seger moaned and withdrew from her. He rose up high, thrust in again and again, and struck that part of her where the pleasure seemed to both begin and end.

Clara lost herself in the luscious sensation—the feverish ache that reduced her to melted butter, dripping all over her new husband. She wanted more and more of this, deeper and faster until she satisfied the sweet, stinging need that was overtaking all her senses.

He rose up on his arms and looked down at her, watching her face as he made love to her with a steady pace in the flickering light. Before long, she felt her climax approach, then it sizzled and exploded through her. She shut her eyes and clutched at Seger's broad shoulders, driving her hips up to meet each of his deep, firm thrusts.

Her body relaxed afterward, and she didn't care about anything outside of that moment. All her doubts and insecurities disappeared, replaced by a physical satisfaction that somehow went beyond the physical—so much so it was confounding.

She opened her eyes and looked up at her beautiful husband. He was still inside her, moving with the hypnotic cadence of a poem. His eyes held hers, and for a brief instant, she felt like she was floating.

She loved him too much, far more than she should.

Seger then seemed to give himself permission to let his own passions take him where they would, and he groaned with a fiery orgasm that pulsed and throbbed within her.

Clara hoped he was planting a child in her womb.

She wanted to create a child with him.

She wanted to do and share everything with him.

Slick with sweat, he collapsed on top of her and held her for a few minutes, then rolled off her and smiled.

"That was incredible," he said, breathing hard and staring up at the ceiling.

"It certainly was. I have only one question."

He turned his head on the pillow to look at her.

"I don't want to rush you, but when is dessert being served?"

He laughed out loud. "As soon as my cake rises, darling."

She rolled toward him to nibble on his earlobe. "How long does it take to cook?"

"Not long."

She slid her hand down his damp, muscled chest and below, then gently took hold of his lower, more supple anatomy. "The main course was delicious, but you're right—even when I'm satisfied, I still want a little more. Strange, isn't it?"

She leaned up on one elbow, then began a trail of kisses down his salt-flavored abdomen. Plunging her tongue into his navel and swirling it around, she asked, "Do you mind if I turn up the heat in your oven?"

Seger lifted his head to look at her. "Kitchen skills too?" He laced his fingers through her hair, then closed his eyes and relaxed back down on the pillow. "I had no idea I married a woman with so many hidden talents."

"I'm a very fast learner." And down she went.

Clara woke the next morning to bright sunlight streaming in through the windows. Seger's arm was stretched across the bed, just below her pillow in the crook of her neck. She was still naked.

This was bliss.

She inched a little closer, admiring Seger's beautiful face as he slept. She touched her nose gently to his, wanting to kiss him but not wanting to wake him, for they had slept very little the night before. Chivalrous to the end, he had given everything to her pleasure, delivering ecstasy again and again, and for that, he deserved another hour of slumber.

Gazing at his face as he slept, looking at his peaceful countenance and the divine structure of his cheeks and nose, she felt drunk with fascination. She remembered the exquisite feel of his hands working her in the darkness, and the way she had opened herself to him. He was a man of infinite aptitude when it came to a woman's needs and desires. His energy was limitless, his desire to satisfy never ending. She had been exhausted when dawn had come, and he'd finally let her sleep, knowing with confidence that he had fulfilled her. And he had. Her hunger for what he offered had been satiated, her thirst quenched, and afterward, she had slept better than any other time in her life.

Oh, how she wanted to taste his lips right now.

Suddenly, a knock sounded at the door. Seger awakened sleepily, filling his lungs with a slow, deep inhalation, gazing around as if he didn't quite know where he was. As soon as he saw Clara's face, he rolled toward her, took her into his arms, and tried to go back to sleep.

"Seger, the door," she whispered.

The knock sounded again and he awakened more fully. "Someone is pounding at my door the morning after my wedding night? This had better be important."

Sluggishly, he rose from the bed, pulled on his robe and went to see who was knocking. Clara recognized the butler's voice when he spoke.

"I'm sorry to disturb you, my lord, but there is a gentleman caller here to see you. He says it's urgent."

"Urgent? Who is it?"

"His name is John Hibbert, my lord."

Seger stepped back and began to close the door. "I don't know anyone by that name. Tell him to come back later."

The butler persisted. "He says it concerns Miss Flint, and it is a *very* urgent matter."

Seger held the door half open. "Gillian? What in God's name . . . ? Tell him I'll be right down."

"What's happened?" Clara asked, tossing the covers aside and slipping out of the bed. She reached for her wrap and pulled it on.

Seger pulled on his trousers. "I don't know, but I intend to find out."

Chapter 16

Seger entered the drawing room where the gentleman had been waiting. The man wore a shabby-looking suit. He held a bowler hat in his hands and straightened uncomfortably when he turned around and met Seger's eyes.

"Sir, you have disturbed me at a most inopportune time. I hope this is important."

The man shifted from one foot to the other and spoke shakily. "It is, my lord. Gillian Flint . . . is she a relative of yours?"

Seger tilted his head at the man. "A relative by marriage, yes. She is my stepmother's niece. What of her?"

The man turned his hat over and over in his hands. "Uh, my lord, Miss Flint fell from her horse in front of my house this morning. She was unconscious and someone brought her to my door. My wife is with her now. The young lady mentioned your name."

All the muscles in Seger's body tensed. "Is she all right?"

"A little shaken up, but I reckon she'll survive."

"Have you summoned a doctor?"

"No, my lord, I came straight here."

Seger nodded. "Thank you for bringing this news to me, sir. Wait here, please."

Seger left the drawing room and requested that his coach be brought to the front door posthaste. He returned to the room just as Clara appeared in a simple gown with her hair in a messy knot, looking as if she'd barely had time to hook her corset.

"Gillian has been hurt," he told her.

Clara covered her mouth with her hand. "Good gracious. What happened?"

"She fell from her horse. I must go and fetch her right away. Will you tell Quintina to send word to my physician to meet me at this gentleman's home?"

Seger questioned the man, who related the address to Clara.

A short time later, Seger was stepping into the coach with John Hibbert, but paused when he heard Clara call his name from the front door.

"Wait!" Without so much as a shawl or gloves or hat, she bounded down the steps and practically leaped into the coach. "I'm coming with you."

Seger helped her inside, and closed the door behind her.

Clara sat in a rocking chair next to the sofa where Gillian was resting in the Hibberts' small parlor, and held her hand. She listened as the physician spoke to Seger out in the front hall.

"She's fine," the man said. "No signs of bruising or any broken bones. I believe she is just shaken from the whole affair, as any lady would be. You might want to take a look at that horse, however. Miss Flint said he bucked suddenly without any cause whatsoever."

Clara watched from the parlor as Seger escorted the physician to the door. "I will, Dr. Lindeman. Thank you."

A few minutes later, Seger entered the room. He smiled at Gillian. "You gave us quite a fright, my dear girl."

Gillian squeezed Clara's hand. "I'm so sorry, Seger. I didn't mean to cause so much trouble. I was riding too fast, I suppose."

Clara sensed the girl's embarrassment. She pushed a lock of hair away from her forehead.

"Why would you ride too fast, Gillian, and why did you go out alone? You've never done anything like that before. You've never been careless in your actions."

She shrugged. "I know it was foolish . . . I . . . I simply couldn't help myself. I felt reckless this morning." Gillian leaned up on both her elbows. Her gaze flitted back and forth from Seger to Clara. "I didn't mean to interrupt you."

An uncomfortable tension twisted and curled around the room. Clara tried to dispel it. "Nonsense, don't be silly. This unfortunate accident has given us an opportunity to get to know each other. I believe it's the first time we've had a chance to really talk."

Gillian smiled up at her. "Yes, I suppose you're right."

Mrs. Hibbert entered the room. "Can I get any of you anything? A cup of tea perhaps?"

"No, thank you, Mrs. Hibbert," Clara replied. "You've been very kind."

The woman smiled and left the room again.

"All this reminds me of the time I fell at Rawdon Manor," Gillian said. "I was only twelve. Do you remember, Seger?"

He smiled kindly at Gillian. "Of course I do. I remember how you cried."

Clara gazed down at Gillian's face and saw a warm radiance in her eyes.

"What happened?" Clara asked.

Seger stepped forward. "Gillian was running, that's all I saw. I don't know where she was running to, only that she fell. You went down very hard. Your nose scraped the rocks."

She touched it. "I still have a small scar."

"Yes, I know," he replied.

Gillian tried to sit up. "But you came to my rescue."

"I merely carried you into the house."

Clara watched the exchange and realized that Gillian was like a sister to Seger. She hoped Gillian would become like a sister to her, too.

Seger glanced toward the front hall. "Perhaps it's time to leave the Hibberts to their day," he said. "Will you be able to walk, Gillian?"

"I believe so."

"I won't have to carry you this time?" he said merrily.

Eyes flashing with delight, she giggled and shook her head. "No, Seger."

"Good. I'll summon the carriage, then. Are you ready, my dear?" he said to Clara.

She nodded and took his hand as he helped her to her feet.

Gillian chose her newest, most fetching gown when she dressed for dinner that evening. Quintina had convinced her that the color amber brought out the best in her complexion, especially in candlelight, and went well with her sand-colored hair. Quintina also chose a pearl-and-diamond choker from her own collection to go with the gown, and had lent it to Gillian.

Gillian watched herself in the mirror as her maid hooked the choker at the back of her neck, and wished she had been inclined to be more daring with her appearance before now, when it was probably too late.

She supposed that if things didn't work out with Seger, at least she would have learned a thing or two from Clara about how to attract a man. She'd never experienced admiration from a man before—at least not a man worthy of her notice.

Gillian touched the pearls at her neck. Yes, if things didn't work out here, she would put this new knowledge to good use and do even better than Seger. A duke, perhaps?

That would be very satisfying. She would outrank Clara at social functions. Her blood quickened at the thought. Perhaps one day, she would have an opportunity to give her the cut direct.

Just then, a knock sounded at her door and Quintina walked in. She waved the maid away and moved to stand behind Gillian, who looked at her aunt in the mirror's reflection. "Well?"

Quintina rested her hands on Gillian's shoulders. "You look stunning, my dear. He will be very surprised. We should have been dressing you like this all along."

"I thought the very same thing a moment ago, Auntie. Why didn't we?"

Quintina's shoulders rose and fell with a sigh. "I thought he would prefer someone demure for a wife. Someone like . . . well, you know."

"Yes."

Someone like Daphne. A merchant's daughter who dressed like . . . like a merchant's daughter.

Gillian bristled just thinking of her. Daphne hadn't even been all that pretty. Seger's affection for her had never made any sense to Gillian. She supposed the girl had been a bit of a slut.

Gillian had always believed that Seger would have realized that eventually. Even if Daphne had not gotten on that ship to America, he probably wouldn't have married her in the end. He would have come to his senses.

Quintina fiddled with Gillian's hairstyle in the back, folding locks into place. "It went well this morning, don't you think? We got them out of bed at any rate."

"Yes, and the Hibberts were very helpful."

"Did you feel badly about lying to them?" Quintina asked.

"Gracious, no. They think they did a good deed, and Seger thanked Mr. Hibbert, who is probably bragging about it at his local pub as we speak."

Quintina nodded. "Well, let us go."

Gillian gathered up her gloves and stood.

They crossed the room toward the door, but Quintina paused before opening it. She turned around to face Gillian. "Remember, look directly into his eyes when you talk to him, darling. You must make him see you in a new light. Meanwhile, I will handle Clara. I know exactly what to do. She won't last long."

Quintina glanced down at Gillian's low neckline, then lifted her gaze and smiled. "I believe you have larger breasts than she does."

"Auntie!"

"It's true, my dear. That gown is perfect. Now come along."

That evening after dinner, Seger retired to his study to attend to some business matters, while Clara played the piano for Quintina and Gillian in the drawing room. Gillian sat beside a bright lamp, embroidering a small pillow. Quintina read a book.

When Clara finished her piece, Gillian set down her needlework and clapped. "You play beautifully, Clara. It is such a joy to have you here."

"It's a joy to be here. You have made me feel very welcome, Gillian."

"I'm so glad. We are going to be wonderful friends, I know it. We must stay up late and enjoy each other's company like this every night. We'll be closer than sisters."

Clara stood and moved to sit on the sofa beside Gillian. "But you're forgetting the parties. The Season is far from over. There were a number of invitations today."

Gillian sighed and looked down at her stitching. "Yes, I suppose we must go out. I certainly must, if I am ever to find a husband."

"You will find one in no time, Gillian. You look radiant tonight. Wear a dress of that color to a ball and you'll be danced off your feet."

Gillian continued to look down at her embroidery. "I don't think I should like that—to be danced off my feet. Some might call me dull, but I prefer to stay at home in the evenings. I've always preferred it. Everything that makes me happy is in this house."

Clara inclined her head questioningly. "Have you been living here long? I thought you were just visiting, that you normally live with your uncle."

On the other side of the room, Quintina looked up from her book and listened.

"Yes," Gillian replied, "but Auntie has been very kind, always letting me stay as long as I like. My uncle doesn't mind. He knows that even when my parents were alive, this was like a second home to me. I was close to Seger, you see."

Clara watched Gillian lift her needle high over her head.

"We've always been friends," Gillian added, "for as long as I can remember. I was only one when Seger's father married Auntie. Seger was eleven, and he used to play with me and teach me things. We've been through a lot together. When my mother died, he was such a comfort to me, and before that, when he was suffering with a broken heart over Daphne. . . ." Gillian paused and glanced up from her embroidery to look at Clara. "I do beg your pardon, perhaps you don't know about Daphne. I have no manners sometimes. I can be so clumsy."

Gillian resumed her embroidery.

"Please, do not worry yourself," Clara said. "I know all about Daphne. Seger told me everything. Sad story, isn't it?"

Clara wasn't sure why she felt such a strong compulsion to inform Gillian that she knew about Seger's first engagement, and why she felt suddenly competitive. It made no sense at all. Gillian was Seger's cousin, for pity's sake.

But she'd known Seger her entire life. She knew so much more about him than Clara did.

You'll catch up, she told herself. *Soon, you'll know him better than anyone.*

She reminded herself that Gillian had never seen Seger naked.

Lord, what a petty, ridiculous thought. All the anxiety of the past week was making her loony.

But it did make her feel better. At least she shared one type of intimacy with Seger, and his sexuality was something that she would come to know better and better. From there, other kinds of intimacies would grow.

She must not let go of that hope.

* * *

"You are the most beautiful creature here," Seger said, escorting Clara onto the terrace of Weldon House, where they had been invited for an assembly.

The breeze was warm on Clara's cheeks, the champagne sweet on her lips and tongue. Seger had not stopped looking at her all evening, and she felt beautiful in her red silk, form-flattering Worth gown, with embroidered pearls on the bodice, and a flowing, flounced train. At her neck she wore a huge diamond pendant that flashed and sparkled. Seger's gaze had dropped many times to her cleavage, though she doubted he was admiring the diamond.

She had met a number of interesting people so far that evening, and Seger had not left her side for one minute the entire time. He had presented her to everyone they met, and had seemed genuinely proud to introduce her. There were very few sinister glances or upturned noses over the fact that he was a former libertine and she an American. Most people probably perceived them as a novel couple, an amusement.

Clara gazed up at him flirtatiously over the rim of her champagne glass as she sipped. "You shameless flatterer."

Lord, she couldn't wait to get home and be alone with him.

She recognized his acute sexual instinct alerting to her desires. He picked up on these things like a wolf catching a scent—always eager to respond and meet her needs, whatever they were.

He gave her a look that offered promises for later. "Shameless is my middle name," he said. "I can flatter you all night long if you wish."

Just then, a woman approached from behind and

grabbed hold of Seger's sleeve. She pulled him around to face her. "Oh, you must flatter me, too, Lord Rawdon. I haven't heard your delicious talk in a dog's age. I'm sure your lady-friend won't mind sharing."

"Sharing?" Clara said, stepping forward.

The woman leaned close. Her breath smelled of whisky. She nearly lost her balance as she whispered in Clara's ear, "Your bed or mine, darling? We can take turns back and forth, five minutes each. What do you say, Seger?"

Horrified, Clara gazed up at her husband. He was staring down at the woman with a blank look on his face. Clara wasn't even sure he knew who she was.

Then he said her name and Clara realized he did know. He was merely flustered. She'd never seen him flustered before.

"Mrs. Thomas, my wife, Lady Rawdon." He gestured toward Clara with his hand.

The woman stared at Clara for a second or two, then finally let go of Seger's sleeve. "Your *wife*?"

"Yes."

"I didn't know. No one said anything," she replied incredulously. She backed up a step and laid a gloved hand on her chest. "Good gracious, I'm frightfully embarrassed. I've been in Paris, you see, and I just returned yesterday and. . . ."

Seger turned toward Clara. "Darling, this is Mrs. Abigail Thomas."

The woman held out her hand. "How do you do?"

"Very well, thank you," Clara replied, shaking her hand.

The woman fiddled absently with a lock of hair around her ear as the three of them stood in awkward silence, then the woman commented on the weather and dropped her gaze to the ground.

"It was very nice seeing you, Lord Rawdon," she said, "and a pleasure to meet you, Lady Rawdon." She smiled sheepishly, turned from them, and left.

Seger watched her go, then faced Clara. "I do apologize."

Clara swallowed hard and tried to keep her voice steady. "No need. It wasn't your fault."

His chest rose and fell with a deep intake of breath. "I hope that sort of thing doesn't happen again. I'm surprised she hadn't heard."

"We married quickly, Seger. It's not likely that everyone would know. The news will get around soon enough."

He downed the rest of his champagne and smiled at her understanding, then escorted her back inside. Clara forced herself to forget about the incident and did not mention it again, but she did notice an unspoken tension between herself and her husband for the rest of the evening.

The next morning, Clara sat in the breakfast room sipping her tea and reading the newspaper.

Gillian entered quietly and sat down across from Clara. "Good morning, did you sleep well?"

"Yes, thank you," Clara replied, stifling a yawn, for she might have slept well, but she had not slept much. She and Seger had made love three times.

"Did you have a nice time at the assembly last night?" Gillian asked.

Gillian had arrived later in the evening with Quintina, and Clara had seen her talking to a number of handsome young men. "Yes, I did, and it looked like you were having a good time too. Who was that man with the blonde hair? He always seemed to laugh at what you were saying. You must have been very witty last night, Gillian."

"His name was Stanley Scott. His father is a baron from the north, so dear Stanley is only a mister. He seems very young, don't you think?"

"I don't know. I thought he looked kindhearted."

Gillian rolled her eyes. "Kindhearted and limp in the head."

Clara didn't know what to say. She picked up her tea and took another sip.

"I noticed that you barely left Seger's side," Gillian said after a few minutes of silence. Her eyebrows drew together. "Don't you trust him?"

The question caught Clara off guard. She set down her cup and tried not to gulp too loudly before she spoke. "Of course I trust him. We simply enjoy each other's company, that's all, and there were a number of people he wished to introduce me to."

Gillian swallowed her food. "Like Mrs. Thomas? I saw her speak to you. You did very well, Clara."

Clara felt her insides begin to churn. "I don't know what you mean."

"I saw you shake her hand. You were quite composed. One would never know."

"Never know what?"

"That you were seething inside."

Clara closed the newspaper and sat back. "I was not seething."

"Come now, Clara, you don't have to lie to me. I know how it is with Seger and all the women who want his . . . *services*. But you were very good. Just the kind of wife he needs."

Clara tried not to choke on her tongue. "Gillian—"

"I'm not sure I could do what you do, being American. I've heard you people have different expectations about marriage, that a man who strays is regarded with contempt." She shook her head at the notion and took another bite of her breakfast.

Clara didn't know what to say. She didn't think she'd be able to speak if she tried.

Somehow, however, she managed to find her voice, and thought it a miracle. "Gillian, I don't like what you are insinuating."

Gillian stopped chewing and stared at her. "Oh, heavens, I am sorry. It does bother you, doesn't it?"

Clara had to swallow over the bile rising up in her throat. "Nothing bothers me, because there is nothing like *that* going on. Seger was very apologetic about Mrs. Thomas's behavior."

"Of course he was. Do pardon me."

Clara took a deep breath. She picked up her paper, but Gillian did not take the hint. She spoke again. "I just don't want you to get hurt, that's all. I see how you look at him."

Clara set down her paper again. "I'm not going to get hurt."

"I just know how I would feel if *I* were his wife. He is a handsome and remarkable man. It would be difficult not to be possessive."

I am going to blow a gasket.

"Permit me to offer you some advice," Gillian said. "You must try to remember that you are an Englishwoman now, and English wives look the other way when their husbands take lovers. If he were *my* husband, that's what I would do. I wouldn't think twice about it, because he is worth it. Not only is he a marquess, but he is handsome and fascinating, too."

By this time, Clara's blood was boiling in her head. Her tone was sarcastic when she said, "So it wouldn't bother you at all if he went off with other women?"

Gillian sipped her tea and tossed her head. "No. I'd be happy that he chose me as his wife above all the rest—especially considering the fact that no one thought he would *ever* marry, because of Daphne. He loved her so deeply. If you could have seen them together, Clara. They were made for each other. They were kindred spirits, the best of friends. Some say that kind of love comes along only once in a lifetime."

She gazed dreamily into space, then wrenched her attention back to Clara. "Oh, but pardon me, I'm straying off topic. As I was saying, if I were Seger's wife, he would know that I would always be there for him and I would put his happiness first. He is a great man who deserves an understanding wife."

For Clara, whose fury had hit the ceiling quite some time ago, it became difficult to even see Gillian. Everything—from the tabletop to the chandelier over their heads to Gillian's mouth moving clownishly as she chewed—appeared red and grossly mutated.

Clara had not expected this from Gillian, who had been very sweet up until now. Why in God's name was she saying these cruel, hurtful things, and reminding Clara that she was not the love of Seger's life?

Then it dawned on Clara. It was like a gaslight exploding brightly inside her head.

Gillian was in love with Seger.

Chapter 17

❦

That night, while waiting for Seger to come to her, Clara was quite unable to refrain from thinking about the things Gillian had said to her that morning. She tried to tell herself that she was jumping to conclusions about the young woman's feelings, but it did little good. She couldn't forget the way Gillian had insisted that she would have been a perfect wife for Seger.

Clara wasn't angry at Seger. The rational part of her mind knew that he had done nothing wrong, at least not that she knew of. She was angry at Gillian for saying what she had said, and she was angry at Mrs. Thomas and Lady Cleveland for reminding her that her husband was coveted by other women, and that he would face temptation every day for the rest of his life.

Women would offer themselves to him. Desperate, lonely women who knew how gracious and selfless he was in the bedroom. Beautiful women, who wanted nothing more than a few casual hours with an expert lover—a man who knew by instinct exactly what they wanted. A man who knew just how to move to give them the most intense orgasm possible.

A small chill cooled her skin at the thought of all the women her husband had made love to, but she was sensible and she knew better than to dwell on it. It was in the past.

Was Gillian beautiful? she wondered suddenly. Not particularly. But she *knew* him, better than Clara herself knew him.

Later, after Seger had come and made love to her, he rolled onto his back and sighed. "I believe I like being a married man."

Clara tried to smile. "More than being a bachelor?"

He turned his head on the pillow to look at her. "If it means I get to bury myself inside of you every night, definitely."

"But what if I became ill and was sick for a month? What would become of our marriage if there was no sex? Would you wish for a different wife?"

He rolled onto his side to face her and rested his cheek on his hand. "I told you before that I desire no one but you."

Desire, yes, but love? Will there ever be love between us?

"You've asked me that question before," he said, "and I've answered you, yet here you are asking again. Is it because of what happened at the assembly last night?"

Clara realized how foolish she was sounding. He was right. She had asked this question before and he kept giving her the same answer. She had to try to accept it.

"I'm sorry, I'm saying silly things. I . . . I think it's because of the conversation I had with Gillian this morning. It made me uneasy."

He frowned. "What did you talk about?"

Clara hesitated, not sure if she should tell him, but then

she decided it was worth discussing. Perhaps it would bring them closer together on an emotional level, which was what she wanted after all.

"Gillian told me that she saw what happened with Mrs. Thomas, and she congratulated me for not making a fuss. She said that if *she* were your wife, she would give you the freedom you needed."

His eyebrows drew together. "I cannot believe you had this conversation."

"Neither can I. All day I've been thinking about it, and I've come to the conclusion that Gillian might be. . . . It's possible that she might be in love with you, Seger. Have you ever suspected it?"

Seger sat up and gaped down at her. "That's ridiculous."

Clara sat up, too, hugging the covers to her chest. "Is it?"

"Of course! She has never so much as glanced at me in that way. She thinks of me as a brother. I cannot even imagine such a thing."

"But if you could have heard her talking this morning. Haven't you noticed how she's been dressing lately? How she's been changing the way she looks?"

"No, I have not. I think you are letting your imagination get the best of you, Clara, and you always seem to think the worst of *me*."

"No, I am not accusing you of anything, Seger. I believe it is all on Gillian's side, and maybe she doesn't even know it herself."

"Know what? That she wishes she were my wife? Good God, if *she* doesn't know it, it hardly seems possible that *you* could."

"I just sensed it."

He got out of bed and pulled on his robe. "This is absurd, Clara. I understood your reservations about marrying me in the beginning, and I understand if you are upset about Mrs. Thomas's solicitation last night, but this, Clara—this is getting out of hand."

Her temper began to twitch within her. "You think I am having delusions?"

He sighed with resignation. "I think you are worried about your decision to marry me because of what happened last night, and it has caused you to be irrational."

Irrational?

"Gillian is just a girl," he continued, "a shy, quiet girl. She's not like Mrs. Thomas, so do not think what you are thinking. To tell you the truth, I'm getting tired of your lack of confidence in me. I told you I would endeavor to be a faithful husband, yet you keep bringing up this sort of thing. I'm tired of discussing it." He crossed to the door.

"Where are you going?" Clara asked, her anger rising. Seger had not understood any of what she was saying. He didn't believe her, he couldn't bring himself to doubt Gillian's sweetness, and he thought she was irrational.

Even if she was completely wrong, he could have at least been sympathetic and tried to ease her mind about it. Instead, he had called her feelings absurd. He had defended Gillian. He was walking out. He did not want to delve into her emotions. He wanted only light conversation and sex.

All he knew was how to be casual.

"I am going to get a drink and read for a while," he replied. "Suddenly I don't feel much like sleeping."

Nor do I, she thought miserably, flopping back down on to the bed after the door closed tightly behind him.

* * *

Clara couldn't sleep. She desperately needed to talk to someone, but she couldn't go to Gillian, nor could she go to her stepmother, who adored her niece and would probably react like Seger had.

Clara wished she could talk to her sister, but Sophia had gone to Bath with James to spend a few weeks with his mother and his sister, Lily, who had wished to escape the pressures of the London Season this year. Sophia had explained to Clara that Lily had gotten into some trouble two years ago, shortly after James and Sophia had wed. Lily had run off with a Frenchman. The whole thing had been covered over, but Lily, unfortunately, had not yet gotten over it. She was uneasy around men and didn't trust her own judgment.

After a moment's contemplation, Clara decided to write a letter to Sophia. If nothing else, it would help to express how she was feeling. She went to her desk, pulled out a clean sheet of stationery, and dipped her pen in the ink jar.

Dear Sophia,

It is the middle of the night and I cannot sleep, for I am distraught. This morning, Gillian said a number of things about Seger that made me uncomfortable, and I can only assume she said them to hurt me, for she is secretly in love with my husband.

I know it sounds absurd, and perhaps I should have waited until I had something more substantial to base my beliefs upon than my womanly instincts before I mentioned it to Seger. But I wanted so desperately for us to be close. I wanted to share my

*worries with him. I told him my suspicions, but it
did not go well. He did not believe a word of it. He
called me irrational, for he cannot believe that
Gillian would ever see him as anything other than a
brother figure.*

*Now I feel worse than ever about our marriage. I
feel as if I expected too much too soon, and I have
pushed him away. He was angry with me, and he
left our bed, and I fear that if he loses interest in me
(you know what kind of interest I mean) that there
will be nothing to keep him from leaving me, for
there is really so little depth of feeling between us to
begin with.*

*I miss you, dear sister, and I will look forward to
seeing you when you return.*

> *Love,*
> *Clara*

"Look what I found?" Quintina said to Gillian the next
morning, entering her niece's boudoir and waving a letter
in her hand. "It was sitting by the front door waiting to go
out with the rest of the family's correspondence, so I decided to take a peek."

Gillian was sitting at her dressing table, trying different
hairstyles. "What is it, Auntie?"

Quintina handed it to her niece. "It's a letter Clara wrote
to her sister last night. I almost feel like celebrating."

Gillian stared at it. "Aunt Quintina, it is unconscionable
to read someone else's mail. Can we be so devious?"

"You can't pretend to believe that Clara wasn't devious
when she did whatever she did to get Seger to propose. I
can only imagine what tactics she used."

Gillian considered that a moment, then slowly opened the letter and read it. "She told him what I said! I could brain her!"

"Now, now, it's not such a bad thing. She says Seger didn't believe it and he called her irrational. *Irrational*, Gillian. He would have absolutely no patience at all for an irrational wife. I believe we've found our strategy."

Still reeling with rage at the image of Clara telling Seger about their conversation that morning, Gillian glared impatiently at her aunt. "Which is what?"

"You must continue to say things that make her mad with jealousy. Hint at things—even things about Daphne—but never be clear. When you are with Seger, behave as you always have. Even ignore him a little more than usual, so that he will think Clara is imagining everything. If we can drive her to tears, that will be even better, because you know how he hates that sort of behavior. He'll think she's unbalanced. Then, I will top it all off with my trump card."

"What's your trump card, Auntie?"

Quintina smiled. "Would you really like to know?"

A wicked glint lighted Gillian's eyes. "Of course."

Quintina sat down on the bed. "As it happens, there is a gentleman from America. His name is Gordon Tucker, and he has agreed to do something for me."

Clara spent the afternoon riding with Gillian through Hyde Park. She had not wanted to go, but nor had she wanted Seger to learn that she'd refused, so she accepted Gillian's invitation, donned her black riding habit and top hat, and pasted on a smile.

The sky was overcast and the air cool, and as Clara galloped over the grass, she was surprised to be enjoying herself. Perhaps it was because Gillian was so quiet. She spoke very little, never mentioning their conversation the morning before. She merely rode ahead of Clara, who gladly brought up the rear. She had no desire to race with the girl.

They were on their way home, however, when Gillian slowed her pace and waited for Clara to ride up beside her. Their horses nickered and flicked their ears.

"What a glorious day for a ride," Gillian said. "We should do this every afternoon."

"It is lovely indeed."

"I enjoy our friendship very much, Clara. I am so happy Seger married you."

The statement surprised Clara, who instantly doubted her feelings from the day before. Perhaps she had jumped to conclusions, and Seger had been perfectly justified to react the way he had.

"I enjoy it, too, Gillian," she replied, patting her horse's neck.

They trotted side by side. "Did you know," Gillian said, "that my father had once wanted me to marry Seger?"

Clara's mood took an abrupt, deep dive. *Oh no.*

"Really?" She did not want to have this conversation!

"Yes," Gillian said brightly. "I refused, of course. I told my father that Seger was only a friend to me, that I could never imagine him as my husband, and then after the scandal with Daphne, and Seger's withdrawal from society . . . well, Father changed his tune after that. He wouldn't hear of it. He wanted someone respectable for me. Of course, I never believed that Seger was not respectable. I knew he had more honor than any other man in London, and he was merely pining away over Daphne, whom he had loved very deeply. But Father could never see that. He didn't know Seger intimately like I did." She gave Clara a sidelong glance. "But you must know him like that as well, because you're his wife. He must share everything with you. He probably tells you he loves you every time you're together." She looked up at the sky. "You are a very lucky woman, Clara."

Clara didn't feel so lucky at the moment. She felt like she was losing her mind. Nothing Gillian said hinted at anything untoward between her and Seger. Gillian had said that Seger had been a friend to her, and that her feelings went no deeper than that. Yet there was something in her tone. Something that goaded Clara—and seemingly on purpose. Gillian's voice was condescending, and she seemed intent to have Clara recognize it.

And she kept bringing up Daphne.

"So tell me," Gillian said, "does Seger say he loves you often?"

Clara swallowed over the urge to tell Gillian to go ride her horse straight into the Thames. She reminded herself, however, that Gillian was a member of Seger's family. Clara could not prove that Gillian was designing to upset her, and she could not, therefore, be so rude.

Lord, for all she knew, she *was* imagining it. She could merely be feeling vulnerable, because of all the other women in Seger's life—whether they were former lovers propositioning him at balls, hateful cousins, or the ghosts from his past.

Clara wasn't sure of anything anymore.

"If you don't mind," Clara said softly, "I would prefer to keep certain things private between Seger and myself. I'm sure you understand."

Gillian shifted her riding crop from one hand to the other. "Good heavens, forgive me. I did not mean to sound like a busybody. I loathe people like that. Don't you?"

Clara merely nodded, and they rode out of the park toward home.

That night, when Seger came to make love to her, she smiled flirtatiously and removed her nightgown, and pushed every thought of Gillian and Daphne, and all those other women, from her mind. She would not again make the mistake of spoiling the only intimacy that existed between herself and her husband.

"Has Seger ever shown you a picture of Daphne?" Gillian asked Clara over breakfast the next morning. "He had a miniature of her at one time. He must still have it somewhere. I can't imagine he would ever discard it."

Clara tried to speak with indifference. "No, I can't imagine he would either."

"Well, she was very beautiful, and the reason I ask is because you are beautiful, too. To be honest, you resemble Daphne. We've all noticed. Auntie mentioned it the first time she saw you. The housekeeper mentioned it, too."

Clara struggled hard not to reveal her animosity. She tried to sound unruffled and merely curious. "In what way do I resemble her?"

"You have the same color hair, and your mouth is the same." She pointed at her own mouth. "It's the lips. Seger has an appreciation for lips, doesn't he? Have you noticed that about him?"

As if you *should have noticed!*

Clara fought for self-control and forced herself to sound as confident and triumphant as Gillian. She smiled wickedly. "Yes, I suppose he does have an appreciation for lips."

She was pleased that her voice hinted at all kinds of sexual innuendo. To her surprise, Gillian's gaze shot straight across the table, and her cheeks flushed red. Clara had hit a sore spot.

So there! she said to herself, and happily sipped her tea.

Gillian was the first to break the awkward silence that followed. "Do you know about the gravestone?"

Clara saw the competitive glare in Gillian's eyes, and began to think that things were spiraling out of control. Gillian's resentful air was no longer subtle, no longer debatable. There was recognition now, for the both of them. Gillian knew she was throwing daggers, and she knew that Clara knew it. The dynamic between them was now a plain, open-field battle.

"What gravestone?" Clara felt suddenly fatigued.

Gillian raised an eyebrow in a hateful, invidious manner. Was she not even going to try to be subtle?

"Daphne's gravestone. He had one erected, you know."

Clara admitted defeat in this one, small skirmish. She sipped her tea and set the cup down in its saucer. "I didn't know that."

"No, I wouldn't think he would mention it. He had it erected in their private meeting place at his country estate, and planted daffodils all around it. Daffodils were her favorite. He told me about that once, when he was lonesome for her."

Clara took in a deep, calming breath, and leaned forward in her chair. "Gillian, your comments about my husband are beginning to give me a headache."

Gillian's chin rose up a notch. "I don't know why that would be the case."

"No?"

"No." There was such challenge in the cursed woman's eyes!

Clara squeezed her fists with fury. "In the future, let us

try to talk of other things. You have other interests, don't you? Music? Books?"

Gillian smiled sardonically. "I understand, Clara. I understand completely."

Clara had just finished brushing her hair before bed, when Seger entered her bedchamber carrying a bottle of red wine and two glasses.

"I thought you might be thirsty," he said, his voice low and seductive, his eyes warm.

Having never shared a bedroom with a man other than Seger, Clara wondered if all husbands were as gracious and charming as he.

Not likely, she decided, feeling quietly aroused. His overwhelming allure was why he was in such high demand as a lover, and why she could not resist him.

"You always know what I'm in the mood for," she replied.

With more than a little appreciation, Clara took in the breadth of his shoulders and the sheer perfection of his body as he moved gracefully across the room. He was flawless beyond contemplation. He looked like the statue of David, if one could imagine David wearing a black silk robe.

She, for one, imagined her husband quite without the robe.

Things were different tonight, however. For one thing, her monthly had begun today, and she wasn't sure how to handle it. What did husbands and wives do when the wife was indisposed?

On top of that, neither of them had mentioned their argument about Gillian. It was as if it had never occurred. They'd made love last night, but Clara had felt distanced from Seger and didn't know how to breach that distance without starting another argument.

She rose from her chair and forced herself to smile, all the while feeling like she barely knew her husband. Nor he her. They were like two casual acquaintances, making light conversation, laughing about trivial things, and making love. Though he picked up on each and every desire she had sexually, and satisfied each and every one beyond any expectation, he didn't want to hear about her anxieties or problems. He just wanted her to smile and be beautiful and amusing.

She was thankful that it was easy to smile and be beautiful when he was making love to her, for that was how he made her feel.

As she watched him pour the wine, however, she realized uneasily that the persona she was forced to keep up when he was *not* making love to her was beginning to try her patience.

There were moments when she wanted to shout at Seger, or throw a vase at him to stir up some emotion between them. But she feared that if she did that, he would think she was irrational again, and she did not wish him to think that. She needed to hold onto his respect, and build their intimacy from there.

He handed her a glass. "Try this, darling. It's the best we had in the house."

She sipped the wine and felt the most pleasant sensation of heat pouring down her throat and relaxing all her limbs. She had needed that.

"It's delicious," she whispered.

He held up his own glass. "Not nearly as delicious as you. To your beauty." He took a long swig.

Clara watched him in the dim lamplight, marveling at his own beauty—the square line of his jaw, his strong, masculine hands. Sometimes it seemed like he had no awareness of the potency of his appeal. Other times, he knew exactly how to use his charm.

Distracted as she was by her husband's attractiveness, she still couldn't get the image of Daphne's gravestone out of her mind. Seger had erected it on his country estate, and the memorial to his first love would always be there, even after Clara moved in.

She wondered if he still went to visit it. Did he continue to bring daffodils? Would he carry on the tradition after Clara was living there?

She shook her head at herself, and tried to sweep those thoughts from her mind. She did not want to spoil their evening together. Instead, she sat down on the bed and asked him about his day, resolving to make this a pleasant, memorable night.

As she watched him saunter toward her, sleek and irresistible, she knew it wouldn't be difficult.

Seger gazed down at his wife and wondered how it was possible that any woman could be so exquisite in every way—from her earthly beauty down to her angelic, bright charm. Her smile was everything to him. Sometimes it was sweet and adorable, other times confident and poised, and still other times, it was sexually charged and drove him around the bend with hot, blazing need. She was the perfect combination of innocence and worldliness.

He had forgotten their conversation of a few nights ago, and she had seemed to forget it, too. She had not mentioned Gillian again, and he was glad. He did not want to be reminded of the fact that Clara didn't completely trust him, when he had done everything to earn and deserve her trust. Nor did he want to talk about Gillian when he was with Clara. Gillian was the last person on his mind.

He set down his glass and climbed onto the bed, then took Clara into his arms. He pressed his mouth to hers and gloried in her wine-flavored tongue as it mingled with his, curling into his mouth and sending hot flashes of eroticism straight down to his sexual core.

God, with the exception of a few small impediments, marriage was bloody spectacular so far.

Though he couldn't imagine it being this good with anyone else. He had never been the slightest bit inclined to take this route with any other woman before.

Well, he had with one woman, but that had been a very different time.

He eased Clara down onto the pillows and began to unbutton the top of her gown, but she stopped him. "Seger . . ."

Stalled briefly—and a tad surprised—he drew back. "Yes?"

"I'm not sure we can do this tonight."

He blinked a few times. "What do you mean?"

"I mean . . ." She rose from the bed and walked toward the door. She folded her arms over her chest, looking cold. "My monthly arrived today."

All the breath sailed out of his lungs, and he realized he'd been a little wary of her response. He'd actually feared she simply wasn't in the right "mood," even after he'd given her his best open-mouthed kiss. He was relieved to discover it was something else.

"I see." It wasn't often he'd had to deal with this problem. Most women he knew simply stayed out of "social" situations when they weren't fully able to consummate them.

Then it occurred to him that this meant Clara was not with child. "Are you disappointed?"

"Disappointed that we can't make love tonight?" she replied, in the sweetest, most innocent tone of voice that melted his heart.

"First of all," he said, "we can make love if you wish, but that's not what I mean. Are you disappointed that we didn't conceive a child?"

Her face softened. Her voice was shaky. "A little, I suppose. I do want to give you a son."

He approached her and took her into his arms. "Don't be disappointed, darling. It often takes a few months, I've heard. Look on the bright side, we will have to try doubly hard in the weeks to come. I don't think I'll mind that very much, will you?"

Clara smiled. "No, I won't. But what will it mean for tonight? Things are rather awkward down there." She touched his lips with her thumb. "Will you go back to your room?"

"Do you want me to?"

"No." Her voice became breathy like a whisper. "There is still your pleasure to consider."

He snickered and felt his arousal grow. "What exactly are you referring to?"

His adorable wife went down on her knees and untied the belt of his robe. Her eyes were dark and mischievous as she looked up at him. "I think you know exactly what I'm referring to."

He cupped her head in his large hand. "I was only trying to be courteous, love. I didn't want to presume. . . ."

"Presume all you like. There's no point wasting a good bottle of wine." Then she put her mouth on him and lit his body on fire.

Seger lay on the bed, stroking Clara's soft cheek and kissing her in the darkness. He all at once realized that he was not the least bit disappointed to be lying in bed with a woman, after having agreed to refrain from making love to her.

Not that he himself wouldn't mind staining the sheets, but sweet Clara seemed self-conscious and he did not wish to embarrass her.

God. He hadn't felt such tenderness in a long, long time. Eight years to be exact. He had forgotten what it felt like.

He suddenly remembered the look on Clara's face earlier when she'd told him she was not with child. She had been disappointed. He had taken away that disappointment with a compassionate smile and a few choice words.

Maybe there was hope for him. Maybe, as he and Clara grew closer, she would begin to trust him, and he would not feel so inept when it came to her more complicated emotions. He certainly felt close to her now, and not just in the physical sense.

He closed his eyes, pulled her into his arms, and went to sleep.

Chapter 18

Dear Clara,

Last night, I made the mistake of asking the hostess at a dinner party to pass me the gravy, and a dreadful silence fell upon the table. No one spoke to me for the rest of the evening. Mrs. Wudsworth, my lovely English governess, has since informed me that one should never ask the hostess for anything. Ask the servants. But you probably already knew that . . .

Adele

Seeing her sister enter the ballroom, Clara excused herself from the other ladies to go and greet her. "Sophia, you're back. How was Bath? Were you able to convince Lily to come home?"

"Bath was wonderful and Lily seemed in good spirits. I tried to suggest that she finish out the Season here, but she wouldn't have it. She has not gained back her confidence."

Clara nodded sympathetically. "It might take some time."

Clara knew because she had been there.

They strolled around the room together, smiling and nodding at the other guests, then Sophia looped her arm through Clara's. "I received your letter."

"I was wondering if you had. I regret writing it now."

"Why?"

"Because everything seems better. I haven't mentioned my feelings about Gillian to Seger since then, and we have been very happy the past couple of weeks."

Sophia stopped and faced Clara. "But you seemed so troubled when you wrote the letter. Has Gillian said anything else like that since then?"

"A few things, yes, but I've learned to ignore it and do my best not to let it bother me. I believe she is rather hateful, but I wouldn't say that to anyone but you. I can't insult or scorn Seger's relations. His stepmother would hate me, and I don't want that. I want to be accepted by his family."

They began walking again. "But if she is saying things intentionally to hurt you, you should tell your husband at least."

"I can't right now. When I imagine myself repeating the things she says, it truly does sound like nothing. She's never said anything specifically damaging. It's merely her tone and the look in her eye that insinuates things. Seger would think I was being 'irrational' again. In his opinion, Gillian is a harmless, shy girl who wouldn't know a nasty thought if it bit her on the nose. Besides, I think it bothers him that I don't trust him."

Sophia spoke softly. "But do you think he would take her side over yours? After you've been married almost a month? He should realize by now that you are not irrational. Certainly there must be some deeper affection between you. Is there?"

Clara swallowed uncomfortably. "I don't know."

Sophia led her behind a potted tree fern where they could sit down on a sofa and speak in private. "Has he told you he loves you?"

Clara dropped her gaze to her hands in her lap. "No, and I have no idea if he is even moving in that direction. He treats me with kindness and consideration, but . . ."

"Does he sleep all night with you?"

"Yes, every night."

"Well, that's something."

"I suppose. He is very tender and loving and he flatters me, but I believe that is his natural way when he makes love to women. It's why they all want him so badly."

Sophia shook her head. "You mustn't think those things, Clara. His bachelor days are over and you are his only bed partner. Unless . . . you don't suspect that he is—"

"No, no. We are together every night and there has never been any evidence of . . . well, another woman's perfume or anything like that."

Sophia leaned back and looked the other way. "I can't believe we are discussing such things. There is no need of it, really."

"No, you're right," Clara replied. "Truly, I have let go of thoughts like those over the past few weeks. Well, for the most part. He really has been wonderful, Sophia."

"I'm glad. And if Gillian continues to behave in a beastly way, it will come about right. Seger's an intelligent man, and as his respect for you grows, he will see the truth." She took on a playful tone and waved her fist dramatically in the air. "Good will triumph!"

Clara laughed. "I don't know what I would do without you, Sophia."

"You would get along just fine."

After meeting with his solicitor to discuss a small financial matter, Seger walked through Piccadilly and found himself dreaming of his wife.

He had never imagined marriage would turn out to be so immensely pleasing; he had certainly had his doubts.

Well, he still had his doubts. There was the issue of Clara not trusting him, which continued to trouble him, but he hoped that would soon fade. He was doing his best to work through it.

Other than that, Clara was beautiful, amusing, enchanting. He delighted in making love to her for endless hours in the night, and he was surprised to discover how much he loved just talking to her. His desire for her was overwhelming.

They often stayed up late, conversing about their days as well as books and art and society. He adored her impressions of life and people. Her original, insightful opinions always fascinated him. Perhaps it was because she was American, and had been brought up with different values. He liked how she made him look at life.

He also realized that he was beginning to feel less awkward in relating to her on a personal level, and the notion pleased him.

He felt closer to Clara lately, as if something inside him had awakened. He didn't know what to say about it, though, if he should say anything at all. Things were so pleasant between them, maybe there was no need. Clara seemed happier with their marriage. Perhaps she could sense what was growing between them, and would learn to trust him over time.

If only he could go back and repeat that argument they'd had about Gillian. He would handle it differently. He would be less defensive. He certainly wouldn't walk out on her.

God, he should have been more understanding. Clara had been through a great deal with a pushy duke threatening to ruin her, then the loss of her virginity outside of wedlock, followed by a hasty wedding and the severance of her American citizenship. No wonder she had felt uneasy about certain things.

Perhaps tonight he would apologize to her about the way he had handled that conversation, and ask if she still felt uncomfortable around Gillian.

He passed a dress shop and stopped to look at a ball gown in the window. It would look stunning on Clara. She would outshine every woman in London. In the world, for that matter, with her delectable smile and her winsome laughter. The color of the dress was magnificent. He moved on and decided he would tell her about the dress that night. She might want to have a look at it herself.

Good God, he thought with a smile, tapping his walking stick along the ground. He must be deeply besotted if he was going to talk to his wife about a dress. Imagine that.

He became aware of his stomach growling so he turned into a small cafe. After being seated in the back, he ordered the lamb and requested a newspaper.

Not five minutes later, he heard someone say his name. He looked up.

"Quintina. Gillian." He set down the paper and stood. "What are you doing here?"

As he rose to kiss his stepmother on the cheek, he realized that their relationship had not been quite so strained lately. He had not thought about his anger toward her because of what had happened with Daphne, which had been the most prominent dynamic between them for years. He wondered if Clara's companionship was affecting him in subtle ways that were influencing other areas of his life.

"I was just about to ask you the same thing," Quintina said. "We've been shopping and thought we would stop for a bite to eat."

Seger gestured toward the empty chairs at his table. "Please join me."

The ladies ordered their meals and told Seger about their purchases—hair ribbons and combs for Gillian, a hat for Quintina. Just before the food arrived, however, Quintina pressed a hand to her head.

"My word, I have developed the most painful headache."

Gillian touched her hand. "Can I get you anything, Auntie?"

"No, no, thank you, dear." She touched her head again. "Ooh. It is quite severe." Glancing around the cafe, she said, "I believe I will skip lunch. Would you mind, Seger, if I leave you to bring Gillian home? I wouldn't want to spoil her afternoon."

"Certainly."

"That's not necessary, Auntie," Gillian said. "I'll go with you."

At that moment, the food arrived. "Don't be silly, my dear girl. Enjoy your lunch."

Seger walked Quintina to the door, then returned to his table. He spent a pleasant hour with Gillian, though as usual, he had to work hard to keep the conversation going.

Clara dressed for dinner and walked to the drawing room. She did not expect to see Seger, for he had told her he would be dining at his club with an old friend from Charterhouse, who now lived in India, but was in London for a fortnight.

Clara entered the drawing room. Gillian stood in front of the window, looking out. She turned and smiled brightly when Clara entered the room.

"You look lovely this evening," Gillian said.

Clara wondered how it was possible that Gillian could be so hateful at times and so intentionally charming at others. "So do you."

Sitting down on the sofa, she wished she had brought a book with her so she wouldn't feel obligated to talk, but she had not thought of it, so here she was.

Gillian sat down next to her. "Did Seger tell you?"

The look in the young woman's eyes made Clara's stomach career with dread. "About what?"

"About the dress? We had lunch together in Piccadilly today, and he told me how much he liked it. I believe he was thinking of it for you."

"You believe?"

And my husband met you for lunch?

They're cousins, she told herself. *Cousins sometimes eat together.*

Gillian stared at her blankly. "Yes, I think that's what he meant when he mentioned it, though I suppose one can never be sure."

Clara decided not to respond to that. In fact, she was

not going to say one single word. She would not help
Gillian spin any tales.

The tense silence made the girl rise to her feet. She
wandered to the fireplace and fiddled with knickknacks as
if she were bored. "It was a very nice lunch, except for
when we talked about Lady Cleveland. I hope I didn't
sound too angry."

The normal response would have been "Angry about
what?" but Clara didn't let herself ask the question, because that's exactly what Gillian wanted her to do.

Nevertheless, the girl chattered on. "I really do hate
that woman. I suppose you must hate her, too. I wish there
was some way we could ruin her, you and I together, but I
don't think Seger would like that very much, would he?"

Still, Clara said nothing, but her teeth were grinding
together.

Gillian continued. "I know I once said that if I were
Seger's wife, I would look the other way, but now I'm not
so sure. I do see your plight. When I actually bumped into
Lady Cleveland today in one of the shops, my blood literally boiled, because I knew Seger had just left her house.
He said he'd gone to see his solicitor, and maybe he did,
briefly, but I knew the truth." She gazed down at Clara. "I
suppose it's our lot to suffer through that sort of thing,
isn't it?"

That was it. Clara couldn't swallow another minute of
this harassment. She stood. "*Our* lot?" Clara couldn't take
it anymore. She raised her chin high in the air. "I've had
enough of this, Gillian."

Gillian put on an innocent air. "Clara, I thought we
were becoming close, and could share things with each
other. I don't like your tone."

Clara almost laughed out loud at the nonsense spurting

from this woman's mouth. "Nor do I like yours. And I doubt Seger would think too much of it either if he could hear you now. You are trying to badger me, and your purpose is ridiculously obvious. You're like a bad actress in a bad play, and if I weren't so disgusted with you, I might even find it entertaining."

The color drained from Gillian's cheeks. "How dare you. I am a member of Seger's family."

"And I am his wife," Clara said. "The mother of his future children. Mistress of this house."

Gillian narrowed her gaze and approached Clara. She pointed a finger at her. "You think *I'm* being obvious, but do you know what is *really* obvious? How much you hate me, but that is not surprising, is it?"

"What are you insinuating?"

"I am insinuating nothing. In fact, I hope I am being very frank. You can't stand the fact that I am close to Seger and you are not. I know that you are not, because I know him so well. He shares his deepest feelings with me, and he tells me that you are little more than a stranger to him. So don't blame *me* for what is missing in your marriage, and don't go complaining to him about me, because he will see right through you. If Seger is distant and that upsets you, it is not my fault. I have done nothing wrong. I assure you I am still only a close friend to him. Nothing has happened, at least not yet, but you hate me anyway, don't you? Even though I've done nothing to deserve it." She turned away from Clara and walked to the window. "If you're going to hate someone, hate Lady Cleveland."

Clara stood motionless. Words failed to come. She couldn't think of how to respond to Gillian's outburst. She was in complete, utter shock.

Just then, Quintina entered the room and kissed Clara

on the cheek. "Good evening my dear. What a beautiful day it was." She sat down on the sofa. "I believe Seger is having dinner at his club tonight, isn't he?"

Gillian raised an eyebrow at Clara, as if to suggest he was not at his club. Her expression was triumphant. It screamed, "I told you so."

When Clara did not respond, Quintina glanced at Gillian in the corner and said with a jolly tone, "Well, you both look famished. Are you ready to eat?"

They wordlessly nodded their heads and moved into the dining room. It was the worst meal Clara had eaten since she'd set foot on English soil.

Clara was removing her earrings, feeling angry and nauseous, when a knock sounded at her bedchamber door. Hoping it would be Seger—yet not at all sure what she would say to him if it was—she went to answer it.

Her mother-in-law stood in the corridor.

"Quintina."

"Hello, my dear," the woman said with a sympathetic tone to her voice. "May I come in?"

"Of course." Clara stepped aside and invited the woman in.

Quintina moved to the center of the room. "You were quiet at dinner. Is something wrong?"

Clara thought carefully about how she should answer that. She couldn't tell Quintina that she'd had a huge fight with her niece, especially knowing how much the woman loved her dead sister's only child.

Nor could Clara tell her that she was worried, rationally or not, that her husband was rolling around in another woman's bed at this very moment.

"I was just tired, that's all."

Quintina nodded, but seemed unconvinced. She let her gaze sweep the room. "You have many lovely things." She picked up a framed photograph on Clara's desk. "Is this you and your sisters?"

"Yes. It was taken when I was twelve."

"Indeed. You were lovely even then. All of you were." She set the picture down and met Clara's eyes again. "Please tell me what's bothering you. Is it the conversation you had with Gillian this evening?"

Clara stared in silence at her mother-in-law.

"I sensed the two of you had argued, and when I asked Gillian about it, she told me you discussed Lady Cleveland. Poor Gillian. She's very concerned about you and feels terrible for bringing it up. Are you all right, Clara?"

Clara wondered how it was possible that Gillian could make everyone think she was kind at heart, when in reality she was pure, unadulterated evil.

Quintina stepped forward and hugged Clara. The gesture was unexpected, and Clara was surprised at how much she appreciated it. She realized suddenly how very alone she was in this house.

Still, she felt she should be careful with Quintina.

"It was nice of you to come and check on me," she said.

The woman touched Clara on the nose. "I couldn't help it. You seemed distraught."

"Truly, I'm fine."

"You're sure?"

"Yes."

Quintina was reluctant to let go of Clara's upper arms. "You mustn't worry about Lady Cleveland," she said. "The woman just appeals to Seger's sense of rebelliousness. It won't last. They never do. The important thing to remember is that he married *you*. You're the one he chose.

I would offer to talk to him about it, but I don't think it would do any good. He would only deny it, as any gentleman would."

For the second time that evening, Clara was at a loss for words. She couldn't imagine what Gillian had said to Quintina. All she could do was stare at the woman before her, while the reminder of Lady Cleveland burned inside her brain.

After a few seconds, Quintina backed away toward the door. "Promise you will come and talk to me if you ever feel unhappy or unsure about anything. I would like us to be close, Clara. I never had a daughter of my own."

She walked out, leaving Clara to contemplate everything that had occurred that day, and finally resolve to talk to her husband about it as soon as he arrived home.

And she would be extremely, assuredly rational in her quest for the truth. No matter how badly she wanted to pitch a vase.

Seger walked into Clara's bedchamber shortly before midnight. His breath smelled of whisky and cigars.

"Did you have a nice time?" Clara asked in an intentionally pleasant voice, even though inside she was reeling with doubts and anxieties about Gillian and Lady Cleveland. Even that wretched dress Gillian had mentioned.

Seger tugged at his neckcloth and began to unbutton his shirt. "I did, thank you. Lord Cobequid is looking well. He intends to return to India in a couple of weeks."

Seger told her about their dinner and their billiards game, and related some of Lord Cobequid's tales of the British colony abroad.

When Seger slipped into bed, he made a move to pull Clara into his arms. "How was your evening, darling?"

Clara stiffened, keeping to her side of the bed. "It was interesting. I talked to Gillian tonight," she said matter-of-factly, not caring if the subject exploded in her face and drove her husband from the room like it did the last time she'd brought it up.

She wanted a fight, dammit. She wanted honesty and candor, no matter how disagreeable it was for her husband, and she wanted it now.

To her surprise, Seger sat forward and raised her chin with his finger, so he could look into her eyes. "I've been meaning to speak to you about Gillian."

Clara felt her brow furrow.

"I wanted to apologize," he said, "for the way I reacted the last time we talked about her. It was wrong of me. I should have been a better listener."

Clara sat up. "Seger, I . . ."

She what, exactly? Lord, she didn't have a clue what she wanted to say to him. She was relieved to hear him offer this apology, but something inside her was suspicious about why he was offering it tonight.

He'd had lunch with Gillian that day. Had he suspected, like Clara, that Gillian had feelings for him? Was he ready to take her side and tell her she'd been right?

Or was he trying to appease her because he was hiding something—a rendezvous with Lady Cleveland perhaps?—and he wanted to keep her happy and prevent her from asking pointed questions?

He pushed a lock of hair behind her ear. "I have come to realize that I haven't always been easy to talk to."

"Well . . ."

"I'm sorry, Clara. Our marriage came to fruition very quickly, and I can admit now that I was apprehensive, but since we spoke our vows, I have learned that the reality of marriage is not nearly as frightening as the idea of it. The decision was the hardest part, and now that it's done, I find marriage more pleasant then I ever could have imagined."

Clara swallowed over her shock.

"I believe," he said, "that we've been getting to know each other better. Don't you agree?"

She gazed up at him with parted lips. "I suppose."

Where was this coming from? She wished she could wholeheartedly accept it as a simple move toward a deeper intimacy between them, but knowing his previous lifestyle, his reckless desire for women—and considering everything that had occurred that day—how could she help but be doubtful?

"You don't feel that you have given up a great deal?" she asked. "Your whole way of life?"

Assuming that he had actually given it up.

Seger leaned forward and kissed her. "Giving it up hasn't bothered me for one instant. What I gave up doesn't hold a candle to what I've gained."

He kissed her again, more deeply this time, and despite her desire to fight with her husband, Clara couldn't help but revel in the feel of his mouth upon hers, probing hotly, causing the most pleasurable stirring within her breast.

He was the personification of sexuality. Charismatic, erotic and enticing, he made her quiver from within and forget all the concerns of the day. All that mattered when he touched her was that he continued to touch her, with his expert hands and his astounding talent to please. All she wanted was his body.

Clara realized all at once that she *wanted* to be appeased. She wanted him to make her forget their problems. She wasn't proud of it, but there it was.

How thoroughly English she had become.

Don't be too hard on yourself. For weeks you've longed to hear those words from him.

If only she could believe them. If only Gillian had not been planting seeds of doubt in Clara's mind.

Suddenly, she felt a violent need to clear the air. She dragged her lips from Seger's, and pulled back. She could not continue to guess and brood about matters when she did not know the facts. That way lay madness.

Perhaps she was not so English after all.

"I heard you had lunch with Gillian today," she said.

He gazed at her questioningly. "Yes, but it was a chance meeting."

She recognized how intent he was to assure her of that. Lord, she hated this.

She reminded herself that Gillian was not to be trusted. The woman was determined to make her feel unstable, and Clara would not under any circumstance let that happen. She had to keep an open mind and not rush to blame Seger. She must not look at the vase on the mantel.

She sat up. "Seger, I must be candid. I'm going to tell you what Gillian said to me today, and you can form your own opinions about it. I just need to relate it to you, for my own peace of mind."

He sat up, too, and began to look concerned. "What did she say?"

Clara faced him. "She said things about Lady Cleveland. She made references and suggested that you were still involved with her. Are you?"

"I am not."

Clara inhaled sharply. One down, one more to go. Then she would judge his responses accordingly.

"Gillian also said that you confided all your deepest feelings to her, and you thought I was little more than a stranger to you."

"I beg your pardon? She said those exact words?"

Clara's heart was clamoring, her stomach churning with dread. What if he thought she was insane and imagining things? What if he took Gillian's side?

What if he really *was* still involved with Lady Cleveland?

"That is exactly what she said," Clara replied as calmly as possible.

Seger sat up on the bed. "Are you sure you didn't misinterpret her words?"

There it was—the suggestion that she was irrational.

"What I told you was almost verbatim. Truly, Seger, I do not want to cause trouble, but Gillian has said some terrible things to me, and I don't think I can bear it another minute. She has tried to make me doubt you, and I must admit, I am a vulnerable target in that regard."

He gazed at her for a long, long time. "Do you doubt me?"

As difficult as this was at the moment, the most important thing was to nurture what intimacy existed between them, and close the emotional distance. She needed her husband to understand her heart, and she needed to understand his. There had to be truth between them. "I must be honest with you. I am not sure."

There. It was out, and thank God the vase was still on the mantel.

Seger sat up and pulled her into his arms. "Clara, my darling, you mustn't believe those things. I adore you, and I have not even seen Lady Cleveland since the night you met her at that wretched ball. Gillian had no reason to say any of that. I don't know why she would even think it."

Clara fought the tears that were filling her eyes. "I don't know either, except what I suspected weeks ago—that she has feelings for you, and she hates me because I am your wife. Even if it were true—that you were seeing Lady Cleveland—why would Gillian want to tell me and hurt me with it?"

He held her close and kissed her cheeks and then her mouth. "It is not true. Clara, have you been miserable because of this?"

"I have tried not to let her get the best of me, but I must admit, I . . . I do not completely trust you."

Seger held her in front of him so he could see her face. His eyes were dark and growing darker every second. "I don't know what to do to change that. I want your trust, and dammit I deserve it, for I've done nothing wrong."

He pulled her into his arms again. "For God's sake, I am not seeing Lady Cleveland! I am changing. I have begun to care for you in a way I hadn't thought possible, because I hadn't let myself care for anyone in a very long time."

Because of Daphne.

Clara almost sobbed. "Your apology means a lot to me, Seger. More than you could ever know. I want to try to make things better between us. I do want to believe you."

He kissed her again, then slipped out of the bed and reached for his trousers.

"Where are you going?" Clara asked.

"To speak plainly with my cousin. She will apologize to you, and if she refuses, she will be packing her belongings tonight."

Clara realized the ramifications of such an action, and climbed out of bed, too. "You mustn't do that. Quintina would be devastated. She would hate me."

"She would not be justified in that hatred."

"Perhaps not, but it wouldn't matter in the end. Emotions don't always make sense, especially when they concern a loved one. Quintina adores her niece, and I do not want to be responsible for a rift between them. Quintina might begin to resent me."

"What would that matter?"

Clara paused a moment. "Earlier tonight, after she learned what Gillian had said to me about Lady Cleveland, she came to my room and was very kind to me. I believe that her intentions were good. She said she never had a daughter of her own, and I feel there might be a chance for closeness between us. I don't want to spoil that. Please, all that matters is that you and I are clear about our marriage. If I am confident in your fidelity and affections, Gillian cannot hurt me."

But was she truly confident? She wanted to be. She wanted to believe that he was sincere in everything he'd said tonight—that he was no longer seeing Lady Cleveland, that his grief over Daphne was fading away, and that he was finally ready to let go of his fears and just love her.

Seger hesitated a moment, gazing at her in the lamplight, then walked around the bed and took her into his arms. "You are a remarkable woman. Are you sure?"

"Yes. I don't want a confrontation over me to divide this family. I will be able to handle Gillian from now on. Now that you know what she is trying to do, she has no power. I will tell her that you know, you can even say so yourself, and I wouldn't be surprised if she leaves quietly on her own."

He shook his head, as if in disbelief. "How was a man like me ever so blessed to meet a woman like you at a Cakras Ball?"

Clara smiled. "I was blessed too."

He eased her down onto the bed. "Let's count those blessings tonight." His voice was husky and sensual. "Starting with this one."

He took her nipple into his mouth and proved once again the indisputable basis for his reputation as every woman's dream lover. Soon, Clara was writhing with pleasure, feeling the heavy weight of the day lifting from her shoulders. Her body grew warm, and she buried her fingers in her husband's thick hair.

"I wish we could go on our honeymoon now," she whispered. "If only we could be alone together."

She wanted to forge a deeper bond.

He kissed her tenderly on the mouth. "I would like that, too, but I have an interview with a business speculator at the end of the week that cannot be rescheduled. I have many questions I want to ask him, and he is only in town on the twenty-third."

"Could we go somewhere closer and be back in time?" Clara asked. "What about your country estate? I haven't seen it yet, Seger, and I am desperate to see your home. Our home."

He stopped what he was doing and looked up at her. "Why not just stay here? We could spend the days together."

Clara sighed. "There are too many distractions. I want to be alone with you. Just the two of us. I want to stay in bed all day and not worry about my mother-in-law knowing what we are doing, or my sister dropping by to visit. I want to go for long walks across country meadows with you and listen to the birds. I want to make love in the woods."

A slow, lazy smile touched his lips. "You know that I am always at your service. Anywhere and anytime."

She ran her fingers through his hair, and replied playfully, "I've come to discover that. Please say you'll take me, Seger. I want to see our home."

Seger inched up on the bed to look into her eyes. "You should know, Clara, that I don't really consider Rawdon Hall to be my home."

Surprised, she gazed at him blankly. "But it's where you were born and raised, isn't it?"

"Yes, but I haven't been there in a long time."

She felt a heaviness settle in her chest. "Why ever not?"

He sighed. "I always go abroad during the winter, and when I return to England I come here to our London House. I've always dealt with estate matters from a distance."

"But why?" she asked again, fearing she knew the answer.

He shrugged. "I don't really enjoy being there."

Clara's eyebrows drew together. "Is it the house? Is it uncomfortable or cold? Or do you not like your neighbors?"

It was all wishful thinking, and she knew it.

He shrugged again. "The neighbors are fine, I just . . ." He sat up, then raked his fingers through his hair. "I suppose if I don't tell you now, you'll hear about it from someone else, because the gossip is rampant in the country, so I might as well just say it. I haven't been home in eight years, Clara, because . . . because I did not wish to be reminded of Daphne."

Clara stared at her husband in bleak silence. *There it was . . . out in the open at last.*

Seger touched her cheek. "You look wounded, Clara."

"No, I'm not." But her voice was shaky.

"I promise you, my feelings for Daphne are ancient history. She might have been my reason to leave eight years ago, but the fact that I have not returned since then is merely because I became a creature of habit. I assure you, she is forgotten."

But until you married me, she was the only woman you ever loved. Perhaps she still is.

"Come, lie down," Seger said, fluffing the pillows. "There has been too much talk of other women tonight, and I don't wish to think of anyone but you."

Clara forced herself to smile. She snuggled close to her husband.

"And you're right, darling," he added. "We are newly married. We need to spend some time alone together. I will send word to Rawdon Hall first thing in the morning, and tell them to expect us the day after. It's time we embarked upon our new life."

Clara rested her cheek upon his warm shoulder, smiled when he kissed her forehead, and wished she could feel better about the new life she had begun.

Gillian stood at the window in her bedchamber and did not even try to fight the tears that were pouring from her eyes like two cascading waterfalls. Her cheeks were drenched. Her nose was running and she couldn't stop sniffling.

She pressed her hand to the cool pane of glass and watched Seger's coach disappear down the road. She cursed that vile American cow. Clara had lured him away with sex. How could Gillian ever compete with that?

But when, she wondered miserably, had she ever been able to compete with anyone where Seger was concerned? She had been fooling herself to think that Seger could ever fall in love with her. She had no idea how to charm a man. How to be coquettish. Everything Gillian had told Clara about her father wanting her to marry Seger had been a lie. He would never even have considered such a thing. He'd always called Gillian an embarrassment.

Gillian should not have let Quintina manipulate her. She should have given up all hope the day of the wedding. Quintina had been wrong to suggest that things could change. She had given Gillian false hopes.

Quintina entered the room, saw her niece sobbing by the window, and immediately embraced her. "There, there darling. Go ahead and cry, get it all out. That's better. All will work out, you'll see."

But Gillian did not see. She pushed her aunt away and wiped the tears from her eyes. "No! I have tried and tried, but she will not be broken! I can't do it anymore. She is not behaving the way you said she would. You said she would be driven to tears, but I am the one who is crying."

"Get a hold of yourself, dear. The war is not over."

"This is not war, Auntie. It is a marriage, and I am an outsider. I do not belong here. I should go home to my uncle's house and forget about Seger. I should prepare for a Season of my own next year, and find someone else."

Quintina moved forward again and took Gillian into her arms. "You are upset because they just left, but they will be back and we still have one more scheme to execute. Please don't give up now. I want Susan, God rest her soul, to know that I made your dreams come true, and to be frank with you, dear, I can't bear to think that my future grandchildren will be half American. Wait until we at least try all the possibilities."

"I'm beginning to think this is more for you than it is for me! You hate the fact that your parents lost their home to a deep-pocketed American, and you can't stand to see it happen again. But Clara is mistress of this house now, Auntie, and there's nothing we can do about it."

"There is!" Quintina replied desperately.

"I can't wait anymore. This is too painful! Too humiliating! I cannot bear to be in this house when he goes to her bed every night!"

"Gillian, calm yourself. Sit down and listen to me. Something significant is going to happen soon. I have been communicating with that man I told you about—the one from America. He has incriminating information about Clara and his very presence will knock her clear off her glowing pedestal. I have asked him to come to London, and I assure you, the situation is going to be deliciously sordid. He is on his way even as we speak."

Gillian sat down and tried to stop crying as she listened in foggy comprehension to what her aunt told her would happen next.

Chapter 19

Adele,

I love Seger more than anything in the world and I want to make him happy, but there are still so many barriers between us. While I believe I have overcome the problem with Gillian, I am still not at ease. I must continue to live with the knowledge that what happened to the woman he loved eight years ago has left a deep hole in his heart. She is the sole reason that his heart is so inaccessible, and while I knew that from the beginning, I had thought my love would fill that hole. I have just learned, however, that he has not returned to his country home since the day he left, shortly after she died.

I am hoping our trip there today will bring us closer, and help him to finally open up to me completely. . . .

Clara

As the carriage approached Rawdon Hall and drove around the circular fountain in front of the house, Seger realized uneasily that an emotional awakening did not come without some discomfort, for he could not stop himself from thinking of Daphne.

He had always been able to stop himself—he had spent eight years teaching himself how to be numb inside—but at this moment, he could not push her from his mind. She was so much a part of his youth and his memories of this house, which was why he had never returned. Until now.

He gazed out the carriage window at the south garden. All at once, a host of vivid images came hurling, spinning back at him. He recalled the excitement and anticipation of running through that garden, sneaking away in the evenings before dinner, to meet her secretly down at the lake.

He remembered how his feet would carry him across the lawns and through the woods, how his heart would race at the thought of seeing her. For four years she had been his best friend, his confidante.

She was—and would always be—his first love. His first lover.

A knot of tension formed in his gut as the carriage rolled to a stop. He remembered the last time he had been here, when he'd driven away devastated and shattered—emotionally bruised and beaten down into a state of complete and utter grief over Daphne's death. He had not looked back. He couldn't. He'd been so full of rage toward his father for sending Daphne away. For being the cause of her death.

Why had she gotten on that ship? he had wondered so desperately afterward. Why hadn't she come to him? If she had, they could have run away together.

The question had haunted him for years. He had wondered what he'd done wrong. In the end, he had accepted that she'd left for his own good. She had always worried about his parents' disapproval. She had not wanted to be the reason his father would disinherit him, as he had threatened to do.

The carriage stopped in front of the house, and Clara squeezed Seger's hand. He smiled at her, glad at least to have her with him to distract him from those memories and to remind him that life was not the same as it was. Now he was married to a beautiful, extraordinary woman whom he desired beyond any imagining.

He had come around full circle, he told himself. He was home, and he was about to start a new life.

He helped Clara out of the carriage and escorted her into the front hall where the servants were standing in two straight lines, eager to greet the new marchioness. Seger recognized almost no one. He supposed many of the former servants must have moved on and been replaced over the years. Even the butler was strange to him.

A short time later they were shown to their rooms, and Clara seemed genuinely pleased with her boudoir and the house in general.

"It's lovely," she said. "I'll be very happy here, Seger. We'll live here, won't we? You won't continue to manage the estate from London?"

Seger took both her hands in his and kissed them. "If you wish to live here, then we will make it our home."

He was surprised to hear himself say those words so quickly, without really thinking about it. He had expected more of a resistance from his deeper self—from the place where the memories lived.

But he supposed he had faced those memories just now, and had not suffered so much after all. Yes, he had remembered things—things he had not permitted himself to re-visit before now, because they were too painful. But they were only memories. Scattered and dim. Small, individual fragments of the four years he had spent with Daphne. Sad memories of a difficult and turbulent time, yes, but there were pleasant memories, too, and for the first time since he couldn't remember when, he had let himself think of them. He had looked at the familiar gardens and remembered how he had felt when he was sixteen.

Perhaps he could let himself remember other things. Face all of it at last, and put it behind him.

Seger smiled and laid a kiss on Clara's moist lips. "We have the house to ourselves," he said. "We'll spend every moment together for two days and nights, and we'll come to know each other better."

Her eyes lit up. "Thank you, Seger. It's what I've wanted since our wedding day."

"It gives me pleasure to know I can give you what you want. You must always tell me what you desire, darling, and I will do my best to make it so."

She smiled warmly. "I will."

Clara spent an hour in her room with her maid, unpacking her things and freshening up after the journey from London. Then she met Seger in the drawing room at the agreed upon time.

He took her on a tour of the house, which she enjoyed immensely for it was a wonderful house, full of antiquities and art and all the modern conveniences. Then they ventured outdoors to the stables where a groom was waiting for them, with two horses saddled.

She and Seger went riding over the green hills and through the trees along a narrow river. Seger told her about the childhood games he used to play with two boys who were sons of a nearby squire. He showed her the squire's house from a distance, and wondered if the family still lived there.

"Would you like to call on them?" Clara asked, but Seger said no, reminding her that this was their time to spend together and get to know one another.

"Another day," he said, and Clara felt a wave of happiness move through her.

Later, they arrived at a lake, and decided to give the horses a rest. Seger dismounted and tethered his gelding, then helped Clara down, too.

"Shall we walk?" he suggested.

A short time later, they sat down on the grass in the shade of some towering oaks. Seger leaned back on his elbows and crossed his ankles. He stared at the calm lake.

There was not a hint of a breeze. Clara breathed in the clean, damp scent of the water and listened to the birds chirping. The trees were still.

"It's so peaceful here. I believe I could come every day and just sit here and do nothing but daydream." She gazed up at the huge, leafy branches over her head, blocking her view of the sky.

Seger said nothing. He was very quiet.

She watched him for a moment or two and wished she knew what he was thinking about, then it occurred to her that he might be thinking of Daphne. Remembering. . . .

Clara felt a tightening sensation in her stomach and cleared her throat. Maybe she should suggest that they leave now and go back to the house. They could go to her bedchamber. They hadn't made love yet. Perhaps they could steal some time before dinner.

Then she reminded herself that she had come to Rawdon Hall with her husband get to know him better. To forge a connection between them—a connection that sustained endurance outside of the bedroom.

"Does all this remind you of Daphne?" Clara gently asked him.

His gaze darted up at her. He looked surprised at first, then his face softened. "Yes."

Clara tried not to feel hurt that he was thinking about another woman now, in this beautiful, idyllic place, when she herself was thinking of no one but him.

Wanting him to feel that she was offering comfort—and *not* wanting him to know that deep down she was fighting a pang of jealousy—she reached out and touched his shoulder.

Daphne is dead. He will get over this, she told herself.

"Did you come here with her often?" Clara asked.

"All the time. We used to swim over there." He sat up and pointed.

Clara didn't know what to say next. He seemed melancholy; he was particularly quiet.

She felt a little sick.

Finally, Seger turned to her. "It was a long time ago, Clara. Don't think that I still want her. I want *you.*"

Clara sucked in a breath.

He leaned toward her and cupped her head in his hand, pulled her close for a kiss. She moaned with sweet, aching bliss at the feel of his mouth on hers and his tongue parting her lips and venturing inside. The kiss was full of reassurance—intentional reassurance, she believed. It was unlike any other kiss they'd shared.

Perhaps they did know each other in certain ways, she thought. Somehow he had recognized her distress, and he wanted to soothe her. He did not want her to feel like she was his second choice. Somehow he knew she needed his affections at this moment.

Gently, he eased her onto the soft grass and covered her body with his own, tilting his head this way and that as he kissed her.

With roving hands, he reached down to raise her skirts. The feel of his fingers feathering over her thighs roused her senses and caused a flurry of butterflies within her belly.

Oh, how she needed to be the object of his attentions at this moment. She wrapped her legs around him and held him close as he kissed her neck, his hot breath tickling her skin and filling her with lustful need.

"Let's make new memories," she whispered in his ear. "I love it here, Seger."

Her husband recognized the heated tone of her voice, the breathy quality that hinted at all kinds of wicked pleasures in the middle of the day in a completely inappropriate location. Sensitive lover that he was, always willing to answer to a woman's longings, he smiled his consent and revived his extraordinary charm.

Clara felt instantly beautiful, as if she were the most important person in the world to him. He had such a talent in that regard. All he had to do was smile in that suggestive way, and she opened for him like a spring flower.

Glancing down with teasing eyes, he unbuttoned the top of her bodice and kissed along her collarbone.

"Tell me what you'd like this afternoon, love." His voice was husky, provocative.

"Why don't you surprise me?"

"It would be my pleasure."

He inched down and freed her from her skirts, then put

his mouth on her—kissing and suckling with great vigor until ripples of pleasure pulsated through her body.

Clara clutched at his head, thrust her hips forward in hot, tense exhilaration, and finally cried out with reckless abandon.

Her body soon relaxed in complete, utter abatement. Seger inched up to lie on top of her again, gazing down at her with an animal grin as he unfastened his riding breeches. A second later, he was easing himself into her, slowly sliding in with grace and control, never taking his eyes off hers.

They watched each other in the daylight as they moved. Neither of them spoke. It was so peaceful by the lake. So fresh and clean. Clara had never known such gratifying contentment, such deep, soul-blazing lust.

Soon, his pace quickened and he closed his eyes. He pushed into her harder and faster, then held himself deep inside—so deep it felt like he filled her completely.

Clara squeezed his shoulders and gloried in the sight of him reaching his climax. She felt him throb and pulse within her, felt the hot, flooding sensation of his seed gushing forth. God, how she loved him. She loved giving him this pleasure.

A moment later, Seger collapsed upon her. "I'm completely spent," he said breathlessly in her ear. "I must have given you everything I had."

"I hope there will be more later," she said playfully.

He propped himself up on both elbows and gave her the rakish grin that always melted her heart. "I'll see to it. A hearty dinner should fill me up again."

With a boyish lift of his eyebrows, he glanced at her hair and picked a few crisp, dead leaves out of it. "I've made a mess of you."

Clara laughed.

He fixed his gaze on her eyes, then pressed his lips to hers while he slid out of her.

"Ah," he sighed, rolling onto his back and tossing his arms up under his head. "I'm glad you suggested this makeshift honeymoon. It's been a delight."

Clara rested her cheek on her hand and gazed at his profile. "Thank you for bringing me here, Seger. I know it must have been difficult for you."

He turned his head toward her. She saw in his eyes that he knew exactly what she was referring to. "No, Clara. It has not been difficult."

"But you were thinking of her for quite a while, and you were so quiet. You looked sad."

He sighed. "Only because I haven't thought of her in a long time, and that was my own choice. I never let myself. Being back here makes it impossible to ignore the memories, that's all."

"Then you'll be thinking of her a great deal while we're here, won't you?" *Just what I want on my honeymoon— my husband embarking on a nostalgic journey back to his first love.*

He hesitated before he answered, and sounded reluctant when he spoke. "Probably, but that doesn't mean I wish she was here instead of you." His gaze narrowed. "Honestly, if she suddenly appeared right now, I would choose you."

I hope so, but I will never know, because you do not have that choice.

Clara dropped her gaze to the matted grass. There was one more thing that had been weighing heavily on her mind.

"Do I remind you of her? Is that why you married me?"

Seger leaned closer. "Of course not." He cradled her chin in his hand. "Clara, look at me. I admit that when I first saw you, I noticed a very slight resemblance. Perhaps it's what made me approach you, but since then I have not seen it. You're different in every way. I don't see her when I look at you. I see you."

Clara accepted his explanation and reminded herself that even though this conversation about Daphne hurt, it was a good thing, because he was being very open with her, and that was what she had wanted.

"I understand if you need to think of her. It's been a long time since you've been here."

He touched her cheek, then leaned back on his elbows. "You've been so calm and reasonable about this, Clara. Most women would have slapped my face and stormed off by now."

She tried to smile. "It means a great deal to me that you were honest with me, Seger, and if anytime, you want to talk about her, I'll listen. I want you to share your feelings with me."

He considered it for a few seconds, then kissed her. "Thank you, but I believe I will keep my thoughts to myself. I don't want to hurt you."

He was right. It would hurt if he talked about Daphne constantly and told her private things about their relationship, because as much as Clara tried to maintain a calm and reasonable demeanor on the outside, her heart was aching on the inside. She was only human after all.

Seger fastened his breeches while Clara arranged her skirts, then he rose and helped her to her feet. He pulled the leaves out of her hair.

As they mounted their horses, she thought about Seger

coming here with Daphne, and how often he must have pulled leaves from *her* hair. She imagined Seger making love to Daphne, telling her unreservedly that he loved her, as he must have done hundreds of times.

He does not love me, at least not yet. Not like he loved her.

The thought came unbidden, made her stomach clench, but she forced herself to banish it.

Chapter 20

Dear Clara,

It sounds like he idealizes Daphne, and now you must compete with the ghost of a perfect woman. I hope he will eventually see how fortunate he is to have you, for I know how deeply you love him. Every man should be so lucky . . .

Adele

Clara was the one he wanted. Seger knew it with a surprising firmness of mind when he climbed into bed with her that night.

Yes, he had thought of Daphne a number of times since he and Clara had arrived at Rawdon Hall, but the memories were distant. They were vague and seemed almost childish, for he had been a mere adolescent when he'd first met Daphne. He had been sixteen, and he had fallen hopelessly in love, but he had changed a great deal since then.

He was no longer that boy. Daphne's death had ripped from him the person he had been. He had lived another existence. He had grown into a man. He was not the boy he had been when he'd loved her.

He wondered how he would feel about her if he met her now, for the first time. He would probably not even notice her in a crowd of other women. He was far too experienced.

"I enjoyed myself today," Clara said sweetly as she inched down under the covers. "I love this house, Seger, and I love the countryside. I will look forward to returning after the Season has ended."

"So will I," he replied with some surprise. He rolled on top of her, pressed his lips to her delicate mouth, and smiled. "Because this bed—with you in it—is like a little piece of heaven."

That experience he possessed had moved him to choose Clara out of a sea of eager, willing females. Now, Clara was here with him in the flesh.

Her patience and understanding—knowing he was thinking of a woman from his past—only served to solidify his respect for her. She was so very sensible. She had understood the complexities of the situation. She had understood *him*. He had admitted he was remembering his first love, and his wife had been sympathetic and tolerant. She knew he couldn't help but think of Daphne after returning to Rawdon Hall for the first time since her death, and his wife had been patient.

How could he not adore Clara for that?

Seger kissed her with an unruly passion and helped her pull her nightdress over her head.

* * *

Seger did not mention Daphne again during their stay at Rawdon Hall, but Clara took note of the times he was quiet and melancholy and knew that he was thinking of her.

Nevertheless, Clara enjoyed their private time together and felt that by being understanding and patient, she had gained Seger's respect. They had, in fact, forged a closer bond.

Now, back in London and riding alone in the coach on her way home from a brief shopping excursion, Clara reflected on their marriage, and began to believe that a deeper love between herself and her husband was indeed possible. Likely even, if they continued in the direction they were going.

They had come forward a great distance since their wedding day, she realized with a smile. Seger had opened up to her completely at Rawdon Hall. He had softened toward her and given up the superficial flirtations. He had held her tenderly in the night, and he had appreciated her understanding.

Clara sighed heavily as a wave of relief and contentment moved through her. She felt optimistic about her marriage now, for the very first time.

The coach stopped at an intersection, and without warning, her door opened and a man stepped inside.

"Sir!" she shouted. "This is not a hackney cab! Get out please!"

Before she had a chance to call to her driver, the carriage lurched forward. The man settled himself on the seat and turned toward her.

She gazed at the familiar face, and her pulse seemed to stop abruptly.

All she could do was say his name. "Gordon."

He smiled. "Yes, it's me, Clara." He stared into her eyes. "My God, you are more beautiful today than you were the last time I saw you. It hardly seems possible."

He placed his hand on his chest, as if he were trying to still his heart.

Panic thrust into her veins and shock settled in behind it. Clara had to struggle to think clearly. "What are you doing here? I thought you were in prison."

"I was released three months ago."

"But you promised you would never contact me again. What do you want?"

He leaned back in the seat and rested both hands on his walking stick. "Straight to the point, as usual. It's what I admired most about you, Clara. You always knew exactly what you wanted. Well, almost always." He smiled again, this time, a sinister, knowing smile. He leaned toward her, as if he wanted to sniff her.

Clara slid away from him. "I am married now, Gordon. I don't wish to see you. I will ask you to get out of my coach immediately. Driver!"

But the driver didn't hear her.

"Oh, I know all about your triumphant marriage," Gordon said. "It was splashed all over the New York papers."

Clara tried to keep her breathing slow and steady. "You still haven't told me why you're here."

"Why do you think I'm here?"

"I don't know. All I know is that I want you to leave."

How could she ever have been so young and foolish as to allow this man into her life?

He shook his head at her. "You must know I never stopped loving you."

Clara frowned. "That's the most ridiculous thing I've ever heard. You never loved me. You wanted my father's money, and you got it when we parted—a great deal of it—so you had better leave now before he finds out about this, and takes steps to see you back in prison for blackmail."

"I don't wish to blackmail you. I only want to see you."

"Why?"

"Because I thought of you every wretched night I was in prison. Surely you must remember what we shared."

She slid away from him again, disgusted by his mendacity. "I remember nothing! You manipulated me and lied to me." When he did not reply, she narrowed her gaze. "Did you send that telegram to my husband on our wedding day?"

He considered the question for a moment. "No, that wasn't me."

"But you know about it. Who did you tell? Who sent it?"

"To be honest, I don't know, and I don't care. I'm here only to see you again for my own personal reasons, and to remind you of what we had."

"The only thing I am reminded of is filth. Get out of my carriage, and do not ever contact me again."

"But I don't want to get out."

He moved closer until she was pinned up against the side of the coach. He moved his face in slow circles in front of hers, so close she could almost feel his mouth touching hers.

She turned her face away in disgust. "Let go of me!"

"I want to be with you again, Clara. We belong together. Surely your husband of all people will be open to his wife taking a lover. From what I hear, he would probably encourage it."

Clara tried to squirm out of his grasp. "I don't know what you've heard, but it isn't true. Our marriage isn't like that."

He continued to paw at her, kissing the side of her head. "You're dreaming if you think he isn't taking lovers of his own. If nothing else, why not get revenge?"

"Let go of me!"

Just then, the carriage bumped and Clara glanced out the window.

"We are almost at Rawdon House," she said in a panic. "Get out of here, Gordon, or I will send my husband out to remove you himself, and I guarantee he won't be gentle."

Gordon glanced out the window as well. "Damn. I suppose I should hop out before he finds out about us." He slid away and picked up his hat. "As the English say, *Cheerio*."

He opened the carriage door and leaped out onto the street, leaving Clara behind to still her racing heart.

"There is no us!" she shouted after him.

The carriage reached Rawdon House and stopped. Clara bolted inside to tell Seger what had happened, for she had vowed on their wedding day that there would be no more secrets.

Seger descended the stairs at his club. He had been informed that Quintina was waiting for him outside with an urgent message.

She had never come looking for him at his club before.

"What's wrong?" he asked, exiting the building and letting the door fall closed behind him.

Quintina was pacing back and forth on the sidewalk. "Seger, I am very sorry to bother you, but can we take a walk?"

He stared at her a moment, then met her at the wrought iron gate and offered his arm. "Certainly."

"I have something to tell you," she said, as they strolled

down the street, "and I don't know how to say it. It has come as a shock to me, and I hope it will not be unduly painful for you to hear it."

"What is it, Quintina?"

She cleared her throat. "I have a friend in New York, and she has informed me that Clara was involved in some kind of embezzlement a few years ago."

Seger glowered down at Quintina. "I already know about that. Clara explained what happened, and she is innocent. But I am curious to know how your friend came by this information, and if this is the person who sent me a telegram on my wedding day. Who is it, may I ask?"

Quintina glanced up at him. "An Englishwoman I knew a number of years ago. She moved to America to become a governess, and when she read about you and Clara in the New York papers, she felt obligated to inform me of Clara's background."

Stopping on the sidewalk, Seger took his stepmother's hand in both of his. "I would like to know this woman's name, if you please. This is a matter that must be cleared up posthaste. I will not have anyone spreading lies about my wife—lies that concern something that is buried in the past."

Quintina sighed. "I'm not entirely sure that it *is* buried in the past, Seger, which is why I came today. You see, my friend wrote to me about this issue quite some time ago, but I chose not to mention it to you, because I like Clara so very much, and I want your marriage to be a success. But I could not keep it to myself any longer after what happened today. Can we stroll again?"

Seger nodded and offered his arm. They walked in silence for a few seconds before Quintina finally spoke. "First of all, I'm not sure that Clara was entirely innocent.

My friend informed me that her signature was on certain documents, but that is not what concerns me now. Like you said, it's in the past. What concerns me is Clara's association with the man who lured her into this embezzlement in the first place. She was engaged to him, I understand."

"Yes, but Clara severed her relationship with him, and he went to prison."

"But he is out now. Here in London, in fact."

Seger found himself clenching a fist. "In London, you say?"

"Yes, but it's worse than that. He came to the house looking for Clara, and she went off with him in the coach. Alone. I don't think she realized that I knew who he was. She said he was an old family friend."

Seger glared at his stepmother, then uttered an oath and turned to summon his carriage.

Seger walked into the house, where he found Clara sitting alone in the drawing room, gazing absentmindedly out the window.

At least she was here, and not somewhere else.

He approached and stood over her where she sat on the sofa. Eyes wide, she gazed up at him.

"Care to tell me what happened today?" he asked directly.

She stared dumbfounded for a moment, then went pale.

He suspected she was recognizing the hostility in his voice and grasping the fact that he had already heard.

"Seger . . ." Her voice betrayed her trepidation. "You know?"

"Yes. But I wish to hear your description of it."

She continued to gaze up at him with dismay, then she

rose to her feet, wrapped her arms around his waist and buried her face in his chest.

"I tried to find you when I came home, but you had gone out." Her voice began to quiver. "Oh, Seger, Gordon has come to London."

He would have liked to see her eyes when she spoke, but her cheek was still pressed into his chest. "I know. What happened, Clara?"

"He caught me off guard. I was on my way home from Piccadilly, when he opened my carriage door and got in. There was no warning. He must have been following me."

"He got into your carriage?"

"Yes. I told him to get out, but he wouldn't."

Seger reached around to pry her arms off of him. He stared at her, trying to see the truth.

Just then, Quintina entered.

Seger held up a hand. "Let my wife explain." He turned his attention back to Clara. "He did not come to the house? You didn't go with him willingly?"

She shook her head.

Quintina stepped forward. "What do you mean, Clara? Of course he was here. Mrs. Carruthers told me who he was, and I watched you leave with him. I watched you from my window upstairs."

A heavy silence descended upon them while Clara and Quintina stared at each other, as if they were each trying to comprehend what the other was saying.

"I didn't leave with him," Clara finally professed. "I don't know what you think you saw, but I did not see Gordon in this house."

Quintina shook her head in disbelief. "You think both the housekeeper and I imagined it?"

"Yes!"

Quintina turned her gaze to Seger and gestured toward Clara with a hand. "Perhaps she wishes to spare your feelings, Seger."

Clara's voice took on a more aggressive tone. "I don't wish to spare my husband's feelings. I did not go anywhere willingly with Gordon Tucker. He got into my carriage uninvited. Seger, you must believe me."

Seger's gaze darted back and forth between his wife and his stepmother. "One of you is not telling the truth."

He looked down at his wife, whose face had gone ashen. He felt a stabbing sensation in his heart. It was fear, and it was sickeningly familiar.

He tried to ignore it and focus on the matter at hand—determining the facts.

"I swear on my honor, Seger, I did not leave this house with Gordon."

"But what motive would I have to lie?" Quintina asked. "And the housekeeper, too?"

Seger was not about to guess anyone's motives. He had not trusted his stepmother in many years, yet how well did he really know Clara? She had kept the secret about the embezzlement from him until he discovered it on his own on their wedding day. Now Quintina was telling him that Clara was not innocent after all, that her signature had been discovered on certain related documents.

He didn't know what to believe. His gut pitched and rolled.

Clara took a desperate step toward him. "Seger, please . . ."

He held up a hand to silence her, then turned to his stepmother. "Excuse us, please, Quintina. I must speak with my wife privately."

"Seger, I am very sorry. Perhaps I shouldn't have said anything."

"Yes, you should have. Now leave us."

Quintina hesitated a moment before she walked out and closed the door behind her.

Chapter 21

Dear Adele,

I pray that all will work out between Seger and me. I believe that if I lose him now, after we have come so far, I would never recover from the heartbreak. . . .

Love,
Clara

"It seems to be your word against Quintina's," Seger said to his wife.

God, the thought of Clara in the presence of her ex-lover—whether she was telling the truth about how she encountered him or not—enraged Seger. He tried to push the fury away, but couldn't.

He wasn't accustomed to such weakness where a woman was concerned. It had been years since he felt anything like it. His hands were shaking.

"I am telling the truth," Clara said. "I don't know how to convince you, except to ask for your trust."

"My trust? You lied to me once before about this matter. I would be a fool to offer my trust blindly."

"I never lied. I told you about Gordon, I just didn't tell you everything, because we barely knew each other. There was so little time."

"But you could have found the time if you'd wished to."

Her chest rose and fell with a sigh of defeat. She collapsed onto the sofa, and buried her face in her hands.

"You're right, I could have. My only excuse is that I was afraid you would change your mind about marrying me, and I wanted you more than anything. If I neglected to tell you, it was only because I loved you."

He almost laughed at the idea. "Love? You just said, Clara, that we barely knew each other."

She looked up at him, her eyes red and puffy, laden with a mixture of anger and bafflement. "Don't you believe in love, Seger? Have you forgotten how you felt when you first met Daphne?"

"I spent four years with Daphne. I've known you little more than a month. And Daphne has nothing to do with this."

"But you told me you fell in love with her the first time you saw her. That you'd decided she was the one for you after a mere week of knowing her. Can't you believe that that kind of magic could happen again?"

He did not want to think about how quickly he had leaped into an intimate relationship twelve years ago, how quickly he had given away his heart. "I was only sixteen, and I am no longer that boy."

"Only because you have given up hope. You have become jaded and you have not let yourself love me, Seger. I deserve a chance to earn your love. I want to be more to you than just a wife in name."

He suddenly wondered why they were having this conversation, when the issue of her ex-lover still hung in the balance. He paced the room.

"What happened today, Clara?"

She sighed in frustration. "I already told you. Gordon walked into my carriage uninvited. I never met him here in our home. Quintina is lying."

"Why would she lie? She told me today that she wanted our marriage to be a success."

Clara spread her hands wide. "I don't know. Maybe she's lying about that, too."

He remembered the day Quintina had explained that Daphne had gotten on a ship bound for America. Quintina had spoken in sympathetic tones and tried to explain and defend her husband's actions. She had held Seger's hand as she delivered the news, but he had known she harbored triumph on the inside.

Today, he didn't know whom to believe.

He watched his wife wipe the tears from her eyes. Something inside him throbbed with deep, agonizing empathy. He hated to see her cry.

Christ! He did not want to feel this pain that was cutting him from the inside out. He wanted to crush it, like he'd learned to crush all feelings for other people years ago.

He didn't want to face the possibility that Clara had been dishonest with him, or that she was somehow involved with another man and was lying about it, as Quintina was suggesting.

He didn't want to face the possibility that she had married him for his title, like so many of her fellow countrywomen did these days, because he could not deny that he'd always felt certain there was something more than that between them. He'd always known Clara desired him in a basic, elemental way, and that had pleased him. It had been his justification for marrying her. Desire was something he understood and could handle. Now, everything was falling into question.

He wanted to leave this room, to shut himself off.

He also felt the urge to protect what was his.

Seger walked to the door.

"Where are you going?" Clara asked.

He did not look back. "Out."

Seger went to five hotels before he found the one that had Gordon Tucker listed as a registered guest. It was an expensive hotel. Too expensive for an ex-prison convict.

He tapped his walking stick on the man's door.

A few seconds later, the door opened and Seger found himself standing face-to-face with his wife's one-time fiancé, a man who had recognized her passion and had taken advantage of it in the worst possible way.

He was a good-looking man, tall with brown hair and blue eyes.

Seger wanted to strangle him.

"Lord Rawdon," Tucker said with a vile grin. "I was expecting you. Eventually."

He opened the door the rest of the way. Seger walked in and glanced around the familiar room. He had been in this hotel—and every other decent one in the city—a number of times, but he didn't want to think about that. He was a husband now, and the sheer, rock-hard density of that role seemed to fill his entire being.

"I presume you have come to ask me to stay away from your wife," Tucker said.

Seger replied with absolute calm. "I'm not here to *ask* you anything. I'm here to tell you that she doesn't want to see you, and that you should get the hell out of England today."

Tucker pulled a cigarette box out of his breast pocket, removed one and lit it. He took a deep drag and blew the smoke off to one side. "I don't think so."

Seger moved forward. "Clara belongs to *me*, and you'll be back in prison by nightfall if you choose to ignore that fact."

"She belongs to you, does she? American women are not meek little lambs, Rawdon. You should have learned that by now. Clara is a passionate woman, and one should not attempt to contain her."

"My reason for coming here is not to contain my wife. It is to get rid of *you*."

Tucker raised an eyebrow. He sat down on the bed, leaned back on an elbow and crossed one leg over the other. "If you force me out of the country, you'll make Clara very unhappy. Is that what you want?"

"She won't be unhappy."

"Yes, she will.

Christ. Seger wanted to end this conversation right now by throwing Tucker out the window, but he smothered the urge because he wanted information.

"I understand that you forced your company upon her today," he said.

"I wouldn't call it that," Tucker replied. "She received me in her drawing room like the proper lady that she is."

Seger cleared his throat. *She received him.*

If that was true, it meant Clara had lied about what had really happened.

But God! Even after hearing Tucker uphold Quintina's claim, Seger still had trouble believing it. He wanted to trust Clara—his instincts were telling him to—but how could he, when three people were now saying one thing, while she said something completely different?

He loathed being in this position—in a battle, unarmed, ignorant of his enemy. Unaware of the terrain.

He decided to take a risk. "She didn't receive you. You forced your way into her carriage."

"Is that what she told you?" Tucker rose to his feet. "She's a sneaky one. You probably shouldn't have married her. I'll tell you what—I'll take her off your hands and marry her myself, if you'll agree to give her to me. A quiet divorce shouldn't be difficult for a man like you. You're an aristocrat, you must have connections in high places. I reckon she'd be happier with me, anyway. She doesn't have it in her to stay in one place for too long. Besides that, we're drawn to each other."

All at once, Seger could hear the rush of blood pounding in his ears. He clenched his jaw, hauled back an arm, and threw a hard punch at Tucker, knocking him flat onto the bed.

"Jesus!" Tucker said, cupping his chin in his hand.

Seger turned to leave. "Be out of here tonight, sir, or I'll be back in the morning to continue this conversation exactly where we left off."

Gillian heard the hotel door click shut, and stepped out of the wardrobe. Heart racing within her, she smoothed a hand over her skirts and observed Gordon sitting on the edge of the bed, clutching his jaw. He glanced up at her with a feeble expression in his eyes. His lip was bleeding.

"He bloody well hit me!"

She crossed over the carpet to stand before him, took a look at his lip, and removed a handkerchief from her reticule. "Here."

He reluctantly accepted it. "I thought you English were supposed to be polite and reserved."

"Not Seger. Well, he's polite when he wants to be, but never reserved."

Gordon shook his head. "I don't know what you see in him. He's a brute if you ask me."

"You were plenty brutish yourself."

He didn't look up at her. He just dabbed at his lip with her handkerchief.

For a long time she watched the top of his head. His hair was a shiny brown color. She liked the way it parted in waves.

"I would have thought you'd be used to fighting," she said, "after being in prison."

He tried to give back the handkerchief, but it was stained.

"Keep it," she said.

He stuffed it into his pocket and stood up. He was very tall. He towered over her, and he smelled like cigarette smoke.

"I had a talent for talking my way out of most fights," he told her.

"I'd wager you did."

The side of his mouth curled up. "Not this one, though. Seemed more like I was talking my way into it."

Gillian shrugged. "It's what you agreed to."

"Yeah, and I agreed to a hundred pounds. I said exactly what your aunt asked me to say, so where's my reward?"

She paused and looked up at him. He was a criminal. She'd never known a criminal before.

"I have it here." Gillian reached into her reticule and pulled out a bank note. She held it up between two fingers and waited for him to take it, but he didn't right away.

His eyes bored into hers.

She felt an electric current surge through all her nerve endings.

Then he smiled, and slowly removed the note from her fingers.

Clara sat up in bed, waiting anxiously for Seger to come home, but he stayed away for most of the night—which gave her plenty of time to think about what had happened today, and why.

Quintina had lied. She had looked Clara in the eye and spoken a complete fabrication. There had to be a reason. She was carrying out some kind of scheme to make Clara look bad to Seger.

As the evening wore on, the reason became very clear: Gillian wanted Seger, and Quintina wanted her niece to have him.

As soon as Clara realized that, she decided it would be best to stay in her room and wait for her husband, for she had no idea what would happen if she encountered Quintina or Gillian. She did not know how far they would take this.

Finally, after spending the entire evening entertaining every possible scenario about where Seger had gone, Clara heard the carriage outside. It was almost midnight. By the time his footsteps tapped heavily over the floorboards in the corridor outside her bedchamber, Clara was wound up tighter than a tallcase clock.

Would he come to her, or would he avoid seeing her and go to his own room?

She barely had time to contemplate the possibilities when a knock sounded at her door and Seger walked in. Every fragment of her being breathed a sigh of relief. She had no idea what his feelings were at the moment, but at least he was willing to be in the same room with her.

He entered, closed the door behind him, and stood at the foot of her bed. "I spoke to Gordon Tucker today."

Clara's heart began to pound faster. "Did he tell you what happened? Do you believe me now?"

Her husband circled the bed and stood over her. "He told me you received him in the drawing room."

Anger swept over her. "He's lying! I can't believe this is happening. It's some sort of conspiracy!"

Clara got out of bed and reached for her wrap. She'd barely pushed her arms into the sleeves, when she felt Seger's hand on her shoulder from behind. "Where are you going?"

"I'm going to talk to your stepmother. She lied today, Seger, and if Gordon told the same lie then they must be working together. Quintina wants to get rid of me. The only explanation I can come up with, is that she must be doing this for Gillian."

Seger took her by the arm and gently turned her around to face him. His eyes were full of tenderness and compassion. It was not what she had expected.

Her vision blurred. "Go ahead and call me irrational. I know that's what you must be thinking. Or maybe you think I'm making this up to cover myself, to hide my affair with my former fiancé. Well, I'm not making it up. I have never been more—"

Suddenly, her words were smothered by the force of her husband's kiss. He crushed her mouth under his, as if he hadn't seen her for an entire year.

A tiny moan escaped her, and her knees turned to jelly. Clara wrapped her arms around his neck and gave in to the sweet pounding pleasure of his hot tongue thrusting into her mouth and mingling gloriously with hers. She could barely even remember what she had been saying only seconds ago. . . .

He kissed her thoroughly and meticulously, then with care pushed her away from him to look into her eyes.

She felt weak. Dazed. She swallowed hard and blinked up at him.

"Do you think I've lost my mind?" she asked ridiculously.

He gave her a tiny trace of a smile. "No, but I spent the entire night thinking that maybe I'd lost mine."

The rage that was devouring her only seconds ago receded, and she took a deep, calming breath. "Why?"

He closed his eyes and touched his forehead to hers. "Because despite what Quintina and Gordon Tucker profess, I still can't stop myself from wanting to take your side in this."

Joy flooded through her. "Do you believe me, Seger?"

"I don't know. I want to, Clara. My gut is telling me to, but three people have said one thing while you say another."

She took his face in her hands, determined to convince him. "Surely, you must know in your heart that I would never do anything to jeopardize our marriage. You must know that I love you, even if you aren't ready to love me back."

He looked doubtful.

"I need you, Seger. I need our relationship to be solid and steady. I need to feel that you are my true and constant mate. I cannot stay in this house and face adversaries if we, as a pair, are anything less than that."

He turned away from her and moved to the other side of

the bed. He closed his eyes and pinched the bridge of his nose.

"Clara, for the past eight years I've lived a certain kind of life, because I was knocked to my knees and couldn't get up. Lately, I have managed to stagger to my feet, but this day has been trying. I wanted to kill Tucker today because I nearly went insane with jealousy. I didn't want to feel any of that. I wanted things to go back to what they were. I wanted to go back to the man I was before I met you."

Clara swallowed over a sudden lump that formed in her throat. "You mustn't believe any of what Gordon said. I tried to get rid of him in the carriage, Seger. Honestly." She heard the desperation in her voice. "I told him I never wanted to see him again."

"I want to believe you, but that's the problem, you see. I can't help worrying that I'm inclined to take your side only because it's what I *want* to believe."

She knew she was grasping at straws. "Quintina and Gillian. . . . This is all their doing. They want me out of here, Seger. Think about that. It makes sense. If you can't trust your heart, trust that. Ask them."

He nodded, and she almost cried out in relief. There was still hope.

Seger moved around the bed to stand before her on the other side. He laid a hand on her cheek and kissed her tenderly. "I will, but not now. It's late, and after what happened today, I want to make love to you. I need to feel that you are mine."

She thought about insisting that he go and ask them now, but the weary look in his eyes changed her mind. All that mattered at this moment was her husband's confidence in her love, so she pulled off her wrap and began to unbutton his waistcoat.

When Clara woke the next morning, Seger was gone.

She took a deep breath and knew this day would either turn out to be the dissolution of a family, or the dissolution of a marriage. There would be a confrontation. Accusations. Someone was going to be ousted and maybe even sent away.

Pray it not be her.

She rose from bed and washed, then rang for her maid. A half hour later, she left her room to go and knock on Seger's door. She wanted to go to the breakfast room on his arm. She wanted to present a united front.

When she reached his room, his door was open. She saw him standing in front of the window, handsome as ever in his dark morning jacket and waistcoat, so she entered without knocking.

He was holding a letter in his hands.

"Seger . . ."

He faced her. "A footman just brought this."

His eyes were dark with concern. Clara took the letter and read it.

Dear Lord Rawdon,

I am the one who sent you the telegram on your wedding day. I have information about your wife. Please meet me at ten o'clock at Hyde Park, under Marble Arch.

"Who sent this?" Clara asked, as panic welled up inside her.

"It doesn't say."

She swallowed nervously. "Have you talked to Quintina yet?"

"No, and there won't be time. It's almost ten now."

Almost ten! Clara's entire body tensed. "Will you go?"

"Yes. I want clarification."

"What do you mean, clarification? I've told you everything, Seger. There is nothing you don't know, nothing this person can say that you haven't already heard, unless what they say is a lie. Maybe Quintina has orchestrated this."

He studied her face, then nodded. "It's possible, but I still have to go. I need to know who sent me that telegram, and why they felt the need to travel all the way here to explain themselves."

"But do you still believe me about Gordon?"

His shoulders rose and fell with a deep intake of breath. "I don't know anything right now, Clara. I want all the information before I can form any decision. Surely you understand that."

She did understand. She always understood, didn't she? But it didn't make any of this easy to bear. "Seger, I want your trust and support. I did nothing wrong."

There was a sneer in his eyes. "You of all people should know how difficult it is to trust your spouse completely, when there are questions."

Clara shifted uncomfortably. She supposed she deserved that. All she'd done was point her finger at her husband and assign blame, make him feel that he was never giving quite enough, without thinking about how it must have made *him* feel. No wonder he had not been able to hand over his heart to her. He felt she had no confidence in him. He didn't believe that he had her trust.

"Take me with you," she said.

He shook his head. "I don't think—"

"Please, Seger. I'll sit in the coach. I need to know who sent this, too, and I deserve a chance to defend myself if need be."

He considered it a moment, then agreed. "All right, but I don't want you to show your face. For all I know, this person might be dangerous."

The Rawdon coach clattered over the cobblestones at precisely ten A.M., causing a flock of sparrows to flutter noisily from the treetops over Marble Arch.

Clara sat across from Seger on the opposite seat inside the coach, feeling sick to her stomach, while her husband appeared completely in control.

The coach came to a slow halt, and Seger reached for his hat.

"You'll be careful?" Clara said, touching his arm.

"Of course." He settled his hat on his head and leaned to open the curtain with one finger. His eyes searched the area, then fixed on something or someone.

"What is it?" Clara asked.

She pushed her own curtain aside as well, and peered out. A woman stood under the arch.

Clara glanced back at Seger. He was still staring at the woman, then he let the curtain fall closed and sat back. He gazed blankly at Clara's knees.

"What is it? Do you know who she is?"

All the color had drained from his face. He was as white as a sheet.

"Who is it, Seger? What's the matter?"

Finally, his eyes lifted. They were deathlike. "It's Daphne."

Chapter 22

Dear Clara,

My lovely English governess gave her notice the other day, and has now left us for another situation. I am extremely disappointed, as I liked her very much. In many ways, she reminded me of you. . . .

Adele

Clara stared numbly at her husband, who was sitting motionless across from her in the coach, with his hands clasped together in front of him.

The whole world seemed to shift beneath her. All she could do was stare at him, waiting. Waiting for a response.

A few seconds went by—seconds that seemed more like hours—then he peered out the window again, as if to ascertain that he had seen what he'd thought he'd seen.

He sat back again, and his chest started to heave. "It's her."

Clara slid across to the other side to sit next to him. "Are you sure?"

"Yes." He covered his face with his hands and leaned forward. *"My God."*

Clara placed her hand on his back. Her first instinct was to calm and comfort him, but then her mind rebelled. What would this mean?

"Jesus!" He sat back and shook his head, as if he were disoriented. "She's alive."

"Are you all right?"

He swept his hat off his head and violently raked his fingers through his hair. "No."

Clara's stomach pitched and rolled. She felt like she was going to be ill.

The two of them sat stiffly in the coach, then Seger finally met her eyes. His were bloodshot. A vein was pulsing at his temple. After a moment, he turned away from her to get out of the coach.

She grabbed for him. "Seger, wait!"

He paused and turned back, but she didn't know what to say.

He didn't either, apparently.

She let go of him, and he left her behind.

Seger had to force himself to put one foot in front of the other as he walked toward Daphne. *Daphne!* His heart was ramming against the inside of his ribs, and his head was spinning dizzily with a chaotic mixture of shock and anger.

How could she be alive? How could she have let him think she was dead all these years?

He stopped a fair distance away, feeling suddenly paralyzed as their gazes met.

Standing against the wall of the arch, she looked the same. Older, yes, but still lovely and slim. She no longer looked like a merchant's daughter, however. She wore a deep purple silk gown of the highest fashion, and a matching plumed hat with black netting over her face.

Seger swallowed hard, and forced his feet to carry him the rest of the way. When he reached her, he let his eyes roam over her face. He had so many questions.

He gazed at Daphne and saw in her face the years that spanned between them. Tiny wrinkles framed the outside of her eyes. Within them, he saw the experience of a life apart from his.

She was not the innocent, buoyant girl she had been when he'd first met her, all smiles and exuberant expressions. She seemed calm. Mature.

She took her time studying his face, too.

Slowly the shock of seeing her again abated. Seger took a deep breath and found the will to speak. "I thought you were dead."

Her shoulders rose and fell with a sigh. "I know."

Her voice hadn't changed at all. Something deep within him shook.

"Why didn't you contact me?" he said harshly. "Didn't you know how deeply I would suffer?"

She moistened her lips and stared apologetically into his eyes. "I thought it was best. I thought it was the only way to get you to forget about me and move on."

Seger clenched his jaw to try and stifle his anger—anger that stemmed from being lied to all these years. By Daphne of all people. He needed to understand.

"So you weren't on the ship that went down. What happened?"

"I was on another ship that left the day after. Your father

was afraid if you knew what ship I was on, you would trace me to my destination in America."

He let that sink in, then his mind groped madly at other questions. There were so many of them, questions that had haunted him and gnawed at him for eight painful years.

"Why didn't you at least tell me you were leaving, and say goodbye?"

"Because you wouldn't have let me go."

"Damn right I wouldn't have."

She shook her head and met his eyes again. "I couldn't let you defy your father, Seger. You would have been disinherited. You would have had no family. I didn't want to drag you down."

"*You* would have been my family."

"But we would have been social outcasts."

His eyebrows drew together in dismay. "You knew that didn't matter to me. I never cared about society's approval. I ended up a social outcast anyway. By choice."

She nodded.

He realized by her response that from a distance, she had been following his path through life. The knowledge gave him a chill. "You knew that?"

"Yes. It was one of my conditions when I accepted your father's petition to see me leave England. I made Quintina promise to keep me abreast of your news."

He tried to stay calm and focus on the questions that still burned in his head. "My father told me you went to him and asked for money in exchange for leaving me."

She shook her head. "No, he came to me with the proposition and the money."

"Which you accepted."

"Yes, and I will not apologize for that. I knew I would have to start a new life, and believe me, it was a meager consolation."

A meager consolation. Seger's chest constricted. A panicky sensation moved through him, and he found himself breathing hard.

He wanted to hear her tell him that it had been devastating for her, too. He wanted to hear that she *had* loved him, because that was the thing that had plagued him all these years and caused his wariness of trusting women's affections. He had always wondered if his only love, Daphne, had not really loved him so much after all. That their years together had been a lie. He had not been able to trust any emotion since then because of that doubt.

His voice shook when he spoke. "Did *you* suffer?"

Her eyes filled with tears, and she took a few seconds before replying. "Yes, Seger, more than you will ever know. I did what I did because I loved you."

He blinked down at her. His blood slowed in his veins. For a long time he could say nothing, do nothing, but stand there staring at Daphne. Daphne.

Then something made him turn and look back at the coach. He thought of Clara and how she must be feeling. His whole body went weak. She was probably wondering if he was going to leave her and go back to the woman she believed was his one true love.

He swallowed hard and faced Daphne again. "Why did you send that telegram? What were you trying to do?"

She nodded as if she had been waiting for that question, and did not wish to answer it. She turned and walked a few steps away from him. She began to pace back and forth under the archway.

"For the past eight years, I've known what kind of life you were living, Seger, and a selfish part of me was glad—glad that you had never gotten over me. I liked knowing that I was the love of your life, and that if things didn't work out for me in America, you would always be there, willing to take me back. Then I read about your marriage in the papers, and suddenly you weren't there for me anymore. Quintina wrote to me, and told me that Clara was a terrible match for you, that she was a greedy, title-seeking vixen. I was more than happy to believe it, and help her put a stop to the marriage."

Daphne stopped pacing and met his gaze directly. "But know this, Seger—I wasn't doing it for Quintina. I despised her and I still despise her now for being the cause of our separation. I was doing it for *me*, because learning about your marriage made me want you back. I began to fantasize that when it did end, I would find the courage to return to you. I imagined being held in your arms again."

She paused, gazing intently at him. Seger made no move to take her into his arms now. He wanted only to hear the rest of her explanation.

"So I offered myself to the Wilson family," she continued, lowering her gaze and pacing again, "as a governess for Adele, hoping I would be able to find something to make you reconsider your marriage to Clara. I took things from Adele's room. I went through her letters and diaries, and the scandal with Gordon Tucker was more than I ever could have bargained for. It was like a gift from heaven, I thought. I was sure that would be enough to bring an end to your marriage."

"But it didn't," he said.

"No, it didn't. And then I . . . I started reading the letters that Clara was writing to Adele, and I realized that she was not what Quintina said she was, and when Clara wrote about Gillian, my heart actually went out to her. I remember Gillian, you see. She was only a young girl then, and she was hateful toward me, too."

Seger nodded. Everything was becoming very clear.

Daphne approached him. "But those letters made me remember how it felt to be with you. I never stopped loving you, Seger, and I never married. My only excuse for doing what I did is that I was too young to understand how lucky I was to have the love of a man like you. I thought I would meet someone else one day, but no one ever compared to you. If only I had known that then."

She stood a mere six inches away, her eyes wide and searching as she gazed up at him. His Daphne. Her face, her lips, they were so achingly familiar. How many nights had he dreamed of kissing those lips again and holding this woman in his arms?

Something wrenched his attention away, however. He looked back at the coach again.

"Seger." Daphne reached up and laid a gloved hand on his cheek to turn his face back to her. "What we had was rare and extraordinary, and if you wanted me back today, I would come. I would marry you if it could be so, but even if it couldn't be, I would be yours regardless. There are ways."

A cold tremor moved down his spine. "You're saying you would be my mistress."

"Yes. Some things are more important than the rules of the world we live in. You taught me that, or at least you tried to eight years ago. It's taken me this long to realize that you were right. I do love you, Seger."

Seger gently removed her hand from his cheek. He held

it in his for a few seconds, then raised it to his lips and kissed it. "I'm sorry, Daphne. I can't."

"Why? Are you afraid I'd hurt you again? Because I wouldn't. I'm wiser now, Seger. I know what's important."

He stared into the depths of that statement and felt a surge of wisdom himself. "So do I."

Daphne slowly pulled her gloved hand from his. "Your marriage to Clara."

He nodded.

She glanced back at the coach and nodded, too. "I'm too late then."

"Yes."

She continued to stare at the coach as if she wanted to see the woman who had, after all these years, redirected Seger's heart, but the curtain was drawn. "She must be very special."

"She is. It's time you and I said goodbye."

Her gaze shot to him, and she shuddered visibly. Then she nodded. "I understand, but first, I . . . I want to give you something."

She reached into her reticule and pulled out a stack of letters tied together with a ribbon. "Here, take these."

"What are they?"

Was this an outpouring of love? he wondered uncomfortably. Were these letters meant to make him change his mind?

She managed a smile. "You probably think they're from me, but they're not. They're Clara's letters to Adele. I took them. You should read them."

He accepted the small stack and stared down at his wife's elegant penmanship on the top envelope. "They're not my letters to read."

"Ask her permission first, then, because you need to understand some things about your wife."

His eyes lifted. Trepidation rippled through him. "Like what?"

"Like how much she loves you."

Seger stared at Daphne, speechless.

She forced a smile that did not seem to come easily. "I knew," she said, "that it would go one of two ways today. You would either take me back, or you would be faithful to your wife. I came prepared for the latter."

He continued to stare at Daphne's troubled face in the morning light. "Why are you doing this?"

"Because when I read those letters, I wept. I realized that she loved you more than I ever did, because I had selfishly allowed you to idealize my memory for eight years, when I should have proven to you that I was not the perfect woman you thought I was. On top of all that, I was ashamed of myself because I was willing to leave you, Seger. For money."

He felt his heart throb with what he realized was an unprecedented sense of freedom. He had thought he was free before, never committing to anyone or anything, but he had not been free. He had been in chains, afraid to love. Afraid to let Clara into his guarded heart.

None of that mattered now. *This* . . . this new understanding of his misconceptions about the past was opening his heart and mind to the extraordinary gift he had in the present.

Still staring down at the letters, he recalled Clara's patience and understanding when he had not been willing to give her his whole heart. He had never told her he loved her. He hadn't known that he had, but now . . . yes, now he knew.

He had desired her from the first moment he saw her across a crowded ballroom. And every day since, that desire had grown and grown until it had matured into love. *Love!* Now that Daphne was here before him, he knew that he loved his wife, and he knew that she had been unwavering in her love for him.

"I don't need to read these," he said. "I already know how she feels." *She has shown me everyday. She has persisted, steady in her constancy, while I have shut her out.*

He heard Daphne's voice as if it were coming from a great distance away. "You should know something else, Seger. Quintina paid Gordon Tucker to follow Clara yesterday. I know because I went to see him. He told me that Clara loathed him because he was a threat to what she had with you."

Seger touched Daphne's arm. "Thank you."

She sighed. "I'm sorry for what I did to you, Seger. You've suffered long enough. You deserve happiness."

He glanced up, then stepped forward and took Daphne tightly into his arms.

Clara peered out the coach window, saw Seger kiss Daphne's hand, and knew she couldn't bear to watch any more of this. She was infuriated. Her fists were clenched so tight, she was surely going to draw blood. She needed air.

She opened the door and got out. She walked around to the other side of the coach—the street side, where she wouldn't have to look at them, and where they wouldn't be able to see her—and leaned her head back against it.

What in God's name was her husband thinking about and feeling right now? Had his love for Daphne come flooding back, and had he already forgotten the fact that he had a wife watching and waiting?

He had a wife.

Little more than a month ago, he had been a free man. He had married Clara so hastily. Was he regretting it now? Had proposing to her suddenly become the worst, most impulsive mistake he'd ever made?

Glancing up at the coachman, who was oblivious to her at the moment, she tried to decide what to do. She had always been understanding when it came to her husband's grieving heart, but this was too much. He was now taking advantage of that understanding, and she couldn't bear the weight of it anymore. She wasn't a saint. She was a woman with passions and fears. Did he ever think of that? No. He was presently kissing another woman's hand right under her nose—a woman he had admitted was the love of his life.

It was just as Mrs. Gunther had said it would be.

Could Clara live like this? Could she survive a marriage that would cause this kind of heartache day in and day out? If it wasn't Daphne, it was Gillian or Lady Cleveland or a score of other beautiful huntresses, who all wanted a share of her husband, and Clara wasn't sure she could ever learn to trust him enough not to let it bother her.

She couldn't go on like this.

Just then, a hackney cab came toward her, and the need to escape this pain and anger displaced all sense of reason. She stepped forward and waved a hand.

The cab came to a stop in front of her, and she got in.

As soon as she closed the door, she looked up at her coachman, who glanced down at her. He lurched forward in his seat, but it was too late for him to do anything. Her cab was rolling again, and she was driving away.

She was glad. It was time Seger knew that she was not

his ever-faithful crutch. It was time he fretted about *her* for a change.

Seger walked back to his coach. He couldn't wait to see Clara and prevail upon her the genuine truth that he wanted no woman in the world but her, and that he now had the concrete proof that she was telling the truth about Gordon. He would assure her that he would deal at once with Gillian and Quintina.

When he approached the vehicle, his driver rose to his feet at the reins. "My lord . . ."

Seger raised a hand. "Not now, Mitchell."

Not giving the driver another thought, Seger opened the door of his coach. His eyes darted from one seat across to the other. The coach was empty.

He stepped back and looked up at Mitchell. "Where is the marchioness?"

The man's face was lined with worry. "She got out of the coach so quietly, I didn't notice until she was driving away. She got into a hack, my lord."

Panic ignited in Seger's veins. He made a fist and pressed it against the side of the coach. "Which way did she go?"

The man pointed. "That way, my lord."

Seger ran around the back of the coach to try and see down the street. "How long ago?"

"Just a few minutes."

There were a number of carriages in the street. There was very little possibility of finding hers among them.

Seger bolted around the back and got in. "Take me back to Rawdon House."

He said a prayer that she had simply gone home.

Chapter 23

Seger pushed through the door of his London house and did not stop to remove his hat or coat. He dashed up the stairs taking them two at a time and went straight to Clara's boudoir.

"Clara!" He knocked once on her door and entered, only to find the room empty. He then went to his own bedchamber and looked there, then headed for the drawing room.

He stopped in the open doorway when he saw Quintina and Gillian both sitting demurely in chairs, embroidery on their laps and a tray of tea and scones on the teacart.

"Seger, you look troubled," Quintina said sweetly. "Whatever is the matter?"

"Did Clara come home?"

She laid her embroidery aside and stood. "No. Why? Gracious, I hope she hasn't gone off with that deplorable Mr. Tucker again. Is that what has you worried? How can we help? Gillian, did Clara mention anything to you? Did she say where she was going this morning?"

Gillian opened her mouth to reply, but Seger moved fully into the room and stopped her with a look. "Don't even bother."

"I beg your pardon?" Gillian said, as if she were bewildered by his tone.

He stood before his stepmother, glaring coldly down at her. "Clara is not with Gordon Tucker, nor did she ever receive him in this house."

"Seger, how can you take Clara's side, when she has been dishonest and—"

"She has been wronged, Quintina. By both you and Gillian, and I will see the two of you gone from this house by nightfall."

Both women were shocked into silence.

Quintina managed to gather her composure. "Seger, you married Clara impulsively, without a clear understanding of her nature. We now know that she is deceitful, and she has seduced you into believing her. It's not too late. We can get you out of this."

He shook his head. "No, madam. You are the deceitful one. You destroyed me years ago when you came between Daphne and me, and informed me that she was dead. You will not do so again."

"*I* didn't come between you. It was Daphne's choice to leave, and you can't blame me for her death."

He took another slow step toward Quintina. His voice became hushed, almost a whisper. "We both know that Daphne is alive."

All the sounds in the room—the ticking of the clock, the snapping of the fire in the grate—seemed to recede into a bleak nothingness.

Eyes wide, Quintina stared up at Seger. "I know no such thing."

"I've heard enough lies." He turned his cold gaze to Gillian. "And I've seen enough cruelty. Clara is my wife, and her happiness is my primary concern."

Quintina made a desperate move to grasp his arm. "You are not thinking clearly, Seger. Jealousy over this Tucker fellow has turned your head."

He moved toward the door. "There has never been more clarity in my mind than there is at this moment." He turned back, however, when Gillian tossed her embroidery onto the floor and called out to him.

"It wasn't my doing, Seger! Quintina was the one who talked me into everything!"

He recognized the desperation in her voice, saw it in her eyes, but it was too late for that. "You have a mind of your own, Gillian. You could have used it." He faced his stepmother. "I will wire your brother in Wales and inform him that you and Gillian are on your way to his home for the time being. I will also ensure that you are settled with an adequate sum to live on, Quintina, since you are by rights my father's widow. All I require in return is that you never set foot in this house again."

With that, he left the room and returned to his coach. "Take me to Wentworth House," he instructed the driver, hoping that he would find his wife there, and that she would agree to hear him out.

Seger stood beneath the portico at Wentworth House, asking the butler if Lady Rawdon was inside. The man didn't answer the question. He simply invited Seger in and escorted him to the duke's oak-paneled study to wait.

Wonderful, Seger thought, preparing himself for the certain advent of the so-called "Dangerous Duke's" infamous wrath. *Bloody hell,* he didn't have time for this. He needed to talk to Clara.

Finally, the door of the study swung open, and James walked in. He stood tall and grim just inside the door. He stared at Seger for a moment, then crossed the room and poured two glasses of brandy.

He handed one to Seger, and said, "This is disturbingly familiar."

Seger accepted the glass, then set it down on the desk without touching it. "Is Clara here?"

James regarded him, then set his glass down as well. "You made me a promise once, Rawdon, that you would not treat my sister-in-law carelessly."

"Yes."

"It seems you have not kept your word."

Seger clenched his jaw. "No, I have not. I've hurt her, and I know that. But you can rest assured that I have not been unfaithful to her, nor have I ever come close to entertaining the notion."

James considered Seger's defense. "That's not what Clara believes—not after what happened this morning."

"She's here, then?" Seger asked, clutching at the hope that he would be able to make things right.

"Yes."

Seger felt the pressure lift from his chest. "I need to see her."

"But she doesn't want to see *you*."

"Did she say that? Or are you just trying to protect her?"

"Yes to both."

Seger swallowed hard over his frustration, and paced around the room. "That woman I met this morning . . . she means nothing to me."

God, why was he explaining himself? The only person who needed to hear his explanation was Clara.

"From what I understand," James said, "Clara has endured a significant amount of distress since she married you. She is my wife's sister, and I consider it my duty to make sure that such circumstances do not continue."

Seger's whole body tensed. "Clara is *my* wife, Wentworth, and any duties regarding her happiness are my concern, not yours."

The duke's gaze narrowed. "I'm not sure you are capable of fulfilling a duty. You have not displayed any such tendencies in the past."

"Maybe not," Seger replied irritably, "but we all grow, and some of us even deserve second chances. I thought you embraced that idea."

Tension hung in the air like a thick haze. "I do," James said, "and you were given that second chance. I'm just not sure you deserve a third."

"I did nothing wrong. I had to see that woman. She said she had information regarding Clara, and when I realized who she was, I had to speak to her. You see, she was the woman I—"

"I know who she was."

Seger felt like he was talking to a brick wall. "Then you must understand why I had to talk to her. But it's over now. I'll never see her again. All that matters to me is that Clara . . ."

His voice broke.

He couldn't finish.

God, he wasn't even sure he could go on standing. "*Please*, James," he said, taking an unsteady step forward and pleading desperately, knowing he sounded pathetic. Knowing that his eyes were becoming wet, his voice was breaking. "I *have* to see her."

James stared at him for a long, agonizing moment, then his chest rose and fell with a deep intake of breath. He went to the door and held it open.

"She is with Sophia in the nursery. Third floor."

Seger regarded his brother-in-law with some surprise, then crossed toward him. "Thank you," he said, pausing before him in the doorway, before dashing up the stairs to find his wife.

Clara sat in the rocking chair by the window, gazing out at the gray sky and the limp, idle leaves on an old English oak, while she rocked Liam to sleep. She leaned her head back, hugged the soft bundle gently to her breast and closed her eyes, but opened them again, slightly startled, when Sophia bent to scoop the babe out of her arms.

"I'll take him now."

"But he's just falling asleep," Clara whispered.

Her sister almost scolded her. "Clara, I'll *take* him."

Realizing something was wrong, Clara glanced at the door.

There stood her husband, filling the doorway completely with his huge, masculine frame.

All her senses trembled and quivered, her heart fluttered like the wings of a hummingbird. Even after what had happened that morning, he was still the most beautiful man in the world. He still made her weak with desire.

"Seger."

He glanced pleadingly at Sophia, who carried Liam toward the door.

"I think I'll take Liam to nap in my bed," Sophia said, "while John is out in the pram with the nurse. Perhaps I'll just go and . . . and . . ." She gazed awkwardly at Seger and Clara. "I'll just go."

She left them alone in the nursery. Clara rose from the chair, her body tense as she tried to resist her womanly responses to him—the same sexual responses that had given him the power to take advantage of her on so many occasions, and talk her into believing that he was the man she had wanted him to be.

She didn't think he really was. He would always enjoy other women. She had simply been denying it to herself all this time.

Seger slowly walked toward her, as if he wasn't sure he was welcome, and had to test the waters first.

"Clara," he said softly, "why did you get in that cab?"

She lifted her chin and wondered how it was possible he could not understand why she had done what she'd done. Or perhaps he was just playing innocent. "Because I couldn't watch."

"There was nothing to see." He took a few more cautious steps closer.

She responded by turning her back on him and walking to the other side of the room. "That is a matter of opinion."

Every instinct she possessed sensed the intensity of his nearness as he quietly approached.

"No, it is not a matter of opinion," he said. "Listen to me." He cupped her upper arms in his hands and turned her to face him. "I had to speak to Daphne to understand what had happened. I was in shock. You must understand that."

"I've understood everything, Seger. I've done nothing but understand, but I can't do it anymore. I can't keep coming up with excuses for my uncertainties about our marriage. I can't continue to be understanding and patient, when I am really frightened to death on the inside. I don't *trust* you. I realized that this morning. I felt sick watching you go off to talk to her. I was sure you were going to leave me."

"I'm not going to leave you."

She looked into his eyes and saw sincerity. Desperation. But after everything she'd been through, she wasn't sure she could believe it. Maybe this was just his way of appeasing her, so she would give him the freedom he needed to . . .

She didn't want to think about the rest.

Clara went to the table beside the crib and began to put Liam's toys back into the toy trunk, one by one.

"She wanted to become my mistress," Seger said.

Clara froze, then forced herself to continue what she was doing. "That's not surprising. There are a number of women in London who want the same thing."

"But I don't want them. Nor do I want Daphne. I told her that. She is going back to America."

Clara whirled around to face him. "How can I believe you? She's the reason you never married for eight years! She's the reason you haven't been able to love *me*!"

He shook his head at her. "Maybe she was the reason I chose to live as I did, but she has nothing to do with what is between us today."

He moved closer and cupped her face in his hands. "I'm sorry I have not been able to love you, Clara, but it had nothing to do with Daphne. It was because I had become so accustomed to a certain way of life, it became almost impossible to imagine anything different. I'd begun to believe that I wasn't capable of loving one woman. But from the first moment I saw you, I knew you were different. Everything about you was different, the way you looked, the way you made me feel. All other women were eclipsed by you, and they still are. You have been my best friend and my lover, my confidante and my companion. You have made every day a fragment of heaven, and I think of nothing but you when we are apart. I could no more live without you than I could live without air in my lungs. I would die if I lost you, and that—I believe—is love."

Clara saw the light in her husband's eyes, and slowly blinked. Could she believe him?

"Seger . . ."

She had no idea what she wanted to say. All she knew was that her husband was kissing her. Holding her in his arms and calming her, soothing her.

He was such a magnificent kisser. His lips and tongue moved with gentle, erotic precision. Her body throbbed at the exquisite sensation of her breasts pressing up against the firm wall of his chest. Heat issued forth and simmered between them where their bodies touched. The tight, close contact began to melt the ice crystals she had worked so hard to forge around her heart.

He continued to hold her face in his hands as he gazed down into her eyes. Her body ached with desire. "I want no woman but you, Clara. I *love* you, and I will always love you."

She felt herself bending to his will as she always did. How could she not? She was melting in his arms, burning to give herself over to his strong skillful hands, quivering with the need to feel his flesh next to hers.

She labored to subdue such weakness. She had to be strong. She could not give in so easily. This was a turning point in her life. She would set the rules now and demand his fidelity and respect, or give him the power to tramp all over her heart in the years to come.

Her voice shook as she spoke. "How can I trust that you're telling me the truth? That you're not going to go back to your old ways as soon as this is forgotten? I can't live like that, Seger, and I won't. I would rather spend my life alone than suffer that kind of anguish, and I *will* spend it alone if you cannot be constant."

He stroked her hair tenderly. "Clara, I will be faithful to you until the day I die, and beyond."

"Those are just words, Seger. I need more than that. I need proof."

"Here's your proof!" He touched his open palm to his chest. "I have changed. Everyday since I met you I've moved farther and farther away from the shallow shell of the man that I was. I feel it inside myself. I'm whole again. Surely you can see it, too." He cupped her cheek in his warm, gentle hand. "Can't you see it in my eyes? Hear it in my voice? Feel it in your heart? God, this morning Daphne appeared, *alive*, and offered to be my mistress, and I sent her away. Isn't that proof enough that you are the only woman in the world I want? That my heart beats for you and you alone? *I love you, Clara.* You are my entire world."

Tears of joy welled up in her eyes as she gazed lovingly at her husband and listened to all he said. Really listened. He was right—he had changed, and she could see it in his eyes. She was just so afraid to trust her instincts.

But she did love him. That much she knew.

"I love you, too," she sobbed.

He gathered her into his arms and held her tight, kissing her cheeks and neck and finally her mouth.

"Clara, you have given me so much, even when I gave nothing in return. I want to spend the rest of my life showing you how much I love you. I want to have children with you and travel with you and grow old with you. I want to prove to you that I will be the most faithful husband England has ever known."

A wealth of emotions cascaded over Clara as she stared

up at her beautiful husband in the afternoon light that was pouring in the nursery window.

"I sent Quintina and Gillian away," he said. "They will never have another opportunity to cause you pain. No one will, if I can help it."

He kissed her again until her lips were burning with heat and need and a flickering, licking flame. She clutched at him, feeling as if all her dreams had come true. She did trust him, deep in her soul she knew he was the man she'd always believed him to be. Today, she had feared the worst. She had thought she would be heartbroken for the rest of her life, but he had pulled her out of that and shown her what was real.

"Please know in your heart," he said, "that I will never leave you, nor will I ever go back to the empty existence that was my wretched life before I met you. You are my whole world, Clara, and I love you with all my heart."

She smiled and gazed up into his fathomless green eyes, then wrapped her arms around his neck and cried tears of pure, perfect joy.

Epilogue

Three weeks later

Quintina entered the blue guest chamber, which was the room Gillian had taken, at her brother's home in Wales. A note lay on the dresser.

A powerful surge of dread throbbed inside Quintina's stomach. She had the distinct feeling this would not be good news.

Dear Auntie,

I'm sorry to disappoint you, but I am leaving. I am going to America to marry Gordon Tucker, because I have fallen in love with him. He is a handsome and exciting man, and he tells me I am pretty. I believe I have finally found happiness.

Love,
Gillian

*P.S. I took the diamond pendent that you lent me, as
we were short of funds.*

Quintina read the note twice, then sank into a chair by
the bed. No, no. No! Gillian could not have gone off with
a prison convict. She could have been so much more! She
could have married a duke or an earl!

What would Susan think if she were alive today? She
would blame Quintina for not making things right, for not
taking better control of her daughter.

Quintina buried her face in her hands and sobbed. She
could not accept that her dear niece—her dead sister's
only child—was going to become an American!

Clara raised the covers for Seger to slide into bed beside her, and inched down cozy and warm. "I've been
waiting for you for almost ten minutes. What took you so
long?"

He smiled that rakish grin that she loved. "I wanted to
make sure my robe was on straight and my hair was just
right."

"Why?" she asked in a coquettish voice. "It's just me."

"Just you? Just you? You are the center of the universe,
my love."

"Not for long," she replied.

He gazed questioningly at her. "What do you mean?"

"I mean, there's going to be a new center in our universe
very soon, darling. In about eight months to be exact."

His eyes sparked with a joyful, loving ray of light. "Are
you sure?"

"Yes. I saw the doctor today."

Seger went pale, then gazed down at her flat stomach
and rested his warm hand upon it. "A baby."

"Yes, Seger. *Our* baby."

He met her eyes and lowered his lips to hers. "I am the luckiest man on this earth. You have made me so."

"Just as you have made me the luckiest woman."

Seger covered her body with his own and kissed her again, more deeply this time with full abandon as his tongue slid into her mouth and mingled with hers. His hips thrust forth, gently but firmly, causing a sensuous arousal deep in her feminine core. She thrust her own hips forward to meet his, and wrapped her long legs around him.

"I love you," he whispered in her ear, his breath hot and moist. He laid a trail of soft, open-mouthed kisses down her neck, driving her mad with sizzling, hungry lust.

"I love you, too. I never knew life could be so wonderful, Seger. Make love to me."

He grinned and nuzzled her nose. "I will fulfill your every desire, my lady. Where would you like me to begin?"

Clara smiled in return. "Wherever you wish. You always seem to know what I want before I know it myself."

She lifted her head off the pillow and kissed his open mouth, then relaxed as his lips made their way down her neck to the open collar of her nightgown. Gooseflesh shimmied down her spine. He slid his warm hand inside and massaged her breast, and Clara sighed with perfect, bewildering enchantment, reveling in the tingling sensation of his mouth closing around her nipple, his tongue flicking over it again and again.

"What did I ever do to deserve you?" he asked, sliding her nightgown up, and cupping her behind in his hand.

"You gave me pleasure."

"More than just pleasure, I hope."

"Yes, much more."

He positioned himself above her and paused there at the entry to her womanhood. She could feel the tip of his sex, creamy against her own. With a flare of impatience, she thrust her hips upward and felt the head of his erection enter her. He went still, grinning down at her.

"I want the rest," she said directly.

His voice was laced with seductive teasing. "You're sure?"

"Yes."

He kissed her on the nose in the flickering candlelight. "Positively sure?"

Her head came off the pillow as her body trembled with need. "Yes!" she cried out, laughing.

Seger smiled. "Then you may have all of me, my love, for the rest of my days and beyond. Thank you for giving me back my life."

Then he slowly, very slowly, pushed the rest of the way into her until she quivered all over with ecstasy.

Author's Note

According to Oscar Wilde, the English gentleman admired the American woman for her "extraordinary vivacity, her electrical quickness of repartee, her inexhaustible store of curious catchwords." If such a woman was also an heiress, all the better.

In the late Victorian period and early in the twentieth century, approximately one hundred American heiresses married British nobles. A fair exchange of titles for money became the business of the day, and millions of American dollars wound up in the hands of impoverished English lords, who certainly couldn't work to replenish their bank accounts. That would have been ungentlemanly.

In that light, marrying for money was nothing new in the British aristocracy. It had been going on for centuries. With modern industrialization in America, however, Wall Street had come into its own. New Money was everywhere, and there was a freshly stocked market for brides who were not only wealthy, but beautiful and spirited.

But why were these American fathers willing to send their daughters and their hard-earned fortunes across an ocean to a country they had fought a war against one hundred years before?

As Marion Fowler states in her book, *In a Gilded Cage*, they longed for "the *poetry* of class." They felt the chill from those with Old Money in America, who turned their noses up at a society who had earned its fortune, not inherited it. The New Rich wanted respectability. Refinement. Something more than mere economic standing.

So it went that in the late Victorian period, red-hot American blood penetrated the more reserved blue-blooded veins of England.

Princess Diana's great grandmother was an American heiress. In 1880, Frances Work of Newport married the Honorable James Burke-Roche, younger brother of an Irish baron. Burke-Roche had traveled to America and spent time in Wyoming, raising cattle, before meeting the woman of his dreams—the beautiful and very wealthy daughter of a Vanderbilt stockbroker. The couple traveled back to England where they had twin sons, one of which was Diana's grandfather.

Winston Churchill is another offspring of a transatlantic marriage. His mother was Jennie Jerome of New York, who in 1874 married Lord Randolph Churchill, second son of the seventh Duke of Marlborough. He proposed to her when she was nineteen, three days after meeting her on board a cruise ship, at a ball held in honor of the Prince and Princess of Wales. In 1895, Randolph died. Jennie married two more times, and devoted herself to her son's political career. Jennie had two sisters who also married Englishmen.

I hope you'll look for the other books in this series, based on three fictional American sisters: Sophia, Clara and Adele. Sophia's book is *To Marry the Duke* (June 2003), and Adele's story will be published in late 2004.

The best in romance can be found from Avon Books
with these sizzling March releases.

ENGLAND'S PERFECT HERO by Suzanne Enoch
An Avon Romantic Treasure

Lucinda Barrett has seen her friends happily marry the men they chose for their "lessons in love." So the practical beauty decides to find someone who is steady and uneventful—and that someone is definitely *not* Robert Carroway! She wants a husband, not a passionate, irresistible lover who could shake her world with one deep, lingering kiss . . .

FACING FEAR by Gennita Low
An Avon Contemporary Romance

Agent Nikki Taylor is a woman with questions about her past assigned to investigate Rick Harden, the CIA's Operations Chief who is suspected of treason. Yet instead of unlocking his secrets, she unleashes a dark consuming passion . . . and more questions. Now in a race against time, piecing together her history can get them both killed.

THREE NIGHTS . . . by Debra Mullins
An Avon Romance

Faced with her father's enormous gambling debt, Aveline Stoddard agrees to three nights in the arms of London's most notorious rake, a man they call "Lucifer." Once those nights of blistering sensuality and unparalleled ecstasy are over, will Aveline be able to forget the man who has stolen her heart?

LEGENDARY WARRIOR by Donna Fletcher
An Avon Romance

Reena grew up listening to the tales of the Legend—a merciless warrior who is both feared and respected. So when her village is devastated by a cruel landlord, she knows the Legend is the only one who can rescue her people. But the flesh-and-blood man is even more powerful and sensuous than the hero she imagined . . .

REL 0204

Discover Contemporary Romances at Their Sizzling Hot Best from Avon Books

IF THE SLIPPER FITS
by Elaine Fox
0-06-051721-2/$5.99 US/$7.99 Can

OPPOSITES ATTRACT
by Hailey North
0-380-82070-6/$5.99 US/$7.99 Can

WITH HER LAST BREATH
by Cait London
0-06-000181-X/$5.99 US/$7.99 Can

TALK OF THE TOWN
by Suzanne Macpherson
0-380-82104-4/$5.99 US/$7.99 Can

OFF LIMITS
by Michele Albert
0-380-82056-0/$5.99 US/$7.99 Can

SOMEONE LIKE HIM
by Karen Kendall
0-06-000723-0/$5.99 US/$7.99 Can

A THOROUGHLY MODERN PRINCESS
by Wendy Corsi Staub
0-380-82054-4/$5.99 US/$7.99 Can

A GREEK GOD AT THE LADIES' CLUB by Jenna McKnight
0-06-054927-0/$5.99 US/$7.99 Can

DO NOT DISTURB
by Christie Ridgway
0-06-009348-X/$5.99 US/$7.99 Can

WANTED: ONE PERFECT MAN
by Judi McCoy
0-06-056079-7/$5.99 US/$7.99 Can

Available wherever books are sold
or please call 1-800-331-3761 to order.   CRO 1103

AVON TRADE... because every great bag
deserves a great book!

Paperback $13.95
ISBN 0-06-056277-3

Paperback $13.95
($21.95 Can.)
ISBN 0-06-056012-6

Paperback $13.95
ISBN 0-06-053437-0

Paperback $13.95
($21.95 Can.)
ISBN 0-06-053668-3

Paperback $13.95
($21.95 Can.)
ISBN 0-06-056075-4

Paperback $13.95
($21.95 Can.)
ISBN 0-06-008545-2

**Don't miss the next book by your favorite author.
Sign up for AuthorTracker by visiting *www.AuthorTracker.com*.**

Available wherever books are sold, or call 1-800-331-3761 to order.

ATP 0204

Avon Romances—
the best in exceptional authors and unforgettable novels!

THE CRIMSON LADY
0-06-009770-1/ $5.99 US/ $7.99 Can
by Mary Reed McCall

TO MARRY THE DUKE
0-06-052704-8/ $5.99 US/ $7.99 Can
by Julianne MacLean

SOARING EAGLE'S EMBRACE
0-380-82067-6/ $5.99 US/ $7.99 Can
by Karen Kay

THE PRINCESS AND HER PIRATE
0-06-050282-7/ $5.99 US/ $7.99 Can
by Lois Greiman

ONCE A SCOUNDREL
0-06-050563-X/ $5.99 US/ $7.99 Can
by Candice Hern

ALL MEN ARE ROGUES
0-06-050354-8/ $5.99 US/ $7.99 Can
by Sari Robins

FOR THE FIRST TIME
0-06-052741-2/ $5.99 US/ $7.99 Can
by Kathryn Smith

BELOVED HIGHLANDER
0-06-051971-1/ $5.99 US/ $7.99 Can
by Sara Bennett

TO TEMPT A BRIDE
0-06-050218-5/ $5.99 US/ $7.99 Can
by Edith Layton

WICKEDLY YOURS
0-06-050759-4/ $5.99 US/ $7.99 Can
by Brenda Hiatt

ALMOST PERFECT
0-06-050911-2/ $5.99 US/ $7.99 Can
by Denise Hampton

THE DUCHESS DIARIES
0-06-051969-X/ $5.99 US/ $7.99 Can
by Mia Ryan

Available wherever books are sold or please call 1-800-331-3761 to order.

ROM 0903